The son of Irish immigrants,  born in 1953. His father was a pioneer Hoffman spent his childhood and Africa, avoiding school wh battle with the English educatic place to read English at New Cc university would accept him. Graduating in 1976 he has had over twenty different jobs, including boardman in a betting shop, messenger boy in the City and teacher. Paul Hoffman is a screenwriter. He used to be one of the senior censors at the British Board of Film Classification and was responsible for replacing the butter in *Last Tango in Paris*.

Jude Law starred in the motion picture *The Wisdom of Crocodiles*, based on one portion of the novel. Paul Hoffman's new novel, *The Golden Age of Censorship*, is now available from Doubleday.

Also by Paul Hoffman

THE GOLDEN AGE OF CENSORSHIP

THE WISDOM OF CROCODILES

Paul Hoffman

BLACK SWAN

TRANSWORLD PUBLISHERS
61 63 Uxbridge Road, London W5 5SA
a division of The Random House Group Ltd
www.booksattransworld.co.uk

THE WISDOM OF CROCODILES
A BLACK SWAN BOOK : 9780552770828

First published in Great Britain
in 2000 by Big Time Press
Black Swan edition published 2002

A CIP catalogue record for this book
is available from the British Library.

Addresses for The Penguin Random House Group can be found at:
global.penguinrandomhouse.com

The Random House Group Ltd Reg. No. 954009.

Penguin Random House is committed to a sustainable future for
our business, our readers and our planet. This book is made from
Forest Stewardship Council® certified paper.

Printed and bound in Great Britain by Clays Ltd, Elcograf S.p.A.
Typeset in 11/12pt Melior by
Falcon Oast Graphic Art Ltd.
6 8 10 9 7 5

For five minutes David Hendrix sat brooding in front of the computer. Then he switched off NEMO's voice and re-read its conclusions from the screen. Then he read them again. Despite the irrationality, he could not forget the sound of NEMO's voice as it spoke the last sentence, nor the sense of mocking distaste. The man from Machine Intelligence had told him what to do if he wanted to discover the source of any remark made by NEMO. The young man had laughed. 'If you ever get the spooky feeling this thing is alive, just press this. Think of NEMO as an incredibly stupid and fraudulent student with the world's longest crib sheet up its cheating arm and you won't go far wrong.'

Hendrix highlighted the last sentence and pressed Curl Alt and S. Immediately half the screen was covered in a drop-down window. It was a page from an article in the *Journal of Nervous and Mental Diseases*, vol. CXXXV, No. 4, October 1962, by Paul MacLean. Highlighted in blue was the line about the horse and the crocodile MacLean had written nearly forty years ago. But Hendrix did not feel reassured, he felt miserable. He did not feel its wit or its elegance. He felt its truth.

How sad Alice felt watching the confusion and alarm at her husband's failing grip, at his efforts, pointless now, to get out of bed without her help. Weary as she was, after so many interrupted and uncomfortable nights, she would not let him worry that he would die alone with no one there to hold his hand. But also, in the cold darkness of three o'clock in the morning, her resentments softly called to her, sour, acid, scalding, eroding the new feelings of compassion she felt for him, wearing them away to anger at having been denied something that was owing to her. Then quickly her habitual antidote to rage: oil of coldness, balm of frigidity, sedative of reserve. The long-term treatment she prescribed to calm herself was blandness of diet, a fast of bread and milk to starve what was afflicting her.

For an hour her bitterness would summon her, testing her new resolve, receding at four o'clock as he woke up calling for water or the light.

During the night Alice sat in the ugly but comfortable reclining chair her mother had given them. For the first few hours of her watch she would doze and wake, not allowing herself to sleep deeply, listening for his faint words or an irregular pattern of breathing, or none at all. She found that at around three in the morning she would become unusually alert for an hour or so. It was a bleak time, soundless outside and dark, little demanded of her because he slept most deeply then. Tonight she was not so much alert as restless. She tried to read a book but could not concentrate. There was a newspaper on the bedside table. Quietly she eased it out from under the papers on top of it. But it was awkward because a chair was in the way and some of the papers fell to the floor. He stirred but did not wake. She picked up the papers, took the *Independent* from the table and sat down again. First she sorted through the fallen papers, some scribbled notes, which she did not read, a few letters. One of them was the letter from the psychotherapist, Hendrix, along with the answer to the crossword puzzle. She looked at it: "senselessness". Then at the clue: E13. For five minutes she tried to work it out. Then, for the first time in a long time, she smiled with pleasure. How very clever, she thought.

'Why are you ...'

She looked up. George was awake, his face contorted with the effort to find the word he was searching for.

' ... smiling,' he said at last, irritated at how much effort it took, at how simple and arbitrary the words that would not come.

'Are you all right?' she said. 'Can I get you anything?'

'No.' He started to shift. She moved quickly and was by his side in a moment, putting her arms around his shoulders and helping him. It was not difficult. He had lost a good deal of weight in the last few weeks. He looked at her, grateful. She did not take her arms away but sat down beside him on the bed.

'So,' he said at last, 'what was amusing you?'

'I don't know if you'd want me to tell you.'

'You're going to confess about your secret life.'

She laughed. It had been a very long time since he had made her laugh. 'No. It's not about my secret life,' she said. 'It's that crossword clue you told me about.'

He gasped with pleasure. 'You've ...' Then he groaned in irritation. 'Damn! You know ... found it ... discovered it ... revealed ... *solved*! You've solved it.'

'Yes,' she said. 'I think so.'

'What is it?'

She looked around the room. 'I need a pen.' She had to move her hands to search and eased him back into the pillows gently.

'In the ...' He pointed at the drawer in the bedside table. She opened it and took out a pencil and the writing-pad next to it. She sat down again and making sure he could see wrote out "senselessness" as three words:

SENSE

LESS

NESS

She did not want to rob him of the pleasure of at least some of the discovery. 'Can you see?'

He looked at it, frowning with concentration. He sighed and smiled, resigned. 'No. Sorry.'

'Don't be sorry,' she said, and felt as if she were going to cry.

'Tell me. I can't bear the suspense.'

She took a deep breath, as quietly as she could so he would not see she was upset. 'It's the second word: "less". Give me another word for less.'

He sighed but wanted to offer something. 'Ah ... inferior!' She shook her head. 'Lower ... nether.' They both laughed at where such an obscure word had come from. ' ... Under ... subordinate.' He stopped. 'Sorry. I know I mustn't apologise. I can't.'

She shuffled closer and put her arms around his shoulder so she could show him the three words again. As if her hand were now his, next to LESS she wrote:

SENSE

LESS (take away)

NESS

'Do you see it now?'

'No.'

She stroked his forehead. 'If you take the letters N-E-S-S away from the letters S-E-N-S-E what you're left with is the letter E. The answer to E13 is sense **less** ness: E.'

It took him a few more seconds and then he began to laugh. 'My God, what a monster. Out ... out ... outrageous. Impossible. Unfair. Unjust. In ...'

He looked at her but she was crying, the tears spilling down her face without her making any effort to stop them. He took her hand and neither of them said anything. Within ten minutes they had both fallen asleep.

An hour later he gasped aloud. 'What?' he called out. 'What?' Afraid, distressed, he waved his hands weakly in front of him as if to push someone away. She was instantly awake. 'It's all right ... It's all right ... Sshh ... Sshh ... calm down.'

Breathing heavily he seemed not to know where he was. Then he looked at her, as if surprised to see her there, and was immeasurably relieved. 'Oh ... Alice ... Oh ... It was a dream.'

'It's all right now,' she said, taking his hand, 'it was a dream. It's all right ... just a dream.'

In his anxiety he had moved upright but unable to keep this position he fell back against the pillows breathing heavily. 'Terrible ...'

'It was only a dream. Sshh.'

'Write it down.'

'What?'

'Write it ... write it down.'

It was the first time since he had become seriously ill that she had seen him truly afraid.

'Would you like a drink?'

'Write it for me.'

'It was a dream ... just a dream.'

'Please.'

She switched on the twenty-watt table lamp. It hurt her eyes, thin though the light was. He did not react. She picked up the writing-pad and the pencil and looked at him. His eyes filled with dread as he stared into the distance and she felt a surge of overwhelming pity. 'Let me get you something.'

He shook his head. 'There is a man ... in his late fifties. He is overweight and cheerful and he's wearing a cardigan and slippers. He is coming out of his front garden. It's a bungalow and there are many others. It's a long street ... many houses all of them neat ... cared-for. But at the end of the road there is a large waterfall ... big ... very wide.'

595

'You're going too fast.'

He did not slow down or look at her. 'He must go down the side of the waterfall to fetch his daughter's husband who is missing. They think he's dead. He sets out and he has a rifle over his shoulder. He's at the side of the waterfall. It's very noisy and there's a rope and he has to use it to climb down because there's no path. Hand over hand he uses the rope to climb down the side of the waterfall and it's very easy for him and he's feeling a sense of adventure ... but as soon as he reaches the bottom and he puts one foot on the ground it vanishes and he feels very uneasy. The waterfall is now huge ... incredibly ... noisy. This is a crater of some kind and it's like ... It's Africa ... it's South Africa or somewhere. And he looks up, and around the rim of the crater are all these bungalows, and they have lights on and the curtains drawn and it's night up there but it's day in the crater. But he can't get back the way he came because he can't pull himself up and the only way out is to go on a long trek to the other side of the crater. It's open at the other side but it's a long way. His spirits are shaken and he thinks of his duty ... to find his daughter's husband ... his body. So now he walks hunting style around the front of the waterfall, which is somehow far away but ... close as well ... and he goes around the other side. There it is ... in the pool ... the body of the young man.'

He paused for a moment, afraid.

'All around the pool are black cats ... ordinary cats but bigger. They don't look at him ... they don't seem bothered but he knows they're very dangerous. They lick their paws and don't seem interested and wash. He takes his gun off his shoulder and a black cat standing on a rock in the pool slowly, casually, slips into the water and goes over to the young man's body and takes it up on to a rock where it folds him over one paw like it was holding him in its arms. It has killed the son-in-law and keeps the body in the pool, guarding it from rescue. The dead man's hair is black and very wet and thick and it's thick over his forehead where the water has slicked it down.'

He groaned softly.

'And he looks down at his gun but when he looks up the cat isn't holding the young man any more, he's holding a woman.' He stopped and his eyes were staring. He looked at his wife. 'It was my mother and – she's alive. Her arms are swollen and she's looking at me and she's calling out to me to help her. "Don't let me die here ... please don't let Mummy die." Then the man aims his gun. Then it's as if I'm looking down the barrel like a telescope pointing at the cat ... then the cat looks backwards and forwards between my terrified mother in his arms and the hunter ... and the hunter is confident because he's got the cat in his sights. And I am confident as well because it's covered. I'm going to save her. The cat looks back and forth making itself angrier and angrier looking at the hunter and my mother's face. Then the cat ... its face becomes a sort of a blur and it has lips and its mouth makes a kind of O shape ... and his mouth moves and changes shape in a rage. The man shoots ... and he misses ... again ... he misses ... and again ... and he misses and the cat turns and starts towards us and I see it coming down the barrel ... it won't stop. He keeps coming and it leaps and the man jumps back and takes his eye from the sight and seeing the cat with his own eyes ... not through the sight ... he shoots from the hip as he falls back. The cat falls down dead.'

George stopped and looked at Alice.

'Shhh,' she said, 'it's all right.'

'The man is terrified ... but he rushes through the water to my mother. She's floating on her face and he quickly turns her round. But it's not my mother any more, it's the man's son-in-law. He stares down at the body, confused and so sad, and I feel as if ... as if I have failed my mother that I didn't ... I don't know how I felt ... bad, terribly bad.' He closed his eyes as if he were about to faint.

'Be quiet now,' she said softly. 'It's all right.' But he began talking again so softly that she had to bend her head to hear him.

'He has to take the body with him and he is so sad, so melancholy. The pool is shallow now and covered in an immense scaffolding ... rusty ... everywhere and there's a kind of roof so it's dark and dripping. He's got to drag the body through it all, climbing over the pipes and pulling the body behind him turning over in the water ... and though he's dead he's ... alive a little bit very deep inside and he knows ... he's been very frightened in the pool all this time ... so cold and wet and alone ... dead but not dead. The man drags him behind him and it's slow and hard ... and with each step it gets darker and colder and now he feels a terrible loss ... terrible, which he never felt for the young man before when it was just a duty he owed somebody else. But he's afraid because he can see outside in the light beyond the scaffolding there are the cats and they're gathering and looking to see him. And then he knows and the body knows too ... that he can't take him back. But he keeps pulling him to the edge of the pool and out of the scaffolding and into the shallows at the edge and he's next to the rope which he climbed down ... but he can't get back up and he can't take the body of his son-in-law with him. He has to leave him behind in the land of the dead even though he isn't completely dead ... moving and rolling under the water ... bobbing and rolling. He has to leave him. There are others waiting on the shore – white hunters and black hunters – but he can't make out their faces. They are shouting at him to come ... They can lead him up a steep path nearby, covered in plants and trees but they won't wait ... there's no time ... he must come now. Terrible is the way he feels. He has to leave the son-in-law behind. He can barely walk because his grief and his loss are terrible. He comes out of the water and the hunters take him away.'

She did not know what to say to him.

'It was only a dream,' she said at last.

He closed his eyes, exhausted.

'I'll get you a glass of water.' She took the jug from the bedside table and went downstairs.

In the kitchen she emptied and refilled the pitcher and quickly returned to the bedroom. He was asleep.

Over the next two days he deteriorated quickly. He had reached the point where he started to look wasted. His skin was losing all colour. The doctor's visits increased from twice a day to four times. It was his habit on leaving to give her a brief summary of George's condition as she saw him out, but at the end of the second day after the dream he asked her to sit down. She took him into the living room.

'Is he talking?'

'Hardly at all ... very little for two days.'

'His sight's going.'

'Yes.'

'It will be quite gradual. He'll probably go in his sleep. He won't be in pain.'

'Really?' she said desperately. 'I couldn't bear it if he was.'

He was touched: she had not shown much reaction before beyond the merely dutiful. But it was clear now that he had been mistaken. How easy it was, he thought, to misunderstand people.

'If there's anything, you can call me at any time ... night or day,' he said.

She smiled, grateful and relieved, then followed him out into the hall and said goodbye.

For an hour she sat in the green recliner, watching him. She felt an extraordinary weariness, as if something heavy were pressing down on her, irresistible, anaesthetic. When she opened her eyes it was more like regaining consciousness than waking. Her chest ached in a strange way, and her throat. She looked at her watch. She had been asleep for four hours. Alarmed, she looked over at George but even before she had half risen from the chair she could hear his breathing, slow, heavy and with a slight sigh on every inward breath.

She stayed with him, mostly silent, sometimes reassuring him, always holding his hand, leaving only twice in the next fourteen hours, both times jamming open the bedroom and the bathroom door. All through the night she did not eat or drink or rest. All through the night, through dawn, he did not move; there was only the regular breathing, the sigh on the down breath and the blinking of his eyes. Then at ten past six his head moved slowly, and with an immense act of will he turned towards the door as if listening for the sound of someone on the stairs who should not be in the house. It held his attention for a full minute. Then he called to her. His voice was faint and indistinct, slurred by weakness, it sounded like a warning. She started to talk to him and, for a moment, he saw her but then, exhausted, his head shifted back onto the centre of the pillow. He opened his eyes and looked at her.

'I don't feel well,' he said weakly. 'In fact ... I think I'm going to die.' He closed his eyes and a faint groan escaped his lips. She froze in horror and pity. Suddenly he opened his eyes and again looked to the door, calling out as if warning off the approach of an intruder.

'Hello?'

The pain in her chest surged, unbearable, filling every fibre in the muscles of her chest and neck and cheeks. She squeezed his hand and began to talk to him. 'It's all right,' she said. 'I'm here. Don't be afraid. It's all right. You're not alone.'

He gave no sign of having heard her or that he knew she was there. He had opened his eyes again and appeared to be focused somewhere far away.

In the distance there was a loud noise, a bang like a truncated clap of thunder. Although she heard it, she was too distracted for it to register.

There was no sound inside the house. It was still, and it seemed to her that the stillness would go on for many hours more. Then suddenly it was as if something powerful stirred in the room. Something huge was leaving, an entire world passing away.

'I'm here,' she said. 'I'm here. I'm with you. I'm here.'

Between her first sentence and her last his hand went cold and his eyes emptied. And then he sighed.

Alice sat back as if astonished, staring at him. After a short while she began to whisper: 'Into thy hands, O Lord, I commend his spirit. Give him eternal rest and let thy perpetual light shine on him, for you are ...'

A terrible constriction in her throat began to choke her and she could not go on. She stayed like this for ten minutes then gave a loud cry, a terrible bark of grief.

———

In a small flat in Finchley, Geoff Healey is listening to the summary of the morning news as he packs up before returning to his wife. The most important story is that the Bank of England has announced that interest rates are going up. Then the newsreader, light-hearted and a little condescending in the way of such signings off, announces that engineers working to prevent the imminent collapse of the Leaning Tower of Pisa have succeeded in moving the tower back by six millimetres to the position it held twenty five years ago. Of John Barton there is no mention. As Geoffrey Healey finishes his preparations for a return to life, for that is how it feels to him, he listens to the weather. The forecast is snow.

The prediction is correct. The men and women of weather have got it right. In the centre of Harrow-on-the-Hill a single snowflake is falling. Formed high up in the clouds as the result of many complex variations of temperature and humidity it gently falls, with its lattices and puckered layers and its fragmented symmetries, onto the lips of a young woman. Her lips are blue; but not because of the cold. She is the source of the noise heard but not noted by Alice Winnicott a few minutes before. The young woman with blue lips is lying in the road. Her spine is shattered and she has no legs. For the moment she is still alive, but it will not be long before her mouth stops gaping like that of a fish drowning on a river bank, and the cold stealing through her stomach will reach her chest and cause her heart to stop. Twenty yards away a red double-decker bus, an old-fashioned Routemaster, lies on one side of the pavement, shattered and skeletonised by the bomb she had been carrying at her feet and which she had been intending to use to kill George Winnicott. The explosive death of the former Head of the Anti-Terrorist Squad was to have been a dissenting reminder that not everyone agreed that even for the gangster the story must change, that coercion now required a female wing. They would not see the future also had to be female for intimidation as for everything else; that even terror has its feminine side; that words must point the gun in politics; that the inquisition of the baseball bat or bomb should only now and then be used as an enforcer to the despotism of the gentle hint. (*They haven't gone away, you know*). A persuasiveness that's rooted in the occasional, spectacular and yet deniable atrocity is the way ahead for wickedness. No one claims responsibility any more. But even reactionary killers are driven to adapt and they had tried to put the future to the service of the past through the young woman dying slowly on the streets of Harrow. Afready she had killed, a husband and his wife who'd been passing as a lorry that she'd parked in Newgate St had blown apart. But she was made uneasy by these deaths; it was too hard to like yourself with blood like this upon your hands. Had she lived, she, too, might have outgrown dynamite and murder and become an entirely novel kind of nuisance: one who needed to feel good about themselves, one of many new kinds coming to afflict us in a new millennium where the nuisance will lie down with the psychopath, and the pest will lie down with the thug; as long as it is remembered that we get our word for pest from the notion of plague, rivers of blood, the death of the first born.

———

At the Fraud Secretariat people are arriving to start the day, ignorant of the death of their helmsman and that with this death their days are numbered. Already with Alice Winnicott's terrible howl they are beginning the vanishing: into the Department of This or the Office of That. For some of them its drift into oblivion will bring opportunity; for others, blight. For now, many and watchful, they begin the daily task of sorting the ins and outs and ups and downs: What is the story of this lie? Who made the decision? Why did they make it?

Should they have acted as they did? Who did what to whom and for how long and for how much and what was their state of mind? What has been stolen? Who was it stolen from? Who was the thief? Each one must make some progress through this mournful day: ponder, rule, decide to prosecute, baulk the submission to dismiss, fearing the appeal and the release, hoping for the confirmation of the prison sentence and the ruinous fine.

———

Waiting for his final resting-place, the narrow valley for his bones now dry and disconnected, the ache in George's back is fifty minutes gone. At close of business all his former workers' heads will throb and all of them will stretch and ease the muscles of their backs commemorating him. The spine designed to take them on all fours through life on horse's hoof or reptile's claw will groan in protest at this unnatural pretence, its upright deviance. Our leaning tower, our Babel of backbones ending in a little tail that still exists between our hips, is always threatening the collapse, the slip, the slow degeneration; straining at something it was never meant to do. We were not made to sit all day to make a bob or two. But economics doesn't give a toss for our biology. At the end of the working day our backs will always ache, we will always be sore. At half past five the workers will unite in harmony and fellowship and celebrate the common ownership of tender joints. They are confederate now, united, made one flesh in honouring their spinal destiny, raising themselves to toast their former boss:

Be upstanding.

ACKNOWLEDGEMENTS

I have had the benefit of reading numerous books and articles, but too many to mention all of them. Some have been essential to various sections of this book. I am deeply indebted to Stephen Fay's account of the workings of the Bank of England, *Portrait Of An Old Lady*. The dialogue in The Dark Figure often relies on interviews or comments made by historical characters quoted in his excellent analysis. I am also indebted to two of Michael Levi's impressively readable books on fraud: *Regulating Fraud* and his Royal Commission report, *The Investigation, Prosecution, and Trial of Serious Fraud*. Richard Sennet's *The Corrosion of Character* distilled some useful thoughts on the life of the consultant. I am particularly grateful to Blay Whitby, Lecturer in Computer Science and Artificial Intelligence at the School of Cognitive and Computing Sciences at the University of Sussex, who commented so thoughtfully on the material about artificial intelligence in the novel. Louis Bris's comments on the fox and the hedgehog are partly stolen from an essay by Isaiah Berlin and another by Keats. The extract of 'For the Fallen' by Laurence Binyon on page 275 is by permission of The Society of Authors, on behalf of the Laurence Binyon Estate.

not now leave the flat for the long postponed walk, he turned the ledger upside down. He thumbed through the figures collated month by month at the back that detailed everything from the number of times he touched her in a week to the minor presents exchanged.

To have refined, or complicated, the categories further would have been easy, but they worked in a practical way only by being simple: phone calls, which he detailed separately, could consist of support or emotion, and they could even be classed as a form of touching or absence. But he was not interested in abstractions, in anything for its own sake. For all their rule-of-thumb crudeness, the categories seemed endlessly capable of producing the unexpected. He tried, for example, to rectify the two for three imbalance that emerged after a few weeks of keeping the ledger, but although his records indicated that obligations were now more or less equal, Maria became depressed and apathetic. He returned slowly to the two for three imbalance and her mood lightened. Equally slowly he started to do less for her and she became nervous and hypersensitive. What surprised him was the ratio of obligation. It could be varied over a short period of time. Over one or two days, say, there could be a drop or an increase; but the ratio had to be restored so that over a two-week period he averaged two acts of generosity for every three of hers. Puzzling at first, the nature of the imbalance later appeared obvious. Although his records clearly showed that she gave more to their relationship than he did, her perception was that the contribution was equal. Restored to a true equilibrium she felt obligated to him, and it was this that made her depressed.

Six months after they had drunk that cup of coffee together under Waterloo Bridge she was in many ways a different woman. For one thing her looks had changed. She had put on a stone, and had needed to; underweight, her bones had shown through on her chest, but now there was a bloom on her. She held herself differently, the victimised stoop of the shoulders having gone with the hesitant look and the worn skin.

One day they had gone shopping to buy him a new suit. She had tired of waiting for him to make up his mind and had demanded a turn of her own when they had passed a Dominguez shop with an ostentatiously discreet sale sign in the window. The dress she tried on was low-cut and he had teased her: 'It's too young for you.'

'Don't be horrible,' she replied, admiring her reflection in the mirror, turning sideways and smoothing the expensive fabric along her thighs. 'I've never had a cleavage before.' She laughed, then looked at herself again. 'I was like a boy until I was seventeen, straight down all the way. I can't tell you how desperate I was to have a bust. I actually used to cry about it at night.'

'I'm sure you looked fine,' he said gently.

'No.' She looked at him steadily. 'No, I didn't.' She turned back to her reflection with an extraordinary seriousness. He had encouraged her to cut her hair short and the new style emphasised the high cheekbones and grey eyes, diminished the large, flat nose. It worked now to her advantage: without the curtain of lank, straight hair, her face now had a surprising strength. 'Not bad, though I do say so myself,' she said, looking at herself with open admiration. He smiled his agreement. She walked over to the changing room, taking a red silk top from a sparsely filled rack. As he waited, he wandered closer to the curtain that acted as a door to the changing room. It was only partly drawn and he could detect movement behind it. He took on the shifty pose that waiting husbands or lovers always adopt in this situation, exaggeratedly calling attention to the fact that they are not gawking. She called out to him. 'It's too small. Get me get a bigger size, a twelve, would you?' He fetched it and returned. Instead of reaching a hand around the curtain as he had expected, she pulled it back completely. She had taken off the blouse and stood in front of him in her bra. It was white, contrasting strikingly with her now lightly tanned skin, and slightly too small, giving an alluring sense of both the soft and the tensely confined. The top of her breast shifted delicately as she reached out. The cup was of a transparent lace that seemed only to accentuate the pink of her nipples. He realised he was in immense danger. Fear and horror rescued him: he looked at her fiercely and threw the blouse at her. Her mouth opened in alarm and astonishment. He turned and walked out of the shop, her cry following him.

Just out of sight he stopped and considered whether or not to allow her to catch up with him. He decided a reconciliation would be a bad mistake and he had made enough of those. He turned into the nearest side street and then again until there was no possibility of her following, although he was sure she would try to do so. After about twenty minutes he found himself in Silver Street. He walked round the corner to the Owl Café and drank tea with a couple of depressed-looking men in their late fifties and a haggard-looking tart wearing a Crimplene mini. With its Formica tables, cracked cups and tired clientele, it was authentically awful in its Englishness. This England will never go away, he thought, no matter what happens. No designer, no architect, no politician, no amount of money, no European ideal could change it: the true ghastliness of the English would endure always, Gibraltarian in its permanence. He started to drink the grey tea in front of him. He felt sick the way you do after you've been hit very hard. He was appalled at his carelessness. For a long time he had neglected everyone but her. If the relationship failed him he would have no one. He had worked so carefully to restore Maria, but he had missed what had been happening while he did so, and it had struck him only when she pulled back the curtain of the changing room. There had been nothing calculated about her exhibitionism. In fact it had not been exhibitionism at all. He was not her lover and yet she had regarded it as safe to reveal herself in this way.

He had supported her too well and for too long. He had become a friend.

MEN AND WOMEN
AT WORK

The best picture of the world economy is the
female body. When I say that the future will be
female – and I will say it often – I do not mean
that from now on women will be in charge of
more things than men, I mean that the future
itself is changing sex. I am not joking when I
say that this is why the future will be more
difficult to understand.

Louis Bris, *The Wisdom of Crocodiles*

At twelve o'clock, precisely, as the dying twelfth
stroke of Big Ben faded to signal the end of one
millennium and the beginning of another, the former
head of the Anti-Terrorist Squad awoke screaming at
the top of his voice, 'I know the meaning of life! I
understand the origin of good and evil!'

'What? My God!' cried his terrified wife, as she was
woken from a deep and dreamless sleep.

'Oh,' gasped George Winnicott, as he recovered himself. 'Oh, God, it must have been a dream.'

'You nearly scared me to death.'

Winnicott sat up, put his head in his hands and
groaned.

'You were shouting,' said his wife, Alice.

The thin middle-aged man took a deep breath. 'I'm
sorry for waking you,' he said flatly. 'What did I say?'

'You didn't say it,' she replied coldly, 'you screamed it.'

He turned his head to one side, a signal that he wanted an answer but would not respond to her tone. The pause continued as her resentment mingled with what she would not acknowledge as alarm. Alice had not heard what he had said but as she woke, in her deep confusion, she had thought the screaming was coming from outside. And that it had been the sound of a terrified woman.

'I don't know,' she said at last. 'I was deeply asleep.'

He stood up.

'My back's hurting. I'm going to get a couple of Distalgesics.' He looked at the clock and then at his wife. 'Happy New Year,' he said, as he left the bedroom.

Downstairs he took the pills, put the kettle on and sat down, staring out into the dark night which every few seconds was lit up by the firework display on the Thames, bursts of light so vast they could be easily seen even from their house in Harrow. Soundless from this distance, it was like big lightning without rain or the start of a terrible but distant offensive.

He had been married to Alice for fifteen years. There had been no particular point at which things had begun to go wrong, no adultery, no thump, no poisonous word which once spoken could not be taken back, no coldly rebuffed sexual request. It had been a slow freeze, a chilly drying out that only a time-lapse camera sensitive to hidden disappointment might have tracked; the missing kind word at the necessary time, the absent gift or the presence of the wrong one, the pursed lip of unspoken disapproval, the imperceptible shrinking when one of them reached out to make it up. But making up was something they did not know how to do. They hardened their hearts so that it would not hurt so much. They were as sensitive as teenage girls.

A few hours later as George Winnicott moped over his tea and waited for the sun to rise, eight miles away in the City of London a couple in their late twenties were making their way to their car after a party. Half an hour earlier and they would have met many of the vast crowd, which had gathered by the river to see the fireworks, still miserably trying to get out of a central London whose masters had failed to predict that the three million who had come to bear witness to the new century might want to go home once they had done so. But now it was deserted. The toss of a coin had decided that the woman would drive and consequently she was entirely sober. Her husband was not.

'You want me to appreciate you and help more around the house.'

'No, that's not what I'm saying.'

'Good!' he replied, and started to giggle. 'Because I wouldn't want our marriage to be … y' know … brought down to the level of washing and cleaning.' He smiled at her. 'Give me a kiss.'

'No.'

'If I promise to do more round the house will you give me a kiss?'

She laughed, then stopped and looked at him. 'This isn't about that.' She put her hand around the back of his neck and lightly drove the heel of her other hand into his forehead. 'Think!'

A look of bewildered effort crossed his face. 'I've been to a party and had too much to drink. You're taking advantage of my weakened ability to change the subject.' She laughed again but said nothing. He looked at her desperately. 'Give me a clue.'

She turned and walked off down the dark and deserted street. He hurried to catch up with her.

'I want you to see how much you need from me,' she said. 'This isn't about housework. That isn't the point.'

'I'll do more.'

'Fine, but that still isn't the point. What I want you to get from this conversation is for you to understand – no, to *feel* how dependent you are.'

'I'll do a *lot* more.'

She stopped again, kissed him then walked on. He called after her.

'Are you wearing those knickers Elizabeth gave you for your birthday?'

'Be quiet!' she hissed, although it was early in the morning, they were in the legal centre of the City and there were no lights on in any of the imposing buildings that surrounded them.

'Look,' she said, as he caught up and she turned off Newgate Street into Warwick Lane, 'I want a great deal more out of this conversation than a bit of badly done ironing.'

'Tell me and it's yours,' he replied.

She stopped again and looked at him. 'All right, but don't pretend tomorrow that you were drunk and didn't take it in, because you haven't had *that* much to drink and, in any case, I'm going to get my way on this.'

He rolled his eyes. 'Oh, *do* get on with it.'

'All right. I want you to *recognise* just how dependent on me you really are. It's not that I want you to be any less dependent because I want you to need me. I just don't want you not to know it any more. I want you to see how needy ... how *greedy* you are for all the things I give you, the support and stroking and ... all the ...' She tried to grasp for the right word. 'Stroking. I stroke you like a cat – a great big, spoilt, over-fed pedigree cat.'

He gasped. 'Come on, you're exaggerating.'

'No, I'm not, and that's the problem. Because that's what you get, but it's not what you give.'

'You're saying that I'm not nice to you?' He spoke with a tone of entirely sincere incredulity.

She sighed with exasperation. 'Forget *nice*. I want you to see how needy and greedy you are so that you'll stop patronising *me* because *I'm* needy and greedy about wanting the same thing back from *you*. If I am a whiny, pathetic, needy little girl from time to time, I want you to say to yourself, "I'm just as bad, only I get my greedy little needs seen to so wonderfully well, I don't even know it's happening."' She laughed and pinched his chin. 'I want you to stop thinking you're a bit of a loner ... cool, manly ... whatever hopelessly, completely and totally incorrect view of yourself you've got and come down here with me. And whenever I want stroking, petting, patting, feeding, watering and smothering in oil, I want you to jump to it.' She looked him in the eyes, cool and amused. 'OK?'

He seemed to be thinking about what she had said as if it caused him physical discomfort. As if to steady himself he put one hand on a parked lorry filled with spare metal barriers for crowd control. He grimaced.

'What's the matter?' she said.

'I've got a stone in my shoe.'

She turned round and walked off towards a side-street about thirty yards away, shouting over her shoulder as she went. 'I've got the key to Mark's garage. You might as well wait here.'

She was just about to turn into the side street when he called out to her. She glanced back to see him holding his shoe in his left hand.

'I ...'

At this point the lorry on which the man was leaning disintegrated at a thousand metres per second. The two hundred pounds of plastic explosive hidden inside disconnected his body joint by ligament, scoured it of stomach, lungs, heart and face, and atomised his blood so that, for a moment, in the aftermath, a fine mist of it hung in the air like a small cloud.

Within a few minutes a policeman walked slowly to

the spot where the lorry had once boon parked, stunned by the impossibility of what he was seeing – an apocalypse of broken glass and masonry. For the moment there was only silence. He stood for a few seconds unable to think and then raised the radio attached to his lapel to contact his home station. It was then that he saw the woman lying on the ground, her body arched slightly over a shattered pillar of stone. He ran over to her. She had been cut in two by the metal tailgate of the lorry as it had exploded. Her skirt, not much damaged, was bundled around her waist and the policeman could see she was wearing a pair of immaculate white knickers on which were printed a small red heart and around it the words "*I love you*".

An hour later, still unable to sleep because of the pain in his back, George Winnicott switched on the radio and heard the first reports of an explosion near the Old Bailey. He thought how odd it was to be sitting in his kitchen when only ten days before he would have been woken within minutes of the bomb going off. The report said that one woman had been killed and that a man, her husband, was missing. He decided to go for a walk to take his mind off the pain in his back. By the time he returned Alice had left with the kids to visit her mother for the day. He found a post-it on the kitchen door: "*Urgent. Ring Jim Vaughan as soon as possible.*" Winnicott looked in his diary, picked up the phone and dialled. It was answered after the first ring. 'Jim, it's George here ...'

'Maria's vanished,' interrupted a desperate voice. 'It's been three weeks.'

'Maria's disappeared before, Jim. She's twenty-five.'

'Not for this long. Five days, that was the longest. I'm worried, George. Monica's beside herself.' There was a pause.

'How can I help?' said Winnicott finally.

'Talk to Hobbs. If you ask him, he'll help – put some-one on it and keep them there.'

'I'm not in the force any more, Jim, you *are*. Hobbs is more likely ...'

'He won't. We've never got on and I'm not senior enough to ask a favour. He'll listen to you. He owes you after the Waldorf business. Please.'

Winnicott tried reassurance once more. 'Why could-n't she have gone off somewhere with friends to celebrate the New Year? Lots of people have strayed.'

'I'm sure something's happened. Please, George.'

Winnicott said nothing, weighing up whether he could refuse. He was pretty sure this was just another of his goddaughter's disappearing acts. But the last time they had met the change in her had been astonishing. Why would she have gone back to her old ways? On the other hand, she was an odd girl. 'Of course, I'll do what I can, but it'll take a few days for everyone to get up to speed after the new year so be patient. Give me the details.' He took a pencil from the back of his diary.

'There's not much – you know how secretive she is. She came to see us the week before she disappeared – said she'd never been happier. George ...' his voice expressed only bafflement, 'she looked wonderful. We were both so happy ... never seen her looking so well ... a different girl.'

'Yes, I know,' said Winnicott sadly. 'I met her about six weeks ago. She was on her way to work. I'd never seen Maria looking so contented.'

'So why should she run away?' asked the voice, plaintive and afraid. 'This psychiatrist she'd been seeing, she said he was wonderful. Really helped her. She had a boyfriend and he'd got her to see things differently. He really cared about her. So why would she run away?'

'Have you spoken to him – the boyfriend?'

'She wouldn't tell us his name. You know Maria. We were so delighted we didn't want to press her. She was a new girl, George, almost like another person. Hobbs could find him. If you speak to him, he might know something. I'm worried, George, really worried.'

About six weeks before the phone call about Marie Vaughan, Michael McCarthy, deputy head of investigation at the Fraud Secretariat, had arrived for work. He made his way straight to the chief executive's office suite and booked in with Sally Brett's personal assistant, then sat down and waited. His grey business suit could not hide the stocky mass of his body. The short frame and wide shoulders looked no more than a couple of generations from the working of a plough or the selling of horses, an effect heightened by the slightly red flush of someone who had been out in the sun and open air recently. It was a peasant face, square with a large nose, open, friendly and at ease. When he spoke, however, it was in the rhythm and tone of the Home Counties.

For the first six months after he had become deputy chief, the PA had been pleasant to him, but he had made the mistake of referring to her as Sally Brett's secretary. She took her revenge by always waiting ten minutes before telling Brett he had arrived to keep his appointment. The result was that McCarthy, a punctual man, had now developed a reputation with his superior as a slovenly time-keeper. Brett frequently dropped hints about lateness, and though he realised she was trying to communicate something to him, he had no reason to connect it with his own prompt arrival. On this occasion, however, he was shown in almost immediately. He entered Brett's office feeling slightly uneasy. He knew that his own lack of involvement in the series of cock-ups that had resulted in the collapse of the Bris case after such a long trial would be overlooked if it was considered convenient to deliver someone's balls to the president of the Department of Trade and Industry by way of conciliation. There had, in fact, been no director of investigations since the previous year when McCarthy's last boss had been bribed by a generous early settlement of his pension to take the rap for the collapse of the second Northern Accident trial. McCarthy had refused the offer to replace him on the grounds that the decision, several years earlier, to place all the most complex fraud investigations under one agency meant that a significant proportion would inevitably fail to result in a conviction because they *were* so complex. Any such failure, he reasoned, was bound to be laid at the feet of the FS because the press took into account neither the special difficulty of these cases nor the possibility that the accused might have been innocent.

'Ah, McCarthy,' said a miserable-looking Brett, standing by the window looking down into the street fifty feet below. 'It's good to see the buses are running on time.' McCarthy grunted in a way that he hoped signified his agreement that standards of public transport weren't all they might be, generally speaking. Brett turned round and sat down looking glum. She was in her sixties and had an odd way of speaking, rather like a pre-war colonial governor, which is what her beloved father had been. Unusually tall, with grey hair and a face thin to the point of gauntness, she had a dress sense that had been arrested in the early 1950s, a time when she had, according to unsubstantiated office rumour, been left at the altar by the only man she had ever loved. As a consequence, she had been nicknamed Colonel Havisham after her clipped manner of speaking and the mad, jilted bride in Great Expectations. There was nothing unbalanced about Sally Brett, however, as those who made the mistake of underestimating her usually discovered. Many were the exiles who had tried to get one over on her only to find themselves gulaged to whatever job passed for Siberia in that particular organisation. She sighed irritably.

'Have you seen this morning's *Times*?'

'Not yet.'

'Read it.' She passed over a copy folded so that only the editorial was visible. The headline ran: *A Cosy Arrangement Fails Again.*

Serious fraud is unique in at least three respects. The rewards for wrongdoing can be huge, far in excess of traditional kinds of theft. The late Robert Maxwell misappropriated several hundred million pounds, while the Brinks-Mat gold bullion robbery, the largest ever traditional theft, netted less than thirty million. There are often, at least in the more technical frauds, no obvious victims and no obvious signs that an unlawful deed has been committed. Finally, the complexity of all but the most unsophisticated frauds means that it can be very hard to prove whether or not there has been any wrongdoing at all – at least of a kind that can be clearly established in a court of law.

The disintegration of yet another major fraud trial means that serious questions must be asked about the Fraud Secretariat and its ability to deliver the goods. The FS clearly needs to be given a good shake-up through clearer direction from the top. Why, for instance, was it necessary to indict Louis Bris on so many counts, or to call so many witnesses who merely echoed each other? However, given the failure of its high-profile director Sally Brett to appoint a successor to the long-departed but not-much-lamented John Rank, there is real doubt whether she has the will to take the initiative with regard to getting the financial professions to put their houses in order and restore public confidence in their ability to deal with the cheats within their ranks.

Self-regulation is a traditional British means of avoiding unnecessary state interference while also saving the public purse. It also satisfies a widespread desire by professional bodies not to wash their dirty linen in public lest confidence be lost, although this is not a facility extended to less middle-class miscreants such as bank robbers or burglars. It is hard to feel much confidence in the smug view implicit in the continued existence of such arrangements.

While it is notoriously difficult to assess the total amount of money lost through fraud, reliable estimates put it conservatively at £3 billion a year. This is twice the sum misappropriated through conventional theft, burglary and robbery. If the Upperworld is not to replace the Underworld as the prime source of public concern about the level of criminality in society, then it is high time the financial sector realised that it can no longer be a judge in its own court. The Fraud Secretariat for its part needs to realise that the days of hands-off regulation are numbered. It is being weighed in the balance and we must hope that it will not be found wanting.

McCarthy put the paper back on her desk. Brett looked at him balefully. 'I also had a phone call from Lafferty. He wants to see me over at the DTI tomorrow morning.

I'll have to give him something solid. Louis Bris stole from a great many influential people and a lot of Tory MPs are getting their noses tweaked. Lafferty is under pressure to deliver somebody and I've got to make sure it isn't us.'

'What have you got in mind?'

'We ought to be seen to be acting in a way that is both substantial and effective. We need to fill the Director's vacancy. I had dinner with Sir John Hapgood on Tuesday. He was after a job.'

'With us?' said McCarthy, astonished.

'Not quite. No doubt Sir John would be willing to take over from *me*, but I've no intention of going anywhere. No, it was for someone else.'

'Ah ... who?'

'George Winnicott.'

'Winnicott?' said McCarthy, mystified.

'Yes,' said Brett. 'Is there a problem?'

'We're talking about the Head of the Anti-Terrorist Squad?'

'That's correct.'

Neither said anything for a moment and it was McCarthy who spoke first. 'He's obviously intelligent ... *Principles of Policing* was an interesting piece of work, very well argued. Not at all what you'd expect.'

'From a policeman, you mean?'

'Yes ... I suppose that's what I *do* mean. There's no doubt he squeezed the IRA dry in London. Until recently, anyway.'

Brett looked offended. 'You can't reasonably expect one man to solve the problems of Northern Ireland. The point is that the Anti-Terrorist Squad was an absolute bloody shower when he arrived. Since then there's been a near universal recognition that the IRA have had a difficult time of it because of him. You said so yourself. His decision to seal off the entire City of London to stop them from bombing the financial centre of the country to oblivion was absolutely brilliant ... decisive, direct.'

'I don't remember many people taking that view at the time,' he said, with restrained relish because Brett had bitterly complained about the plan to put road-blocks at all points of entry into the financial district. She ignored the reminder. 'Anyway,' continued McCarthy, 'why would he want to come here? He can't be much more than forty and he's already head of the Anti-Terrorist Squad, so why would he leave? It sounds fishy to me.'

'It's simple. Winnicott's got a bad back, an injury from years ago apparently. He's failed his police medical and he's got to take a desk job. He needs a job that isn't physically demanding but which keeps him mobile.' Brett coughed. It was not a clearing of the throat, it was a black cap to signal the death of their conversation. 'He'll have fresh eyes ... see things differently. He's got a reputation for getting results. Sounds like just the man.'

George Winnicott sat in one of his chiropractor's treatment rooms eyeing a model of the spinal column complete with an assortment of typical back problems defined by different coloured plastic: spondylitis, compression fractures, prolapsed discs. He felt as if he were suffering from every one of them.

'How are you?' asked the chiropractor, as he walked through the doorway with the briskness of a man who could charge twenty-five pounds for every ten-minute consultation he could fit into an hour.

'Not too bad,' Winnicott lied pointlessly. 'A bit stiff.'

The chiropractor gestured towards a padded couch that rested on a plinth hinged so that it pointed vertically. 'On you go.'

Winnicott walked over to the couch, which was slightly taller than him, and rested against it, face down, with his arms above his head. The chiropractor pushed a pedal with his foot and the couch slowly settled to the horizontal, taking Winnicott with it. The chiropractor prodded the fifth lumbar vertebra.

'Ow,' said Winnicott.

There was a grunt of Holmesian inference from the chiropractor, as if he had once again detected the handiwork of some Moriarty of the spinal column. He paused for a moment and then spoke decisively. 'Right then, over this way.'

Reluctantly, because he knew what was coming, Winnicott shifted onto his left side. Long familiar with the violent nature of the assault about to be perpetrated on his body, Winnicott tensed. The chiropractor waited. Winnicott tried to fool himself into relaxing. The chiropractor moved almost imperceptibly and Winnicott stiffened instantly in anticipation. The chiropractor backed off. They made polite diversionary conversation.

'Keeping busy?' said the chiropractor.

'Yes ... you?'

'Oh,' he said complacently, 'we're always busy. We've got a joggers' boom on at the moment. All those middle-aged men who took up jogging in the late Seventies before the arrival of running shoes with decent cushioning. Loads of problems.' He grunted with grim satisfaction. 'God designed us to walk on all fours, basically. From the spinal point of view, standing upright is a terrible idea. People's backs are always going to ache, business will always be good.'

CRACK!

The chiropractor had struck, fast as any kite or snake, pushing and pulling in opposite directions simultaneously. Winnicott could never quite rid himself of the fear that after so many sessions the treatment must be weakening his spine. One day perhaps it would be violently twisted once too often and he would burst open, scattering his vertebrae all over the floor like pearls from a broken string. They went through the same performance on his right side. Then the chiropractor pressed the pedal and Winnicott started to point skyward. As Winnicott slowly returned to the vertical the chiropractor made his habitual joke.

'Be upstanding.'

Fortunately, because Winnicott's face was buried in the leather cradle of the couch, no response was required to a remark that he had heard on nearly forty occasions and which had not been very amusing in the first place.

Inspector Geoff Healey and Sergeant Alan Roache sat in the office of Chief Superintendent Robert Hobbs of the MPD. The initials, reflecting the seriousness with which the department was taken inside the Met, were generally held to stand for Morons, Psychos and Deadbeats, the first two describing the relevant members of the public, the third referring to the fact that the Missing Persons Department was generally disdained as a graveyard for officers of whatever rank who had allowed the wheel to fall off their investigations once too often.

Hobbs was well aware of this lack of regard, particularly by members of the Murder Squad, and this accounted for the sour atmosphere in the room. It was clear that Healey and Roache were unhappy at becoming involved in the case of the missing Maria Vaughan.

'Look, sir,' said Healey wearily, 'we're being taken off inquiries into already proven murders in order to investigate someone who has a history of disappearances. I don't see the logic of that. Unless of course the logic is that it's now become the policy of the Met to investigate possible crimes against relatives of its members as opposed to actual crimes against ordinary members of the public.'

'No, *you* look, Healey,' replied Hobbs, irritated both by Healey's manner and that he agreed with him. 'Let me tell you what the policy of the Met is. The policy is for its officers to do as they're bloody well told. The fact that she's the daughter of a serving officer is irrelevant and I'd better not hear of you or Sergeant Roache saying otherwise in the canteen. The reason we're investigating this case is partly because it has certain unusual features, namely that Maria Vaughan had apparently been cured of her mental problems some time ago, and partly for reasons to do with this new computer program the Information Technology Crime Unit are developing. Your boss thinks this MEMO, or whatever it's called, could be useful in distinguishing early on between people who've just gone absent without leave and victims of serious crime. We want you to gather as much evidence as you can and then we'll evaluate it with the IT people. That's all there is to it. There's nothing sinister and it has nothing to do with any other officers in the force. All right? Now, I suggest you get cracking.'

A week later in Brett's office, the introductions and pleasantries over with, George Winnicott, the new director of the Fraud Secretariat, was taken downstairs to his office by Michael McCarthy.

It was five or six times larger than anything he had occupied before and Winnicott felt a surge of pride at the ownership of such luxury. There was a polished Regency table with eight seats in red and white period stripe, a deeper red, a serious person red to the carpet, and an imposing Queen Anne reproduction desk. There was a brass lamp and a leather blotter, with thick white blotting paper, the size of a pillow case, lying expectantly on it.

He sat down in his chair – more dark wood and leather and not very comfortable – then leant forward to stretch the tense muscles of his lower back, complaining as a result of the unsupportive sofa in Brett's office.

'Congratulations, Director,' said McCarthy, smiling.

Winnicott returned the smile, disconcerted that McCarthy should see what he was thinking. But, of course, it was natural to feel this way, anyone would. McCarthy sat down. 'It would be useful if I went over the history briefly. Unless you feel you've covered all that.'

'Not at all. It's best to assume nothing. I've read a good deal ... not that it's all that easy to get hold of anything on you. I've talked to people. But assume complete ignorance. That's best.'

'Fine. I'll go over the history, set out your specific powers and give you rather a lot of homework. You'll need to review the history of the bigger cases – Britannia Park, Barlow Clowes, Guinness and Blue Arrow should give you what you need.'

'Sounds formidable.'

'Yes, but Shakma does damn good summaries. I think you'll find them a good read. The Upperworld is a fascinating place.'

'Upper world?'

'As in Underworld.'

'Ah, very good.' He laughed not altogether convincingly.

'There's one thing it's important to understand about the scale of what's going on here, if you don't mind me saying so.'

'No, of course not.'

'Imagine you were to put all the robberies, car thefts, muggings, burglaries, all the solid gear stolen by working-class criminals, in a big pile. Then you put next to it all the money defrauded by middle-class people from other middle-class people mostly: the tax evasion, the expense-account frauds, the mortgage frauds where people end up driving around in their new kitchen extension, and then the big stuff, insider deals, share-support scams, trading while insolvent, thefts from pension schemes. This second pile is three ... four ... five times larger.'

Winnicott was clearly surprised. 'I realised from what I'd read that this was a big problem, but I didn't come across anything that indicated it was so serious.'

'Yes, it's pretty odd when you think about it that there isn't more of a fuss. I suppose it's because it's all so undramatic – no guns, no loveable cockney rogues who love their mums, no psychopaths nailing informers to the floor for blabbing to the filth. Welcome to the Upperworld.' McCarthy struggled to think of what else he had to tell his new boss. 'Oh, by the way, your PA's name is Lucy Bradd.'

'We only had secretaries at the Met. What's the difference between a secretary and a PA?'

'About four thousand a year, I understand.' McCarthy looked uncomfortable. 'It might be as well to tell you about a disagreement which has caused some bad feeling. The head of personnel, Allan Gribben is a ... he's very enthusiastic about introducing short-term contracts. To cut a long story and all that, a few years ago he managed to find a perfectly legal way of taking the secretarial staff off their permanent posts and putting them on two-year rolling contracts. I have to say I strongly opposed it – but your predecessor and Sally Brett were quite happy, so that was that. But there's a lot of animosity because of it. Your PA, Lucy, was vocal in opposing Gribben. There's some awkwardness there.' He thought about telling Winnicott that Gribben was not a man to allow opposition from anyone less powerful to go unpunished and that he had been doing everything he could to make life so awkward for Lucy that she would leave voluntarily. Perhaps it would be better to wait until he knew him better. 'Anyway,' McCarthy said, anxious to get on, 'the FS has about fifty lawyers and accountants, and a detachment of about twenty police officers. The accountants try to find out what's been going on in a fraud by following the paperwork and doing interviews. The police mostly handle the evidence resulting from what they find. The lawyers advise on prosecution then bring the cases to trial.'

'The accountants and lawyers ... how do they get on with the police?'

'It's a relationship that could do with improving.'

'In what way?'

'Well, the police don't think that accountants are the right people to interrogate suspects, not on their own. They think the police should be a major part of every investigation as well as being in charge of the documents arising from it. The accountants and lawyers ... well, nobody wants to give up power, do they?' He paused for a moment. 'Perhaps it would be better if you had a nose around yourself. We could compare notes.'

'How do the accountants and lawyers feel about a policeman becoming director?'

'To be honest, I don't know,' lied McCarthy. 'This has all happened pretty quickly.'

Winnicott looked at him. 'And how does the Deputy Director feel about it?'

'He thinks that because the previous directors were all lawyers, all prosecutors, what they understood was how to go about structuring a case once it was clear, broadly speaking, what the case was. What they didn't appreciate, or not appreciate enough, is that we're also an investigative organisation. A gendarme at the top is no bad thing in my view.'

Winnicott stood up and walked over to the window facing Barter Street. The headaches caused by the deterioration in his back were getting worse. 'Is a policeman at the top no bad thing as long as this policeman listens to your advice?'

'Yes.'

Winnicott turned back from the window. 'That's very clear. Thank you.'

McCarthy reached into his briefcase and took out several books and placed them on the desk. 'I'd look at Kirk first; he's thorough on the law. There's a couple of good summaries of the DTI and so on. It's quite technical, a good reference. Try Michael Levi's Royal Commission report next. He's a good read, too. No rush.' He paused. 'Friday will do.'

Winnicott looked at the pile of six books and was not sure if he was joking.

'Shall we go?' said McCarthy.

Evidence Room Four was the size of a small classroom but considerably higher. Large cardboard boxes were stacked on shelves from floor to ceiling around all four walls. But for a narrow corridor, the centre of the room was also taken up with shelves filled with the same buff-coloured boxes roughly the size of two milk crates.

'This is the documentation on the simplest case we're currently investigating,' said McCarthy. 'It's a pretty big sum involved, fourteen million, but there's only one charge.'

'All this for only one charge?' interrupted Winnicott.

'No,' replied McCarthy, with obvious pleasure. 'The paperwork for this case fills another seven rooms just like this one.' Winnicott advanced deeper into the room as if to get the measure of his opponent. McCarthy watched him. 'Your predecessor said that doing this job was like herding cats.'

Winnicott laughed. McCarthy wondered whether he'd still be laughing a year from now. 'I'd better be off. Places to go, people to see. I'll take you back upstairs – it's easy to get lost down here, everywhere looks like everywhere else. Lucy'll go through your diary with you. But the highlight will definitely be the trip to the Bank of England on Wednesday.'

'Really?'

'They're keen to give you the once-over. You'll like Charley Varadi. I'll be interested to hear what he's got to say for himself. The Bank have got very pally over the last three years since he became deputy and I don't know why. Still, they do a nice steak and kidney pie. There's a book on the Bank by Stephen Fay. It's a fine piece of work,' he said with admiration. 'Even though he's a journalist.' He said this as if describing an occupation widely suspected of involvement in the ritual sacrifice of small, blond children. 'I've got a copy. I'll get my PA to pop it down, if it isn't beneath her to do such a menial task.'

Inspector Healey and the young sergeant he had brought with him sat across from George Winnicott in his opulent new office.

'You don't have any idea where Maria Vaughan might be?' asked Healey.

'None.'

Healey nodded. 'Would it be right to say you were close to her?'

'I'm not sure that I'd go as far as that. She was a secretive girl. There were long periods when I didn't see her for months on end.'

He paused for a moment. 'But you are her god-father?'

'Yes.'

'And I'm correct in thinking that she was your children's nanny for several months?'

'Nanny would be a grand way of putting it. She helped my wife for a while when she was recovering from an illness about three years ago.'

'Was she good at helping out?'

'She was rather scatty, I'd say. She was a nice girl. She meant well.'

Healey smiled. 'Shall I put that down as "not a great help"?'

Winnicott smiled back awkwardly.

'Did your wife get on with her?' Healey noticed that the question made him seem ill at ease.

'She was ... irritated by her. She needed the help but Maria was more the kind of person who needed support rather than someone capable of giving it. Don't get me wrong, she was a kind person and generous, but she was unhappy, I suppose.'

'Not a good choice, then.'

'No. My fault. I thought it might help them both. I was wrong.'

Healey nodded as he wrote in his notebook. 'Did she leave under a cloud?'

'No, not at all. My wife had a relapse. Maria found it difficult. There was relief on both sides when we decided it would be best to make other arrangements.'

'But you got on well with her personally throughout this?'

'Yes.'

'Do you have the names of any people she might have been seeing when she was staying with you?'

'There *were* people but I can't remember anyone in particular. As I said, she was very secretive, even as a child. Have you been able to find her boyfriend?'

'Yes. Well, he found us really. He reported her missing a few days ago. A Steven ...' He took out his notebook and searched inside. 'Griltch – God knows if that's how it's pronounced. He did tell me on the phone. A name like that, you'd think you'd remember it.'

Healey took out a photograph from the file he was carrying. It was of a young woman, drably dressed, far too thin and with waist-length, slightly greasy hair. He passed it to Winnicott. 'Her parents said she'd changed a lot since this was taken about six months ago. Would you agree?'

'Yes, a different woman. I think it would be fair to go that far.'

Healey made a brief note. 'Could you give us a description?'

'I'll do my best,' said Winnicott. 'Her hair had been cut shorter than this to about half-way down her back ... expensively cut, with a fringe just about here.' He drew a line across her forehead with his finger. 'But it was still long. She'd put on weight and she needed to. I never thought I'd describe Maria as curvaceous but she'd be about a stone heavier now. But it wasn't fat. She was wearing makeup, not a great deal but it had been put on with skill. She must have learnt that recently – on the rare occasions when I saw her wearing it in the past she'd always looked a bit of a fright, to be honest.'

Healey asked a few more questions, most of them concerned with double-checking things he had already been told. He changed back into an affable former colleague, then he and his silent partner left.

WOMEN IN LOVE

The masculine and the feminine do not describe two sets of qualities in the human heart, but four: good maleness and bad maleness; good womanliness and bad womanliness. When evil men and women discover their feminine or masculine sides they do not become nicer or more resolute, they simply discover a different way of being evil.

Louis Bris, *The Wisdom of Crocodiles*

'He's in a meeting. I did see your proposal on his desk.' There was a pause. 'I *think*. Can he call you back?' Steven Grlscz gave the secretary his number. He almost pointed out that she had said the same thing the last time he'd called. But he didn't.

When people expressed interest in his life as a consultant it was always with the sense that this life was to be approved of and even prized. Consulting seemed to be the epitome of the modern: he was embracing change and did not worry about what was coming next. He was nonchalant about shift and slip, thrived on chaos. In fact his life consisted of long-term unease and short-term drudgery: he had to do his own photocopying, buy stamps and toner, paper in reams; every call had to be answered, even the briefest business acquaintanceship had to be followed up. He must network. He must accept without question the schedules of those who paid, people who had no obligation to give him work, answer his calls, or respond beyond the perfunctory to the hours of effort that went into every proposal. The contracts he signed were fictions. Even lies. If he wanted to work with them again, and such repeat business was the only hope of some stability in all this flux, then he had to accept that they were like beautiful women with many fish in their sea. They had to be stroked, their whims acceded to. And while they could be disagreed with, they could never be crossed. How were you to find satisfaction in this? How were you to find peace of mind? People were aspiring to the condition of sharks, not because they were becoming more predatory but because they could not rest or they would sink and drown. The gurus of business, pimping for instability, were always saying that the Chinese pictogram for problem was also the sign for opportunity. But he knew they must be wrong. It must have been a translation thing. The synonyms for problem were pretty much invariant no matter what the tongue: difficulty and riddle, puzzle and doubt, quandary and snarl and mess.

Steven put down the phone and sat in his high-sback chair with the special lumbar support which cradled his aching back. He began staring out of the window, wondering where he had gone wrong with Maria. With hindsight, nothing he could think of would have improved on his decision to walk out of the shop. It was the right choice. He drifted back to the hours after he had left her, half-dressed, staring after him as he angrily walked away. When he left the Owl Café, he had walked around for several hours wondering what he could do to rescue the situation. Finally, tired and feeling dreadful, he decided to go home.

He heard his phone ringing from half way up the

stairs. He ran up the remaining flight and fumbled desperately for the key, dropped it, swore and managed to get the door open. As he got to the phone, she hung up. 'Fuck!' he shouted, realising he had forgotten to set the answering- machine. He switched it on. Then it rang again. He went to pick it up but decided to listen instead. 'Hello, I'm not in at the moment. Please leave a message at the sound of the tone.'

'Steven? Steven, if you're there please pick up the phone.'

The dread began to lift. There was desperation here. She must have decided either that he was out or wouldn't answer. 'Whatever it is, Steven, I'm sorry. I ... I'm so ...' This must be tricky for her, he thought. The wrong apology could make things worse. 'I'm so clumsy. You musn't be angry with me ... I have to go out. I'll ring back at eight-thirty.' There was a pause. 'I don't really understand a lot of things. People are a m—' She stopped and put down the phone.

He listened to her message over and over. All in all, he was reassured rather than otherwise, although not greatly. He worried about her going out: it seemed to distort the implications of the desperate tone of her voice. If she was as worried as she seemed, why had she left the flat when her absence meant that this anxiety could not be allayed by a call from him? If it was vital then it would be all right, but if it was not, he was finished. He sat and thought about it for some time. After about an hour he was violently sick, bringing up the tea he had drunk in the Owl Café.

At eight twenty-five the phone rang. At the last moment he again decided not to pick it up. She did not ring again until nearly midnight and yet again, uncertain to the point of terror, he did not answer. Beyond identifying herself, she left no message, nor did she the next morning. He took the next day off work and waited. She did not ring. He grew more and more alarmed, afraid that he had overplayed his hand.

He waited through the early evening until nearly nine. A ferocious anxiety gnawed at him, but he couldn't bear to stay in any longer and decided to go for a walk. He pulled the door firmly behind him. It was sticking now in the damp winter, and as he turned for the stairs he saw her waiting in the shadows at the end of the corridor leading up to the next floor. For the first time in his life he was unable to speak. She moved forward into the light. Her eyes astonished him: wide, fearful, the pupils large and black. She called his name then stopped.

'Thank God you've come,' he said. His sincerity pulled her into his arms and with her eyes staring full into his she kissed him. She pushed up against him, forceful in a way that caught him off-guard, and he stumbled against his door awkwardly, catching his back on the handle. He grunted with pain but either she didn't hear him or didn't care. Her hands grasped him around the small of the back and she pulled him tighter into her. She grabbed his hand and forcing it downwards pushed it between her legs. Then she pulled her thick woollen skirt up around her waist. He tried to find the top of her tights but fumbled. With her skirt bundled around her waist she dragged frantically at them, forcing the tights down her thighs. She shifted her legs apart and his hand moved between them. Her left hand cupped the front of his trousers. Then someone moved on to the landing above. She groaned. He reached into his pocket, took out the key, and with a hefty shove to the sticking door they were in the flat.

He tried to steer her to the bedroom but failed. Something had taken hold of her. She pushed him to the floor, stepped out of her shoes and rolled down her tights and knickers. But she was too excited to take them off completely. One foot still sheathed in a train of nylon and cotton, she sat astride him and forced him into her. He winced. In only seconds she was twisting and arching as if shaken by a terrible pain. She fell forward on his neck and said wearily, 'Oh, God.' These were the first words she had spoken since he had found her waiting outside his door.

She stayed there immobile but for her laboured breathing. He could feel her breasts pushing against him rhythmically as she slowly recovered. She said nothing more. He heard heavy breathing again growing louder, and realised it was his own. Still she did not speak.

'Look at me,' he said finally.

Staring at the wall, she replied softly, 'I can't.'

'Why?'

'I'm embarrassed,' she said.

'It's a bit late for that, isn't it?' he said smiling, although he felt sick again.

She pulled herself up. 'I suppose you're right.' She looked him straight in the eye. 'If I'm going to be shameless, I'd better do it properly, don't you think?' She began to undo her blouse, reached behind to unclasp her bra, fumbled for the hook then laughed as she remembered it opened at the front. She unclipped it, pulling the bra away from her without either coyness or overt sexuality. He reached up, taking the weight of her breasts in his palms. How wonderfully soft the skin was, how warm, and how heavily, despite their size, they took to the shape of his hand.

They went to his bedroom and they talked all night, stopping only twice. It was fascinating, if disconcerting, to listen to her as she gave him an account of her state of mind during the previous year. He had spent uncountable hours guessing at the effect of his remarks and actions. Now he was hearing directly what she had really been thinking. Events of which he had been barely conscious or had forgotten turned out to have been of great significance to her. Others that had

pleased him with their subtlety and effectiveness
had made no impact at all, although in one instance
particularly she had seemed at the time to have been
moved deeply. But she also talked of things he had
done or said, or not done or said, which were detailed
in his ledgers in their imagined, hoped-for impact,
sometimes almost word for word. He could not
remember a time of greater pleasure, or relief, as she
poured out her heart to him.

After a long time the spate slowed and between one
sentence and the next she fell asleep. It would have
been nice to sleep too; he could have done with a good
night's rest. But tonight he felt unsettled, as if he
needed to keep listening or moving. His breathing was
shallow and his pupils contracted. Vindication is a
powerful drug, he thought. Be careful. He slipped her
head gently from his shoulder and slid out from under
her legs. He stood by the bed, his arms hanging loosely
by his side, and looked at her for a long time. After
about ten minutes she stirred, missed his presence,
opened her eyes half-way and saw him standing by the
bed watching her. She smiled almost without moving
her lips then closed her eyes and settled into the white
pillow. He looked at her face. It was relaxed, entirely
itself.

In the end he went to the kitchen to make himself
tea. He drank it and made more, trying to think calmly
of what to do. He went back to bed at six-thirty and
within ten minutes he was falling into his habitual
semi-conscious doze. When he woke it was nearly
twelve and Maria was sitting, dressed, on the edge of
the bed with a cup of tea in her hand. He was oddly
startled, and disguised his nervousness by yawning.
She was smiling but he could think of nothing to say.

'Would you like tea or coffee?' she said.

'Tea, please.' He was acutely conscious that he was
not meeting her gaze, and to hide his eyes he rubbed

his hands over his face, as if trying to wake himself properly. Fortunately she left, and when she returned a couple of minutes later he was ready to face her.

'There doesn't seem to be any toast,' he said.

'What did your last slave die of?'

He reached for her and pulled her down beside him. She squealed as she fell, her legs splaying inelegantly apart. Off-balance still, she struggled to close them but he pushed his hand and elbow between her knees, the skirt taut across her thighs. He shifted his weight, jamming her against the wall on one side. Placing his left hand just above her knee he slowly pushed it along her cool, white skin and between her legs. She had kept still at first but now she started to struggle. This caused her skirt to ride up towards her waist. He hooked one finger around the tight elastic of her knickers and gently pulled them to one side. It was not difficult for him to avoid being sentimental but even after all this time and all these women he was still astonished by its beauty. It surprised him because it was so unexpected. All other parts of the human body seemed predictable, to belong to one another, but somehow the connection between this combination of hair and softly folded skin and the body it served eluded him. He did not understand pornography, nor was he interested in it. Once in the 1960s he had looked through a collection of pin-up photos in black-and-white he had found lying on the pavement. The pubic area had been airbrushed to remove all traces of hair and labia so that they looked like naked mannequins in a shop window: smooth and impenetrable. Odd as this was, and though the implications were absurd, the pictures somehow seemed more logical, what you would have expected. Looking up at Maria, he noticed how touched she was by his gaze and how safe his appreciation made her feel.

An hour later she returned from taking a shower. As

she walked naked and unselfconscious around the room, it occurred to him how vital it had been, this disinterested sense of the beauty of women. They felt the sincerity of his appreciation and imagined always, every time, that this arrived hand in hand with a capacity for love or being genuine or a whole range of related virtues.

Distractedly she searched the room. Unsuccessful, she stood, biting her lip thoughtfully.

'What are you looking for?'

She turned her head away, laughing. 'I can't find my knickers.'

He pulled back the sheets, picked them up and held them out to her.

As she took them from him, she turned and sat on the bed to put them on. Then she stood up and looked at him. 'I was beginning to think you might be keeping them for a souvenir.'

'Me?' he said with genuine surprise. 'I'm not much of a one for keeping things.'

'You're not, are you? There are no bits and pieces here, no photos, no old letters on your mantelpiece. I don't really know anything about you at all.'

He looked at her thoughtfully, then said quietly, 'You never seemed particularly interested.'

She turned and started to dress too quickly, then stopped. Still with her back turned she said, 'I'm sorry.'

'There's no need to be. If I'd wanted to tell you my life story I would have. If I'd wanted you to think about my state of mind rather than your own then, frankly, I wouldn't have taken the trouble to get to know you and then I wouldn't have fallen in love with you.'

Her eyes rounded. 'I want to know about you now.'

And so he began to tell her about himself, his child-hood on an obscure RAF military base in Germany;

how after he had drunk purple rat poison his mother
had saved his life by forcing him to swallow salt water
and repeatedly making him sick by sticking her finger
down his throat; his elder brother's death by drowning
and his own inability to persuade a passer-by who
could have saved him that it was not a childish prank;
the day he inadvertently set fire to the school's grand
piano and how a year later, having got away scot-free,
he confessed because he'd misunderstood what was
intended to be a jovial remark from the headmaster;
university, jobs, the accident, not his fault, in which
he had run over and killed a small boy; the story that
always turns out to be more morose than you had
expected. He talked for several hours without
stopping, Maria contributing only occasional laughs
and touches. When he had finished she said, 'Now I
really am sorry.'

He laughed. 'After three and a half hours I'm not surprised.'

She smiled back. 'Thank you for telling me.'

'Would you like to see a photograph of my brother?'

She nodded and he went over to his desk drawer,
searched for a moment, then returned with a single
black-and-white box-camera photo. It was of a coltish-
looking blond boy of about thirteen, whose smile was
breaking out of the unreal grimace of the carefully
posed family photograph and into the grin of someone
who wasn't taking the photographer seriously.

'My mother took it about a week before he died. I
was an orderly little boy, terribly tidy about my clothes
and toys – just like now. He used to burst in on
me, wreck everything in his search for whatever he
needed, then vanish. He doesn't look much like me,
does he?'

'No.'

They talked more about his brother's death and
the effect it had had on his family. He admired the

delicacy with which she listened and responded: a comment here, a question there, a readiness to laugh when he shifted from bitterness or loss to an amused and telling evocation of the dead, in one of those bewildering switches so typical of those talking about their grief. She made no claims to know exactly how he felt, avoided intrusive sympathy, yet she was clearly moved. He was impressed.

Finally she left.

Some people have a thirst for understanding, some have a hunger for it. Some are even desperate, but not in the way that Steven Grlscz is desperate. The peasant farmer staring at his horse's arse twelve hours a day is not in tune with nature and the natural world. It must be done to stay alive. The natural world is always threatening to break his heart and anyone who can choose to do these things is never going to understand. Thinking is what Steven has to do and what he does is like breaking the ground with a blunt plough, tending a sick horse, having too many mouths to feed and insufficient rain. Except that it's not just hard: it's complex, tricky and fathomless.

His head ached and he felt drained rather than tired. He decided he must ring Maria and put her off returning so that he could get some more sleep. That he dozed so lightly meant that he needed a great deal of this half-sleep to maintain his strength. She answered quickly, pleased to hear his voice and obviously thinking his call was a demonstration of romantic impatience for her return. She was caught off-guard by his request. Her silence and the hurt tone of her response alarmed him. He tried to withdraw and asked her to come as soon as she could but he knew it sounded lame and she was unconvinced. 'Please come now.'

'Look, it's all right.'

He could almost see the tautness of her lips. 'I want you to come.'

She laughed but in a way that sent a chill across his heart.

'Don't be silly. I understand. Just get some rest, it's fine.'

He knew there was no point in continuing. 'I'll see you tomorrow,' he said, aiming for a tone somewhere between tiredness and gentle anticipation.

'Yes ... fine.' The hurt tone had increased in its intensity.

'Bye, then.'

'Bye.' Her farewell was almost inaudible – iciness warmed by disappointment.

He went to bed and dozed, waking at midday with the winter sun shining powerfully on his bed. Although he preferred the heat of summer, he liked the sharp, severe lines produced by the sunny days in December and January. Despite the cold, anything was preferable to the predominant greyness of an English winter. He felt better after his sleep and the sunlight in the room cheered him up. He rang a local flower shop and ordered a dozen roses to be sent to Maria at work. The choice of flowers was not an unthinking reflex but the result of experience: he knew to his cost that it was foolish to put aside rituals of this kind on the grounds that they had become devalued by habit.

He left several messages on her answering-machine knowing that there was no chance of her being in. He called her as soon as she arrived home from work and quickly sensed her desire to forgive him, and, after the urging of his first apology, her nervous hope that he would observe all the forms of contrition. She was like a mother anxiously watching her son's first piano recital where all that was required was for him to finish without pausing or striking too many false notes. It would not be so easy a second time or, if it were, a third. The power of a breach made up to bring two people closer had proved itself to him before, but so had its capacity to erode. And you could never tell for certain which was which.

He returned to his ledgers with renewed heart. To his relief their account began to approach a point where they matched. They were becoming equals. When they were balanced it would be the right time. At night when he was not with Maria he would work at the ledger with the care of an interpreter on the final draft of a complex technical manual full of obscure terminologies for which there was no exact translation.

———

'Are your eyes closed?' he said to her. She was sitting on his sofa half-way across the room from him smiling and with her eyes shut. She was dressed in a business suit because she had arrived straight from a book launch at work. Her skirt, fetchingly, was just a little too short and, perched on the edge of her seat, she uncrossed her legs to give herself a greater sense of security while she waited uncertainly but pleasurably for what he was going to do. The result of this was that her legs splayed slightly too wide. Other than when they were making love there was a modesty about her and she was as careful about bending and sitting elegantly in company as a 1950s debutante. He could make out the dark V between her legs lightened by the white cotton of her knickers; it made her seem especially vulnerable.

'Do you trust me?' he said.

'Of course not,' she replied opening her eyes widely.

'Shut your eyes.' She did as she was told, laughing in nervous anticipation.

'Do you trust me?'

'I don't know. What are you going to do?' She sensed him coming close to her and then she felt his hot breath on her face. She forced her eyes to remain shut. She waited. Gently, hardly noticeable at first, she felt him brush against her lips, and then he was kissing her softly. The desire to open her eyes was almost impossible to resist. She gave in. His hand was raised in front of her a few feet away and between his thumb and forefinger he held a ring. He said nothing as she looked at it, her lips slightly parted. He felt for her left hand and slowly slipped it on to her ring finger. She looked at it, watching the light refracting through the three diamonds, and for several seconds he felt as if she were somewhere else entirely. She looked at him.

'Yes,' she said.

They said nothing more for a long time but when they began to talk it was quietly, as if trying to avoid waking an invalid in the next room. She sometimes rested her forehead on his, sometimes leaned back slightly in order to look at him. Without their noticing, the light began to fail until they realised they were talking in the dark. She stood up to switch on a table light but he stood up with her as she did so. She could feel that he was in the grip of something powerful as he pulled at the skin on the back of her hand. She sensed the emotion in him as an almost physical push and she was excited by his excitement. She pushed back and he pulled her towards him, one arm around her waist. He kissed her then let her go and, without looking back, walked towards the bedroom. As she followed him through the door, he grabbed her hand and pulled her behind him. She came to him and then, supporting her weight behind her shoulder-blades, he laid her gently across the bed. She felt an unfamiliar harshness between the counterpane and thin sheet and with it a noise that was familiar but which she could not place.

'What's that?'

'Nothing,' he said.

She raised her upper body and shuffled backwards to gain a comfortable purchase on the bed. He moved on top of her and handled her roughly with a desperation that was both alarming and exciting. His usual control, intriguing yet also slightly off-putting, had deserted him. His left leg came across her lower body and pushed her firmly into the mattress. She was dimly conscious of the unfamiliar sound and texture again. He slewed his body so that his weight pinned her down while leaving her right side free. He looked into her eyes, his own wild and oddly unfocused, and she felt swept by strange emotions: curiosity, a submission in the face of something at once distasteful and exciting and also subterranean, which she did not recognise as the beginning of fear. His left hand fastened across her forehead and he intertwined the fingers of his free hand with hers. She was deeply moved by the gentle way he did this, as if he were sifting for a lost valuable in warm sand. He arched his back so that he could look at her from the furthest distance possible. He held this look for a long time until he could see the first signs of uncertainty and puzzlement, then gently placed the flat of his hand over her eyes, held it there for a few seconds then covered her mouth. She tried to call his name but only half the sound emerged before he smothered it then pushed her head into the bed with terrible force. She started to struggle but he tensed his whole body, except his neck and head, and she could barely move. He bit her with all the strength in his jaws. She bucked in agony and his body jerked upwards. His teeth were not sharp enough to break through the skin and he pulled her head sideways so that he could tear at it with the force of the immensely developed muscles of his shoulders and neck. Her body heaved again in pain and terror and her face slipped briefly from his grasp and she screamed. It was a terrible sound, which resonated through her whole body, centred in the bowels. He bit and tore again. She thrashed beneath him and the blood sprayed out of the tear in her neck, pumping over his face, covering her bare shoulder and staining the counterpane. His mouth stretched open in an attempt to cover the tear he had made, but still the blood leaked. He began to drink, interrupted only by the fitful heaving of the woman beneath him.

He drank for about five minutes until the struggling stopped and the first involuntary shivers began, as if she were being fed tiny electric shocks. He stopped as soon as he felt this, slowly lifting his mouth from her neck but by no more than half an inch, relieved to be able to breathe through his mouth again. Then he pulled himself up further, his hand still tight on her mouth. Holding his breath, he looked into her eyes. Horror was clearer now than terror, and the physical shock of her wound and loss of blood had left her weakened and dazed. He searched her eyes and seemed to see something. Underneath the growing paralysis something in her was still alert. He bent down and sucked at the wound for about twenty seconds, then raised his head as if he were bringing a hidden thing deep inside her to the surface and this was now what mattered. Slowly the balance shifted until he was gazing almost continuously into her eyes, with only the occasional dip of his head to drink. He searched her eyes again and marshalled all that he found there: incomprehension, fear, pain, disgust, shaping and ordering them until he could get a clear sight of what would keep him alive. He let his hand slip from her mouth. For the five minutes before she became un-conscious he watched her sense of his betrayal of her love deepen and spread like a terrible stain until it coloured everything, even her terror at her approaching death. Her eyelids fluttered then closed. He shook her and they opened but her sight was failing. He shook her again and for the last time she saw his face clearly and felt his rapt attention, lacking either pity or malice and then she was gone.

She was still alive, however. He got off the bed, knelt beside it and pulled her limp body to one side. He began to suck again at the wound until he could feel the flow of blood grow sluggish as her heart slowed. Suddenly her body twitched as she suffered a heart attack. He stood up and walked to the bathroom to wash his face and hands. When he returned, she was dead.

Standing by the bed he felt under the counterpane, reaching for the sheet of thin polythene underneath. Without the bedcovers to muffle it, the sound was unmistakeable. He pulled it up and used it to roll her body into the centre of the bed, covered her with one side of the counterpane and polythene, walked to the other side and did the same. He carried the body into the bathroom, laid it on the tiled floor, took off his shirt and went back to sit down on the bed.

Carefully, as if protecting an injured back, he turned and pushed the pillows on to the floor, then slowly lowered himself onto the bed. After about five minutes a faint flush of red appeared on his chest which then began to deepen and spread like an allergic reaction up to his neck and shoulders and then to his face. It faded, but then appeared on his stomach, now enlarged and taut like the belly of a starving child or a bald head going red in the sun. Then it, too, faded, leaving his skin a delicate pink. His eyes, half-closed, blinked slowly every few seconds like those of a small child about to fall asleep. During the next half-hour a slow and irresistible peace seeped into every muscle. When it reached the tip of his toes he fell into a sleep that was rare, excellent and still.

When he started to wake up it was without any idea of
how long he had been asleep. It had been, in fact,
about three hours. He heard a groaning noise and,
groggy, for one terrible moment thought it might be
Maria, somehow still alive. Just as he realised that the
groan was coming from him, he felt an unpleasant
surge in his stomach, massive and palpable like a
child turning over in its mother's womb. There was an
unpleasantly metallic taste in his mouth. He tried to
swallow but the mucus covering the back of his throat
was choking him, and he had to reach deep into his
mouth with his finger to clear it. He looked at the
sticky substance on his forefinger. It was red. Then he
recognised the taste.

The skilled oenophile can trace a glass of wine not
only to a vineyard but also to a particular place and
time of pressing. Steven inhabited a world without
smell or flavour. Milk was much the same as alcohol;
garlic and chocolate differed only in texture.
Everything in him was reserved for blood. A little
went a long way and though he, too, used it as a fuel,
what he was mostly nourished by was something
more complex than sugars or amino acids. At first this
evidence of the supernatural disturbed him: its
ghostliness failed to match up with the grim drive
to live that nagged at him every minute of the day,
irritating even his twilight attempts at sleep. But after
a while it seemed just common sense: babies lacking
the touch of adult skin decline to grow, well-fed
children suffering abuse will fail to thrive, men's
hearts stutter given sufficient aggravation as they
work. The lump in the throat, the swallowing of pride,
the eating of humility in a pie: these are not poetry.
Emotions have a taste and their flavours are stronger or
more discreet depending on their nature. Strong
flavours mask those more subtle. The love she had felt

for him was briefly tainted by terror, disgust and fear –
but she did not feel these things for long enough to
stop him getting what he wanted. But love, in turn,
concealed: inside Maria there had been many hiding
places, many dead-ends, many oubliettes where things
were bottled up in strictest confidence, most of
them irrelevant to Steven's need – except for one. This
had needed several hours to make itself apparent,
hidden so deep in her that even she had not been more
than fleetingly aware of it before she put it aside. The
taste he recognised was that of reservation. She
had been holding back. Something in her was dissatisfied with him; something deep, minute and very
poisonous.

His stomach heaved. He ran to the bathroom, fell
over Maria's bound body and cracked his head on the
toilet bowl. He vomited with a painful retch. There
was surprisingly little. It was dark red, almost black,
and liverish. He vomited again until he was drained
and sobbing with exhaustion; and still he retched. He
slumped to his knees and rested his head on his arms,
his breathing laboured and irregular like a toddler
after a lengthy tantrum.

He remained like this for perhaps half an hour until
his breathing slowed and became rhythmical, his heart
stopped racing and the pain in his head settled to a
dull throb. He undressed and got into the bath and ran
the taps until it was half full. Weakly he washed himself. The water turned a pale rust colour rippled with
strands of undissolved blood. It looked, he thought, as
he lay back exhausted, like liquid marble. He dried
himself with immense care so that no blood would
drip onto the carpets and left the bathroom. Wearily he
saw that the blood had already seeped under the door
and had stained the bedroom carpet.

Although it would take time to do it properly, the
bathroom was completely tiled and could be steam-

cleaned. The blood-stained carpet would have to be cut out and replaced. The real danger was the small drop of blood left unnoticed from the killing. He padded towards the kitchen and, passing the full-length mirror in the living room, caught a fleeting reflection: old-looking and startled, his body white, as if he had been soaked in bleach.

The unusually large stainless steel sink was built low so it was easy for him, even in his weakened state, to sit on one of the double drainers with his feet perched on either side of the sink. He half filled it then mixed in some low-sud automatic washing powder. He let his feet and fingers soak for twenty minutes until they puckered like miniature mountain ranges. While he waited, he rested his head on his knees and tried not to be sick. Feeling slightly better, he took a wooden toothpick from a box on the window ledge and began to clean under his nails, wiping the contents onto a small sponge that he would burn with his clothes and the sheets. He would also clean her body before disposing of it, careful as the most painstaking manicurist. He filled a jug with water and meticulously rinsed the sink again and again. At last he had finished. He stood in the middle of the kitchen and looked around, checking that he had not forgotten anything. Suddenly he felt cold. A thrill of pain and nausea struck him and he sank to his knees to stop himself fainting. He remained on all fours for several minutes. When he tried to move he felt a sharp pain in the back of his head. He lay down and the pain receded, to be replaced by an uncomfortable pumping sensation. He tried to move again. The pain was worse. Slowly he crawled out of the kitchen, across the living room and into the bedroom where he pulled himself onto the bed. It took him forty minutes to make the journey. He lay there letting the pain fade and getting colder: the sheets and blankets from the bed were wrapped around Maria. He lay still for an hour, freezing, thinking about the blood hardening in the bathroom and how endless the task of removing it would be. At last the central heating came on and slowly warmed the room. The hairs on his body, erectile with cold, sensed the increasing warmth and began their slow decline to lie flush against his skin. He fell asleep.

It was the cold that woke him up again eighteen hours later when the heating had gone off for the second time. His back muscles felt as if they had been tied in thick knots by clumsy hands and then lubricated with sand. He swung his legs over the side of the bed, sat still for a moment, breathed out heavily and slowly stood up. All things considered, he could have been in worse shape.

He took things easy for the rest of the day, and as it wore on he felt better although still delicate. The various pains and aches dissipated but were replaced by a sense of fullness. He stayed away from the bathroom.

Over the following two days he began to feel stronger and by the end of the third day he could see that his skin had lost its patchy, dull appearance and looked increasingly sleek. This puzzled him because he had been keeping at bay the fear that he was now faced with slow starvation. After a time it occurred to him why this was probably not the case. Some of the complex chemicals in wine or beer are toxic, but even when taken in sufficient quantities to poison they also contain food: minerals, vitamins, liquid solids. Drunks slowly strychnined by their addiction seldom eat but do not starve. He would live to regret his mistake, whatever it was.

He waited until the next morning before tackling the bathroom so that his neighbours would not hear him making odd noises at suspicious hours. People notice small things that are out of the ordinary: pink suds, minor changes in behaviour, odd smells and the moving of rolled-up carpets at three a.m. It had cost him many scares to learn that real secretiveness involved a powerful awareness of routine. He went to the Do It All store at Staples Corner and hired a carpet cleaner and another machine for steaming wallpaper. At first he tried to liquefy the blood in the bathroom using the wet heat of the wallpaper stripper, but this was messy and therefore dangerous. He learned that with the right amount of heat he could simply soften the blood so that it would remain solid yet slip away from the tiles using the scraper. The mixture of digestive juices and blood warmed by steam gave off an appalling stench, which even several cans of air freshener could not entirely hide. Within a surprisingly short time, about four hours, the bathroom looked clean to superficial inspection. Hours of work remained with many different kinds of blood-obscuring cleansers and abrasive powders: Sparkle, Kilrock, Sugarsoap and Shiny Sinks; Kleenoff, Ajax, bleach, Bar Keeper's Friend; and Mr Muscle, Vanish, Viakal and SOS.

The cleaning was all made more difficult by the increasing discomfort in his lower abdomen. It was not so much a pain as a sense of being full. His head began to ache mildly, although this could have been because of the chemicals evaporating in a confined space. Then the fullness in his lower abdomen became an uncomfortably hot sensation. He tried urinating, but although he wanted to, nothing happened. Repeatedly he stood over the toilet waiting, but the sensation went away. Finally a slow dribble came out, stinging and hot. Then a powerful pressing sensation began, but as if it were being held back. He gasped as a sharp pain hit the base of his urethra. It started to move upward as if he were pissing needles. He tried to stop but the relentless slow grind continued as his eyes bulged in agony. Another dribble emerged, this time yellowy-red. There was a pause, a sharp stab, and then a gush, and looking down he could see something hard and pointed poking out of the top of his penis, enfolded in the delicate softness of his urethral skin. It stuck with the bloody urine leaking around it and he was forced to squeeze it out with a stifled scream. It emerged slowly like an obscene crystalline tongue. Then it was out and in his hand. A rush of urine burned its way like acid over the torn skin.

This happened seven times. He took three Kapake analgesics every four hours to dull the pain. It worked. The level of pain remained merely unbearable. After three days it stopped and he was left with a handful of muddy coloured crystals which shed a powdery residue. He crushed one easily but found that it would not dissolve in water or anything strongly acidic or alkaline. Carefully he tasted a tiny grain. It was overpowering and nastily familiar. He spat it out immediately but could taste it for hours afterwards, and it caused the muscles in his neck to knot again like an old tree. But at least the pain was explicable and therefore priceless. The incentive to avoid mistakes next time would be very great indeed. Nevertheless he felt sore, weak and humiliated because only luck had saved him, and he resented luck like a favour from a magnanimous rival you knew would not be there to bail you out a second time.

———

Disposing of the body was a practised routine, but her body had lain unattended for much longer than normal. Having finished smearing Maria in Nutradol gel to disguise the smell of decay he zipped her into a thick rubber body bag and carried her downstairs in a Day-Glo orange hold-all. At about eleven a.m. he took it downstairs and put it in the back of his twelve-year-old Mercedes 350 estate. Within ten minutes he was heading around the City and out towards the bridge which had replaced the decaying Blackwall tunnel. The old Mercedes swept over the wide roadway which gave a fine view of London. Downstream the Thames fell to the sea washed in a brilliant sunlight softened by a thin layer of cloud. For perhaps this one day in the year it gave the remains of the brutal heavy industries on either side of the river – cement, iron ore – a derelict pastel grandeur.

There was a short queue to pay at the toll booth and when his turn came he had only a ten-pound note. He held it out to the sullen attendant. She pointed to a large sign: Exact Change Only.

'I don't have any. I'm sorry.'

'I need the right change.'

Steven searched his pockets to show willing, although he knew they were empty. 'This is all I've got. I know it must be a bind for you ... I didn't know the bridge was open yet.'

'You don't have anything smaller?'

'No ... if I had it, I'd give it to you.' He let her realise that he was controlling a justified impatience but that she had the power to force him to keep it under control.

She looked at him flatly. 'You're supposed to have the right change.'

'I haven't been through here before. Next time I'll have the right money.'

She looked at him without responding. He handed her the ten-pound note and the barrier lifted. As she turned to the next driver, her face showed neither triumph nor irritation.

He drove to the Suffolk coast with the windows down, enjoying the warm wind on his face, taking a couple of hours to reach a small place near Sizewell where he rented a hut next to the beach. Once in the hut, he locked the body in a steel padlocked chest. He hired a boat in Harwich where he also bought six 15-kilo weights. Four hours later, he was back at the beach and loading the body into the boat. Cloud had dimmed the sun so that the grey stones of the beach merged with the grey sea and the grey sky. The only colour in the deserted landscape was the dark blue of his track-suit and the bright electric orange of the bag.

Ten miles out, in deep water, with the weights tied to the body, he rolled it over the side. Its fall was visible for half a second as the black of the body-bag merged with the blackness of the undersea. He watched for a moment, feeling the gentle swell of the sea as it shifted the boat. He plunged his face into the water for ten or fifteen seconds, and pulling himself back, he wiped the freezing water from his face, smoothing it over his dark hair. He sailed into Harwich as the light failed and he was back in his flat by eleven p.m.

———

The weariness of pursuing a life where the opportunities for failure were endless left Steven alternating between boredom and terror. It was such hard work being the way he was. He could rely on nothing. Mistakes and successes often masqueraded as one another. With Maria, poor judgement had saved his life, thoughtfulness and insight almost lost it. Careful planning and patience had allowed their relationship to settle into a deadly friendship. But his storming out of the shop in anger had forced her in the most dramatic way to reconsider what she felt about him. He should have killed her weeks ago but he was confused both by the failure as well as the success. Unplanned victory was itself a kind of defeat because it was vital not only to succeed but also to know exactly why. Where you might unconsciously charm you might also unwittingly offend. In letting her live long enough for her reservations to crystallise, what would have been pure enough to keep him safe for years had been adulterated to the point where it had poisoned him. All he had now was breathing space, and little enough of that. It had not been indecisiveness alone that had delayed her killing but a certain gratitude that she had returned, and a desire on his part to take it easy for a bit. This, thought Steven, had been his unforgivable mistake: the thing that distinguishes man from the animals is that animals don't take holidays. Nature doesn't believe in breaks, in time off. There's paying attention or there's death. Down in the jungle it's work, work, work.

He realised this because he learnt quickly. But you could never learn quickly enough, for there were so many complicated ways in which to make mistakes. This complication was not matched by the brutally straightforward consequences of getting it wrong. There was starvation in every compliment, in every kiss bestowed and touch reserved; what you did and what you did not do. It all mattered, all of it, all of the time.

He flicked through a copy of *Vogue* he had bought at the newsagent's the day before. For a long time women's magazines had been a puzzle to him. All of them – whether for the young or the middle-aged, cheap or pricey – seemed identical in their triviality: no politics, no economics, no sociology, no history, no analysis. Everything was reduced to the golden rule of four: food, relationships, disease and looking good. He liked and admired, and was often amazed by, the richness of the women he had known, and so the repetitive similarity of these magazines did not reflect his experience of women in any significant way. Until one day he twigged.

Most men led simple, if aggravating, lives consisting of money and the work they did to get it. Women, on the other hand, were on the go from dawn till dusk, just as they had always been: gathering, watching, preparing, teaching, fetching, carrying, mending, arranging, delivering, putting things back. Now they were free to live lives of money and work as well. The High Priestesses of liberation had given them something else to do, and only the inventive generosity of men – Mr Hoover, Mr Zanussi – had prevented them from grinding to an exhausted halt. Women liked to read women's magazines for the same reason that he enjoyed them: in a life where there were always other things to think about, always another task you had to do, it was nice to switch off for a bit.

And no wonder, he thought, that women's magazines were full of recipes: mothers rewarded and withdrew through food; anorexics punished; seducers and plain women fed their way into the hearts of others; grandparents sweetened their daughter's toddlers and in doing so turned their daughters sour. Every bottle has its message, every meal its manifesto. Here were the missing economics, the absent politics, the disappearing sociology. Many bitter Christmas dinners with many different families had taught Steven that you could even eat history. Since he survived on something that could not be touched, what had seemed implausible to him at first was suddenly obvious: abstractions can be boiled or baked or fried.

At some point in the fairly recent past, he had realised that he was harbouring an ideal. He had read in *Vanity Fair* about a family refurbishing an ancient, run-down, large ancestral home. They had discovered while rebuilding that it had two bedrooms they hadn't known about. He considered himself to be exactly like a house – finite, known, needing to be adapted to changing circumstance by sharp tools – but this story captured his imagination and unsettled what had become a fixed way of viewing himself. Some time later he'd listened to a woman at the next table in the café in Liberty's who was troubled by a recurring dream in which she discovered that her house contained large rooms she'd never seen before. He was particularly struck by her recollection of opening an airing cupboard door and finding, instead of the dark accumulation of out-of-fashion clothes or the warm smell of hot cotton, a spacious room: light, well-proportioned and with a view. He was possessed by a certainty that there was a way out, that if he could find the right woman and persuade her to love him perfectly, then when he killed her it would stop.

In the days that followed, his body reacted erratically to his near-failure with Maria – nausea, blurred vision, an occasional attack of the shakes – but all in all he was reassured. He would manage for a year or so, he guessed, maybe more. The headaches and the stiffness were more pronounced, particularly if he could not doze for an hour during the day, but whether he slept or not, at four o'clock came the sudden dip, the sense that he had been disconnected and allowed to drain away. His fear, great at first, receded to a nagging presence at the back of his mind.

After three weeks he called the police and reported Maria missing, then went shopping for clothes. He spent nearly two hours with one of the assistants in the Paul Smith shop in Covent Garden. The man's initial enthusiasm waned as Steven chose and replaced, matched one set of clothes with another then rejected everything he had chosen. His attitude changed again as Steven arrived at a collection of suits, jackets, ties and trousers which suggested a taste which was original but restrained. He wrote a cheque for just under two thousand pounds and walked round the corner to Windles. He gave the hairdresser a photograph cut out of a magazine of a man in his forties, a businessman, with a neat but uninspiring haircut, and asked her to do his hair in the same style.

When he returned to his flat there was a letter for him. **This is Not a Circular**, the envelope announced. He opened it. The Nationwide building society was pleased to declare a half per cent fall in the interest repayments on his mortgage.

THE DARK FIGURE

There is no such thing as an individual man or woman. There is only society.

Louis Bris, *The Wisdom of Crocodiles*

From time to time the head gatekeeper at the Bank of England turns away members of the public who waggishly ask him to show them the cash machine, or ask where they need to go to get a loan. He treats them as he has always done, with tolerance and courtesy. He gently points them to a commercial bank, Lloyds on Poultry, perhaps, or the National Westminster on Bishopsgate. If he curses them he does so under his breath and the curse is a mild one, as you would expect of a man with such fine silver hair, a red waistcoat, pink tails and a top hat.

It's true, there are a few current accounts. The Chancellor of the Exchequer may have one, also the Lord Mayor of London, even a few companies, but only if they've had money deposited since before the Indian Mutiny. Some employees keep their money in a chequing account, although until recently the Bank refused to allow them overdrafts: debt of any kind was declared imprudent. The decision to allow individuals at the Bank to borrow had been the most important event in British banking history because it marked the point at which money changed its attitude. It changed from being hard to being flexible, from being a constant worry to being a plastic friend.

'Fuck.'

It is three minutes past nine and money in the Bank of England has fallen short. Two hundred million pounds cannot be accounted for. The man who is cursing is no more than irritated and only he can hear the language which had he been overheard using when he first came to the Bank would have got him fired. Pencil and rubber in hand he scans the number-laden paper in front of him: vast columns of unimaginable sums made up of innumerable giros paid to unemployed welders, redundant middle-managers, single mums; the price of an MRI scanner here; the final payment for a submarine there. A call to the Treasury has failed to find the missing millions and the manager is doing his sums again, rubbing out and filling in. He will not use a calculator or a computer, not out fuddy-duddiness or an unwillingness to learn new tricks, but because he knows technology is thoughtless and liable to make mistakes, and if he is going to get it wrong, the mistakes which have emerged from the tips of his fingers are easier to find. He speaks to these figures and they talk back to him.

Elsewhere it's clear that the markets must be calmed. A discount house is offering to buy bills one thirty-second of one per cent over the prevailing interest rate. Charley Varadi considers the meaning of this twitch. Knowing that at one p.m. figures will be released to reveal that inflation has risen slightly above expectations, he considers the ways in which the market can be stroked. He talks to the dealing room: 'Stress that the numbers last month were lower than they expected. Encourage them to look at the figures together. Tell them we're taking a long view.' There is laughter at this, Bank laughter, gentle, knowing and private.

The head of Foreign Exchange knocks on his office door and enters. In the old days, say three years ago, they might have had a conversation about the wisdom of intervening in the markets, buying pounds to bolster the price of sterling. But the days when the Foreign Exchange dealing room could fight off raids on sterling and defend a fixed exchange rate have gone for ever. 'Intervening in the foreign exchange markets these days,' Charley was fond of saying, 'is like walking into the middle of the M1 and trying to stop the traffic by raising a disapproving eyebrow.'

Now the Bank is only able to advise and warn. It's not that no one is listening, but that there is no longer anyone out there to hear. There is only money, volatile, on the move, following the flow of itself: here, there, everywhere. Charley Varadi would sigh. 'You know, I used to think that if there was such a thing as reincarnation, I wanted to come back as the President of the United States ... but now I want to come back as the bond market. Then I could intimidate everybody.'

The phone on his desk rings.

'Mr Varadi, your visitors are here. Shall I bring them up?'

'No. I'll come down.'

The secretary is surprised and looks more carefully at the man and woman in front of her. They do not look important enough to bring down the deputy governor of the Bank of England. But to Charley Varadi, Sally Brett and her new director are very important – more important in their way than the increasingly ungovernable flow of money of which everyone believes the Bank is custodian. *That* can no longer be controlled.

'Sally, how are you?' Varadi took her hand and gave her a peck on the cheek. Winnicott saw at once that they had known each other for a long time.

'Charley, this is George Winnicott, our new director.'

'How are you? I was talking to Tim Fowler the other day.'

Winnicott looked surprised.

'He speaks highly of you. Says it'll take you six months and you'll know the City better than any of us.'

'He's very kind but I know enough already to know he's wrong.'

'Perhaps you'd like the Cook's tour before we go up, Mr Winnicott?'

'Yes. Very much.'

As he moved them past doors made of Cuban mahogany as solid as the sheets of Derby stone that faced the walls, Varadi turned to Sally Brett.

'And how is the Icarus of the Fraud Secretariat?' he said, teasing.

'I take it you mean Daedalus, Charley. Icarus was the one who flew too close to the sun and fell into the sea.' She turned to the puzzled Winnicott. 'Charley is being droll about Michael McCarthy. In his spare time, Michael is a free-fall parachutist.'

'Really?' Winnicott realised that his surprise had come out as graceless disbelief, but before he could correct the impression, Varadi interrupted.

'Come now. He's not just a bit of a daredevil, we're talking about the Champion of Europe no less. Isn't that right, Sally? He's quite a hero at the Bank, Mr Winnicott. Whenever people accuse us City regulators of being dreary we all bring up Michael. That soon shuts them up.' Varadi looked at Sally Brett as if he were a small boy about to pull a pigtail, 'Never thought of having a go yourself, then, Sally?'

She looked at him witheringly and he thought better of continuing. Winnicott was keen to know more about this surprising side to his deputy but he, too, could see that Sally was not in the mood. Varadi stopped beside a mosaic of the two-faced god, Janus.

'Rumour has it that one of the privately wealthy Bank men paid the artist to give it the face of Lord Cunliffe, reputedly one of the nastiest men ever to have been Governor.' He looked over at Brett to see if she was ready to be placated. 'You remember old George Routon who came in just after the First World War? He wasn't exactly renowned for expressing a strong opinion on anything.' Brett smiled – a private joke. 'He described Cunliffe as a real pig.'

His bluntness took Winnicott aback.

'Do you still print money here, Mr Varadi?' Winnicott knew that all the notes were printed in Debden because one of the IRA cells he had interrogated had been casing it as a target, but he had been trooping along silently, like the new boy at school and he thought that asking a question would stop him feeling like a dope.

'We did until 1921 when we moved it just down the road into a building in Old Street.' He laughed, a high-pitched, pleasant sound, almost a giggle. 'It was the old lunatic asylum.'

'Mind you, at times it doesn't seem quite so amusing,' said Brett indignantly. 'Look at all the fuss in the papers this morning because our former Chancellor had the temerity to suggest that as the economy keeps growing ordinary people should be careful not to over-stretch themselves when they borrow large sums of money. Hysterical outrage at a rather straightforward notion, I would've thought.'

88

'Yes, but he wasn't just urging good sense on a prof-ligate electorate, was he? I think there was just a touch of his trying to avoid responsibility for all the people who got up to their gizzards in negative equity as a result of his policies. He encouraged people to borrow as much as they liked without thinking about the consequences. People haven't learnt how *personal* economics is becoming. Once you're in debt, you're part of the international banking system whether you like it or not. The U.S. Federal reserve decides on Monday, your higher mortgage lands on your breakfast table on Friday ... and if your household budget deficit is critical, you're out on the streets by March.' He grinned, aware that he was on a hobby-horse. 'I'll just show you one of the wells we still use to draw our water.' They moved towards a small door hidden at the end of the corridor. 'You know,' continued Varadi, 'when my father started work on the railways in the 1920s it was impossible for a working man to obtain a loan. By the middle of the 1980s it was barely possible for him to refuse one. Happy days.' He smiled, mock-ingly, to himself. Opening the low door, he gestured Winnicott through.

'Mind your head as you ...'

There was a loud crack as Winnicott's head hit the lintel of the doorway and he fell unconscious to the floor.

———

When Winnicott opened his eyes he was flat on his back. The room was enormous. In fact it was not really a room at all but a circular space the size of the Albert Hall, with a domed roof and a skylight at its apex. He sat up, wincing at the sharp pain in his head. On one side of the hall there were about twenty people lying vertically on couches similar to those in his chiro-practor's treatment rooms. The couches were arranged around a long table on which there were a number of lamps. They were dim, and merely defined the area without giving enough light to see clearly what lay beyond. The people on the couches looked up at the ceiling, eyes fixed, uninterested in where they were or in anyone around them. Just behind Winnicott someone coughed. He turned, startled.

A tall man stood holding out his hand.

'Mr Winnicott,' he said. 'How do you do? I'm the Dark Figure. If you wouldn't mind we'd better get started. I'm not sure how much time we have and there's a lot to get through.'

He offered Winnicott his hand and helped him to his feet.

'What is all this? How did I get here?'

The Dark Figure looked at him, raising his chin to give himself a noble aspect. 'This,' he said in a low and stately voice, 'is a government regulatory inquiry.' A sudden look of panic spread across his carefully composed features and he spoke more loudly, as if to someone hidden in the darkness. 'I mean a regulatory inquiry *independent* of government.'

'Into what?'

'An independent regulatory inquiry into the three things central to every regulatory inquiry: Who made the decision? Why did they make it? Should they have acted as they did?'

He walked to the centre of the room.

The couches were laid out in a narrow horseshoe shape. The Dark Figure pulled up a small chair and gestured for Winnicott to sit. As he did so, the Dark Figure pulled out a table attached to the chair and swung it over Winnicott's lap. 'It feels a little like a high-chair, I'm afraid,' said the Dark Figure, 'but it was all we could come up with at short notice.' He took out a notebook and handed it to Winnicott. 'It's important you take notes.'

'Why?'

'Because this is complicated and, I can assure you, you won't get a second chance. Do you have a pen?'

'No.'

The Dark Figure took one from his inside pocket marked *Property of United Biscuits*, gave it to him and then turned away into the oval. His eyes now used to the dim light, Winnicott could see that the back of the couches, just behind their occupants' heads, bent over to form a cowl, like the hood of a salon hairdryer. From inside a light shone onto each of them, illuminating their faces. There was only one woman, but rather than mitigating the maleness of her surroundings her presence emphasised it more strongly. A voice boomed from high up in the darkness.

'THE LORD CHIEF JUSTICE! PRAY BE UPSTANDING!'

A light flashed on from a point high above, where the roof began to curve, illuminating a figure in a judge's wig and robes slowly emerging from the prone position on a chiropractor's couch. The judge's couch was motorised like the one Winnicott was used to, but this one was now folding to become a chair.

'Proceed,' said the judge, and the light went off immediately. Even though he had only seen him for an instant, Winnicott recognised him immediately. Despite an absurdly exaggerated wig, an excess of enormous, dusty legal tomes, a pair of tiny, impractical rectangular bifocals and a huge false nose, it was patently the Dark Figure addressing himself in disguise.

He turned and raised his voice past the dimly lit oval. 'M'lud, I would like to introduce my first witness.' The Dark Figure walked towards the furthest couch, stopping about ten feet away. The lights went out in all the others so that the faces could no longer be seen. 'Be upstanding!' announced the Dark Figure. The man the Dark Figure was looking at raised his head and stared back calmly as the motorised couch moved to form a chair. He was in late middle age, dressed in clothes that belonged to a wealthy citizen of the 1860s. 'Please state your name and profession for the record.' The Dark Figure nodded at Winnicott to take notes.

The man spoke firmly, the nineteenth century was in the timbre of his voice: sureness of tone, clarity of expression, the absence of any acknowledgement of doubt or neurosis. 'I am Hugh McCulloch, Comptroller of the Currency of the United States of America.'

'Is it the case that in the spring of 1863 you were deeply concerned about the declining standards of prudence and probity in the United States banking industry?' asked the Dark Figure.

'I was indeed, sir.'

'What did you do about it, Mr McCulloch?'

'I gave the banks some advice – by which I mean I made clear to them what would be done while I was in the office of comptroller.'

'Could you possibly tell us what you said to them? And,' the Dark Figure simpered apologetically, 'if you could be brief -- we have much to get through and very little time.'

McCulloch stared at him. There was no change in his expression, no eyebrow raised, no alteration in his tone beyond the fact he spoke a little more quietly. 'Sir, I am always brief.'

McCulloch was not a handsome man: his head was slightly too large for his body and his skin was pallid against the shadow of his beard, which must have required shaving at least twice in a working day. What he knew, he knew absolutely and what he did not know was of no interest to him. He continued. 'The essentials of good banking practice are simple enough to state. First: let no loans be made that are not secured beyond a reasonable contingency. Give facilities only to legitimate and prudent transactions – and encourage no extravagant speculations. Second: do not concentrate your loans in a few hands as large loans to single firms are generally injudicious and frequently unsafe.'

The Dark Figure opened his mouth as if to ask a question. McCulloch stared at him and he closed his mouth. McCulloch continued. 'Third: treat your customers liberally but never permit them to dictate your policy. If you have good reason to distrust a customer, close his account. Never deal with a rascal under the impression that you can prevent him from cheating you.' He paused and again the Dark Figure waited, nervous of interrupting him.

Hesitantly he started to speak, 'Um ... moving on. Would it be accurate to say that you do not accept the propriety of advancing loans to individuals?'

For the first time uncertainty appeared on McCulloch's face. 'You refer to individuals wishing to finance a business enterprise who can be accounted for with regard to their integrity and who have sufficient collateral?'

The Dark Figure, taken aback, said nothing.

McCulloch smiled – not an altogether pleasant sight, thought Winnicott. 'I can see you do not mean that, sir. What you refer to is a heresy little spoken of in polite banking society, and then only in hushed whispers and not in the presence of ladies.'

'Personal loans to ordinary members of the public cannot, in your view, be justified?'

'*My view* be damned.' McCulloch was annoyed now. 'It is not and never can be the business of banks to furnish the desires of the working man. A bank is not a shop in which a man may buy his way into the illusion that he is worth more than he is, and that he owns more than he has.'

'Banks have always made loans to individuals, Mr McCulloch.'

'Indeed they have, sir, just as they have always gone out of business.'

'Are working men not to be trusted, Mr McCulloch, to judge for themselves?'

'They may *judge* as they like, sir, but I will not help them to gamble without good cause. Debt is a measure of confidence in the belief that there are more sunny days in this world than those on which it rains. It is a risk, a gamble, to be undertaken by an imprudent optimist or those with a sound knowledge of the science of meteorology and a ready supply of umbrellas. In this second group should be bankers and reliable business-men. It is my task to ensure that money is invested wisely in sound businesses in order that ordinary men may have steady work and reliable wages to put food on a table for which he has paid ready cash. Debt for the common man is a house of illusion: an easy place to build but a draughty place in which to live.'

McCulloch sat back and calmed himself, aware that he had become heated.

The Dark Figure began to speak, 'Mr McCull—'

Immediately McCulloch leant forward again. 'Let me add,' he said, 'that any loan made to splendid financiers who lack proper aims, soundly arrived at, is equally an illusion, however splendid the mansion they attempt to construct. Sooner or later it will fall, and when it does so the houses of many working men will fall with it.'

'Let me be clear about what you are saying, Mr McCulloch.' The Dark Figure looked over at Winnicott to indicate that he should write this down. A shadow crossed his face as he saw that Winnicott was sitting and simply staring. 'Are you saying it is immoral to give loans to working men and splendid financiers, as you call them, or that it is bad business?'

McCulloch's face stiffened and he leant forward again, one of his hands tightening around the arm of his chair. 'I do not well understand your distinction, sir. If it is immoral it can never be good business. If a bank cannot prosper without immorality then it will eventually fail. And it will fail not because the good Lord punishes wicked bankers, sir, but because no good man was ever a greedy man and all greedy men are fools. Pursue a straightforward, upright, legitimate banking business. And as for the splendid financiers: never be tempted by the prospect of large returns to do anything but what may be done properly. Splendid financiering is not legitimate banking, and splendid financiers in banking are generally either humbugs or rascals.'

'Mr McCulloch, thank you for agreeing to speak to us.'

McCulloch sat back, and as he did so the chair folded back to become a couch and the light above him went out, covering his face in an impenetrable black. Irritated, the Dark Figure walked towards Winnicott. He stopped in front of him and spoke quietly as if he was afraid he would be overheard.

'Mr Winnicott, you are acting against your own interests. You must keep the best record you are able.'

With this he turned away and, smiling ingratiatingly, again addressed himself to the judge.

'I would like to call my second witness, m'lud.'

'Proceed.'

Again a brief flash of light revealed the judge in his ridiculous ensemble: the nose, if anything, was even larger.

'Thank you, m'lud,' said the Dark Figure, eliding his last word like the sound of a stone dropping into a bucket of thick wallpaper paste. He approached a couch half way up the oval. 'Be upstanding and state your name and profession, sir, for the record.'

The light above the man's head came on as the couch folded. In his early sixties, the man's dark suit was cut with the lack of imagination available only to the truly well-off Englishman. His skin was of a strikingly healthy pink but its warmth was diminished by the remote blue-grey of his eyes. He spoke with an authority that was part natural, part assumed, or if not assumed, certainly cultivated. He was completely bald but the shape of his head gave him a monumental authority, as if his features had been carved in stone. 'I am Samuel Letherby, Governor of the Bank of England from 1968 to 1984.'

The Dark Figure assumed a banker's briskness. 'Mr Letherby, I'd like you to outline the events surrounding the loan required by the Labour government from the International Monetary Fund to bring an end to the sterling crisis of 1976.'

From the judge's bench high above came a lugubrious remonstration: 'Dark Figure, I must remind you that there is a considerable amount of evidence to be heard in the limited time we have available. Fascinating as it would be,' he paused to allow the full judicial sarcasm to take effect, 'I feel we must press on to matters that perhaps in your view are less stimulating, but in my view are more relevant.'

The Dark Figure turned his face upward, smiling at himself in oleaginous appeasement. 'I can assure you, m'lud, no one is more cognisant of the need for brevity, but I'm confident that the relevance of my request will be apparent by the close of these proceedings.'

'Very well,' conceded the judge reluctantly. The light snapped off.

The Dark Figure motioned for Letherby to begin. 'In 1976 it became clear to me that in the preceding five years the world economy had undergone the most radical change since it had become appropriate to speak of such a thing.'

'Could you explain, briefly, why this was so?'

'Just before the end of the war – at the Bretton Woods Conference – the United States, to all intents and purposes, assumed responsibility for the effective running of the international financial system.'

'Why was this significant?'

'It meant that the world economy was stable. Because the American economy was so vigorous it could absorb an enormous amount of pressure. The United States led, everyone else followed.'

'What happened to change this impressive equilibrium?'

'As always, there were many factors, but the prevailing view is that Lyndon Johnson's response to the cost of the Vietnam War was the central cause.'

There was a theatrical clearing of the throat from high up in the dark. Letherby stopped, irritated by the implication of the interruption.

Alarmed, the Dark Figure hurried him along. 'And this response was?'

'In 1966 Johnson was under pressure to increase taxes to pay for the War. But he was nervous of domestic reaction and complacent, frankly, about an economy that had prospered for such a long time. So he decided he could pursue what became known as the guns and butter policy – increasing spending without raising taxation. This led to the beginnings of an inflationary spiral just as the West German and Japanese economies began to compete successfully in American markets.'

'How did the Americans react?'

'First they refused to convert dollars automatically into gold, and then they devalued the dollar. Then there was a free-for-all in international currency policy. By 1973 world currencies no longer stood in stable, fixed relationship to each other, which for a generation had allowed us to manage the world economy. The world of Bretton Woods was dead. Perhaps extinct would be a better word. It was a free market in money.'

Winnicott saw the Dark Figure's expression change to one of deepest malice. 'I'll remember where you live,' he said under his breath, his eyes hooded like those of a small-time gangster.

'What did you say?' replied Letherby, aghast at what he thought he had heard.

'I'm so sorry, Governor, I said, I've a *memory* like a *sieve*,' said the Dark Figure pleasantly. He moved on briskly. 'Now because my recollection of the general reaction to the sterling crisis of 1976 is not all that it might be,' he smiled at Letherby with mock deference, 'compared with an economist of *your* eminence, I was wondering if it would be fair to say that, at the time, overseas politicians and central bankers had lost confidence in the Labour government's ability to manage the British economy?'

Winnicott watched Letherby's face carefully as he tried to make sense of what he had heard from the Dark Figure. Letherby was clearly unable to grasp that he had been threatened as if he were a small-time thief. Nothing like this had ever happened to him before. It could not therefore have taken place and he must have misheard. Nevertheless, he was rattled.

'They made it pretty clear, yes,' he replied hesitantly.

'And is it the case that they regarded Harold Wilson and Tony Benn as the main architects of this economic misfortune? Indeed, is it not the case that Mr Benn was described by the President of the Bundesbank as the "Bertie Wooster of economic management"?'

'I couldn't possibly comment on such a remark,' said Letherby coldly.

Winnicott could see that Letherby had found his feet

again and wondered what else the Dark Figure would do to try to unsettle him.

'What I *can* say,' continued Letherby, regaining his confidence, 'is that at that time the Labour government was spending twelve billion pounds more than it was raising in taxes, inflation was at nearly twenty-four per cent and the balance of payments was deteriorating alarmingly rapidly.'

'And you feel that these somewhat terrifying figures speak for themselves?'

'If they speak for themselves, there can be no point in my making any further comment.'

The Dark Figure sniffed loudly and gave Letherby another poisonous look. 'It is the case, is it not, that the Treasury wanted to attempt to deal with the deficit by devaluing the pound?'

'Not exactly. It was considered too open an admission of government failure to devalue in such an overt manner. The Treasury attempted a camouflage devaluation.'

'And how was this to be done?'

There was another loud throat clearing from the shadows.

Letherby ignored the interruption. 'The Treasury … *scheme*' – he used the word as if referring to an attempt to sell deep freezers to Eskimos – 'involved their belief that if they reduced interest rates, sterling would be made less attractive to the foreign exchange markets. In the Treasury's view, dealers would sell sterling in a gradual, orderly manner with the result that the pound would fall gently by about five per cent or so and no one would notice the cunning subterfuge that had been worked upon them.'

'What was the Bank of England's view of this ingenious soft landing?'

Letherby stirred in his seat.

'We pointed out to them that foreign exchanges

were extremely volatile for the reasons I've outlined already.'

'The breakdown of America's role as the guarantor of economic stability?'

'Quite so. We tried to make it clear that the markets were now intrinsically unstable, and that the notion that one could reliably manipulate the currency was deeply unsound. The markets were unlikely to behave in a structured way just because ministers and civil servants thought it would be helpful to them if they did so.'

'Did they take your advice?'

'They did not.'

'With what result?'

'In early March of 1976 it became clear that there were an unusually large number of orders for sterling.'

'Why was this a problem?'

'It would create further demand for sterling and push up its value.'

'The exact opposite of the Treasury's intention.'

'Yes.'

'What did you do?'

'In line with the Government's strategy we sold sterling.'

'With the intention of holding the price down?'

Letherby nodded irritably.

'Then you had some bad luck.'

'The Nigerian government had decided to sell an enormous amount of the sterling they'd been holding so that they could benefit from the rise in its value that we were trying to stem by also selling. You must understand that these events happened quite independently of each other. It was just a dreadful coincidence.'

'With the result that now the market was flooded with people trying to sell sterling?'

'Yes.'

'So its price started to fall?'

'Yes.'

'But wasn't that what the Treasury wanted?'

'It wanted it to fall slowly to a predetermined point of about a dollar ninety ... but the markets assumed from such a flood of sterling sellers that something was up. Not wanting to be left holding an asset whose price was falling, they also sold.'

'They panicked?'

'Within a week sterling had fallen to a dollar ninety.'

'But forgive me, Mr Letherby, let me repeat – isn't that what the Treasury wanted?'

'Indeed it did, but it hardly needs pointing out that the fall to a dollar eighty involves going through a dollar ninety along the way. It was supposed to stop at a level agreeable to the Treasury, but it kept on dropping.'

'What did the Treasury do?'

'It took its lead from the markets,' said Letherby, his eyes glinting with malice. 'It decided to panic as well. We were instructed to stop the fall at a dollar eighty-five.'

'And how was this to be done?'

'We bought sterling in a rapidly falling market, spending one billion dollars in the process.'

'And did this expensive strategy work?'

'At the beginning of June sterling stood at, I think, a dollar seventy-one.'

'So, it was not successful.'

'In the same sense that you could say the maiden voyage of the *Titanic* was not successful, no.'

The Dark Figure's eyes narrowed at Letherby's tone and he reached into a pocket on the front of his waistcoat. Carefully, so as not to be seen, he took out a metal object. He pressed a button and there was a loud click as a six-inch blade shot into view. It was a flick-knife.

Without taking his eyes from Letherby, the Dark Figure began to clean under his thumbnail with the point of the blade. Because of the surreptitious way he had done this, only Winnicott could see what was going on. Letherby looked on, his face a mixture of alarm and incomprehension. Then he collected himself. He was, after all, the ex-Governor of the Bank of England. He was about to protest when the Dark Figure spoke first.

'I wonder if I might interrupt you for a moment, Mr Letherby.'

As if he had been switched off, Letherby sank back, expressionless, into his seat and his light went out. The Dark Figure closed the flick-knife and replaced it in his pocket with almost magical dexterity. He turned and walked towards Winnicott, gaining momentum as he went until he was almost running. Winnicott stood up in alarm. Impeded by the awkward table connected to his chair, he struggled to free himself as the Dark Figure descended on him, grabbed him by the hand, pulled him free of the chair and launched them both into the air. Winnicott screamed, in astonishment as much as fear. Up and up they went, circling the giant dome, gaining height and speed until they rushed towards the glass apex, and with a terrifying whoosh! shot out into the dark and snowy night.

Hand in hand the Dark Figure and Winnicott performed one swift turn about the dome and then sped off in the direction of the Thames. They followed its grim sparkle and then suddenly banked to one side, like a fighter plane attacking an armoured column, and headed straight for the Houses of Parliament. Aiming for one of the stained glass windows, the Dark Figure overshot and with a thunderous crash of wood, brick and glass they demolished twenty or so feet of Pugin's masterpiece.

The Dark Figure coughed once then strode along a

corridor and through a door, still with his hand clasped around Winnicott's wrist. He came to a dead halt in front of a man wearing a suit similar to that worn by Letherby. But this man was sleeker: self-satisfaction shone from his skin as if he had been polished with oil of smugness. His guest seemed to have come straight from a performance in a provincial theatre that required him to play a drunken journalist. His face was florid, the veins on his nose broken from a life of alcohol abuse. His fingers were stained with the dirty yellow of unfiltered cigarettes and in the ribbon of his battered trilby there was an equally battered card that bore the inscription "Press".

The journalist leered at the man in front of him. 'So, what's a Treasury official doing in the Houses of Parliament, as if I didn't know?'

The sleek man smiled. 'You musn't be so suspicious, Peter. This is temporary while my office at the Treasury is being redecorated.'

'Papering over the cracks, are they?' giggled the journalist.

'Very droll, Peter. What a wag you are.'

The sleek man was irritated, but the journalist was barely sober enough to notice.

'Look,' said the sleek man placatingly, 'all joking aside, this is a serious situation. Sterling is at a dollar seventy-one, and things could get a lot worse.' The journalist sat forward, interested. The man from the Treasury leaned forward also. 'What really worries me,' he said softly with the tone of a concerned parent, 'is the Bank of England's role in this.'

'Everyone knows you hate each other's guts. That's what you *would* say.'

The Treasury official held out his hand in a gesture of acknowledgement. 'I'll admit we've often had pretty severe disagreements.' The journalist sniggered. 'But it's a complicated world out there and getting more complicated by the day. The Governor and his deputy ... their approach to things was shaped in a world of Bretton Woods agreements, fixed exchange rates.' He made a slight but eloquent gesture to signal an etcetera of redundant notions: the theory of phlogiston, that the blood circulated via a system of buckets. 'It's all much trickier now, and of course that's bound to mean we all make more mistakes, the Treasury too.'

'Can I quote you on that?'

The Treasury man smiled and went on. 'But this wasn't that complicated a manoeuvre. Lowering the value of the pound from two dollars to one dollar ninety was a straightforward exercise in market management. The Treasury – the country for goodness' sake – had got to be able to rely on the professional expertise of ...'

The Dark Figure decided they had heard enough and, grasping Winnicott's wrist, pulled him out of the room and along a corridor. Winnicott floated behind him like a balloon. They went through a door that led into a small gallery from which they looked down on a chamber packed with middle-aged men. It was noisy, hot and claustrophobic, and many were standing in the aisles.

At one end, a man in a long wig was shouting, 'ORDER! ORDER!' and being ignored. 'ORDER! ORDER!' he shouted again, and slowly the muttering, loud conversation, shouting, barks, laughs and sneers dwindled to a low rumble. This was less in response to his call than from a general desire to see what would happen next. The man in the wig spoke again.

'The Right Honourable Gentleman for Bolsover.'

There were loud boos from the opposite side of the room and a brief but indistinguishable shout.

The MP for Bolsover, a thin man with the face of a much-used hatchet, began to speak in a voice that declaimed, taunted and prosecuted all at the same time. 'It is perfectly clear—'

He was interrupted by loud boos and a shout of 'that you're an idiot', followed by forced laughter. He carried on, clearly familiar with the routine. 'It is perfectly clear why the Bank of England made such a monumental cock-up. It's perfectly clear. We know who runs the Bank of England and we know his fat cat pals in the City, and what they wanted was to put an end to the government's agreement with the trade unions on an incomes policy—'

This brought roars of laughter from the other side of the house with cries of 'RUBBISH!', and more grunts and snarls and a gabbled 'RAH! RAH! RAH! RAH! RAH! ORDER! ORDER!'

The Right Honourable Member continued, ' ... an incomes policy. It wasn't a cock-up at all. It was deliberate sabotage!'

'RAH! RAH! RAH! RAH! RAH! ORDER! ORDER!'

'The Bank doesn't want this government coming to an agreement so we can save the economy. It wants a Labour government out!'

'RAH! RAH! RAH! GOOD! RAH! HA! HA! HA! RAH! RAH!'

'And it doesn't care whether it destroys the economy to do it. I call upon the Governor to RESIGN!'

The end was a signal for more uproar, cries of 'WHY DON'T YOU SHOW HIM HOW?'

As the chamber exploded into roars of hilarity and outrage, the Dark Figure pulled Winnicott away and within a few steps they were through the door and running towards the large hole in the wall made by their entrance. Then they were off over the Thames, the City, down through the dome and back into the court.

———

The Dark Figure let go of Winnicott, brushed himself down and walked over towards Letherby's darkened couch, which lit up as he approached. The former Governor of the Bank of England eyed the brickdust-covered figure in front of him dubiously.

'Mr Letherby,' said the Dark Figure, his tone having shifted from that of knowledge-sharing interlocutor to starchy inquisitor, 'what is your response to the comments of the Treasury official? His version of events ... what was it?' The Dark Figure took a notebook from his pocket and flicked his way pro-fessorially through the pages. '"A straightforward exercise in market management" was how he put it.'

'Whoever said that was either a fool or a liar. I wonder whether I might have a drink of water.'

The Dark Figure curled his lip and clicked his fingers with the self-importance of a City trader order-ing a bottle of champagne on company expenses. Without any visible means of support, a glass of water floated into the light and set itself down next to Letherby. He looked at the water longingly but the Dark Figure did not pause to let him drink.

'Baldy!' he whispered to Letherby.

Letherby looked at him in horror. 'What?' he gasped.

'*Baldly* speaking,' said the Dark Figure pleasantly, 'what was the long-term result of all this?'

Letherby was clearly furious. 'You said something else.'

The Dark Figure was the picture of innocent confusion. 'I don't think so,' he said jovially.

'Yes, you did,' said Letherby angrily. 'You said ...' He stopped. There was no one to support him, and the Dark Figure had provided himself with an explanation that would make a complaint look hysterically paranoid.

He was saved by the judge. 'Dark Figure,' he called

out reprovingly, 'this is not the first time the defendant … I'm *so* sorry, the *witness* has failed to catch what you were saying. You must speak up.'

The Dark Figure nodded apologetically. 'I'm extremely sorry, m'lud, but I fear that the necessity for so much talking has had an effect on my voice.' He turned back to the grey-faced Letherby.

'So the crisis was over?'

'Yes,' said Letherby, barely able to control his fury.

'And what were the lessons, Mr Letherby?'

'That regulating an economy isn't like herding cats – it's like herding cats using *dogs*.' He looked at the Dark Figure coldly. 'There's no such thing as a simple exercise in market management.'

'But your claim is that you already knew this – it was the Treasury and the government who learned that modern money markets were inherently volatile.'

'Yes.'

'*You* learned nothing?' said the Dark Figure accusingly.

Letherby had regained his composure. He put his hands together thoughtfully as if about to pray. 'I'm not sure if a Governor of the Bank of England should really be heard to quote Louis Bris …' A low hissing emerged from the shadows. The judge, infuriated, began banging on his bench with an enormous Day-glo rubber gavel that squeaked at every blow. Slowly the hissing ceased. Letherby continued as if he had heard nothing. ' … but I remember reading something of his that struck me at the time and still does: "*Economics is the sum of all the strengths and weaknesses of the human heart expressed in money*". In my opinion …'

The Dark Figure interrupted by looking up at the judge. 'I was wondering whether I could have a drink of the witness's water, m'lud. My voice …' he said apologetically.

'Very well, get on with it,' said the judge irritably.

Smiling triumphantly, the Dark Figure took Letherby's glass and drained it. He replaced it on the table with a hefty crack and a loud gasp of appreciation. 'Thank you, Mr Letherby, I think we have had quite enough of your opinions. That will be all.'

A frightened Letherby sat back and vanished into the dark again. The Dark Figure walked briskly to his next witness.

'Be upstanding! Identify yourself!' The Dark Figure was more peremptory now, growing arrogant as he became more certain that he was in control. The man in the folding chair was in his early sixties with a luxuriant head of brilliant white hair. 'I am Harold Glover, Head of Bank Supervision at the Bank of England.'

'You were a kind of Dixon of Dock Green for the City, Mr Glover, would that be fair?'

Glover looked at him. 'No, it would merely be sarcastic.'

'You'll forgive me, Mr Glover, but as an outsider I'm afraid it does all seem very cosy: the City as a gentleman's club full of the right sort of people but, as with even the best institutions, regrettably marred by the occasional Terry-Thomas rotter with a gap in his front teeth and a loud check jacket.' Glover opened his mouth to reply but was cut off by a question phrased more as an accusation. 'What is the definition of a bank, Mr Glover?'

This change of tone unnerved him and his reply was cautious.

'Mr Letherby took the view that a definition as such was unhelpful. They were like elephants – difficult to define in the abstract but perfectly clear when you saw one.'

'And in practice this meant the clearing banks and the merchant banks? Lloyds, Barclays, and Warburgs,

Morgan Grenfell ...' he leered at the distrustful-looking Glover, ' ... *Barings*. All blue chip.'

'Yes, in effect.'

'Is there no definition in law of a bank?'

'The power of determination is, in law, a matter for the Bank of England.'

'So, a bank is a bank when the Bank says it's a bank.'

'Yes.'

'I see.' The Dark Figure smiled as if enjoying a private moment. 'Now!' The move to a brisk let's-get-on-with-it unsettled Glover again. Winnicott could see him trying to work out where the Dark Figure was going with the sudden changes of direction. He realised that the Dark Figure was trying to make Glover think he knew a great deal more than he was letting on.

'I wonder if you would tell us, as briefly as you can,' again the self-absolving passing on to Glover of a reputation for prolixity he had done nothing to deserve, 'something about the secondary banking crisis you mentioned as the cause of all this unnecessary rush to regulation. These secondary banks were companies licensed to take deposits of money from the public, but not banks as the Bank of England defined them.'

'No.'

'Not elephant-shaped banks?'

'No.' Glover's face was impassive.

'These secondary banks ... these ...' he looked around the chamber with a waggish smirk, 'these lesser-spotted banks were, am I correct, not banks for which you were responsible in terms of supervision?'

'No.'

'But you were forced to become involved, and in a central role, when twenty-one of these *fringe* secondary banks got into financial trouble. Why was that, if you were not responsible for regulation?'

'You have to understand that banking is about confidence. Banking is a belief system interconnected in all kinds of ways which have nothing to do with things you can touch. Once fear gets into that system, the results can be catastrophic.'

'That sounds most alarming, Mr Glover. I wonder if, again briefly, you would describe how these apparently unimportant institutions could wield such calamitous power.'

'I did not say they were unimportant.'

'But you did not consider them banks?'

'No,' admitted Glover flatly.

'They were licensed to take deposits, make loans, all the things that banks do. I appreciate I'm not an expert, but isn't that what a bank does, putting it simply: a bank takes deposits and makes loans?'

'They're similar but not the same thing.'

'Well, Mr Glover, to pick up on the Bank's own analogy of dumb animals, all ducks are similar but not the same. However, if it looks like a duck, quacks like a duck and swims like a duck then are we not entitled to the view, given that all ducks are similar but not the same, that what we are seeing is, in fact, a duck?'

Glover was furious. 'It's absurd to—'

The light flashed on from above.

'Dark Figure! Would you please stop squabbling with the witness. For goodness' sake get on with it!'

The Dark Figure nodded theatrically to his disguised self and turned to Glover, whose reply had been most effectively stifled.

'Mr Glover, I wonder if you would give us an account of how such a banking crisis unfolds.'

Glover brought himself quickly under control but he spoke coldly. 'Stage one of a crisis involves a liquidity problem in a secondary bank. Depositors get nervous about their money. They withdraw it and put it – usually – in a clearing bank.'

'Lloyds, Barclays ...' prompted the Dark Figure.

Glover nodded. 'Clearing banks don't pay as much interest as secondary banks but they are more secure. Stage two begins when the secondary bank can't meet its obligations in the money market. No other bank will lend it money because of the same fears that led to the depositors withdrawing their cash, and so the bank doesn't have enough money to redeem debts when they fall due. Stage three drags in the clearing banks. Their creditworthiness becomes suspect because of the loans they've made to the secondary banks.'

'So they *are* connected?'

Glover ignored him. 'The clearers borrow in the international money markets and when the international banks see that the clearers are going to incur heavy losses on the collapsing secondary bank, they refuse to roll over loans to the clearers. If one of the clearers is particularly heavily exposed, a run on the banks begins. Stage four, fear spreads to the currency markets, there are heavy exchange losses. Financial institutions who have loaned into weak sections of the economy – property, say – are now in danger of collapse. Stage five ... the international banking system breaks down.'

Glover sat back stony-faced.

'And stage six, Mr Glover?'

Glover leaned forward again. 'There is no stage six. What I've outlined is the collapse of the world economy.'

The light flashed on from above. 'Let me say, Mr Glover, I had no idea banking could be so exciting ... so apocalyptic.' The judge beamed and looked around the dark empty space. The Dark Figure laughed appreciatively. The light switched off. The Dark Figure's

111

expression instantly turned to one of utter disdain. He looked at Glover.

'And what did the Bank do to prevent this terrifying prospect?'

'We launched what became known as the lifeboat. We got the clearing banks to advance money to the secondary banks to match the sum of money that worried depositors had withdrawn from them: four hundred million in all.'

The Dark Figure looked puzzled and for a considerable time said nothing. He started to speak and then stopped, considered for a little longer, then spoke quietly. 'Let me get this straight, the clearers paid four hundred million pounds into the secondary banks.' He paused again. 'Where did the four hundred million pounds come from, Mr Glover?'

'It was the money that worried depositors had taken out of the secondary banks and put into the clearing banks.'

'I see. So ...' the Dark Figure seemed to be working something out, ' ... what you're saying is that the depositors fearing for their savings in the secondary banks withdrew their money and put it in the elephant-shaped clearing banks – Lloyds, Barclays – then the clearing banks took the money so deposited and lent it back to the secondary banks?'

'Yes.'

'The money just went round in a circle.'

'In a manner of speaking.'

The Dark Figure looked at Glover and for some time said nothing. Then he sniffed loudly and began again. 'The upshot of all this being that the Bank decided to become involved in the supervision of all banks.'

'To be pedantic,' said Glover with obvious pleasure, 'we merely extended the definition of what a bank was.'

'Ah, but, Mr Glover, not quite, I think. It was most

certainly not the case that you extended the definition. The elephant-shaped definition didn't alter at all, did it? There were still proper banks – the clearing banks – which were large creatures with long memories – and not-so-proper banks – the secondary banks ... the duck-shaped banks.'

'If you're referring to the two-tier system, that's one way of looking at it.'

'Oh, I *am*, Mr Glover,' said the Dark Figure, in the sonorous voice of someone who has worked long and hard to get to this point and who sees victory just ahead. 'I *am* referring to it.'

He declaimed to his audience of two. 'Your Honour, we come now to the crux of our presence here today.'

'A presence can't have a crux.'

'Thank you, Your Honour. We come to the heart of the matter that brings us here today: the two-tier banking system.' He announced it as though it were the name of an infamous train robbery or a particularly unpleasant massacre. 'An act of regulatory incontinence that will live long in the annals of regulatory shame, a supervisory device that will go down in the history of superintendence as a defilement, a desecration, a disreputable disgrace that forever befouled, besmirched and blemished the entire—'

'Get on with it!' cried the judge, hammering his rubber gavel squeakily on the bench.

The Dark Figure gasped with frustration. He swore under his breath and turned back to Glover. 'Mr Glover,' he said stonily, 'would you please explain how you set about dealing with the secondary banks.'

'We formed a new office—'

'Is it not the case', interrupted the Dark Figure, 'that many in the City felt that this was *all* you did? Was it not the case that forming a new office, as you put it, actually consisted of no more than screwing a wooden plaque onto a door with the word *supervision* printed on it in gold letters?'

'That's what was said by some.'

'And I suppose you're going to suggest this wasn't fair?'

'It was not. We significantly increased our supervisory staff, applied strict criteria with regard to the risk-asset ratio. They had to provide proper statistics and submit themselves to questions about their balance sheet.'

'And did these admirable new checks and balances apply to the banks who used to be your only responsibility – the elephant-shaped banks?'

'No.'

'Really? And why was that?'

'*They* had not been the problem. Indeed, it was largely the elephant-shaped banks, as you insist on putting it, which were responsible for rescuing the secondary banks. It hardly seemed fair to reward them for the considerable risks they took by lumping them ...'

Glover realised his mistake but he had gone too far.

'Go on, Mr Glover, you were saying.'

Glover did not reply.

The Dark Figure continued. 'You were saying, lump them in with the lower classes, the barrow-boys of the banking business.'

'I was certainly not saying that.'

'I would hope not, Mr Glover. The *proper* elephant-shaped banks you defend so passionately for running what one of our earlier witnesses called upright, straightforward, legitimate banking businesses rescued the secondary banks, no doubt partly for the highest motives but also because they had lent money to the banks at risk. It follows, therefore, that they, too, had been imprudent – in a number of cases, very imprudent indeed. The lines between your two tiers were seriously blurred even before the two-tier notion was decided upon. Thank you, Mr Glover.'

The light went out over Glover's head and the Dark Figure intoned theatrically to the vast, empty space, his hands behind his back:

'It is now ten years later. Governor Letherby has retired. A Conservative government has been in power for five years and, after much hardship, the economy is beginning to boom. Private industry is leaner, many nationalised industries are dead, dying or under notice that they will be privatised. There is money about, a lot of money, and it's flowing in and around the City in unthinkable amounts. Old restrictions are being cleared away and the market in money is free. This is a world of risk, venture, of ambition and opportunity. This is a huge world, enormous, splendid – and enormous, splendid borrowings are needed to feed its appetite for yet more borrowings. The Bank, too, has changed. Jobs have been shed and overmanning is a thing of the past. In a world fat with money, its custodian is lean, hard-bodied.'

The Dark Figure paced up and down. 'It is April 1984. In the department of banking supervision a woman, thirty-eight or so, is working late. She has money worries – not electricity bill concern, or mortgage rate angst but big money, fat money, splendid money worries. Her pale face and tired blonde hair are caused by economics. Her dry skin is due to the collapse of the Bretton Woods agreement, to the freeing of money from its cage; her stiff neck cracks when she moves it wearily from side to side because of an IMF loan to a dying government with its three-day weeks and unburied dead. Her never-quite-satisfying sleep is caused by Milton Friedman whispering in her ear all through the night. And because government expenditure must be reduced, she has too much work to do, too many banks, too far

115

apart, to try to understand. As she labours late into the night, she does not realise, as she tries to make sense of the returns lying in profusion on her desk, that thirty years of history is about to collapse on top of her.'

The Dark Figure approached another of the couches. It lit up to reveal the woman he had just described.

'Be upstand— Oh, sod it!' he said irritably. 'Just state your name for the record.'

'Marianne Fraser, Deputy Bank Supervisor.'

'How many banks were you responsible for at this time, Ms Fraser?'

'Two.'

'Was this an unusually large number?'

She seemed uncertain as to her reply and did not answer quickly.

'Come along, Ms Fraser,' said the Dark Figure irritably, 'it's not a difficult question.'

'It doesn't seem to me to be necessary to badger the witness,' boomed the judge.

The Dark Figure turned sourly. 'As your lordship persists in reminding me, there is a great deal to get through and little time in which to do so. But if your lordship now takes a different view ...'

'No, I don't. I want you to get on with it *and* I want you to stop badgering the witness.'

The Dark Figure gave a contemptuous nod of acquiescence.

'Was being responsible for two banks particularly burdensome?'

'In this instance, yes, it was.' There was a sharpness in her response that contradicted the sense of passive defeatism which until then had seemed almost as much a part of her as her hair.

'And why was that?'

'The two banks were Continental Illinois, which was on the verge of collapse because of bad debts in the oil and gas industry, and the Johnson Mathey

Bank, JMB. On its own, Continental Illinois was a full-time job and JMB should have been.'

'Should have been?'

'I knew that something odd was going on but I couldn't identify what it was.'

'But that was your job, finding out what was wrong, wasn't it? A supervisor's job is to supervise. You must have had a specific remit. Did you follow it?'

'Yes.'

'Why didn't you know what was going on, then?'

She breathed out heavily, annoyed.

'We were expecting JMB to report on its financial status for the quarter ending in March but it didn't arrive. I repeatedly pressed them for it and finally it turned up in Juno.'

'And what *did* you find?'

'JMB had loaned the overwhelming majority of its capital base to just three people.'

The Dark Figure looked down disapprovingly. 'Breaking one of the cardinal rules of banking in doing so.'

'Yes. Even if they'd loaned the money to ICI and GEC it would have been ... imprudent.'

'And this unholy trio were very far from being ICI and GEC, is that not so?'

'They were not the kind of *good names* we consider it wise to lend such enormous sums of money to.'

'And what were these names, Ms Fraser. I think we should be told.'

She wrinkled her nose in bankerly distaste.

'Nogbad the Bad. Dennis the Menace. And Ming the Merciless.'

'What kind of sum are we talking about?'

'Sixty million pounds, thirty million pounds, ten million pounds.'

'What did you do next?'

'I requested a meeting for July. They held out for August. I agreed.'

117

'That was good of you. Do you regret your generosity?'

'Anyone can be wise after the event. There was no evidence that any of the three were ...' She broke off.

'Splendid financiers?' prompted the Dark Figure patronisingly.

'Yes,' she said. 'As a result, there was nothing more I could do. After all, this wasn't a second-tier bank.'

'Ah, indeed!' exclaimed the Dark Figure triumphantly. 'As defined by the Bank's own published criteria, JMB was a proper bank, reputable, of good standing, with appropriate professional skills. It was prudent, a quality so much admired by the Old Lady of Threadneedle Street that it is mentioned three times in as many pages in its annual report of that year. In short, it was an elephant-shaped bank.'

She did not answer this barrage of rhetorical sarcasm and the Dark Figure was content to let it sink in. 'I owe you an apology, Ms Fraser,' he said finally. 'Here I was, I have to confess, thinking that someone had blundered and that this someone was you. But in fact you could not have done otherwise than request a meeting, allow a delay and make a few suggestions, *could* you? Because JMB was the kind of bank that, in Governor Letherby's words, did not require,' he looked down at his notebook, '"*an elaborate statutory system of supervision which might only succeed in rendering trouble at the expense of initiative*".' He turned with his most theatrical swirl. 'I put it to you,' he said, in an accusatorial rush, 'that JMB were nothing less than financial satanists, and that their version of running around a cemetery in their birthday suits chanting the mass backwards and disembowelling a black goat over the figure of a supine virgin expressed itself in their taking the advice of the Comptroller of the United States currency in 1863 and reversing every single one of his laws of sound banking. They fostered speculation, put enormous sums in the hands of a greedy few, gave the benefit of the doubt to rascals, treated extravagance as a virtue and not the handmaiden of crime. They were tempted by large returns, bankrolled splendid financiers ...' he looked triumphantly around the hall, ' ... and when it came to the straightforward, the legitimate and the upright, they showed only a genius for the Byzantine, the aberrant and the grotesquely recumbent! Thank you, Ms Fraser, that will be all.'

The Dark Figure turned to another couch. 'You are Roy Doyle, a colleague of Marianne Fraser?'

'Yes.'

'Did she share with you her concerns about JMB?'

'She discussed them frequently – it had become a bit of an office joke about whether JMB or Continental Illinois would crash first.'

'Very amusing, no doubt,' said the Dark Figure pompously. 'But did she seem alive to the problems with JMB as early as she should have been?'

Doyle looked irritably at the Dark Figure.

'Have you any idea how complicated the affairs of JMB or any bank actually *are*? They employed eight thousand people. Do you know what it takes to find out what on earth is really happening in a structure of that size when the only information you've got is late, incomplete and put together in a way that makes it difficult to know what's going on? And that was only half her job. She was trying to sort out the mess at Continental Illinois as well.'

'So, the entire economy of the western world was brought to the brink of collapse by one over-worked female regulator? How simple, and how convenient for your superiors. There are no guilty senior men, there are only guilty junior women. What should this inquiry recommend, Mr Doyle? That the next great world economic crash can be avoided by firing all the women at the Bank of England and hiring twice as many men?'

'Don't be absurd!' said Doyle angrily.

'So, what are you saying? That it was the arrival of all these new secondary banks that lowered the tone? Is that what you mean? Deal with the rotters with gaps in their teeth and go back to the good old days when we all went to the same school?'

Doyle smiled sardonically. 'JMB wasn't a secondary bank so ... no, that's not what I mean.'

There was a sudden movement of the Dark Figure's lips at this sneer, an I'll-get-you-for-that rictoid flicker. But he did not respond directly. 'Mr Doyle, your immediate boss was Clive Howatt, the assistant director.'

'Yes.'

'Was he informed of Ms Fraser's problems with JMB?'

'Yes.'

'What did he do about JMB when it was drawn to his attention?'

'To be honest, there wasn't all that much to be done. JMB was a primary bank – we're not the police. The two-tier system was all about trusting the trustworthy old banks and concentrating on the unknown new ones. I think it's a rational way of doing it.'

'So you agreed with the system of two-tiers?'

'I didn't say that, I said it was a rational system. I didn't say it was right.'

'Well, we'll come back to that later. Go on.'

'Howatt saw that Marianne Fraser was asking for better statistics more frequently but, based on what they were telling us, she was doing the right thing.'

'And that was it?'

'He had other things to deal with.'

'Indeed?'

'He wasn't there all that often,' said Doyle with deep reluctance. 'He'd been appointed to sort out the department in 1982, but as soon as he came in he was also given a major responsibility for representing the bank in New York over the South American debt crisis.'

'Which involved ... *briefly*?'

'Most of Central and South America couldn't repay their international debts and were threatening to default. If they went ahead, to put it simply, the entire world banking system would have collapsed.'

'So Mr Howatt took his eye off the ball?'

'Well, it depends,' said Doyle indignantly, 'whether you see an entire continent defaulting on its loans as more important than a bank that's being lazy about its returns and is pushing its luck with regard to its spread of debt. What we didn't realise then was that the collapse of a single bank could mean the collapse of the world economy as well. Howatt was travelling back and forth from New York practically every week for most of 1983, and when he returned full time to the department, just as the situation at JMB started to look more serious, he got shingles.'

'A most unpleasant condition,' interrupted the judge. 'I've had it myself, leaves you exhausted and you can't do anything properly. Took me months to recover.'

'What makes you think you did?' muttered the Dark Figure. He turned back to Doyle. 'So, Mr Howatt was in bed with his Concorde-aggravated conniptions, having saved the world from financially incontinent Argentinians, with the result that the private joke between the hapless Ms Fraser and her colleagues as to which of the banks she was responsible for would crash first remained all too private. So it was that when JMB informed the Bank towards the end of September 1984 that their two largest loans to their splendid financiers were not backed up by anything more substantial than the fog that surrounded their wheeler dealings, it came as a shock for which the senior men at the Bank were ill-prepared. However, at first it seemed merely serious – a question of a trip in another lifeboat round the ragged rocks where financially ragged rascals ran then pump in some money from the clearers to make up for the bad debts and all would be well. Pleased by his donnish wit, he clasped his hands behind his back and walked towards the now furiously writing Winnicott.

'However, for the clearers this was one trip around the bay of bogusness too many and, not to put too fine a point on it, they told the Bank of England to get stuffed. This hurtful rebuff quickly became immaterial when JMB's accountants reported there were many more bad debts than they had originally thought. JMB was bust. The figures were of the horrific kind that bankers use to terrify their small children when they spend all their pocket money in one go on gob-stoppers, Curly-Wurlys and other short-sighted investments. Bad debts equalled two hundred and fifty million pounds. Moreover, there was the matter of JMB's eight thousand employees and the inevitable questions in the House as to who was responsible. And, of course, lurking in the shadows was the Treasury, ever hungry for revenge after the success of the IMF loan in 1976 in pushing the balance of power in the Bank's favour.' He walked past Winnicott and stopped in front of a nearby chair.

'The weekend this disaster struck coincided with the annual meeting in Washington of the IMF and the World Bank. Like Actaeon to Diana in the spring, back rushed a senior director of the Bank, Robert Kingsley, only to discover that a deeply alarming prospect was about to get significantly worse.'

He turned to the man in front of him. 'Mr Kingsley.'

'*Sir* Robert Kingsley, actually.'

'I *do* apologise, Sir Robert.'

'And, to be accurate, when I first returned things actually started to look up for a while.'

The Dark Figure's eyes filled with loathing, galled at the double correction. 'Perhaps you could explain, Sir Robert.'

'When we had a closer look at JMB's books, they gave the impression that while the banking side of JMB was on the rocks, the gold bullion business was pretty healthy. In other words, JMB apparently had a life-saving asset in its vault consisting of a hoard of gold bars. A Canadian bank expressed an interest, so swearing the members of the fixings to secrecy—'

'The *fixings*, Sir Robert?' said the Dark Figure, in a tone that conveyed that while he, of course, knew what the fixings were, it was surely clear to *anyone* with a bit of common sense that it required explanation in a hearing involving non-specialists.

Kingsley's face wrinkled with distaste as if he were being asked to explain a dubious sexual act to the annual conference of maiden aunts.

'The gold bullion side of JMB was part of an informal group of similar gold bullion banks called the fixings. If one needed rescuing we had to have their advice about how to do it. The bullion business isn't really an area in which we have much expertise. We called them in over the weekend when we were still fairly optimistic because we thought that the bullion side of JMB represented a significant asset because of all those gold bars lying about in their vaults.'

'And why was this ... optimism unjustified?' the Dark Figure asked.

Kingsley paused for a moment, as if considering a distasteful family secret he would rather not have discussed in front of strangers.

'They began to explain what you might call a somewhat *delicate* aspect of the gold bullion business.' His use of the word carried a note poisonous with disdain.

'Which is?'

'A firm like JMB, it transpired, doesn't actually keep all their customers' gold in the vaults.'

'And where *do* they keep it?'

'Apparently they lease it out.'

'*Lease* it out?' said the Dark Figure in a tone that would have won the envy of Lady Bracknell.

'Yes,' replied Kingsley with a lofty contempt that almost matched that of the Dark Figure. 'To companies who use gold in their manufacturing processes – jewellers and so on. Apparently they line the engine bay of the Maclaren F1 with gold. I'm given to understand it's an excellent insulator.'

'Let me see if I understand you correctly. Individuals and governments from all over the world keep their gold in various bullion banks in London. And these banks, including JMB, then rent out some of that gold to industry?'

'Yes.'

'The banks' customers are aware of this?'

'It seems not,' he said.

'You mean "No"?'

Kingsley sniffed. 'I suppose I do.'

'What did you do, Sir Robert, when they pointed out that much of the gold you thought was in JMB's vaults was actually honeymooning in Torremolinos on the fingers of newly-weds, or driving around Monaco in an overpriced sports car?'

Kingsley coughed, deeply uncomfortable. 'I asked them what they thought would happen if JMB couldn't return its customers' gold.'

'What was their reply?'

'They didn't say much at first. They seemed finally to be coming to an understanding of just how dubious this leasing business was.'

'One commentator described it as a practice more appropriate to a gang of second-hand car salesmen than an alliance of respectable financial institutions. Would you agree?'

'I wouldn't put it that way myself,' Kingsley said in a manner that made it perfectly clear that this was altogether too generous a comparison. 'These people were subjecting their customers to a risk of which they were unaware and for which they received no payment.' Sir Robert drew in a deep breath of disgust. 'However, I had a more pressing problem on my hands than the business ethics of the fixings. If the practice of leasing became widely known at that particular juncture there was bound to be a massive rush to withdraw gold. For obvious reasons customers who had deposited gold in the City would want to protect themselves from the same thing happening to them. And if there weren't enough gold then the gold market would collapse.' He snorted with derision. 'It's a fragile thing.'

'I could think of another word, Sir Robert.'

'I entirely agree.'

'So what did you envisage would be the consequence?'

'Pretty grim. It would spread to the British banking system as a whole. The Midland Bank was deeply involved with an American subsidiary that was in serious trouble. Customers lost confidence in American banks as a whole when Continental Illinois got into difficulties and a wall of money got moved out of America and ended up in Europe and Japan. If the same thing happened over JMB, then God knows where it could end.'

The Dark Figure paced back and forth for a few moments. He took a deep breath, as if steadying himself for the task ahead. 'Sir Robert, what did you do when you realised the implications of the somewhat insubstantial nature of the gold market and its ... delicate secret?'

Sir Robert sighed. 'The City doesn't exactly have nerves of steel.'

'In a word, spineless.'

He considered this for a moment. 'Not spineless, no.' He looked thoughtful. 'The notion of a run on the banks is immensely tricky. It's not a matter of solid things. Everyone thinks banking is a dull, money-for-its-own-sake business. In fact nothing could be further from the truth. A currency isn't just made out of solid things like economic performance.' He stopped again. 'Its value is based on confidence, and fear, and nerves and the soothing of nerves. It's about belief and faith. When everyone has faith then it all works. Economics is made of emotions.'

'So it's an illusion.'

'No, not an illusion. It's difficult to explain because it's difficult to understand. There are so many contradictions.' He paused before continuing, as if unable to decide where to begin. 'In 1974 this country was running a budget deficit of one per cent and no one believed in us economically so we had to borrow from the IMF who then told the government how to run its own economy as if we were a kind of banana republic. Because of unification, Germany is running a deficit of two per cent but the markets everywhere still believe in it with pretty much absolute faith.'

'Isn't this merely a sign,' said the Dark Figure, 'that the herd instinct has been electronically globalised?'

Kingsley pursed his lips disapprovingly. 'Chancellor Lawson is an able man, but it's not altogether wise to sneer at the herd instinct: it's one of Nature's most effective ways of not finding oneself isolated in the presence of lions, jackals and hyenas.' The Dark Figure's face fell, although Kingsley clearly didn't realise he had intended to pass off Lawson's remark as his own.

'Lions, jackals, elephants,' said the Dark Figure sourly, 'the Square Mile seems to be a bit of a menagerie.'

'I'm sorry,' said Kingsley, 'I don't know what you're talking about.'

The absolute confidence of this dismissal pierced

the Dark Figure and he lost his temper. 'Did you not say of the JMB crisis that the real problem was that the Bank of England left it in the hands of a damn woman?'

Kingsley was shocked. 'Absolutely not!'

The Dark Figure opened his mouth in surprise at the genuine indignation of the man's response. He then turned with a *hah!* of disbelief, his back to Kingsley, as he desperately searched through his notebook, all the while moving away from his witness and towards Winnicott. Eventually he stopped and frantically scanned a page. His eyes closed in disbelief. Winnicott heard him mutter, 'Shit!' under his breath just before he turned back to Kingsley.

The Dark Figure looked at Kingsley murderously and, again keeping his back to everyone else in the court but Winnicott, took out the flick-knife from his waistcoat pocket. He walked towards Kingsley, pressing a button to flick open the knife and another to close it. Click! Click! it went, a sinister, high-pitched chirrup. Click! Click!

As with Letherby, the obviously tough-minded Kingsley was both alarmed and at a loss. He looked about for support but there was only the shadowy sightlessness of the other witnesses. He was about to call out to the judge when the judge himself intervened. His voice was not curious or irritable, but fearful and paranoid. 'What's that sound, Dark Figure?'

Again with magically invisible dexterity the Dark Figure returned the flick-knife to his waistcoat pocket. 'Sound, m'lud?'

'That chirrupy, clicky sound,' said the judge, nervously.

The Dark Figure halted his menacing advance on Kingsley and turned with an expression of deepest concern to look up at the judge.

'I wonder,' he said musingly, 'if it might be bats, m'lud.'

'Bats!' echoed the judge, rising alarm in his voice.

'Yes, m'lud,' replied the Dark Figure. 'I wonder if perhaps your lordship has bats in his belfry.'

For a moment the judge forgot his fear as he wondered whether the Dark Figure might be treating the court, which was to say himself, with contempt. 'What do you mean, bats in my belfry? Are you trying to ...' A look of fear and loathing crossed his face and he looked into the Stygian darkness that surrounded him. 'Do I have bats in my belfry?'

There was a brief pause, then a voice, oleaginous with many years of malign deference, spoke out of the darkness. 'Yes, m'lud, I'm afraid you do.'

There was a gasp of terror from the judge. 'Get rid of them at once!' he demanded.

'I'm afraid,' said the unseen voice, 'that will not be possible, m'lud.'

'Not *possible*!' replied the judge in a tone of absolute incredulity. 'What can you mean? That the Lord High Chancellor should have bats in his belfry, it's ...' The judge stopped dead, clearly at a total loss to find an adjective befitting such an affront. 'It's unconscionable,' he said at last.

'Yes, m'lud.'

'I refuse to accept this. Remove them!'

'Government regulations, m'lud. The 1982 Wildlife Act, which makes the bat a protected species, forbids any person to disturb a bat in any way without a licence from the appropriate regulatory authority.'

'Then get one immediately!' said the increasingly fearful judge, looking about for any sign of flying mammals.

'I'm afraid *that* is the problem, m'lud. The appropriate regulatory authority is in the process of being sold into the private sector in line with government policy which, I am given to understand, takes the view that there should be as little public ownership as is consistent with the efficient running of the state.'

'Then get a bloody licence from whoever bloody well bought it,' cried the judge.

'Unfortunately,' said the voice, 'no buyer has yet been found. Apparently the private sector has taken the view that public demand for bat-handling licences is unlikely to be sufficient to provide a realistic return on their investment. At the moment all traffic in bat-handling licences is at a standstill.'

The judge groaned with frustration. 'Damn! Well, go and get me a tennis racket and be quick about it. That should keep the buggers at bay.'

There was a cough from the floor of the courtroom. The judge looked down irritably. 'What is it, Dark Figure?'

'I was just wondering if it was all right for me to continue questioning the witness?'

'Yes, yes, get on with it.'

The Dark Figure was now standing next to Winnicott, a look of quiet satisfaction on his face. He spoke to Winnicott so that no one else could hear. 'The useless old lunatic is terrified of two things: bats and ducks. I'll teach him to give me a hard time in court.'

'Why would anyone be afraid of a duck?' whispered Winnicott.

'I told you,' replied the Dark Figure. 'He's a useless old lunatic.'

Then he stood up, all smiles and menaces, and readdressed Kingsley. 'Sir Robert, I'm afraid I'm unclear as to the point you were making: are you telling us the markets believe that Germany is such a manufacturing powerhouse it will pull itself out of these problems?'

Kingsley considered for a moment, perplexed as to

how he should proceed. But there was nothing obvious he could do and, warily, he said, 'That is the general view, I would say, but it's not mine.'

'Which is?'

'It doesn't really have as much to do with how much they produce as what lies behind what they produce. It's really ... though I'm sure the markets wouldn't see it like that ... about faith in ...' He paused, 'I'm not sure what the word would be – morality, perhaps, or grace.'

'I'm afraid it isn't any clearer.'

'It's what the financier Louis Bris calls the pyramid of virtue.'

From out of the dark shadows a low hiss began again. Belonging to many voices, the sibilance was filled with hatred and malice as long matured as the most exclusive single malt.

There was a furious squeaking of the judge's gavel and he shouted, 'No hissing. I will not have hissing in my court!'

As if turned off by a switch, the sound stopped.

'I'm not sure that anyone in a British court of justice wants to hear what Louis Bris has to say about morality,' said the Dark Figure. 'Will this take long?'

'Bris puts it succinctly in my view, in his book, *The Wisdom of Crocodiles*.' Kingsley smiled like a small boy able to use rude words in the presence of disapproving but powerless adults. The Dark Figure's nostrils flared with disdain. Kingsley, once again the government banker, continued. 'Bris argues that behind every solid object manufactured, or service provided – a fridge, a bulldozer, insurance, a loan arrangement – there lies a pyramid of decisions, attitudes and values that are solely responsible for the kind of product it is. These values are the key to understanding the underlying strength of an economy. The reason no one wanted to invest in the British economy in the 1970s is that the tip of the pyramid consisted of things like Austin Maxis. The reason they still want to invest in Germany, despite the problems of unification, is that then, as now, the tip consisted of Volkswagen Golfs. We now see that Lloyd's of London has been making Austin-Maxi-shaped decisions whereas, for example, the Bundesbank has been making Volkswagen-Golf-shaped ones.' Sir Robert smiled. 'Economics is the sum of all the strengths and weaknesses of the human heart expressed in goods and services.'

'It's as simple as that?'

'If you think that building the base of a pyramid that ends up in a Volkswagen Golf is simple then you haven't understood the point.'

'Perhaps. But if you're right then there's no need to worry about runs on the banking system. You could have let JMB go to the wall and as long as everyone else was not similarly exposed then the run would come to an end. Or had the Bank created an Austin Maxi-shaped banking system? Is that what you're saying?'

Kingsley realised he had put himself in an awkward position. 'No, I'm not saying that,' he replied defensively, but said nothing more.

The Dark Figure enjoyed his revenge. Confidence restored, he pulled out his notebook. 'So, the upshot of all this activity was that you couldn't persuade anyone else to rescue JMB, so the Bank of England had to do the job itself. Would you now say that this was the right decision?'

'How could you possibly be certain whether or not people would panic, or by how much?'

'Many commentators argued that it was unnecessary to intervene – and also unjust. At that very moment the miners were on strike because they wanted public funds to keep open unprofitable mines.

Why did JMB deserve to be saved when it had such an appalling and bizarre record of incompetence and mismanagement?'

Kingsley sighed. 'It wasn't a question of what it deserved.'

'Bank employees are more important that miners, then?'

'Don't be ridiculous.'

'Is it ridiculous? You don't think you panicked, Sir Robert?'

'JMB deserved to be sunk in the lowest pit of the inner circle of hell. It wasn't a question of virtue, it was a question of what the consequences would be if its collapse started a run. To close down a mine involves the loss of the jobs of a few hundred people. That is to be regretted. But a bank isn't made up of coal, it's made up of confidence. If confidence is lost, you can't know what will happen. There was one moment when I saw what *could* happen ... with terrible clarity. First the gold markets, then one of the clearing banks, then the other clearers. A financial collapse would have brought about the worst depression since the 1920s. So, to answer your question, yes, I came pretty close to panic. But I did not. I do not know if there would have been a banking collapse ... perhaps, perhaps not. No one else does either. I don't mean that I felt disquiet or concern or unease or any of those bankerly expressions, I mean that I was frightened. It was easily the worst night of my life.'

The Dark Figure spoke sympathetically. 'I can see it must have been difficult, Sir Robert. Particularly since you had to take such enormous risks to solve a problem for which you had no responsibility.'

Kingsley looked wary and said nothing. The Dark Figure leant forward and said softly, 'So, Sir Robert, who *was* to blame for the Austin-Maxi-shaped decisions which brought about such a terrible prospect?'

132

Kingsley shifted awkwardly in his seat. 'I don't see what pointing the finger would achieve.'

'The Treasury seemed to have held *you* responsible.'

Kingsley's face became instantly impassive, as if in an effort not to allow any emotion to register. The set expression betrayed his anger.

'Is it not the case that the Treasury postponed your reappointment as Deputy Governor for several months out of spite?' said the Dark Figure.

'I couldn't possibly comment.'

'Who was responsible?'

'Surely everything you've heard makes it clear that there's no fair answer to that.'

Suddenly there was a commotion from the judge's bench. The Dark Figure, Winnicott and an astonished Kingsley looked up to see the judge waving the Day-glo rubber gavel desperately around his head.

'Bats! Bats! OW! Get away! Get away!' He dived under the table with a howl of anguish, then everything went quiet.

'Are you all right, m'lud?' said the Dark Figure at last.

Slowly the judge's head appeared above the bench looking for evidence of his leathery tormentors. He ignored the Dark Figure and held out a tiny apple the size of a gobstopper. 'Look at that!' he said indignantly. 'That bat hit me on the head with an apple.'

'Yes, m'lud,' came the voice from the dark. 'I understand the creatures in the belfry are fruit bats, a species known for the disagreeable behaviour you have just experienced.'

'Why me?' asked the judge tearfully.

There was a discreet cough from the dark, the sound of a disapproving underling about to deliver an unwelcome criticism of a clearly familiar nature. 'I believe the fruit bats are attracted by the squeak of your gavel, m'lud.' Slowly, a beautifully carved wooden gavel was proffered from the dark inlaid with brass and heavy with legal seriousness. 'If m'lud were to take this in exchange, I dare say the bats might find it less easy to locate your lordship.'

With huge reluctance the judge took the wooden gavel with one hand and held out the rubber one with the other. Unseen hands took it away. The judge sat down sulkily.

A look of the purest malice crossed the Dark Figure's face. He turned away from the judge and winked at Winnicott. 'Quack! Quack!'

It was a soft sound, barely audible but brilliantly accurate. It barely carried up to the judge but a look of horror crossed his face and he shrank back into his throne-like seat as if to hide in one of its corners.

A delighted Dark Figure turned back to Kingsley. 'Just one thing, Sir Robert, just to get it clear in my mind.'

'Yes?' Kingsley was deeply suspicious now.

'The two-tier system led to there being two quite different ways of supervising banks.'

'Yes.'

'And because there was a lighter supervisory regime placed on the top tier it was extremely difficult to know what was going on in a bank like JMB because supervisors had no real power to demand information.'

'Yes.'

The Dark Figure seemed to be thinking something through. 'And this system just ... happened?'

'I'm sorry?'

'The two-tier system just evolved of its own accord the way poor structures sometimes do in large organisations?'

'I'm not sure I understand you.'

'Well, you said that no one person was really to blame for JMB and for the unimaginable, world-wide misery that might have resulted from its collapse, the millions thrown out of work, the divorces, the repossessed homes, the suicides, the blight that would have poisoned a generation. It was the system that was at fault. It surely follows that it must have been a bad system that just grew up haphazardly, in a piecemeal fashion, without any specific aim in view. The system was wrong and you're saying no one set it up?'

Kingsley did not reply. The Dark Figure allowed the silence to fill the enormous hall. 'I can see that you understand my problem, Sir Robert, because I can't accept your view that no one was responsible but the system, and I can't accept it because the system, as we have heard here today, did not happen by accident. The two-tier system was designed, planned, contrived, drafted, arranged, devised, elaborated and lobbied for. Is that not so?'

Kingsley paused for a moment. 'Yes.'

'And there was one person at the heart of all this devising and planning, wasn't there?'

'Yes.'

'Who was that person, Sir Robert?'

Kingsley paused and shifted in his seat. 'Samuel Letherby, Governor of the Bank of England.'

The Dark Figure looked around the cavernous hall, then spoke in tones of profound triumph.

'Thank you, Sir Robert. That will be all.'

'But,' protested Kingsley, 'I have to say that when it was being set up there were many in favour. I was one of them, at first. There were good reasons to preserve the informality of the way things had been.'

The Dark Figure interrupted firmly. 'That will be all.'

'But you must understand that it wasn't as simp—'

'THAT WILL BE ALL!' shouted the Dark Figure.

Kingsley sank back in his chair and his light went out.

'You needn't worry about writing down that last outburst from Kingsley,' said the Dark Figure affably to
Winnicott, as he walked over to a spot between two
chairs. He called out in a loud voice, as if he were con-
juring spirits, 'Ladies and gentlemen of the jury!'

The space in front of him shimmered and slowly
twelve people materialised. Each was sitting in a toy
bus, the front of which was clearly marked: Clapham.
They were dressed as if for a terrible village pageant in
which they were to represent a typical member of a
particular class: a plumber holding a toilet plunger, a
City gent wearing a bowler hat and carrying a furled
umbrella, a Pakistani holding a shop sign that declared
he was open, a large, smiling West Indian woman
dressed in a hat for a Sunday prayer meeting, an
Irishman holding a shovel, and so on. Winnicott suddenly noticed what was truly odd about them: all the
men were women in disguise. 'Ladies and gentlemen
of the jury ...' He paused for effect. 'I accuse Samuel
Letherby, Governor of the Bank of England, of placing
at risk through his obdurate pursuit of the two-tier
banking system not only the financial well-being of
every man, woman and child in the country but every
man, woman and child in the entire world. When Wall
Street crashed in flames, out of the ashes grew the
monster of Fascism and the deaths of millions. Who
can say what the consequences might have been but
for ... but for what? Only the regulator lies between us
and the chaos of total collapse. We demand of these
men and women that they strive with courage to hold
at bay the seven-headed hydra of the marketplace with
the bright sword of policy and the burnished shield of
procedure. Not just our livelihoods but our very lives
themselves rest on the skills of men such as Samuel
Letherby. We deserve better than this. We require that
matters be regulated better than this.' His voice rose,
filled with indignation and swollen with wrath. 'WE

DEMAND IT! The men, women and children of the world, now and in the generations to come, they DEMAND IT!' He turned to the jury, a single tear slowly forming in the corner of his left eye. 'Gentlemen of the jury, I beg of you, send a signal to all those who would fail in their duty through their vanity and contempt for the little people, the defenceless children, your wives, your servants. Protect them now and in the future with the simple sword of truth and the trusty shield of decent British values.' The Dark Figure drew himself up to his full height, his face noble with sorrow, yet stern with righteousness. 'Ladies, er, I'm sorry, *gentlemen* of the jury, I beg of you to censure the delinquent, castigate the culpable, condemn the reprehensible, blame the ... uh ... blame worthy, and send a signal to the world that Albion will not tolerate the malfeasance of infamies such as ...' he was hardly able to say the words 'the two-tier banking system'. He pointed his finger at the former Governor of the Bank of England. 'Look upon the face of the defendant, Samuel Letherby, and let right be done. Gentlemen of the jury, how do you find him?'

Letherby sat, amazement and fear written into every line of his face.

The jury rose as one and shouted aloud as if with one voice: 'GUILTY! GUILTY! GUILTY!'

The judge, grim-faced at the terrible majesty of the law, allowed a careful hand to place a small black cap on his head. 'Prisoner at the bar,' he said, in gloomy exaltation.

The Dark Figure nudged Winnicott heavily in the back. 'What?' gasped Winnicott, alarmed and confused.

'He's talking to you, fuckwit!' said the Dark Figure malevolently.

Standing up in open-mouthed protest, Winnicott looked up at the judge. 'I'm not on trial. *He* is.' He looked around wildly for Letherby. But Letherby was also wearing a black cap, as was everyone else in the court, and he was smiling.

'The Dark Figure was right about you,' said the judge accusingly.

'What do you mean?' said Winnicott, his helpless terror growing with every passing moment.

The judge looked at him with absolute contempt. 'You *are* a fuckwit!' He gasped in disbelief. 'Did you *really* think you were going to get away with it? Now, shut up and listen to the judgment.' He closed his eyes to recover his equanimity. 'Prisoner at the bar, you have been found guilty of a most grievous case of *implacabilis inscitia de anima.* I therefore sentence you to be hanged by the neck until you be dead.'

Winnicott fell to his knees sobbing with terror. Everyone in the court stared down at him with utter contempt. There was a brief pause followed by a discreet cough from the shadows behind the judge. 'Excuse me, m'lud.'

'What is it?'

'I'm afraid that's the wrong verdict.'

'No it isn't,' said the judge, truculently. 'I'm the fucking judge, you're just an usher.'

'Very well, m'lud, it's the right verdict but the wrong defendant. You'll notice that you turned over two pages. The death penalty you have passed on Mr Winnicott is actually meant for a Miss Ruth Ellis.'

The judge looked down furiously at his papers. He swore under his breath as he realised that the usher was right. Something seemed to trouble him.

'Isn't Ruth a woman's name?'

'I believe so, m'lud.'

'You can't hang a woman!' he said indignantly.

'I think you'll find that you can, m'lud.'

'A gentleman should never hit a woman, no matter what the provocation,' he insisted.

'Quite so, m'lud,' said the usher emolliently, 'but in death by hanging, the aim is to snap the neck of the prisoner using a carefully contrived placement of the rope and employing the prisoner's own weight as the means of effecting the fatal injury. I don't think that it is unreasonable to claim that this is not a blow, hit, thump, strike, rap, knock or impact in the sense that your lordship rightly finds so objectionable. And besides,' he added reassuringly, 'the bitch deserves it.'

But the judge was no longer listening as he read the page he had previously missed. He looked down at Winnicott who was now staring up at him wildly. 'Right, you, you've wasted enough of the court's valuable time. In addition to the previous charge, which is jolly serious whatever it means, you have also been found guilty of the crime of allowing your wife to become a miserable cow. No *proper* man allows his wife to become a miserable cow. I therefore sentence you to explain the meaning of life and eluci- date the origin of good and evil, the sentences to run concurrently. And may God have mercy on your soul!' He smiled malevolently at the bewildered Winnicott. 'By the time you've finished with that lot you'll wish I *had* been able to sentence you to death.'

'You can't sentence him to death, m'lud.'

The judge groaned irritably. 'Yes, I know, I heard you the first time. Shut up.'

'No, m'lud, you can't sentence him to death for the simple reason that he already *is* dead.'

The judge stared into the dark, a look of the deepest exasperation on his face. 'What are you talking about? Is that supposed to be clever, or something? Is it?' Before he could receive a reply he turned to Winnicott. '*Are* you already dead?'

'No, of course not.'

'See!' said the judge triumphantly looking into the

dark as if he had won a great victory over a previously undefeated opponent. 'He says he's not dead.'

'He most definitely *is* dead, m'lud,' came the unperturbed reply. 'He just doesn't know it yet.'

'I've never heard such a complete pile of camel dung in my life!' said the judge furiously. 'What do you mean by—'

Suddenly a small, round, hard object bounced on the table in front of the judge. It rebounded up into the dark then fell back onto the table. It did this several times as the judge and the courtroom watched, mesmerised. Finally it stopped and before it could roll away the judge picked it up and examined it carefully. It was a fruit-flavoured gobstopper covered in tiny tooth marks. He turned it over in his hand, puzzling over what it might mean.

Everyone in the courtroom stared at him. Then the Dark Figure cocked his head to one side, listening. In the almost complete silence, Winnicott could hear a distant sound. Gradually it became louder and louder, like the whining of an aeroplane going into a steep dive. Winnicott looked up at the source of the noise. Far above in the high-domed roof, a huge fruit bat was aiming directly for the judge who was staring down, puzzling over the nibbled gobstopper in his hand. The bat was the size of an eagle and heading for him at a ferocious speed, its huge teeth bared. Winnicott watched in amazement as it went into a shallow dive aimed straight at the judge's head. Everyone in the court bellowed a warning: 'DUCK!' they shrieked.

The judge stood up in terror. 'WHERE?' he screamed.

And as he heard the horrible SPLAT! of giant fruit bat and Lord Chancellor meeting at a hundred miles per hour, Winnicott fell to the ground and began to lose consciousness.

The Dark Figure leaned over him and smiled. 'You

were told to keep your mouth shut about the meaning of life, Winnicott. We've got Maria, and if you want to see her again, button your lip.' By now the jury of women had taken off their disguises. They were staring down at him menacingly. One by one they began to speak.

'Yeah, keep it mum, chum.'

'Leave it in the dark, Mark.'

'Cover your tracks, Max.'

'Keep it discreet, Pete.'

'Don't blow the gaff ...' There was an awkward pause from the woman disguised as a City gent holding a furled umbrella. 'Look, I'm most *awfully* sorry but I can't think of a name to rhyme with gaff.'

'What about Taff?' suggested one of them.

The disguised City gent wrinkled her nose. 'Strictly speaking, shouldn't it really be Taffy?'

'I don't see why,' came the reply. 'My uncle ...'

'SHUT UP!' barked the Dark Figure, who then bent down so close to Winnicott that he was no more than two inches from his face. Winnicott could feel the wet heat of his breath mingle with his own and see every crack and fissure in his yellow teeth. 'The point about secrets, Georgy Worgy, is that no one is supposed to know. We're going to make an example of you so that no one else who squeals thinks they can get away with it. Nobody likes a snitch. You think that telling secrets is such a good idea? Well, we'll see if you still think so after you listen to one.'

Then the Dark Figure's face began to stretch and buckle, short black hairs emerged from every pore, and he transmogrified into a huge and malevolent black cat, his hot breath blowing like a gale into Winnicott's mouth as he opened it to scream. There was a terrible pressure in his lower back as the weight of the huge cat began to crush his spine and then it was as if he were dissolving.

Brett and Varadi, like anxious mothers, were looking down as Winnicott opened his eyes.

'Who are you?' he muttered.

'I'm Sally Brett,' said one of the faces, astonished and alarmed, 'and this is Charley Varadi.'

Winnicott blinked. 'I have a secret to tell you ... terrible secret. You must listen. I know the meaning of life.'

Then his eyes rolled back into his head and he passed out.

———

Later that day Varadi and the Governor he was soon to replace were having their usual end-of-day informal meeting, over a malt whisky for the former and a cup of tea for the latter. They were worrying. This was not personal or millennial heartache, this was the kind of worrying they were paid to do. Varadi's salaried unease was about interest rates or, to be more specific, the rate of interest as it applied to mortgages.

'You know what the buggers are like, Governor. As soon as the public sees mortgage rates fall they start behaving like bloody lunatics. House prices are rising and I don't like it. A half a per cent cut was too much – the committee should have kept it to a quarter, or preferably no rise at all.'

'But, Charley, let's be honest, if it was up to you, you would have increased it by half a per cent.' Smiling, the Governor changed the subject. 'So, Charley, what did you make of Winnicott? I *do* hope he's not the litigious kind.' Varadi ignored the attempt to tease him.

'He's difficult to make out. He's certainly not ...' he hesitated, ' ... one's conventional idea of a police-man.'

'I take it that by conventional you mean not very

bright. It's quite all right, Charley,' said the Governor, enjoying his end-of-the-day cup of tea, nothing fancy, British Rail tea as he called it. 'No one feels it necessary to be politically correct when it comes to policemen.'

Varadi smiled. 'At any rate, Winnicott is an able man.'

'So, will he fit into your grand plan?'

'We'll have to wait and see. The important thing is that he's meticulous and thoughtful. He wrote a document for the Met in the early 1980s ... what was it? *Principles of Policing*. It was good stuff. And you have to hand it to him, until a few weeks ago the IRA had gone very quiet. It was a shambles when he began, a shambles.'

'I don't call what they did to the Baltic Exchange going quiet – four hundred million pounds worth of damage caused by one bomb.'

'Yes, fine, but how did he react? That's the key thing. The IRA put their finger on a real weakness – the City is a small place and one bomb can do immense economic damage. What if it had been the Stock Exchange, or they'd hit the top six merchant banks on the same day? That's what they should have done. Then what? You have to say Winnicott's solution was spot on.'

The Governor put down his cup and poured himself another. 'Come on, Charley, it was hardly that impressive. He just put roadblocks on every road into the city. Effective but hardly as brilliant as you suggest.'

'I'm sorry, Governor, I disagree. It seems obvious once it's done, granted. So does the solution to the Gordian knot. But before Alexander the Great solved the problem of how to unravel it by just cutting it open with his sword, great minds had puzzled over it for centuries.'

'And Sally Brett?'

Varadi hesitated for a moment. 'Smart as she is, if Sally makes it to Christmas without an invitation from Lafferty to retire to the snooker room with a loaded revolver, I'll eat a weasel, as my old dad used to say. If Winnicott is any good, and if he's lucky, he could be running the FS before long.' The Governor finished his tea, both of them comfortable with the silence. 'So, Charley,' he said at last, 'if Winnicott *is* the coming man, do you really think that this is the way we should go? You know my reservations. I was never happy about handing over the power to regulate the City to the Financial Services Authority. The Bank has always regulated the City. Nobody should ever give up power.'

'What power would that be, Governor? Have you been in a supermarket recently? I went to get my grandson a packet of cornflakes the other day. You could have landed a jumbo jet in the aisle just given over to boxes of cereal. What's all that about? I don't understand. And that's just a *shop* for God's sake. All the forces there are in the world, all the lunatic energy that means people can choose between eighty different kinds of cornflakes, it's all flowing through the City, and any attempt to regulate it is going to be a mug's game. Heartache and grief, that's all there is to be had there. We were right to get out.'

The Governor looked at his deputy who was distractedly staring out of the window. After a long pause, he said, 'Is there something else on your mind, Charley?'

Varadi started to speak, stopped, and then began again. 'This afternoon when Winnicott regained consciousness, he said he had a terrible secret he needed to tell. He said he knew the meaning of life.'

'Goodness me,' said the Governor of the Bank of England, his eyes widening with surprise. 'But then people say all kinds of odd things after they've taken a blow to the head.' He laughed, teasing. 'Still I'm not sure you should be considering handing over the job of regulating the City to someone who thinks they know the meaning of life.'

Varadi smiled. 'On the contrary, Governor, it should be a minimum requirement. And, in any case, I was only giving him the once-over.' He stopped smiling. Clearly something else was on his mind. 'But it wasn't just what Winnicott said that was so strange. It was the *way* he said it. It sounded like somebody else entirely.' He paused. 'It was a woman's voice.'

GEOFFREY HEALEY:
HIS EARLY LIFE

Men start out female in the womb and are
simplified. This is why they are so obsessed
with sex – always trying to return to the uterus
so that they can recapture the peace of mind
that was once theirs.

Louis Bris, *The Wisdom of Crocodiles*

Inspector Geoff Healey answered the phone. It was
his wife, from whom he had been separated for two
months. The term must have been coined, he thought,
by some great poet of disintegration since it described
exactly how he felt: separated. He had always assumed
that the word straightforwardly summarised the
business of being in the first stages of divorce, of being
apart from someone you were still married to. But he
now realised that this was not what the word referred
to at all. He now spent all his time being separate from
himself. He had left her only a month ago, but there
had been plenty of time to feel just how impressive the
word was. Whatever the opposite of quality time was
– efficiency *and* purity – he had it in abundance:
shady time, shabby time, shoddy time, base time,
mean time. That was what he had, mean time, and lots

of it. When you left someone you loved that was what happened to you: you were separated. It was as if his body and personality had been replicated in some way, but badly, and the smudged facsimile had gone into exile to manage its replica world, its poor photocopy of an existence, as best it could. Bits of his story were now missing. Important bits. He was rubbed out. He was missing stuff. All the humiliation had come with him, though, all the grief. In the incomplete transmission to his new life, none of the shame had failed to be duplicated with digital clarity.

This was the first time his wife had called him at the new flat since he'd moved in. At first he was alarmed, but there was nothing wrong with either of their two children; he could go back to feeling miserably ashamed.

'Are you all right?' she said.

'Yes. Fine. You?'

'Yes.'

This uneasy exchange went on for a minute or so. Then there was silence.

'Are you busy?' she said at last.

'I'm stuck with some office politics. Someone who used to be big in the Met has pulled in a favour from Myers, so I'm on a goose-chase trying to find a missing woman relative of his.'

'I can't see why someone like you should be put on a missing persons case.' Did he detect a tone of irritation on his behalf? That would be a good sign.

'Well, there is one odd thing. She had a history of mental problems, anorexia, even a suicide attempt. But by all accounts, in the last nine months she'd changed completely. She'd put on two stone, had a boyfriend and was as happy as Larry, according to all the reports. There's probably a simple explanation, but it's odd all the same.'

There was another awkward pause. The past seeped back.

'I've got a problem at work. I wanted your opinion, if you wouldn't mind,' she said at last.

'Anything I can do, you only have to ask.'

There was a moment's silence for which the word painful was entirely inadequate and then she began. 'I'm doing a big audit for a company. I have to sign the accounts as being true and fair. But I don't think they are. I think they might be up to something. A fraud. Perhaps a big one.'

'Do you have any proof, I mean, is there solid evidence?'

'This is not a murder case, Geoff, there isn't a body and a blunt instrument hidden in the coal scuttle.' There was another silence. 'I'm sorry. I'm worried.' But they both knew that she was angry too.

'If there's no solid evidence why do you have to do anything?'

'Because I've got enough to warrant an investigation. At least I think so. The problem is that I'm damned if I report them – because they can sue me for breaking client confidentiality or for defamation – but if I say nothing and it all comes out I could face the end of my career. That's to say nothing of the possibility that the police might accuse me of being involved.'

'What do the lawyers at work say?'

She gasped with irritation. 'Wexler's a nasty little oik. They want me to keep my mouth shut.' She laughed bitterly. 'They don't want to get a reputation in the City as a copper's nark. They think I can sign the accounts in a strictly legal sense as being true and fair, but they don't give a damn about whether they're true and fair in the would-you-allow-your-blind-granny-to-invest-in-this-company sense.' She paused. 'I want to do the right thing, but I don't want to ruin my life. Any suggestions?'

He was silent for a moment. He was worried about her but he was also anxious to help for another reason. If he could come to her aid in an important way, if he could rescue her, then perhaps there would be a way back, of being less humiliated and exposed in her presence. 'Can you give me any details?'

'I can give you as much as I know, but the company is important in the City. It would be too easy to identify if you start asking questions.'

Ten minutes later he put down the phone and at almost the same time he heard the clatter of the letter box. He walked into the hall and was surprised, given that he had been in the flat for only two weeks, that the letter was addressed to him personally. It was a begging letter. It was from Barclays Bank, begging him to take out a loan.

'We're police officers. We're looking for Mr ...' Roache looked down irritably at the piece of paper on which was written an address and the name Steven Grlscz. 'Grillesk,' he hazarded.

Even through the tinny crackle of the intercom Healey could hear the tired good humour in the correction. 'It's pronounced *Grilsh*.'

Roache looked at the intercom with total loathing. 'However it's pronounced, we're still looking for him.'

There was a pause, then a buzz. The front door of the apartment block clicked open.

'Third floor, number six. It's the second on the left after you come out of the lift.'

The foyer was impressive, a carefully restored and maintained art-deco marble vault, like the mausoleum of a megalomaniac with good taste. The lift was an elegant construction of the period, but it was faded and rather grubby. When they came out on to the third floor landing, it seemed as though they were entering yet another level of neglect. The floor was covered in brown lino, cracked in places, the lighting was dim and thoro was the faint odour of old cabbage water. Healey and Roache reached flat number six and found the door half open. Healey looked at Roache, who hesitated and then pushed the door further open, calling, 'Mr ...' He had already forgotten the pronunciation. 'Hello?'

Steven Grlscz was standing at the far end of a long, simply furnished room. Both Healey and Roache were impressed. There was an absence of clutter about the place and yet no sense of an attempt to present the room as some kind of minimalist exhibition. It was as if a discreet person lived there who had tidied up perhaps too carefully, as if in doing so they were providing a distraction for themselves.

They came in, feeling – unaccountably – that this was an intrusion. The atmosphere of unhappiness was unforced but clear. The man was just under six feet tall and in his mid-thirties. There was a warmth that made him attractive, thought Healey. Without being obviously charismatic, this was a person to whom you were drawn. It was not charm and it was not, he felt, deliberate. He seemed likeable, that was it. Roache felt this, too, but it only irritated him further. He began with an even greater degree of insolence in his voice than usual. 'We're investigating the disappearance of Maria Vaughan, sir. Thank you for contacting us.'

Grlscz nodded.

'We understand you were having a relationship with Miss Vaughan.'

'Yes,' said Grlscz softly.

'Can I ask why you didn't report her missing before? After all, her parents reported her missing three weeks ago.'

There was a brief pause before he replied. 'The last time I saw her we had an argument.'

He clearly realised the risk of saying this, but Healey could see that he was ashamed of having taken it into account before replying.

Roache's predatory instincts were alerted. 'It must have been quite a row if you've made no attempt to see her since then. What was it about?'

'She wanted to get married.'

'To you or to someone else?'

'To me,' said Grlscz, so softly he could barely be heard.

'Was it a violent argument?'

Grlscz looked at the young policeman and Healey saw something pass across his face: a kind of judgement, an evaluation. It was without aggression or defensiveness. Roache had been weighed in the balance.

'You mean, did I hit her? No.'

Roache grew more irritable. 'Was it a *heated* argument?'

'She was heated. Very. I was not heated.'

'That's interesting, sir.'

'Is it?'

Healey found it hard not to smile at the tone of annoyance in Grlscz's voice; it let Roache know what he thought of him. And it was pretty much exactly what he thought of Roache himself.

'Yes, it is interesting, sir,' continued Roache, 'because we've talked to a fair number of people about Miss Vaughan, and she didn't seem the type of person who became heated. Rather the contrary.'

Grlscz sat down, motioning for the two men to do likewise. Roache did. Healey did not.

'When I first knew Maria, I would have said the same.' He considered carefully, as if trying to explain something he hadn't yet put his finger on. He smiled sadly. 'It wasn't love at first sight, believe me. She seemed completely washed out as a person. I remember someone saying that about her at the time. But we were both as wrong as it's possible to be. She was passionate ... I mean in the sense that she felt things with an incredible intensity. Inside she was ...' His voice trailed away, partly because he couldn't seem to say precisely what he meant and partly, thought Healey, because talking about her in this way to strangers seemed like a betrayal. 'Inside she was a whirl of emotions. She could be funny – no one realised that about her. But she was an angry person. But she kept it hidden – so well hidden she couldn't see it herself.' He laughed, and Healey could see the affection he had for the missing woman, not only in his expression but also in his tone. 'If you said she was angry she would become absolutely furious at the idea.'

'And she was furious on the last occasion you saw her because you refused to marry her?'

'Not exactly. It started because she became angry when I told her I'd had lunch with an old colleague of mine – a woman.'

'An old *girlfriend* colleague?'

'No. Just someone I used to work with.'

'And this lunch was entirely innocent?'

'This colleague was not someone I even liked. Maria knew this perfectly well. She'd met her several times. It made no difference. She worked herself up into a real fury. She said either we should marry or finish it.'

'And what was your reply, sir?'

Grlscz looked at Roache but his expression was impossible to read.

'I said that threats like that were hardly the basis for marriage. Something stupid like that anyway.'

'But you weren't angry?'

'I was very angry.' Roache was at a loss. 'I said I wasn't heated. I didn't shout or express any strong emotions. But I felt them. It had been a bad week. Six months hard labour had just gone down the drain at work and I was in no mood for Maria's nonsense. This was the third outburst in a couple of months and I'd had enough. What she wanted was reassurance and she would have been fine given a couple of hours of intense effort. For once I didn't feel like making that effort. I was seriously pissed off, if you must know. So ...' He stared out of the window. 'I knew she thought it meant that I didn't love her and I let her go.'

Roache paused, trying to create the impression he was weighing up what he had heard carefully. 'Still,' he said, casually, 'three weeks before you attempted to find her. I have to say I find that strange. Weren't you worried at all?'

'I told you, I was furious. Twice before when she became jealous over nothing she vanished.'

Both Roache and Healey reacted to this.

'For how long?' said Healey sharply.

'Once for a week. The second time for ten days.'

'And she just turned up?'

'Not exactly. I left messages on her machine and she'd eventually answer when she got back.'

'And where did she go?'

'I don't know. She wouldn't tell me. That's why I wasn't surprised by such a long absence this time. It was a much bigger row.'

'What made you change your mind?'

Grlscz sighed. 'I began to get worried. The idea crossed my mind ... but I told you, I was angry ... pride ... all the usual things. But, given her past, I suppose worry overcame my basic feeling that she was punishing me and trying to control me by using the fact that I knew about her problems in the past and could always be relied on to back down. I didn't feel like being controlled in that way. Who would?'

Neither of the policemen reacted to his question, and Healey could see Grlscz felt shabby for trying to win their sympathy. 'I still think she'll turn up. I think she *is* punishing me. I'm just not sure any more.'

Healey looked at Roache, who leant back to signal he'd taken the point. 'I'm sorry to ask you this but do you think it's possible she took your argument more seriously than that. Is she capable of committing suicide?'

Grlscz seemed to shrink slightly. His sense of misery, guilt and loss was almost strong enough to touch. Healey had felt it when he'd entered the flat. 'Of course, I've thought about that.' A troubled look crossed his face. 'It's possible ... but I don't think so, not now. I know what I've told you makes Maria seem just awkward and difficult. And I know what other people will have told you, that she was colourless ... but she was a strong woman too, much stronger than people thought, and she was happy enough most of the time. She'd changed a great deal.' He looked at them both. 'Not enough, perhaps. I think she's – I don't know what the term would be – gone into hiding.'

'Any idea where?'

'She was quite a wanderer before I met her. She'd lived in some real dumps with a lot of lowlifes – one of her flatmates turned out to have been a bomber with the IRA.'

'Any names, addresses?'

'A few names but not where she lived.' Grlscz looked at Healey directly. 'I'd like to ask you something.'

'Of course,' Healey said gently.

'Why have you gone to so much trouble over one missing person? I didn't think the police were generally interested unless there was real reason to suspect something.'

Healey felt sorry for Grlscz because his question made it clear that their interest was more worrying than their indifference. It made it seem more likely that something had happened to her. It was impossible to answer his question without revealing information that would only make things worse and that in any case he was not in a position to reveal. The explanation that *would* be reassuring, namely that her father was a policeman and well connected, was not the kind of information it was wise to reveal to the general public who might reasonably feel that this was an improper basis on which to pursue an investigation. Still, given that the first reason for their investigation was, in Healey's view, a lot of balls, and that Grlscz was obviously not going to complain about privileged treatment, given that his missing girlfriend was the one receiving it, he decided to take a risk. 'Do you know much about Miss Vaughan's background?'

Grlscz sighed. 'Some. She was pretty evasive about her past. It depended.'

'Did she say much about her parents?'

'They were a pretty sore topic. Why?' Grlscz could see that Healey was trying to lead him somewhere.

'Did you know that her father was a *senior* police officer?'

Grlscz did not answer. Healey turned slightly towards the door. 'Thank you, Mr Grlscz. We'll call you in a couple of days, unless we hear anything. Perhaps you could write down any names that might be useful.' He looked at Roache, who produced a business card. 'If she contacts you, or you ...'

Grlscz nodded.

The two policemen walked to the door. As he was just about to leave, Healey turned to Grlscz. 'One more thing. Did she ever mention someone called George Winnicott?'

'Yes. She talked about him often – for her, anyway. He was her godfather. They got on well. He seemed to be the one adult she had a decent relationship with when she was a child.'

'Did they meet often?'

'I don't think often, but she was secretive about that kind of thing so it's hard to know. They certainly kept in touch. She told me they met a few weeks ago.'

'I understand she lived with his family for a while as a kind of unofficial nanny.'

Grlscz smiled. 'Yes, she mentioned it once. She was funny about how bad she was at the job.'

Healey nodded. 'But it all finished quite amicably?'

Instantly Healey saw that it had not, and that Grlscz realised there was a point to the question and that his answer might lead to an unpleasant experience for someone else. Healey's was not a job that was likely to lead to a generous view of human nature, but over and over again, even among otherwise profoundly vicious people, he had seen a similar look on the face of a witness: the look of someone who suspected they might be about to get someone else into trouble. 'I remember her hinting that there was bad blood between her and Winnicott's wife.' He added softly, 'But I don't know what it was.'

'Well, thank you,' Healey said, 'we'll let you know if we find anything.' He opened the door. 'There was one other thing. Your name. We put everything on computers these days and it didn't bring up a National Insurance number.' He paused, waiting for Grlscz to offer it. 'Could you give it to us?'

Grlscz seemed nonplussed, as if he'd been asked a question he didn't understand, but then he walked over to his desk and took out a diary.

'YX207616/2.'

Roache copied it down in his notebook.

'Perhaps you'd better get in touch with the DSS, Mr Grlscz,' said Healey. 'You wouldn't want any problems with your pension.'

As Healey and Roache waited for the lift, a woman and a girl of about six joined them. The child was dressed in a striped school uniform, clearly that of a private school. He smiled at her. She stared back at him as if he were the kind of man she'd been warned about. The lift arrived and they followed the pair into the grimy cubicle. By now the little girl was in a world of her own, talking earnestly to herself. But this was no fantasy of secret friends, speaking to voices no one else could hear. She was rehearsing her times table. 'One times three is three,' she whispered. 'Two times three is six. Three times three is …'

But she was not the only one whose mind was in another place. Geoffrey Healey had returned to 1963.

One times seven is seven.
Two times seven is fourteen.
Three times seven is twenty-one.
Four times seven is twenty-eight.

The teacher sitting on the desk was in her late twenties. To the modern observer the brown ribbed top, the texture of her nyloned legs, the cut of her short skirt and its unpleasing texture would have given her the look, for all that it was the early 1960s, of someone from the remote past. Her shape also seemed to belong to another time. The way her breasts were supported was accentuated by her beating time heavily on the desk to the rhythm of the numbers being chanted by the children. Her upper body, rigidly held in, did not seem to respond in any way.

' … Svens svens are forty-nine …' they chanted, suddenly and inexplicably changing the rhythmic pattern: 'Eight svens are fifty-six.'

There was a pleasantly boring mood in the room, an atmosphere of security in the repetitious nature of the schoolroom tasks: the children enjoying the irresponsibility of rote, the paintings on the wall of Mum and Dad. The obligation to be the engine of endless creativity was still a few short years away. Single parenthood hovered unseen.

Quietly an internal door opened and a woman entered. Only part of her face was visible and nothing of her shape, except that she was slim. She had no hips, no breasts, no hair; neither did she have feet. Her eyes were cast down and she moved without sound, only the click of the opening and closing door signalled her presence. The teacher stopped talking and moved to one side as the woman took her place. She had been expecting her. The woman put a pile of blue exercise books down on the table. There was an extraordinary calm in her expression, an absence of fear or doubt or unhappiness. The children stood, silent in a way they had not been silent before. There was expectancy here, but it was of an odd kind. All of them, even the inattentive ones who had been whispering or daydreaming throughout the lesson, spoke as if with one voice. 'Good morning, Sister Grace.'

She waited, without responding, her eyes moving once from side to side. Then, slowly and slightly, she nodded and they sat. The extraordinary quiet of the children continued.

The nun took one of the blue exercise books from the top of the pile and smiled. It was an attractive smile, if slightly forbidding in its way because not easily given, and incongruous because of the impossibility of reading anything about her from her appearance. She was encased from head to foot in black, except for the white wimple that enclosed her head, neck and ears, revealing only the middle of her forehead to just below her chin. The hem of her habit brushed the ground.

The nun opened the exercise book in the middle, and showed the class a picture of a harlequin, and beside it, a carefully written account of its history.

This was predictable enough in its childish way, copied neatly out of a book. But her most admiring remarks were for the drawing. She praised not only the care with which it had been coloured but also its vigorous sense of movement. The nun's strange smile showed the depth and warmth of her admiration for the work – but the girl whose book it was seemed neither pleased nor indifferent; she looked as if she were waiting for the attention to stop.

The nun walked over and dropped the book on the girl's desk, then turned to the pile. None was praised in such terms; a few were commended. Most were handed over silently. Although she could be pleased, it was clearly not easy to do so. After about fifteen books, she stopped and looked carefully at the pile, then faced the class. The children sensed something, for the watchful silence seemed to deepen. At no time during the handing out had the expression of the young teacher altered; nor had she taken her eyes from the distant point towards which she had been looking. When the nun spoke again, it was quietly but her face was stern. 'Every year I look at the work you have done, a practice I have always observed in the fifteen years since I became headmistress here. But,' she continued softly, 'never have I seen, and never do I expect to see an exercise book like this.' She turned and picked up the book on top of the pile. With a sudden movement like an angry bank teller slowly counting notes, she flicked through the pages. In the absolute silence the sound of the pages being turned, harsh, angry, filled the room. She stopped. She looked up, her lips tight together, and stared around the room. Then she held up the book and panned the centre pages around the class for all the children to see. There was a terrible anticipation as the children stared. The girl whose book she had praised did not lift her eyes at all, and some of the others whose books had been returned quickly looked away. As she brought the pages to bear on the desks by the far wall an expression of shock and dread came over the face of a boy in the middle of the row. The colour drained from his cheeks, his eyes opened wider, then everything seemed to stop – his breathing, the movement of his eyes, the hands.

'Geoffrey Healey,' said the nun. 'Come here.'

The boy stood up. Eight or nine years old, he was short compared to the other children but sturdy, even a little fat. His black hair and navy blue sweater, dishevelled and with a small hole in one seam, framed the colourless face. He walked to an adjacent desk and the seated child hurried to let him pass by shunting his seat into his desk. In his desperation to give him space to pass he seemed to have squeezed his stomach so that he was only three or four inches wide. The frightened boy slipped past and walked up the aisle towards the nun who held his book open like a beacon. He came to a stop in front of her, dazed by terror. His face was now completely white.

The blow, when it came, seemed to arrive from a great distance. With astonishing speed, she had raised one arm behind her head and then turned her body into the movement with the timing and grace of an athlete. It was not a slap. Her open hand took him just above the ear. He staggered back from the force.

'Stand still!' she screamed. 'Stand there!' She raised her arm again as she waited for the boy to move back into position. Slowly he did so, head held away from the direction of her arm. Again she swung it with all her strength; again the boy staggered back from the weight of the blow.

'Don't you move!'

The scream made the girl in the desk next to the boy wince. The young teacher blinked but kept her eyes in the distance. There were no tears from the boy but a terrible whimpering sound emerged from some-where at the back of his throat – a terrible whining of pain and horror. She waited and he moved back into his place. Still she waited. She made a feint with her upraised hand, once, twice and each time it was echoed by the boy moving his head away from the direction of the blow and the holding up of his hand to protect his head. She waited, staring at him. Slowly, the defending hand fell to the sound in the back of his throat, a noise like whooping cough.

'Don't you move,' she said, barely audible.

When the blow came, his head seemed to bounce but he had set his legs wider apart to obey her and he stayed where he was. She hit him again. The noise in his throat was now continuous, exhausted and high pitched, like the grizzle of a two-year-old. She started to point to the book and, page by page, shared the source of her anger with the thirty children. With each new blasphemy, an inept drawing, a clumsy-crossing out, an unmade punctuation mark, she would hit the boy: a blow, then an error pointed out, and then another blow. And throughout, the terrible noise from his throat and the deadly white face. The boy stared ahead, seeing nothing. He seemed to be in a private world in which there was only pain, humiliation and fear. And the woman in front of him defined its begin-ning and end, its limits in every direction. She could do whatever she wanted, and there was no one to stop her. And she had not finished.

'Come here!' She turned and walked around the table. She picked up a piece of white chalk from the blackboard and held it out to Geoffrey Healey. He looked at her, stupefied.

'Come here,' she said quietly. The boy approached and took the chalk, his hand shaking so badly he could barely hold it.

Again she spoke in a low voice. 'Write a nine on the

board. Go on.' The boy hesitated then awkwardly scrawled on the blackboard. She looked at the number he was trying to draw neatly. Terror was causing him to lose control of his hands. As he tried to draw the loop of the nine her cheeks darkened and then slowly spread across her entire face like a stain, as great a contrast with the white of her wimple as the boy's black hair to his pale face. Her rage, unappeasable, unrestrained, seemed almost ready to spread into her clothes and infect the floor, the wall, the board itself. Again she struck him. Again he fell back. A terrible low moan came from the boy. She looked at the number nine drawn clumsily on the blackboard and turned to the class. 'Do you see that?' she asked incredulous, wanting them to share in her inability to understand what was in front of her. Two white spots formed in the middle of her dark red cheeks. She grabbed the boy's hand and forced him to redraw the nine, guiding his hand with her own until it was nearly identical in shape to the one he had made. Then she took the chalk from his hand and corrected it by adding a slight tail to the loop of the nine. 'A nine has a tail. It has a tail. Do you understand?' She drew another tailless nine. 'Put it in, Geoffrey Healey.'

An enormous sob broke from the child as he took the chalk and clumsily drew the tail. She looked at what he had done with loathing. She turned to the class, appealing to them: 'Look at the tail on the nine! Look what Geoffrey Healey has done!' She hit him again across the face and he began to cry. Too big to roll down his cheeks, the tears fell in large drops onto the dusty floor. His nose started to run and she stared at him, her eyes full of earnest hatred. A sob erupted from deep inside his chest. For a moment there seemed to be a terrible struggle within her, as if her rage threatened to break the very flesh and bones of her body. Then she raised her hand again.

'You all right, sir?' said Roache, who was standing in the foyer of the flats and looking back insolently into the lift at Healey.

'Oh.' Healey blinked. 'Yeah. Miles away.'

The little girl, still muttering her times table, was walking through the front door.

Jane Healey sat on the edge of the bath, towels around her head and breasts. The effect she created when naked was striking because her nipples were remarkably large and a dark rose pink. The contrast with her skin produced a riotously erotic effect. In changing rooms at the local swimming pool, even fastidiously heterosexual women were struck by her body or, rather, by its colours, because she was in other ways an average enough shape for a woman in her early forties: bottom large, waistline a little thick. She had nice breasts, and good legs, not long but shapely.

She smoothed the white foam over her wet shins giving the hairs plenty of time to soften and the blood vessels in her legs a chance to cool down so that she would not bleed too easily. For years she had shaved straight out of the hot water with the result that the bathroom often gave the impression, according to Geoff, that she had been using it to butcher a small, short-haired mammal.

To shave her pubic hair she put on a pair of white knickers that looked cream-coloured against her skin. She put on a pair of high-heels because they made her taller so it was easier to raise her leg to the sink. She filled it, took off the right shoe and lifted her leg over the edge. She rubbed more foam over the hair that had grown down the inside of her thigh and began, head bent low and breasts brushing her raised thigh, to shave as close to the crotch as she could. Her hair fell in a curtain almost touching the water and for five minutes she thought of nothing but what she was doing. It was only when she had finished, had taken off the now soaking knickers and was patting herself dry again that a sudden desolation swept over her. She sat on the edge of the bath and tears large enough to splash rolled down her cheeks and on to her breasts, wetting them then falling on to her stomach and thighs. But despite her best efforts – she was tired of crying, tired of that awful pain in her chest – she could not stop. I don't want this, she thought. I don't.

It was the dog that had destroyed her life. If there had been no dog everything would have been all right. She was not foolish enough to blame her as such – she still petted her and took her for walks – but if it had not been for the dog she would not have known, and as knowing was what had destroyed her life it was straightforwardly true. But for the sake of something that might easily never have happened, her life was in ruins.

Unusually she had been working at home on a week-day during a long and complicated audit trying to get to the root of the nonsense in the financial records of TLC. Numerous sheets of paper, reports and pages of figures were spread over her desk as she worked on her computer. A couple of hours earlier, she had made herself a cup of tea but she had put it down at the back of the desk and then forgotten about it as she became engrossed in her work. She had gone to the kitchen to make herself lunch and about ten minutes later she heard a crash. Running into the study she found Millie under the desk licking up the puddle of cold tea. She shouted at the dog, which bolted as she aimed a furious swipe at her. Groaning with irritation as the puddle seeped into the pale carpet, she went to get a towel and some water. She started soaking it up as quickly as she could but most of the liquid had fallen down the back of the desk against the wall and was awkward to get at. After a few minutes of sponging and pouring water on the carpet in a desperate and not very successful attempt to get the stain out, she was on the point of deciding that it wasn't worth the trouble. The stain wouldn't be seen because of the desk, but as she put her hand on the floor to steady herself, one of the floorboards wobbled. She lifted the carpet and was mystified to see that two of the boards had been sawn to create a square about two feet by two. She pulled the carpet back so that it was uncovered completely, then tried to lift the boards. They had been glued together so that they came up in one piece. The space below was dark but not deep. There was a large book inside, like a brown wedding album but thicker.

As she lifted it out, she was aware of her pounding heart. She shuffled out from under the desk, stood up and placed it on the table. She felt eighteen again and about to open the manila envelope that contained her A-level results. She opened it about a third of the way through, looked; then turned to half-way, looked; turned to about three-quarters in then shut it and sat down. For five minutes she tried to understand what she had just seen. Shock fought bewilderment, anger and disgust.

Then she examined the album page by page. The series of pictures, all cut out of magazines, began with women in their mid-thirties but the majority were in their mid-forties. The oldest was sixty-three, though she looked younger, or rather her body did. All the women were naked, many graphically so, and all the pictures had originally been taken on Polaroid, presumably by husbands or boyfriends. These were not the airbrushed models of the pin-up magazines or Page Three but ordinary women: wives, girlfriends, few of them beautiful, some strikingly unattractive. Many of the photographs were modest enough, smiling women without their bikini tops, sharing a joke with their husbands; others, often of the same women, wore of legs held wide apart, fingers opening themselves to the camera, faces abandoned to something overpowering – bold, shameless. There were hundreds of them, row upon row of the pretty and the plain, the riotously buxom and the painfully thin, large thighs and tiny breasts, or uniformly plump without a sign that they were anything but absolute in their desirability. Some had a printed caption giving their name, presumably false, their age and their greatest sexual desire: sex outdoors with other women, groups of men. Whether they were true or the women had invented them to make themselves more desirable hardly seemed to matter. There were no simpers, no carefully contrived pouts, just a mixture of friendly smiles – as if, above the neck, they were on holiday or posing at a Sunday barbecue – and frank, unambiguous invitations to gawp at breast and cunt, belly and thighs. After ten minutes she hid it at the back of one of the larger drawers of the desk and went downstairs.

For the rest of the day she felt wounded, not only as if she had found him in bed with another woman but also as if, on noticing her, he had kept on having sex. And what offended, insulted, bewildered her most was their ordinariness. The pouting tarts of *Penthouse* with their unattainable mien and artificially flawless bodies would have been a shock, but somehow the fact that they were from another world, an unreal one, of hours of make-up and careful light, would have allowed her an escape. No one could be like them, not even the beauties in the photographs themselves. But everyone could be like those women in the album, even, or especially, Jane herself. She understood that he, like every man, looked at and desired the occasional beauty in the street, but these pictures revealed an endless riot of desire for middle-aged women, the fat, the thin, the everyday, the pretty, the plain, the badly dressed. These women, too, were part of it – and she was not. She was outside whatever deal it was that they had struck. And such a contradictory deal, so intense sometimes, the gaze captured by husbands or boyfriends in their instant cameras, but sometimes like a wedding photo, a snapshot where the woman had simply forgotten to put on her dress or underwear and didn't seem to mind one way or the other.

She had been coldly distant when Geoff had returned at about seven that night. He asked her what was the matter and she had said that there was nothing. He realised that this was not true because he was a solicitous husband, and he asked her again. Again she denied there was a problem and he did not pursue it. But he knew she was upset, and seriously. He waited till their two children had gone to bed, then tackled her a third time. She left the room while he waited with a growing sense of dread, seeing that she was more quietly angry than he had ever seen her, and when she returned carrying the album he went white.

'What's this?' she said.

He did not reply. He could not. She asked him again, but he seemed to have become a different person, utterly shattered by her discovery, as if the kind, thoughtful, loving, occasionally bad-tempered man she had known for sixteen years had broken into pieces. To her astonishment and fury he continued not to answer her increasingly angry demand for an explanation. He was deprived of speech.

'I want you to tell me what this is!' She was almost shouting now.

But he could not bear it. Suddenly he left the room. She heard the door close, and he was gone.

He did not return until two in the morning, and stayed downstairs. She fell asleep, weeping. When she woke up, feeling as if something in her had died, he had already left. What had died was respect. Betrayal she would have been able to deal with given time, but this made him squalid – he had diminished and shrunk. It was the anger of distaste and disdain, and it was poison to the great love she had for him. She had always admired him, had seen him as a worthy person. He had worth and he had weight. He was solid, a rock. She loved him because she had the deepest respect for him, and because he showed her the same respect she felt as if she had the same weight and worth. He might have been hard to live with at times, but in the last few years she had loved him more deeply than she had ever imagined possible. She felt something had grown around her and through her and that a powerful and abiding love would always sustain her. And this feeling was all the greater because as a young woman she had always considered the notion of a great and abiding love something she would try never to long for. Her parents had been sour and drab and miserable with each other, and while she'd had higher expectations for herself, they had not been that high – just something better than she had witnessed. And then after ten years of good marriage she gradually realised that she had found her great love. She loved him intensely and passionately. And he knew it.

They tried to talk again the next day but it was even worse. He kept trying to explain himself but the words would not come. Words failed him. He radiated humiliation: he had been exposed and he knew it. Someone who loved him had seen him at his most squalid, and neither of them could bear it. Within three days he had moved out.

In the following week her sense of dispossession intensified. Her desirability had been stolen from her. And she could not see why. The unfairness of her exclusion left her crying bitter tears of disappointment. Sex was something she enjoyed; she was not a prude.

She found herself fighting the grief that threatened to numb her like one of the homeless struggling to maintain the appearance of being part of the normal world. She'd seen a programme once about American women married to rich men and who'd proved unsatisfactory in some way and had been replaced by younger or more pliant versions of themselves. Once privileged and powerful by proxy, they haunted the stores along Rodeo Drive, still thin and elegantly dressed, but as the sun went down they returned to spend their nights in cars packed with the leftovers of a vanished life.

For a month she existed as if a sixteenth of an inch separated her from the real world. She functioned perfectly and even began pursuing old interests, but not because she wanted to re-awaken something. Like keeping clean for people without a proper place to wash, it was necessary to perform these everyday tasks in order to prevent an irreversible decline.

A friend had once described her as well-read, and she took to filling every spare moment with reading. The children had stood by, uncomprehending, as their lives collapsed around them. She felt guilty but she could not explain it to them, although they asked. It was inadequate: they had a right to know at least something, but she could not bear to say anything other than that they had a problem which it would take time to sort out. They guessed their father had been having an affair and were resentful when they met him at weekends. But as the weeks passed this faded to a resigned bewilderment, and neither parent would tell them what was going on. The only contact she had with Geoff was over the phone. If she had not been at her wits' end about the implications of the fraud at TLC she would not have contacted him at all. The children's future as well as her own was at stake. Their conversations, however, were fraught with worry, anger, resentment and loss. Her disappointment in him was scalding. But strongest of all was a raging, restless incomprehension.

Since she worked in Covent Garden, it was quite natural that she would head for Charing Cross Road and its collection of second-hand bookshops to fill her appetite for reading as an exclusionary drug. It was a hot day with the area full of tourists gawping at the Cambridge Theatre – still showing *Les Misérables* – and at the Marquee further up the road, headlining a band she'd never heard of. It was a disappointing trip, the shops full of books that had been remaindered for obvious reasons, but as she went back to work through Endell Street, log-jammed with the grumbling diesels of black cabs and the showy roar of dispatch riders on dirty super-bikes, she noticed a new bookshop on the other side of the road.

She was pleasantly surprised to find that the books had been chosen rather than delivered. The shop had its share of coffee table detritus, but there were numerous copies of books by good, if usually unfashionable, writers.

She browsed and within fifteen minutes had chosen two books: *The True and Only Heaven* and *1984*. She had been looking for the latter for some time. Then she realised that having found it she did not feel pleasure at putting her hands on something for four pounds that she could easily have afforded at fifteen, but only a recognition that this was how, once, she would have felt. Jane was in the early stages of negotiating a contract with disappointment. In exchange for modest quarters, a living wage, a uniform consisting of a shapeless dress, thick tights and plain shoes, she would be caretaker to herself; prevent intruders, ensure the doors were locked, the roof impermeable to rain, the carpet curtained against the sun. The terms were ungenerous, the clauses eardrum tight; and if she had not noticed the odd way a succession of men held themselves as they went past her on their way down to the basement of the shop, she would have signed this contract and been buried above ground along with her resented husband.

At first she had been conscious of them without taking them in. It was as much a question of their way of moving as their presence. Every two or three minutes someone would go down or come up. On the way down they moved with an unconvincing gait. There was something odd, something that didn't match up. Now and again a man would enter, exhibit a fierce interest in one section for twenty seconds, then a sudden and equally fierce interest in something incommensurate with the previous topic. After about a minute they would make a beeline for the stairs leading to the basement. It was this extravagant behaviour that lured her towards the wide, winding staircase that led to the basement. She was filled with the sense that something strange was waiting at the bottom. Down she went, winding her way into subterranean London, and as she turned the final circular sweep she stopped. Still high on the stairs she could see the men in the room, for there were only men, packed around the walls but facing inward as if this were a class so full of naughty children that there were not enough corners to accommodate all the miscreants. There was so little room at the walls that some men were excluded and had to wait their turn. They stood looking aimless and awkward. Every man at the wall was holding a magazine and all were flicking through them, not casually like a waiting woman at a hairdressers, but intently, searchingly. Even from the stairs it was quite plain what was in them: uncountable vulvas signalled to her, rippling across the room like an erratically choreographed genital semaphore. A man supervising from a desk looked up at her from his book and went back to it without a trace of curiosity.

She turned and left quickly, not realising until she got back to her office that she had left the shop without paying for the two books she was carrying. She stared at them blankly for a few seconds: she had just stolen two books. Then she began to laugh at the implausibility of trying to explain this away if she'd been caught, of the shaming condescension, or the inevitable distortion: DESERTED WOMAN ACCOUNTANT STEALS FROM PORN SHOP.

She considered what this humiliation would have meant on top of everything. But the fact that she had got away with it left her with a feeling of exhilaration. Her first impulse had been to rush back and pay for them, but this passed quickly. She remembered something she'd read somewhere: if you wanted power over a rival, steal something that belonged to them – nothing significant, a pen, an ornament would do – just as long as they didn't know you'd taken it.

On her way home that night she realised that if she did not do something about the album she'd never be free of it, and something about the accidental theft of the two books made her feel as if she could face the prospect. The next day, a Saturday, she looked at it, closed, fat and heavy. Both children were out with their friends, and she decided to get rid of it. She put it in a plastic bag and took it down to the bottom of the garden where they kept the barbecue. It had a curiously altar-like appearance because it was made from white bricks taken from an old night-storage radiator. She built a fire out of the dry sticks by the side of the garden shed. The heat was ferocious, for the barbecue was unusually large and the sticks were dry. But she did not burn it. She stared into the flames until the fire went out. Then she returned to the house and put the album and its Polaroids back in its hiding place.

CANTERBURY

If we wish to understand how the last century
arranged its dissolution, where should we look
for the milestones? In the minds of many, the
images of the twentieth century will be fields of
French mud, a Panzer, a soldier eviscerated on a
beach, emaciated corpses in a pit, a mushroom
cloud. But the image should be that of middle-
aged men in suits signing an agreement just
before a pleasant lunch. Do not think Somme or
Stalingrad, Normandy or Auschwitz; think
Versailles, Wannsee, Bretton Woods, Yalta. All
misery and all happiness have their roots in a
conference of one kind or another.

Louis Bris, *The Wisdom of Crocodiles*

George Winnicott and Michael McCarthy arrived at
the Chaucer Hotel in Canterbury a good half hour
early for the presentation to be given by the beautiful
and, considering the esoteric nature of her profession,
celebrated Anne Levels of Machine Intelligence PLC.
They went into the Pardoner's Tale bar and ordered
coffee. While they waited, Winnicott looked around
the room at the Chaucer-related murals. All of them
were ghastly but one excelled in the sheer brilliance of
its awfulness: it was a huge drawing of a beefy-looking
miller quaffing mead or ale – considerable artistic
effort had gone into ensuring he would not be seen as
merely drinking. He was winking conspiratorially at
the viewer. The bar was filling up with men and
women who, from their formal clothes, were clearly

here for business rather than tourism. The PR woman from Machine Intelligence began her rounds, ticking off names on her clipboard and handing out identity tags. 'I hate wearing those bloody things,' said McCarthy. 'They make me feel like a double-glazing salesman.'

He looked at Winnicott who was clearly about to ask him a question, although there was an odd hesitancy in his manner. 'When I was at the Bank of England ... before I hit my head on that damned door, Charley Varadi said that you were a parachutist – a European champion, no less.'

McCarthy laughed. 'Not now. Fifteen years ago.'

'Still. I'm impressed. You don't do it any more, then?'

'Oh, I still jump – but no competitions. I gave that up after I won the title.'

'Why? If you don't mind my asking.'

'Not at all. I used to take it very seriously. And then I thought – why? This is supposed to be fun. And it wasn't fun; it was serious. It was like work. That's the way sport is now. It's been turned into work. I mean, just go along to any gym. It should be like going to a sandpit for grown-ups. But it isn't. Everybody's a professional sportsman these days, even when they're the ones doing the paying. It's supposed to be play – only people don't know how to play any more.' He laughed. 'Sorry ... a bee in my bonnet. Anyway, I stopped. I just jump in the summer now and a couple of weeks in California at Christmas.'

'Nevertheless, not many people can say they're champions of Europe. Whatever you say, that's quite something.'

'You're right – too pious. I do like having won it, it's true.' McCarthy nodded at the newspaper Winnicott was holding. 'Talking of play, I couldn't help noticing on the train that you were doing the crossword. Are you a fan?'

Winnicott laughed. 'You'll disapprove. It's not just fun for me, I'm afraid. I think addict would be more accurate. I have a habit that stretches to three a day. A tame obsession by your standards.'

'I like to do them myself,' said McCarthy. 'But I'm definitely only a fan. My brother sends me them sometimes from America. In fact the other day he sent me just a clue someone had told him about, supposed to be the hardest ever devised. Two weeks I've been trying to work it out – absolutely damn all. But perhaps you know it?'

Winnicott brightened. 'Well, I've come across a few monsters in my time but I've never anything that claimed to be the most difficult. What is it?'

'E13,' said McCarthy, wondering if Winnicott knew this as some shibboleth of real crossword puzzlers – old-hat stuff. But from his expression it was clear he had never heard of it.

'A postal district?'

'Oh, no. At least, not on the face of it. It's just an E, with thirteen letters in the answer, whatever it is. Of course it could still be something to do with a postal district. Anyway, I thought you might enjoy it.'

'Oh, absolutely. Though I probably won't be able to sleep till I solve it. Does your brother know the answer?'

'Yes, but he says he won't tell me till he comes home next Christmas.'

What Winnicott wanted to do was get out a pen and master it like some lexicographical lion tamer, but he felt this would be rude. Conversation was being made with him and he was obliged to return the favour. 'Do you think this new computer is going to be useful?'

'It might be. It's just a field trial, but if it does half of what they're hoping we should definitely be involved. It won't cost us anything, so on the face of it we've got nothing to lose and quite a lot to gain, maybe even in the short term.'

Ten minutes later Anne Levels waited to begin her lecture in the Troilus and Criseyde Media Centre, feeling more like a second-hand car-dealer than a scientist. This was a sales pitch as much as a lecture, and Anne was the true daughter of devout shop-owning parents in whom a genuine piety, a profoundly held faith in the notion of *caveat emptor* and the deep beauty of a balance sheet in the black had no need of reconciliation. Whether it was an idea or a computer program, she loved to sell.

Anne smiled her most winning smile. As a young woman she had become notorious for the devastating trick she had pulled in America on an audience filled with the most eminent men in the field of artificial intelligence. At the time she had felt only youthful delight at being the one to smash a deeply held orthodoxy, but over the years she had often regretted that she had made a fool of so many influential people in such a public and humiliating fashion. In the years since she had upset so many at her show-off debut she had learnt to be more careful. She was now ready to stroke those who needed it. Some of those present were academics. There were the pure scientists, as unsullied in their vocation as any nun, and the age-defining business dons, Mekons of money, all technology parks and BMWs. Many of them loathed her. The third audience consisted of three Japanese executives from Hitachi, accompanied by a translator. Hitachi were paying for the trials that she was formally about to announce. There was also, unknown to her, someone else present: Steven Grlscz. Although she knew him only from his occasional articles in some of the less well-known medical journals, she was immediately drawn to the ideas she found there, essentially because they were like her own. She had sent him an invitation but he had not replied. A deeply worried man, he had only decided to come to Canterbury at the last minute as much as anything for the distraction.

But today her peers were here as guests to witness the beginning of what she hoped would be a landmark occasion: the beginnings of a revolution, the biggest technological advance since the invention of the motor car. At the age of thirty-eight she was coming into bloom like some extraordinary flower, and not even the modesty of the way she dressed could prevent the impression she gave of being about to spill out of her clothes and surround you with a riot of white skin and curve and long black hair. She seemed to be growing as you watched, her hair lengthening, her lips opening; everything about her seemed full of juice, like a great warrior champion of the erotic. Since she was thirteen, Anne Levels had known how much she was desired, aware of lechery for her breasts and thighs and the turn of her throat. But she was about to set in motion the discovery of how deadly it can be to be loved for what you are: lusted after for your intelligence, craved for your understanding; that there is lechery over sweetness of temper, greed for compassion. Lust for love.

Within six months four of the people in the room would be dead. She stepped up to the podium and began to sell the ideas that, in time, would be responsible for three of those deaths.

———

'I am delighted to announce that over the next few months NEMO will begin an extended field trial. Some of those involved have asked for the details to remain confidential but I can confirm that we will be working with the Department of Social Security, the Fraud Secretariat and the Department of Structural Engineering at Imperial College. It is, I must stress, merely the first phase of what will undoubtedly be a long process. In the short-term, nothing of great immediate practical value may emerge. The long-term benefits, if we succeed, may be incalculable. NEMO has the potential to become the most important technological innovation since the motor car.'

Having startled the audience with this deliberately provocative claim, she went on to settle them down by drawing an apparently more familiar picture. Knowledge about the world, she said, had probably doubled between the birth of Christ and 1750. It had taken another hundred years for it to double again. Now it was doubling every five years. She realised, of course, that they were all aware it was becoming difficult in the light of all this to keep abreast of developments – even in their own fields. There was a stir of regretful acknowledgement. No one could disagree. Keeping up was hard to do. 'The greatest disaster in the history of knowledge,' she continued, 'took place at the end of the third century AD, when most of what the world knew was destroyed in a single night when the great library of Alexandria burnt to the ground. We can scarcely imagine what the scholars of the city must have felt as they stood next to the ruins to bear witness to this dreadful loss. They must have felt that civilisation itself had come to an end in only a few hours, and all because of a simple act of carelessness.' She looked around the room. 'We are facing a similar apocalypse.' The audience was satisfyingly stunned by this assertion.

'We hear much about the information superhighway, with all that this implies in terms of coherent flow, of slipways, lanes, speed of exit and ease of distribution.' She looked up and paused for dramatic effect. 'But the highway is not delivering information, it is dumping it. Then it's immediately dumping more on top of what it has already dumped, and then dumping more on top of that. In the future, knowledge will not be consumed by fire, as were the half a million scrolls in the great library of Alexandria. It will be smothered. And it will be smothered by itself. An increasing number of things will be understood, but we will not know that we understand them.' She added regretfully, 'Where, indeed, is the knowledge we have lost in information? Even as I speak, a scientist is discovering things that have already been discovered by someone else. Another could make a breakthrough if only he knew one piece of information that lies buried in a book next to the one he's looking through, or in a memory bank unlooked-at for want of the right question typed into the computer.'

With the mention of the computer she had reached the next stage of her pitch, for she was most definitely selling them something, thought Grlscz, as he watched with increasing attention.

She tore into the uselessness of computers. They were expensive, cumbersome, over-hyped, a huge drain on company resources, fickle, inefficient, absurdly difficult to use. 'Despite the commercially hyperactive nature of the computer industry, recent research makes it clear that in parallel with the gains being made in commercial and corporate efficiency, huge amounts of money, probably in the thousands of millions, are being wasted trying to make computer systems deliver on promises which are often perilously close to fraudulence. And speaking of fraudulence, the final bill for the millennium bug has been calculated as approaching four hundred billion dollars. Ask yourselves what good the money wasted on this one failure alone could have done had it been spent on something useful.' She paused to let this

179

denunciation sink in, looking like some voluptuous Calvin of the digital age railing against the soft and hardware whores of Babylon.

'The problem, of course, is the software. Computers themselves are on direct line to ever-greater speeds and memory capacities, all at a falling cost. But the means of exploiting these advances lags further and further behind, although this is often disguised by the pseudo-usefulness of many systems. The most pressing issue for those of us involved in artificial intelligence is how we can make our systems usable and effective rather than indulge ourselves in grandiose posturing about the innate humanness of our creations.'

Grlscz saw that this barb was an act of deliberate provocation since several of the men in the audience looked as if they'd been forced to swallow bleach.

The next stage of the pitch had been reached. She took a sip from a glass of water and then continued. 'We have a saying in this country to describe the way someone combines two previously unconnected pieces of information to produce new knowledge: I just put two and two together. Adding two and two is a function that the cheapest kind of pocket calculator can now accomplish more quickly and accurately than the best mathematician. But *putting* two and two together is a product of desire, will, commitment, inventiveness, individual autonomy. It draws on a memory that has nothing in common with the banal storage of a computer. Our memory is a living, growing capacity that creates and forgets, then reconstructs the world in the shape of something entirely new. This is something forever lost to the world of the computer. But something forever lost to us is the ability to store anything like the vast amount of knowledge that there is about the world in the straightforward way that we need to process it and make it work for us. We are losing contact with what we know and unless we can create something to mimic that autonomy, mimic not the adding of two and two but the putting of two and two together, then the future of human knowledge is doomed to a terrible dysphasic inefficiency.'

There was a ripple of discussion among the Japanese. One of them, the interpreter, raised his hand.

'Ah ... dysphasic, Dr Levels?'

This threw her, not least because she could see O'Connor, the CEO of Machine Intelligence, looking at her darkly from the back of the auditorium. 'It's ... ah ...' Her mind went blank. There was an embarrassing silence.

'It's a symptom of brain damage,' said O'Connor coldly, 'where the—'

'Where there's a damaged access to language,' Anne interrupted in a desperate rush. 'You have trouble finding words.' She laughed weakly at herself. 'You can't get ... access to ... you can't find the words to express complicated thoughts.'

She looked at he translator hopefully but his expression was full of doubt as he turned to the others and spoke in Japanese. Whatever he was saying, his uncertainty required no translation. The room waited anxiously for them to finish, but when the man haltingly stopped, the other Japanese nodded self-critically and smiled, as if the blameworthiness of not knowing the meaning of dysphasic was profoundly mitigated by the sheer usefulness of the term now at their disposal.

Anne started again, chastened and cursing the insomnia that had kept her up half the night. She knew she had to speak to a mixed audience and to have left in such a word was *so* stupid. She had missed an obvious problem because of tiredness. She knew the revisions should have been done earlier. Everything in her life would be all right if there were only three and a half per cent more time in the world.

'With this problem in mind, I began in 1989 to observe people in the act of creating hypotheses. This was unhelpful at first because I concentrated on my colleagues, assuming, reasonably enough, that being expert hypothesisers they would repay the closest study. But it was only when a young family moved into the house next to my flat, which overlooked their garden, that I started to see where I was going wrong. I began to watch their three children, and it was then I started to realise there was something fundamental to creating new knowledge that was too readily hidden by experts in such creativity. That something was the capacity to make frequent implausible errors. My neighbour's son was particularly helpful. At the age of six he is old enough to perform complicated actions skilfully but not old enough to have devised too many abstract mental models of a kind that would prevent him from carrying out his more eccentric hypotheses. On one occasion he spent nearly an afternoon trying to work out a way of knocking an apple from the tree at the bottom of the garden. He tried standing on a chair, poking it with long sticks, but when he finally started to try and knock it down by throwing a sharp knife on the end of a string, I was obliged to put my role as a good neighbour ahead of that of disinterested scientist and shout at him to stop.'

The audience chuckled indulgently at this.

'On another occasion when I was looking after him in his own house for a couple of hours I found him scraping a piece of burnt toast with a screwdriver while wearing a pair of swimming goggles. When I asked him what he was doing, he explained that the goggles were to prevent the dust from his scraping of the burnt bits of the toast from getting in his eyes. In watching him arrive at a solution to the problems that faced him, I asked myself how he had arrived, not at the correct ones, but at the incorrect ones. He was making guesses about the world and how it could be manipulated in line with his wishes. But how many, I wondered, before he arrived at the one he decided to act on. How are they generated and, if hypotheses are rejected before testing, on what basis are they rejected? Maybe we will find this out, but not in my lifetime and not, I suspect, in any other. I have become convinced that the nature of human creativity lies in its relationship to error and instability, its endless capacity for making wrong hypotheses that are not wild guesses but which may be very close to that. Like fractal mathematics, it is possible that the human mind takes shape at the boundary between chaos and order. This is the essence of our success as creatures: we make mistakes all the time but still manage to survive and prosper. But I felt defeated by the unfathomable nature of the way in which human beings make mistakes in useful ways ... guesses, intuitions, idle dreams, the putting together of goggles and toast with a screwdriver.' She gestured with her left hand in a circling movement as if to indicate the airy ungraspability of such things.

'So I tried putting two and two together myself. Revealingly enough, one of the most important insights in the development of NEMO came about through pure luck. I picked up a magazine left in the waiting-room of the Accident and Emergency department of my local hospital when I was waiting for a friend who was having an X-ray after falling over and banging his head. The magazine was the *International Journal of Aeronautics*. Goodness knows what it was doing there – it was at least two years old. One article concerned a radical new approach to fighter-plane design. Apparently the problem with building such planes is that, conventionally, they are designed to be aerodynamically stable. It turns out that this very stability is the problem. It means that a great deal of effort has to go into making them change course, something extremely important for a war plane as it tries to dodge attacks by rockets and other planes. Manoouvrability is of the essence. Someone wondered what would happen if you made a plane inherently aerodynamically unstable but used computers, monitoring and adjusting continuously, to keep it stable during normal flight. The advantage of the plane being inherently unstable is that when it's attacked, much less effort is needed to get it to turn and twist its way out of trouble. I began to wonder if the human brain works in this way. Why is the brain so much unlike a computer? It jumps here, there and everywhere. Its immense complexity seems to thrive on being able to make the kind of leap that aerodynamically stable computers find impossible. My guess is that we have a system in the brain for keeping it stable for ordinary everyday functions and for work that requires the intensely methodical – but that its extraordinary creativity is a by-product of a fundamental instability. In the human brain, evolution has created a mixture of the reptile, mammal and human, which combines maximum instability with maximum order to create the most effective result. This must be a staggeringly robust alliance given the extreme contrasts involved. But it would explain why there is so much contradiction in human nature, and why the claims that computer software is a model for the human mind are such nonsense. Natural selection is brutal. If we did not need the non-rational, the emotional if you like, we wouldn't have it. Rationality is only one part of understanding, and I include scientific understanding.'

She looked around the room.

'If the supreme triumph of reason is to recognise its limitations, then we must recognise that it is illogical to believe that the non-rational is the same as the irrational. Whatever they are, emotions are not a form of bad reasoning. Intuition may be a name for the program that mediates between reason and emotion, but I can't even think what form such a program might take or even if talking about it in such terms makes sense. I doubt we will ever convert emotion into knowledge.' She paused for a moment.

The next stage of the hard sell, thought Grlscz.

'Fortunately I am convinced that we don't need to engage in such a potentially fruitless search. I am going to suggest that a way out of the problem of too much knowledge will not elude us. It occurred to me that we have another model for the generation of highly complex and useful errors: evolution itself. Evolution is a mechanism where error happens creatively – inefficient errors are eliminated, useful ones survive and prosper. But this is the product of a blind mechanism that works every second of every hour across vast stretches of time without pity or remorse. There is no respite, neither good nor bad intentions, no desire – there are no intuitions or dreams to try and encode. In short, at this level, evolution has nothing in common with the species it has placed so overwhelmingly at the top of the heap. My belief is that we can take hints from this tireless mechanism because it shows us that while being empty of intention or understanding it can produce enormous complexity and coherence. Given the right kind of programming I cannot see why a computer, just as tireless but able to operate at vast speeds, should be unable to generate similar complexity and coherence. The task of trying to understand what makes us human in order to build something similar out of silicon and binary digits is not just futile, it's unnecessary.'

She stopped, her mouth dry, and took a long drink of water. The men in the audience took the opportunity to gaze at her breasts as she raised her right arm.

'In taking the hint that error is central in some way

to having successful ideas, I have concentrated on creating a program that makes mistakes in very large numbers. Unlike evolution, we have not, until the development of NEMO, created a space for error in our attempt to write computer programs. On the contrary, we have tried to eliminate it, regarded it as a sign of incompetence. We have built a rational creature and we wonder why computers are so inflexible. We have tried to make everything one hundred per cent useful. Nature never does this. We can ask ourselves why and answer by pointing to the success of the mechanism of evolution: if it were not necessary for error to be omnipresent it would not be everywhere. We may never fully know how nature makes error work for *it*, but that need not be a problem as long as we can learn to make error work for us. If NEMO processed information at the same speed as my neighbour's six-year-old son in trying to solve the problem of the apple it would probably find it quicker to wait for it to drop off the tree. But, given the potential speed and size of computer memory, we can afford to be much cruder in developing a system of this kind than if we tried to imitate the mysterious short cuts and fuzzy logic of the human brain.'

'NEMO allows us to produce numerous reasonably sensible, but usually wrong, hypotheses. NEMO does not *think*, but it imitates thinking in a way that may help us unite the capacity of the computer to remember everything with the human capacity for turning what it remembers into something new.' She looked down at her notes in order to create a pause before the climax, one that she was sure would not only amaze the room, but also seal the contract with Hitachi. With a thrill of anticipation she began.

'The biggest killer of adults over the age of forty in the West is heart disease. If cardiovascular diseases were infectious – every year they kill two hundred thousand people in the UK alone – we would now be living during the worst ongoing plague since the Black Death. I will shortly be introducing you to Professor David Turner, Research and Development Lead at North Thames Region. We have been working with Professor Turner on an experiment using NEMO to search a huge medical database which links medical files from twenty different universities around the world. Vast numbers of files have been scanned optically into these databases. Some of them go back over a hundred and fifty years. In other words, many of these documents will not have been read by any person living today. Professor Turner,' she nodded at a grumpy-looking middle-aged man in the front row who, at this admiring glance, lit up like a reflective road sign caught in a headlight, 'who has for many years championed the use of computers in his research, and is a gifted programmer himself, provided us with invaluable information in devising ways in which to teach NEMO about cardiovascular disease.' This praise for Turner was a hefty exaggeration and the goblin of truth in Anne's soul heckled and jeered; it was both noted and ignored.

'At any rate, we had gradually been giving NEMO more and more information about heart disease while it was also being taught more information about the world in general. Including, as it happened, information about the fauna of South America. One of the things it learnt was the way in which leeches are able to feed off animal blood by secreting an enzyme to thin the blood of its victims so that it can be more readily absorbed. Having been programmed to search the medical files using such knowledge as we had been able to provide, NEMO astonished us by unearthing a scientific paper on the giant Amazonian leech written by Filippo de Filippi. I'll ask Professor Turner to go into the details of the implications of what NEMO found in a moment, but in his view there is the potential in the discovery of the way in which the enzymes from this animal act on human blood to lead to the development of a new breed of drugs. These drugs could be as important in the treatment of cardiovascular disease as the discovery of penicillin to the treatment of infectious disease.' She looked around the hall at her audience and felt the rapt attention. For the first time she understood what it meant to have people in the palm of your hand. 'As far as we know, no one had read this paper on the unusual qualities of the secretions of the giant Amazonian leech since the paper was submitted to the archive from which it was retrieved by NEMO.' She paused and looked out at the audience. 'Filippo de Filippi's paper was written in 1846.'

The silence deepened.

'Nothing,' she continued, in an ecstasy of hidden pleasure, 'could more dramatically illustrate the problem of buried or hidden knowledge than the discovery I've outlined here. Nothing can illustrate more dramatically the benefits of solving that problem. Thank you for your attention. I will now hand you over to Professor Turner.'

———

Half an hour later the guests mingled in the Wife of Bath's banqueting and reception room, warm white wine in one hand, and sandwiches that managed to be both limp and stale at the edges in the other. Steven Grlscz watched Anne Levels carefully, making sure not to be seen by her. He had considered introducing himself there and then, but the police investigation into Maria's disappearance was too much on his mind. It was best to leave well alone until there was a resolution. He watched as she was buttonholed by a silver-haired, sardonic-looking man in his sixties with silver hair, the CEO of Machine Intelligence, Andrew O'Connor. 'Very well done, Anne. You excelled yourself. Pity about the dysphasia business. An uncreative error if I may say so.'

But Grlscz was not the only one watching her. Across the room Martin Beck was wondering whether his attempt to make a breakthrough in his frustrating courtship of Anne by showing an interest in her work (and neglecting his own as a teacher by claiming to be ill in bed) had deepened her affection for him. He watched as Anne turned away from O'Connor and came towards him, smiling. It was a warm smile, a pleased-to-see-you-and-thank-you-for-coming smile. But it was devoid of what Martin wanted to see: longing.

In the corner of the room George Winnicott was pretending to listen to someone who said he was a soil scientist working on preventing the Leaning Tower of Pisa from falling down. What he was actually doing was thinking about E13.

ALICE WINNICOTT
AND DR WHITE

Many would deride the assertion that a failing
economy and a failing marriage are similar
problems. It is, of course, absurd. They are the
same problem. The difference is merely one of
scale.

Louis Bris, *The Wisdom of Crocodiles*

Alice Winnicott was thirty-eight, blonde and tired.
Her shape, ill-defined by her clothes at hip and
bust, also gave the impression of habitual fatigue. Her
tiredness was not temporary, not the product of a bad
night, or too much work. Over the years, the superficial
weariness of too much children business, shopping
business, washing business, a too-demanding job, had
seeped into her inner life. She was almost spent. Her
desires had suffered a terrible depletion. The pupils at
her school, where she was a senior teacher, were afraid
of her. No one wanted to go and see Mrs Winnicott in
her office. But her own children were not afraid. At
home she seemed both resentful and becalmed: the
power she wielded so readily in school seemed to
desert her as soon as she walked through the door. Her
relationship with them was now confined to having

remembered to buy the correct kind of onion-free beefburger that would forestall the disappointed whimper of her son at tea-time, and the avoidance of yet another pointless spat with her fourteen-year-old daughter. In her rare periods of reflection she thought that she was reducing to someone who merely ran things – but she was mistaken about this. Something much deeper had gone wrong with Alice Winnicott. Her hair had gone wrong. It had been slightly untidy for nearly ten years. One minute's more attention to her hair a day would have made all the difference. But she did not have a minute.

'I don't think going tonight is a good idea.'

'My head hurts whatever I do, so I might as well do something useful.'

There was a pause as she looked at the livid bruise on her husband's forehead. She was not so much unsympathetic to his pain as resentful of it, as if it were another affront. What she liked about these resentments, though this was not consciously acknowledged, was how plausible any denial could be about bearing them. These were things that could not be resented. Any accusation to the contrary could easily be denied as absurd. On the other hand, she felt so many of these satisfying grudges that she also felt profoundly unreasonable. As a result she was ashamed of herself all the time because she felt angry with him all the time, and yet there was nothing to pin on him. Without acknowledging anything openly to herself, she was in a continuous state of shame and anger. Had anyone pointed this out to her she would have become more ashamed and even angrier. Because it was *just not true.*

'I still don't see why you want to come to the parents' evening tonight. It's only two days since you were knocked unconscious and you've just come back from a long day in Canterbury. After all, I *am* the head of a department at the school – if you have any questions when I come back I can just ask them the next day. I don't see what you coming could possibly achieve.'

He did not say anything for a moment. His silences were eloquent rebukes to her testiness. But, still, she was not testy and he was not silently antagonistic. None of this was happening.

'I think it's important to go *because* you teach at the same school. It can't be easy for her sometimes. It doesn't seem fair to have to ask for more information about her. I get the impression she thinks she's being watched all the time as it is.'

'Of course she isn't being watched.'

'All the same,' he said, and went back to his reading.

———

Although he had insisted on going to the parents' evening, Winnicott felt sick by the time they entered the large gymnasium. It was not, however, possible to reveal to her that he was feeling unwell.

The floor space contained about fifteen tables, and behind them sat the teachers with their hand-written signs: PHYSICS, GEOGRAPHY, FRENCH. He had seen this unremarkable identifier of subject teachers many times before but a strange, distant sensation in his head gave the sight a bizarre aspect, as if he were watching an exhibition of a surreal conceptual tableau. The essence of ECONOMICS was embodied by a gangly man with greasy hair and spots wearing a brown suit, the soul of HISTORY by a jolly woman with a tight perm that might itself have formed part of an exhibition on the fashions of 1974, the incarnation of ART was an empty seat and a queue of indignant men and women.

They were late, and not only were all the tables

occupied but there were queues everywhere. One desk, however, was free. Sitting behind it was a man in his late twenties he had not met before, and whose desk bore the sign ENGLISH written in Gothic script so ornate it was practically indecipherable. A surge of nausea swept through Winnicott, too intense to ignore.

'Let's sit down,' he said, 'My head hurts.'

'I told you not to come.'

'I feel much better now that you've reminded me.'

The English teacher looked up. Had Winnicott been feeling better he would have seen the animosity between his wife and the good-looking young man, who stood up, held out his hand and introduced himself to Winnicott, smiling coolly at Alice by way of minimal acknowledgement. 'Martin Beck,' he said and sat down again, placing his finger in his mark book and following the list of names down to *Sarah Winnicott.*

He began talking, but the favourable remarks drifted as the buzzing in Winnicott's head grew louder and louder.

As he went through the motions of qualified approval, it occurred to Beck for the first time that Alice was once, and could still have been, not just an attractive, but even an alluring woman. The clothes she wore were well-made and even fashionable up to a point, but they had been worn too often. There were no missing buttons or frayed edges, nor were they creased. They were just exhausted. When he finished going through his judgement, Beck shut his mark book with a dismissive finality.

'She seems to be doing fine. Is there anything you want to tell me? She doesn't say much.'

'She likes to be asked things,' Alice replied. 'She's a bit of a show-off under it all, really. It just needs bringing out.'

Beck noted the rebuke, but as he was about to

respond he could see that Winnicott had gone white. 'Are you all right, Mr Winnicott?'

'Oh ... I've had a bit of a knock on the head,' he said, pleasantly dismissive. Then he collapsed.

Alice gasped with alarm and knelt beside him. Winnicott spoke before he became unconscious, but so softly that only she and Martin Beck could hear his voice. Except that it was not his voice.

The next morning Martin Beck drove, slightly late, into the car park of Mabey's Grammar School for Girls. One of the sixth form was about to take the last parking space reserved for teachers. He noted mournfully that she was driving a car considerably better than his own. He wound down the window. Hers slid smoothly downwards as she pressed the electric switch on the dash.

'The expression "sling your hook" comes to mind,' he said pleasantly. A large girl, she sighed with the resignation of a particularly put-upon Buddha and backed out. Beck parked, locked the door and headed towards the main building. The school was surrounded on three sides by mature trees, which in the autumn offered a striking display of reds, golds and browns of astonishing variety. The school geographer claimed this autumnal technicolor was virtually unique in Europe and was caused by the unusual combination of rich topsoil and barren, flinty subsoil. Another more recent side-effect was that because of global warming there were still some leaves on the trees in January.

As he walked into the foyer he saw Alice Winnicott looking down at him from the balcony next to her first-floor office as if she had been waiting for his arrival. Then he heard the sentence that makes the hearts of underlings everywhere sink with disquiet and apprehension. 'Mr Beck, I wonder if I might have a word.'

As he walked up the stairs to her office he wondered why the "word" people wanted to have with you was never 'Here's more money,' or, 'I just want to say what a privilege it is to work with a man of your intellectual distinction.' It was always doom of some kind: at best, one of the parents had complained, at worst, he had overheard the Head using the same phrase as the victim had been ushered out of the staff room to hear that her husband had been killed in a car crash.

He sat down in her office and waited, growing less nervous as she failed with uncharacteristic awkwardness to come to the point. 'How's your husband?' he said at last.

She smiled wanly. 'Actually, that was what I wanted to talk to you about. To explain.'

'Explain?' He was puzzled by her unease.

'My husband had been involved in an accident at work. He'd been knocked unconscious. I told him not to come to the parents' evening but ...' She sensed Beck's puzzlement and was offended. It was George's fault. He had put her in this position. 'I just want to ask you ... what he said just before he lost consciousness.' This was agony for her, he thought, feeling slightly sorry for her but also enjoying her intense discomfort. 'I'd rather ... I'd prefer it if you said nothing to the other teachers. You know what people are like.'

He said nothing for a moment then nodded as if he knew only too well what they were like. 'As it happens, I didn't really catch what he said anyway. Something about a secret, that's all. He was obviously very unwell – distraught. I know what's that like. I was in a car accident when I was a teenager. I was rambling for hours after. Anyway, I didn't really hear what he said.' He shrugged to indicate there was nothing for him to be discreet about. 'Is he all right?'

'He seems fine now but he's having another X-ray just to be on the safe side. He went back to work too soon.'

Now that she realised Beck had barely registered the nonsense that George had spoken in *that* voice she felt irritated. She had been forced to make up to someone she disliked and over whom she had to exercise authority, and all for no reason. She might even have made things worse. It might be as well to look for an opportunity to remind Beck that she was not someone to be taken advantage of.

Winnicott was playing host in his office to the seven policemen who were responsible for the collating and safekeeping of documents at the FS. They had been moaning for ten minutes about the lawyers and the accountants, their arrogance, their smugness and their general uselessness. As there was no sign of their irritation with the FS blowing itself out, he decided it was time to get down to business.

'Of course you're curious to know why I've asked you to come and see me today. I want you to be frank. And I can assure you that nothing you say will go beyond this room.' He did not expect them to believe this, and in their position he would certainly have waited until he knew more about him before offering any opinion that might rebound later. However, he felt that McCarthy might be testing him and he had no intention of being caught off-guard if he could avoid it. One of them might be usefully indiscreet.

'In what way do you want us to be frank, sir?' said Stowell, a plump, bullet-headed, twenty-year man with close-cropped hair and an Open University degree in sociology.

'Let me begin by being straightforward with you myself, then. It's been put to me that if the FS has a weakness, it's in the matter of investigation. I have no opinion. It has been put to me and I do not expect to hear any rumours that this is what I think emerging from this meeting. Is that clear?'

He felt satisfied that the pointlessly stern warning would create the impression he was not the type to ingratiate himself, while the implication that their skills were being under-used would obviously please them. He was tough. He was on their side. It did not, in fact, matter to him whether they repeated what he had said or not. If the accountants and lawyers were to fear changes to come it would be no bad thing. 'So, the floor is yours.'

There was a silence. The policemen became uneasy and a fixed expression appeared on each face that emphasised their awkwardness at not answering a direct question from a superior. Still Winnicott said nothing. The silence became more and more oppressive. It was impossible to tell from his expression whether he was angry, or embarrassed, feeling foolish, or that he even recognised how awkward the situation had become.

'Well, sir ... ' A collective but soundless wave of relief flooded through the room. Winnicott looked over at the officer who had spoken and smiled. 'Not to put too fine a point on it, sir, we should be training the lawyers. The way they piss about when they interview suspects ... I mean, you hear the tapes of them doing the interrogation – Christ! It's like listening to bloody day-time television sometimes. And when they do get some hard evidence, half the time they won't go for it and charge anybody.'

'Basically the lawyers are too cautious.'

'No bottle is a better way of putting it.'

'We let too many people off just because they want to be certain they'll get a result.'

'To be fair,' said Winnicott, calming the flow of

criticism, 'the FS has taken a lot of flak for failing to get convictions. Louis Bris, after all ...'

'Yeah, OK, but that's the job. We're supposed to be doing the tricky cases – that's what we're *for*!'

Stowell spoke again. The rest, who freely interrupted each other, sat back to listen.

'I agree with Allan. I think we all do. The success rate is bound to be lower with the kind of crimes we deal with here, but we need to put together a tighter case before trial so it stands up better in court. This place is run by people who think they can prosecute their way to a result when what we need to do is concentrate on the evidence. And you've got to remember, these aren't villains we're dealing with.'

There was a ripple of indignation at this. 'I don't see why not. They're thieves ... only they get away with it more often because they're rich and know how to milk the system.'

'I'm not saying they're not evil-doers, Mike. My point is that they aren't part of a criminal class. It's not OK to be arrested – or even questioned – by the police. Not in Esher or Harrow or among your pals in the City. We got Smallwood to sing because he felt it would look bad for him even to *consult* a solicitor.' Stowell turned back to Winnicott, who was listening as intently as at any time since he had walked into the building. 'For these people the punishment *is* the process. That evil bugger Bris may be sticking two fingers up at us, but nobody accused in Guinness is, no matter how many get off on appeal or get some doctor to say they're unfit to stand trial. However much of a fiasco Blue Arrow was from our point of view, they'll be putting bull-bars on a Ferrari before anyone tries that kind of stunt again.'

He sat back, enjoying, thought Winnicott, the chance to speak his mind about things he had clearly been mulling over for years. The essentials of police culture, even at the highest level, were to analyse by assertion and scorn, mixed with an aggrieved sense of being misunderstood. It was not that policemen were stupid but that they were aggressively reluctant to discuss contradictions or counter-arguments. Doubt was considered a weakness. Stowell was a working-class intellectual. Winnicott could almost feel his thwarted ambition to describe the world as he saw it to someone who would listen and perhaps do some-thing with what he heard.

'The thing is, Mr Winnicott, when the lawyers are deciding to prosecute it isn't just that they don't have the bottle to take a chance, it's also because their training is bound up with the whole notion of fairness and due process. Even the ones who think they're dead cynical have got pretty rose-tinted notions when you give their tyres a kick.'

Winnicott smiled. 'I'm not sure that even an ex-policeman like me would see a belief in due process as a fault.'

'Fair enough, but due process has to be based on what's actually being processed … its nature. We've ridden a coach and horses through the right to silence for financial crime …'

'Yeah,' interrupted one of the others, who had not spoken before, 'but what a balls-up that's been.'

'Perhaps we should let Sergeant Stowell finish,' said Winnicott firmly.

'The law stops us from forcing someone to answer questions if we think they might have committed murder or robbed a bank or raped someone … but if they've only sold preference shares in a marmalade mine to someone with more money than sense then we're allowed to dump these rights we're always being told are so bloody important if we're not to become a police state. And the reason we can do this, apparently, is because it's difficult – sometimes almost impossible

– to find out what really went on. So we've changed the basics of due process so that we can get to big time fraudsters. Fine. I'm all for it. But the lawyers have carried on treating fraud as if it was like murder or car theft, and it isn't. If we carry on with the way they bugger about up there, worrying over whether or not they've got totally firm, completely unambiguous evidence of primary involvement, then we're going to end up with total bloody paralysis and none of the buggers will ever get charged at all. It's not about getting convictions, it's about charging people to set an example to all the others wondering if it's worth taking the risk. I'd like to read you something I put in my dissertation.'

There were fairly friendly groans all round as Stowell reached into his inside pocket and took out a notebook.

'Jesus, it's Jeremy Paxman.'

'Here it is. "*Some persons will shun crime even if we do nothing to deter them, while others will seek it out even if we do everything to reform them. Wicked people exist. Nothing ...*' sorry, I can't read my own ... ah ... '*nothing* avails *except to set them apart from innocent people and many people neither wicked nor innocent, but watchful, dissembling and calculating of their opportunities, ponder our reaction to wickedness as a cue to what they might profitably do.*' He sat back, putting the notebook in his inside pocket. 'James Q. Wilson, *Thinking About Crime.*'

'I'm thinking about lunch.'

'It's the ones in the middle we need to get the attention of. And the only way you're going to do that is by disembowelling a few of them on the floor of the Stock Exchange. Encourage the others, Mr Winnicott.'

There was unanimous head-nodding at this.

'Thank you, gentlemen. I'm afraid we must end there. We'll talk again.'

They stood up and filed out, winding up Stowell as they left. It was a mockery that would be improvised on and built up, as Stowell must have known, with jovial accusations of being a big head and a show-off and sucking up to the boss. Refusing to be intimidated, Stowell turned as he left and held out his hand. 'Welcome to the Fraud Secretariat, Mr Winnicott.'

As Stowell left, the intercom buzzed. 'It's the police,' said Lucy.

'What?' he said, as he looked at Stowell's retreating back.

'Not *our* police, the real police. On the phone – an Inspector Healey. He was wondering if you might have a few minutes later today. I told him you were very busy.'

Winnicott looked at his diary. 'Ask him to come at three-thirty.' He sat down and stared glumly at his reflection in the gilded mirror on the far wall. What he noticed with a much greater pang than that caused by the sight of yet another bruise on his forehead as a result of the fall at the parents' evening, was that only two or three years ago most of its grey and purple hue would have been covered by his hairline. He was becoming concerned for Maria, but he felt pretty sure that she had just vanished for a longer than usual spell and would turn up. That was what usually happened when people of her age went missing. And then there was the strange business of what he had said when he regained consciousness at the school, and how oddly Alice had reacted later, saying something about his voice and then immediately changing the subject and evading his questions. Then he gave in to the temptation not to think about these things any more. Feeling thirsty, he went over to the office fridge. Given the tastefulness of the rest of the office, it was an incongruous-looking object. Instead of the usual white, it had been covered in a plastic imitation walnut veneer so hideous it looked as if it had been reclaimed from the dashboard of the executive model of an Austin Maxi. Bottle of cold water in hand, he sat down, took out a pad of paper and wrote E13 at the top. For the next five minutes he sketched ideas, notions and guesses. E is the fifth letter of the alphabet. The word *thirteen* has eight letters in it. Eight and five add up to thirteen. Is there an anagram to be made from the words eight and five?

———

Three hours later Geoff Healey sat in George Winnicott's office giving him an account of what had been happening in his investigations into Maria Vaughan's disappearance. It was important to make Winnicott feel that he was on his side but that this could not be presumed upon and that he was in a position to help or hinder the future of the inquiry. It was important for Winnicott to feel indebted.

'Do you have anything?' asked Winnicott.

'I'll be frank with you, Mr Winnicott,' continued Healey. 'This is an odd case. On the face of it there isn't much to suggest there's a crime involved.' He paused, as if troubled. 'You know the score in these things. In confidence, there have been a few raised eyebrows that I'm spending so much time on this. My job is to investigate actual murders, not possible ones. You understand?'

Winnicott considered this for a moment. 'This is a widespread view?'

'I wouldn't say it was widespread.' He was pleased with this reply; it sounded both honest and ominous.

'And does the fact that it's not your view make a significant difference to how things might proceed?'

'At the moment, yes.'

'And why do you think it's worth pursuing?'

Healey had not expected this and he did not reply immediately. 'Instinct,' he said at last.

202

'You don't think the facts of the case, as such, justify continuing?'

'To be honest, no. But, to put it simply, it doesn't feel right.'

'I'm not sure if I were your superior I would consider that a sufficient reason.'

'It's not a reason at all, I told you. My intuition tells me there's something odd about this case.'

'And you always trust your intuition?'

'Not always.'

'But in this case?'

'I don't know. But I want to do the right thing by Maria Vaughan. I can't go on indefinitely, but I can continue for a while longer.'

'But if your superiors aren't willing to let you continue ...' Winnicott was guarded, but he wanted the case continued, that was now clear.

Healey pressed on carefully. 'It's all a question of presentation, isn't it?' He looked serious. 'I want to get to the bottom of this case,' he said.

Winnicott's expression was doubtful, worried. 'Thank you,' he said at last. 'I'm grateful for your concern.'

'As it happens, I was reminded recently of what it feels like to worry about people close to you. You need that reminder from time to time, I suppose.'

Winnicott nodded but Healey was alarmed to see by the way he shifted in his chair that he was about to bring the interview to an end and hadn't picked up at all that from Healey's point of view it was just beginning. 'In fact,' he continued quickly, 'you might be able to ... if you have a moment.'

Winnicott settled back into his chair, guarded. In a few seconds he reappraised the significance of their conversation.

'It's about someone I know. She's an accountant, an auditor. She's come across some discrepancies. Its tricky stuff, there might be something ... untoward, but there are big problems. It's not an area I know much about. There's the possibility of fraud. I'd appreciate your advice.' He paused. 'If you wouldn't mind.'

'Of course not. But I'm still pretty new at this. Anything you say, I'd have to go over it with my deputy.'

'Oh.' Healey looked crestfallen.

'Is your friend implicated in any way?'

'No, not at all,' replied Healey, 'definitely not. It's a reporting problem ... whether she might be sued for defamation if she brings in the authorities and they can't get enough evidence to prosecute.'

'Well, if you give me the details I'll be able to see what we're dealing with. Perhaps it would be possible to put the situation to Michael McCarthy without naming names. Obviously this might be awkward, but let's keep it hypothetical. That should cover things for the moment.'

They talked for about twenty minutes, during which it became apparent to Winnicott that whoever Healey was talking about it was someone close to him and that he was deeply anxious about her. He promised to get back to Healey quickly. It was clear the policeman would put every effort into finding Maria, as long as Winnicott helped him.

They shook hands and Winnicott saw him to the door.

———

Jane Healey was not a woman who cared for facile optimism in her fiction. As a serious reader she was often more satisfied with unhappy endings, with books where there were more funerals than weddings. But she liked facile optimism a lot in her life. She expected it, that everything would work out. Up until a few weeks ago she believed that the narrative of the possible future that everyone has inside them was certainly capable of sustaining shocks, of imagining horrors – the kidnap by the paedophile, the heart attack, the road accident – but it was not capable of sustaining *this* shock. This was an unimagined unexpected twist, an unforeseen implausible turn. Unfortunately it had completely altered everything that had preceded it, so that now she had to go back to the beginning and rewrite a lifetime's work, her secret, private, and public drama. She had to start the story all over again so that she would make sense. But she didn't know how. And this was why she began looking at the album of photographs again. She had lost the plot and all she had was a picture book to help her get it back again. To her surprise a sense of detachment began to take over as she moved from page to page. Something in her shook, certainly, but after a while, twenty minutes or so, she felt as if she had no body, no attitudes, no position. She simply looked. Although now and again something would flare up – amazement or shock – she began to understand that many of these women were not just, as she had first assumed, delighting in breaking a taboo but cultivating a special interest. There was, to her, a confusing lack of shame. It seemed a foolish thought, for obvious reasons, but this was a world entirely, absolutely and completely without modesty. There was not even a homeopathic trace of a quality she thought nearly all women shared at some level, as much a part of them, of their genetic inheritance, as large hips or a monthly cycle.

She started to read the captions alongside the photos. Claire remembered making love in a truck; Kay liked to watch herself being penetrated in a mirror. There was a Jane, who sometimes went to work without her knickers on, Millie in a car, Carol in a train, Jackie who's always had this thing about appearing naked in a magazine. *Sue is game for anything but she doesn't know I've sent these pics.* Elaine fantasises about threesomes and having sex with another woman – a gormless male fantasy, Jane would have said, but for the woman lying on her stomach with her legs apart. On their faces the expressions ranged from the frank to the thoughtful to the absolutely lewd. A shy smile from Jennifer, incongruous because her fingers are simultaneously pulling apart the lips between her legs. Christine with her genitals shaved, wearing thigh-high rubber boots and with a disdainful look on a face you'd see behind the till at any bank. Alison is poking out her tongue, one breast eased outside her dress.

Another woman turned up several times with different names (Helen, Lucy, Fran) and different coloured hair, but always cut unusually short, almost like a boy's. She had a thin face but a curvaceous body and some of the photos gave the impression that they belonged to two different people. With a sudden stab that almost brought tears to her eyes, Jane realised that perhaps ten years separated her first photograph, when she must have been forty-odd, and her last. It now occurred to her that many of the pictures must be at least as old. It was not just the style of the few clothes in the pictures, but the kind of make-up that bore witness to the depth of this obsession. These older photographs were also more discreet, she thought, recognising that this was not the right word. The expressions were more coy and they tended to keep their knickers on. The first one of this woman, Helen or Lucy or Fran, had her in bra and pants, one finger hooked into the elastic at the waist and pulling it down slightly to tease the watching audience. In the second, her legs were wide apart, her hair now dark instead of blonde, but still strikingly short, and with an elegantly manicured hand covering her crotch, though she was clearly naked underneath. In the last, she would have been fifty and had aged noticeably but well: her breasts were fuller, her waist slightly thicker, the lines around her eyes deeper. She looked like a matron in a hospital or the department head of a chain store. This time she wore only a pair of hold-up stockings, and the fingers of both hands were pulling herself as wide apart as she could. And on her face, a look of sheer delight.

Jane went into the bathroom and looked at her face in the mirror. She had always liked looking at herself in this particular mirror because of the way the light fell on her face from the window, softening the tone of her skin and diminishing the lines around her mouth and eyes. She had no neurotic fear about her looks, at least not until the discovery of the album. She had suffered occasional panics about the wrinkles, the double chin, the enlarging pores and fitfully spent money on treatments that she knew she would not keep up: the cleanse, the scrub, the tone, the moisturise. But if anything the slightly too-thin face, pretty enough but a trifle sharp, had been softened by a gradual increase in weight across the years. Certainly Geoff had said that she improved with age and there was no falling off in his desire for her or, with one exception, in hers for him. He was six foot two and muscular. Without vanity, he was nevertheless proud of his strength and he visited a gym several times a month, never took the car if he could walk and still played squash. She had never liked men who were too interested in their appearance and had thought herself indifferent to mere looks. This was not so, however. While she acknowledged the pleasure of his muscular body next to her in bed, the ease with which he could pick her up and the sense of security this gave her when she was out with him at night, she was ashamed when she realised that he was losing his hair and that this mattered to her. She had been surprised at how much it had bothered her, how it dulled slightly her natural desire when she looked at him across a room or watched him undress for bed. Had he known that she was feeling as she did, she was certain that things between them would never have been the same again. Thankfully his lack of vanity solved the problem. Tiring of the wispy ungovernability of his thinning hair, he just shaved it off. To her immense relief she came to like this new look, particularly as he made an effort to keep a tan so that the oily pig-like pink of exhausted follicles was not allowed to mock his handsome face. Still fit, still muscular, the honesty of a close shave allowed her off the hook and she had quickly forgotten how uneasy she had felt.

Looking again in the mirror at the face in young middle age, but still attractive, it struck her again, and the more she thought about it the more extraordinary it seemed, that it was, more or less, the same as the faces of the women in the album.

Over the next few days she tried to persuade herself to forget it. She was, after all, a grown woman. It was hardly a surprise to her that men were voyeurs, that they liked pornography. Geoff had once said as much in passing: 'I like it. I don't really approve of it, but sometimes I quite like it. Not that I see a lot, I hasten to add.'

The subject had been of little interest to her one way or the other, and she had let the moment pass. She wished now that she had questioned him further. But what would she have asked? She would never have thought about discussing the pictures in the album because she had never imagined their existence. Would she have been as affected by a collection of the magazines she saw on the top shelf in every newsagent?

She bought two in London, horribly embarrassed,

and took them home as a comparison. One, *Penthouse*, was full of beautiful women. Occasionally very slim, most were curvaceous, big-breasted but with narrow waists and long legs without a blemish, a wrinkle or disproportionate ripple of subcutaneous fat. Hair immaculate, bodies made up and fed through soft lenses and softer lighting, they seemed not to belong to the same species as the women in the album. It wasn't just a question of the make-up, good looks, clever light and skilled photographers, because, as a prize of some kind, the women in several pictures in the album had been given the same glossy treatment as the models in *Penthouse*. Despite this, beneath the fake pouts and sexy smirks which the photographer had clearly told them to adopt, the original woman unmistakably shone through. But the *Penthouse* models were entirely reduced to the status of an abstraction. Jane was reminded of the sculpted heads on Easter Island: some large, some small, the same look, the same position, staring out to sea, their blank expressions given shape by a culture obsessed with an idea that they could only, endlessly, repeat.

The second magazine was something else again. The girls were pretty rather than beautiful, although many were certainly that. The lighting, however, was designed for detail – like pictures in a text-book showing the aetiology of a disease – not harsh or unflattering but meant to put you in the room. The poses were entirely different: very pretty girls of twenty-two, with legs up in the air and fingers pulling themselves apart showing every detail of lip and sphincter. Partly horrified, partly amazed, Jane realised she had never seen a woman's genitalia in such obsessive clarity before. She assumed that, unlike noses, lips or breasts, women down there were pretty much alike. Here were an astonishing variety of shapes and hues and hair. Otherwise, like *Penthouse*, they were all the same, the vision more lewd but just as repetitive. She wrapped them both carefully in a plastic bag, sealed it with Sellotape and put it in the bin.

In the end she decided that she would still have been shocked if she had found these instead of the album, but it would have been easier to fathom. They were young and perfect. This was an adolescent weakness. But what she'd found was not so easy to dismiss, not least because of the care he'd taken, the sense of someone pursuing not just a tawdry desire but a tawdry obsession, a longing. That this revealed itself in something she could so strikingly have fulfilled herself began to bother her more and more. If she had been indifferent to his desire it might have made more sense, but she had taken great pleasure in the fact that he had never seemed to tire of making love to her.

She tried to divert her attention through work or reading, or a few too many drinks at night, but it was like some persistent thief always probing for the weak lock or the window left ajar. In a taxi the next day returning to work from a meeting, and without anything to distract her attention, she had the chance to brood. Every morning when she woke she felt exactly the same as the morning before and the morning before that. It was just like that film about the sleazy cynic forced to live the same day over and over again until he learnt his lesson. She found herself wishing for some deep fault she could correct. Anything would be better than this, whatever it was – this failure to add up, this catastrophe to her life-story, this senselessness. That's what the deserted spouse must feel after the wife or husband who'd popped out for a loaf of bread disappeared and was never seen again. Not knowing the story behind the vanishing kept you stuck in time.

Given the more or less permanent traffic jam that

afflicted London during working hours and that the pornshop from which she'd accidentally stolen the books was close to a major road works, it wasn't surprising that she should be trapped for a few seconds directly outside it. Long enough to see an advert in the window:

WANTED: PART-TIME BOOKKEEPER
Good rates. Apply within

The taxi took off and Jane sat in the back feeling deeply shocked by the speed with which she had decided to take the job.

———

George Winnicott was lying asleep on the floor of his office when there was a knock on the door: 'Sorry to interrupt … My God!'

Winnicott woke instantly and looked up to find McCarthy staring down at him. He got to his feet.

'I was just doing my back exercises.'

'I thought you'd … fainted.'

'No. It was just my exercises. I must have fallen asleep.'

McCarthy looked puzzled. 'I could've sworn I heard Lucy Bradd in here,' he said. There was a silence. 'Hearing voices, the first sign of madness.' He shook his head and did not notice the alarm on Winnicott's face. 'Your back, does it give you much trouble?'

'Not as long as I do the exercises twice a day. These meetings all the time don't help. The chairs in these places never seem to give any support.'

'Talking of meetings, we'd better be on our way. It's quicker to walk – it's only in Cripplegate.'

———

It was hot outside and lunchtime. The piazzas were full of office workers in shirtsleeves or summer dresses enjoying the early spring sun. The sweet smell of Ambre Solaire hung in the gentle breeze. They walked through Warwick Lane, still devastated after the explosion, the buildings draped in acres of blue plastic sheeting like a badly executed piece of conceptual art. As they turned into Newgate Street, Winnicott felt an intense alertness. Something in him beyond intelligence, beyond even intuition, was awakening a powerful and primitive instinct.

He was being watched. And whoever was watching him felt only one thing:

I hate you.
I hate you.
I hate you.

PSYCHOTHERAPY

In Greek drama it is often awareness which
destroys kings. For Shakespeare the opposite is
sometimes true: they are saved by ignorance.
There are two kings who you know will die in
their beds at a ripe old age with a loving family
around them and be deeply mourned by their
subjects: Theseus in *A Midsummer Night's
Dream*, who thinks that the imagination is for
children; and Fortinbras in *Hamlet*, who does
not think at all. Caught between the two possibilities of death by knowing too much and
death by knowing nothing, the English have
decided that the safest option is to be numb.

Louis Bris, *The Wisdom of Crocodiles*

'I would be less than honest with you if I implied
that psychoanalysis is a field I've ever had much
time for. I understand that you're reluctant normally to
take a patient who isn't whole-hearted.'

David Hendrix looked at George Winnicott, pale and
ill at ease, sitting upright in the comfortable leather
chair.

'Actually, unreservedly whole-hearted patients can
be a bit of a nuisance. This isn't an easy process, but
you're right, of course. A patient who's unwilling to go
through that process ... it hardly seems worth it for
patient or analyst.'

'Do you mind if I ask why I had to be assessed by
another analyst before I came to see you?'

Hendrix smiled. 'Essentially we believe in the notion of getting a second opinion first. It helps make one more objective.'

There was a short silence, broken suddenly by Winnicott. 'Look, I hope you're not going to be asking me endless questions about my sex life. I really don't think I could bear going through my dreams, turning every little thing into some ... I don't know ... *thing* about my repressed homosexuality or my desire to murder my father and marry my mother.' He stopped as if able now to dam his burst of irritation.

Hendrix considered what he had said. 'Did you want to murder your father and marry your mother?'

'No.'

'Well,' said Hendrix expansively, 'that's got that one out of the way.'

Winnicott looked at him, intrigued.

'What about my repressed homosexuality?'

'Are you a repressed homosexual?'

'No.'

'Goodness,' mocked Hendrix, 'we *are* doing well. Are you sure you haven't done this before?'

Winnicott looked at the man behind his desk. He was over six feet tall and beautifully dressed in a blue suit of expensive cut. He was almost off-puttingly elegant; the sign of a man who was vain of appearance. At first the thin face seemed almost severe, ascetic in its sharpness, but he had a pleasant smile and an easy manner. The handsome face, though, was marred incongruously with a long scar on his left cheek. Winnicott's expression softened. Hendrix sat upright in his chair. 'I'm an analytical psychologist, basically a Jungian. Psychoanalysts are followers of Freud. Jungians are rather less interested in the sexual origin of psychological distress, so you needn't worry too much on that score. I'm afraid the differences between the two schools are rather extreme. You shouldn't imagine that because we're analysts we're above squabbling. On the contrary, I think that collectively we could show the average Middle Eastern country a thing or two about factional in-fighting. Instead of bombs, we simply ignore one another to death.'

Winnicott looked at him slyly. 'It doesn't sound as if the average shrink is any less childish than the rest of us.'

'Absolutely not,' replied Hendrix. 'But, then, as I keep telling my patients, nobody's perfect, and it would be pretty unbearable telling your troubles to someone who was. Not very effective, either.'

'So, what *is* the difference between you?' asked Winnicott.

'We could spend a long time on that one, but ... you could say that Freudians are concerned with uncovering secrets, while Jungians believe in trying to reconcile conflicting personalities within individuals.'

'And that's what you think is wrong with me?' Winnicott had moved from an almost relaxed mood into one of cold reserve.

Hendrix spoke softly. 'I don't know what's wrong with you. But it's not as exotic as it sounds. Another way of looking at it is that we've all got different sides to our personalities and we have to show those different sides in the right way at the right time. My wife doesn't much care for me talking to her like an analyst. It's a habit I slip into from time to time. An analyst is what I am but it's not *all* that I am. Sometimes what we call the persona – the face we present to the world – sometimes it takes over. The doctor is always a doctor; the accountant always an accountant; the novelist always a novelist. When that happens the other sides of ourselves will either die away and something of us dies with them – or they rebel. Sometimes violently. Civil wars are usually the most brutal conflicts.'

215

'I've read a bit of Freud,' said Winnicott. 'I found the obsession with sex tiresome, as I said – but some of the things about repression struck me as convincing. He understood that it's what makes life possible. My job over the last twenty years – well, I wouldn't have had one if people were better at repressing their emotions. Repressing how you feel is what stops you from rape and murder and theft and everything else. I'd say my experience pretty much supports the view that getting in touch with your inner child usually means someone else is going to get it in the neck somehow or other. Emotional incontinence is what pays the wages of the police.'

Hendrix nodded, acknowledging the point was well taken. 'Nevertheless, I'm quite sure you're going through a crisis of a fairly serious kind. And so are you, otherwise, as you've made pretty clear, I don't think you'd be here.' He paused for a moment. Winnicott looked unhappy but did not reply.

'I've read your account of the dream about the financial collapse. I have to say that such a degree of detail is rare in a patient, indeed in anyone. In my experience it's unprecedented.'

'I have an eidetic memory,' said Winnicott.

'Really?' said Hendrix. 'How interesting. I've never had a patient with total recall before.'

'Total recall would be an exaggeration. When I was younger I used to be able to keep details in my head for a considerable period of time. Now I have to write them down within a week or so or they just go.'

'Still,' said Hendrix, 'a useful talent.'

'Not as much as you'd think. Forgetting has its uses.'

'Do you mind if I ask why you chose to come to me?'

'My goddaughter was a patient of yours and she spoke very highly of you. Maria Vaughan. I don't

216

know if I should say that ... you know, patient confidentiality.'

Hendrix looked troubled. 'Obviously I can't discuss her case but there's no reason not to talk about her in any other context. In fact I had a call about Maria yesterday, from the police. They want to talk to me about her.' He paused. 'No sign?'

'No,' replied Winnicott, 'nothing.'

'I'm sorry. I don't think it's breaking patient confidentiality to say that I'm surprised by her disappearance. She'd been doing well. I was about to persuade her to stop seeing me, though I don't think she would have needed much. It's very odd, to be honest.'

'I think she'll turn up eventually. She's vanished before.'

Hendrix could see that Winnicott did not want to discuss the girl's disappearance further. He changed the subject. 'Given your scepticism, I'm wondering what made you decide to come to me for help.'

Hendrix noticed the brief look of evasive unease that passed over Winnicott's face.

'I should have thought that was obvious. I'd collapsed three times in less than ten days. Although I'd had a bad bang on the head, the hospital tests said there was nothing physically wrong with me. I had to do something.' Winnicott looked up defiantly. 'Though I have to say it's not entirely unknown for hospitals to fail to identify a physical ailment, is it?'

'No,' said Hendrix reasonably. 'Did anything else happen to change your mind?'

Winnicott looked at him, thought Hendrix, rather in the way a young child looks at an adult on being accused of taking a chocolate biscuit without asking. Sounding tired and afraid Winnicott said, 'When I go out in the street ... I think someone is watching me ... following me.'

Hendrix was taken aback by this. Winnicott stared at the carpet, miserable with shame.

'Have you seen this person following you?'

Winnicott's eyes narrowed with irritation. 'If I'd seen them there wouldn't be a problem. Someone *would* be following me.'

Hendrix was confused briefly, then remembered. 'Oh, yes, I was forgetting about your past life. Why couldn't it be the IRA, or a criminal from the past?'

'It could be. But I've seen nothing. I can just sense it ... very strongly but not all the time, only now and again.'

'Tell me what you feel on these occasions.'

Winnicott seemed to sag into the chair. 'This person ... this person hates me.'

'Are you sure you're not being followed?'

Winnicott sighed. 'When I was head of the anti-terrorist squad I was sometimes trailed by people from various undercover services. It was an exercise ... making us aware of the possibility ... what to look for. During three years I was followed for twenty-four hours on several occasions. I never saw a thing. I never felt a thing.'

Hendrix waited, but Winnicott stayed silent.

'Tell me about what you feel when you're being watched.'

There was a long pause. 'This ... person ... I feel hatred and anger. It sweeps over me ... strong.'

'Is it someone you think you might know?'

'No.'

Again there was a silence.

'I have the feeling you're not being entirely open, Mr Winnicott, and I think you know you must. What do you know about the person watching you?'

There was a long silence. For almost a minute neither of the men said anything: Hendrix looked at Winnicott, Winnicott looked at the floor. Eventually he gave in and told the truth. But not the whole truth. Far from it.

'It's a woman.'

Conclusion

I'm surprised he's come to me, given the obvious resistance to analysis. This is the kind of man who would put off going to a shrink at all costs. The fainting is disturbing given that there's no medical reason – but he claimed (perfectly reasonably) that the doctor might be mistaken. A man like this would seize on the fact that hospitals frequently misdiagnose as a good reason not to come to someone like me. He'd get a 2nd medical opinion or a 3rd – he wouldn't go to an analyst. He claims, for example, that the origin of the banking dream is entirely straightforward. He had been reading a book the day before [Portrait of an Old Lady. Get a copy and check out the similarities], an account of the workings of the Bank of England and the financial collapse outlined in the dream. He dismissed the Dark Figure as typical of the nonsense you get in dreams but it may be a symbol of the extent to which he is feeling profoundly persecuted. After all, at the close of the dream he discovers that he's the one really on trial. Allied to the belief that he is being watched by a woman who hates him, this might be evidence for a diagnosis of schizophrenia with severe paranoid tendencies. On the other hand, its severity is mitigated by the fact of his clear sense that this is abnormal. Possibly he can't bring himself to tell me what's really brought him here because it's just too embarrassing for such a repressed individual to talk about – he wouldn't be the first patient I've treated to suffer from Lying-Bastards Syndrome. Still, while misleading other people about your interior state of mind is a symptom of schizophrenia, it's also a symptom of being human.

As Hendrix laboriously finished typing with two fingers his receptionist buzzed him. 'The police are here.'

'I'm Inspector Geoffrey Healey and this is Sergeant Roache,' said Healey.

'Sit down, please,' said Hendrix, irrationally nervous at being interviewed by the police, yet unable to rid himself of a vague feeling of guilt. The avuncular smile of the man sitting in front of him seemed only to make matters worse, as if he knew facts so incriminating he had no need to be intimidating in any way. Affability would do it.

'How long was Maria Vaughan your patient?'

'Nearly two years.'

'And why was she coming to see you?'

Hendrix moved awkwardly in his seat. 'Normally, I'd be very reluctant to discuss a patient with the police for obvious reasons of confidentiality. Let me make it clear that in this case the circumstances alter that general principle.' His integrity established, he got to the point. 'She came to me suffering from serious clinical depression. I don't mean she was just unhappy, I mean that she was close to becoming what we used to call "a danger to herself".'

'That's pretty much what I've been hearing. But she got better under your care?'

Hendrix laughed. 'No, not really. You see, the fact is, I was pessimistic about her long-term recovery. I couldn't get through, not really. People with her kind of depression, deeply rooted in childhood, seem to go through some kind of point of no return. To most people she would have come across as a nonentity – drab, a defeated person. In fact she was a disappointed, angry woman, but it was all turned inward. The violence was aimed at herself. To be honest I felt that there was little I could do. During the first year I came close to having her committed under the Mental Health Act.'

'So do you have any idea what caused this change?'

'She turned the corner very slowly indeed at first. But after a few months it was ... actually, miraculous is a pretty good word. Within a couple of months she must have put on about twenty pounds. She was seriously underweight, not much better than anorexic when she came initially. I have to say that I've never seen anything like it, not really.'

'So if it wasn't the treatment that caused this change of heart, what was it?'

Hendrix laughed. 'My professional opinion – technically – is that she fell in love. Or, perhaps more accurately, someone fell in love with her.'

———

'It's odd, isn't it?' said Healey to Roache, as they sat in the window seat at the Finsbury Park tea room. 'Why middle-class people are so nervous of the police they're too scared to offer you a cup of tea. I mean, if you go to question a working-class person in their home and you haven't actually turned up to drag them away to the nick ... seven times out of ten they'll offer you a cup of tea. You're from a good home, Roache, why *is* that?'

Roache pushed the sugar around in the bowl using his spoon to break the slight crust that had formed from exposure to damp air and central heating. 'They're all guilty,' he said at last.

Healey enjoyed mocking Roache, not so much about his middle-class origins as about his lack of interest in books. He was mildly irritated that Roache had been given a good education yet had done almost nothing with it beyond getting a degree in a subject in which he had no interest. 'You mean they're all guilty in some existential sense?' teased Healey.

'I don't really know what existential means,' replied Roache, unashamed. 'But I don't mean anything deeply psychological, I mean most middle-class people are on the take in one form or another … paying builders in cash, fiddling their expenses, finessing their tax returns, you name it. They know it's wrong but they pretend they're not really doing it even when in the process of exaggerating the insurance claim on the stolen car or the burn hole in the Axminster. But because they're middle class they haven't got the guts to admit it to themselves. Deep down they feel guilty. That's why they're terrified of policemen. That's why they never offer you a cup of tea – they're too shit-scared to think of anything but the clang of the prison gates they can hear in the distance.'

'Your education was wasted on you,' Healey said amiably and without resentment. He couldn't understand Roache. He was smart but he just wasn't interested in anything.

'Yeah,' said Roache, equally amiable, 'you should have had it. I agree. Absolutely.'

Healey stood up. They left the café and walked back to the car they'd left near Hendrix's house. As Healey was waiting for Roache to let him in at the passenger door, he looked across at the therapist's front door. A man was ringing the bell. It was George Winnicott.

About a hundred yards away from behind a telephone booth a tall, angry-looking woman, young and with long, expensively cut hair and a shapely figure, was watching them. In the far distance there was a boom. It sounded like, but was not, thunder.

———

At the same time as the woman was watching the policemen outside David Hendrix's house, Anne Levels was stuck in traffic on the M25. She had been becalmed for nearly an hour. A policeman walking past had informed her that one of the IRA's splinter groups had planted a device at an unspecified bridge on the motorway, and that was that. Of course, by now everyone knew that there was probably no such bomb and the interesting thing, thought Anne, was why it had taken the men of violence so long to work out that this was the way ahead for brutality. Like everything else, cruelty had to keep up with changing times. In the future perhaps there would be hardly any real bombs, few actual bloody murders, there would mostly be relentless inconvenience, a virtual terror in which people would be annoyed and aggravated into compliance. The mad dog would be replaced by the pest and the nuisance, the outrage by the endless irritation. From now on the bully would only rarely twist, shatter or punch, mostly he would just get on your nerves. Permanently.

Anne picked up her mobile and dialled.

'Fraud Secretariat.'

'Could I have the Information Technology department?'

She was put through and put back her presentation to four o'clock.

When, as a young woman, Anne set out to make her mark, the world of artificial intelligence had been like the alchemical world of 1670. Here were the origins of a true science: systemisation, the rudiments of chemistry. But what really drove these seventeenth-century magicians, hucksters and conmen were transformations and universals: alcahest, gold from lead, a way of making life itself. Artificial intelligence was a new science at a time of magical inflation in which the snake-oil salesman lurking in every scientist – his shadow self – had leapt the boundaries of methodology, disinterested purity and thrown itself into a marketplace where visionaries of every kind were promising the wonders of the earth from a device given the breath of life by an inspired employment of noughts and ones. What these men were offering was the reproduction of life itself in wire, glass and silicon: a machine that thought, understood, perceived, outclassed. It was Anne, disdainful scientist and daughter of the commercial manse, who pointed out that this new version of the dream of something from nothing was all a matter of mirrors, secret drawers and sleight of hand.

———

It was at the Fourth Annual Congress of Artificial Intelligence in Chicago that Anne Levels, gorgeous twenty-five-year-old nobody, stunned this new world with a demonstration that made her famous overnight and earned her the hatred of a flock of department heads at Yale and Harvard, MIT and Rand. Like all scientists, they were as vengeful as Sicilians, and the humiliation she had heaped on them that afternoon had returned to haunt her many times since.

Because the organiser of the congress forlornly hoped to get her into bed, Anne had been given a prime spot before a keynote speech by Arthur Gein, in which, it was widely known, the top man in the field would claim a breakthrough in the search for evidence of true machine intelligence. The hall was packed for Gein, but interest in Anne was plain to see among the assembled largely male audience, not least because her reputation as a beauty had preceded her. Her lecture, of which she knew the audience would approve, attempted to demonstrate a program that implied a general solution to the problem of computer understanding of natural language. Called ZARDOZ, it ran a simulation of a non-directive psychiatrist interviewing a patient. She produced an unlikely-looking machine about four foot square, apologised for its string-and-sealing-wax construction and made a joke about poor British funding, which was patronisingly well received. She talked about the origins of the project, and to the surprise of the audience proposed a demonstration using a real patient who would interact with ZARDOZ protected by the anonymity of a phone line specially patched in for the demonstration. She apologised for the machine's slow speed, stressing that it was a prototype. A court stenographer was produced and Anne explained that she would type the woman's responses into ZARDOZ as the audience heard them. The woman being interviewed would receive the questions from ZARDOZ printed on a monitor in her room somewhere in the recesses of the conference centre. The questions would be shown simultaneously to the audience on another monitor next to the podium.

The woman's voice was as uncertain as the hands of someone feeling for the light switch in the dark. 'Hello, is anybody there?'

The monitor flashed up a soothing greeting. 'Hello, could you please tell me your first name?'

'Madeleine.' The shy uncertainty of her voice captivated the audience.

'Hello, Madeleine. How are you?'

'Not too bad ... Well ...' She paused and there was an awkward laugh made up more of defeat than humour. There was a silence. The stenographer stopped. 'Hello ... are you still there?' came Madeleine's uncertain voice. The stenographer's hands raced.

'Hello, Madeleine.'

'This is kinda difficult,' said Madeleine. She paused again.

'In what way is it difficult, Madeleine?'

'I'm not really used to talking 'bout my problems, I guess.'

'Tell me about your problems.'

'My problem is me, I guess ...' She was starting to talk more naturally, ' ... my husband.'

'What's your husband's name, Madeleine?'

'John.'

'Tell me about John.'

'We're not getting along too well right now. We're arguing a lot more ... all the time.'

'Why are you arguing?'

'I don't really know. I reckon just about everything these days ends in a row – money, the kids and ... You know how it is.'

'Tell me how it is, Madeleine.'

'We used to get along real well, least I thought so. I thought we were happy. I mean it wasn't perfect now, it wasn't a rose garden or anything. I mean he always used to drink a lot. His buddies use to call him "Miller", after the beer, y'know; but he was good to me. He was a nice man.' She said this with evident pride. 'Now he's just mean. He's real angry.' She stopped. The silence was heavy with a sense of loss as well as resentment.

'Why is he angry?'

'Hell, I don't know. If he can't find his shaver he gets mad. If the kids are making a noise he gets mad. If someone drives a car a way he don't like, he gets mad; if the Yankees lose a game you'd think they did it on purpose, just to make him feel bad. I'm fifty years old and if I can talk to my husband depends on whether the Yankees are gonna win or lose. Is that living?'

'What do you think?'

226

'*I* don't think so. Everybody thinks he's turned real strange.'

The disconnected sentences resonated oddly around the hall.

'Are you thinking of somebody in particular, Madeleine?'

'No,' she said, revealingly quickly. 'I want ...' She stopped.

'What do you want?'

There was no reply.

'What do you want, Madeleine?'

Still there was no reply.

'Perhaps you need time to think,' came up compassionately on the monitor.

'Yes, yes, I do,' said a relieved voice. 'Thank you.'

'Thank you for talking to me, Madeleine.' The intercom went dead and the screen remained blank.

Anne wound things up while Gein, the speaker who was to follow her, realised with a rueful smile that she had stolen his thunder. The flattering applause began. Anne looked modest and waited for it to die. To her surprise it swelled until it filled the hall, but when it slowed she brought it to a stop. The audience realised that she had more to say. It watched, perplexed, wondering if she would outstay her welcome, overplay her hand.

'Ladies and gentlemen,' she said, 'since you have been so kind I'd like you to meet ZARDOZ.'

Anne walked over to ZARDOZ, moved behind it, bent down and opened a door. She reached in and led someone out. It was a little girl. Hand in hand they returned to the podium. 'Ladies and gentlemen, may I introduce ZARDOZ, more usually known as Diz Baker.' Turning to the girl, she mouthed silently, 'Introduce yourself, Diz.'

The little girl curtsied proudly but shakily. 'My name is Diz Baker. I am ten years old and I am in the sixth grade at the St Aloysius Convent School.' The voice was strange, high and blurred. Diz walked off the stage smiling broadly.

Anne turned to her audience. 'I'd also like to introduce Madeleine.' The horrified audience watched as a pretty woman in her early thirties walked onto the stage. 'Madeleine, as you will now have guessed, does not exist. This is Martina Gassner, actress.' Martina bowed theatrically and left.

'You are entitled to an explanation.' Anne was beginning to realise that her audience was not amused by the way in which she had duped them. 'We chose a ten-year-old in order to demonstrate that no understanding of Madeleine's complicated emotional state could be taking place. But even if she had been a psychological prodigy capable of leading a middle-aged woman through some of her own complex personal problems, she didn't hear any of it anyway. Some of you may have realised when Diz spoke that although she is a happy, confident little girl, she is also profoundly deaf.'

The audience, appalled, stared at Anne uncomprehendingly.

'If you look at the monitor, we can see all of the information given to Diz.'

She pressed the keyboard.

The audience looked at the two columns of words as they appeared on the large screen. The left hand column was headed 'Madeleine', the other, 'ZARDOZ'.

Madeleine	ZARDOZ
1. Hello	Hello, what is your first name?
2. Madeleine	Hello Madeleine
3. Hello	Hello Madeleine
4. This difficult	In what way is it difficult?
5. My problems	Tell me about your problems

6. Husband	What's your husband's name?
7. John	Tell me about John
8. We arguing	Why are you arguing?
9. You know	Tell me
10. He angry	Why is he angry?
11. ?	What do you think?
12. Everybody	Are you thinking of somebody in particular?
13. I want	What do you want?
14. 0	What do you want?
15. 0 (2)	Perhaps you need time to think?
16. End	

Anne shifted the podium to reveal a keyboard at about waist height. 'Madeleine spoke nearly three hundred words in her *exchange* with ZARDOZ. Of course, much of the information contained in what she said was implied and unspoken. However, ZARDOZ — or rather Diz Baker — received only twenty of these words and *I* was the one who typed them onto a printer in front of Diz. She took about three hours to get the general idea and two days' practice to get up to speed. Aside from being impressively unflappable, she is also top in her typing class. If you take input Number Five,' said Anne, gesturing at the monitor, 'you'll see that whenever I type in the word "*My*", Diz typed, "*Tell me about your ...*" What Diz — or the computer — asks to be told about will depend on whether the possessive "*my*" refers to "*my holiday*" or "*my last suicide attempt*". A real computer program having all of Madeleine's three hundred words fed into it would only recognise these twenty words and respond blindly to them. Any proper noun such as "*John*", for example, will prompt it to ask, "*Tell me about John.*" There is, and can be, no connection between this automatic search for recognisable input and the search for understanding of a human counsellor. Such a counsellor would have endlessly rich attitudes to what they are hearing, commitments to what they ask, a capacity to read significance both in what is said and unsaid by the person talking to them. They will, of course, use professional techniques to get at the problem. But a human being *employs* a set of strategies; a computer *is* a set of strategies. A computer processes information and so does a human being, but the human being alone has an attitude to what it's processing.'

The audience eyed her watchfully. She continued but her sense of unease at having alienated them quickly evaporated as the true iconoclast's pleasure at smashing deeply held beliefs began to intoxicate her.

'Nevertheless, there is work to be done of a revealing kind. If you program ZARDOZ to ask the question, "*How long have you been ...*" whenever someone states "*I am* something", then the response to, "*I am unhappy*" will be "*How long have you been unhappy?*" Sadly, if the statement is, "*I am murdering my husband,*" the response will be "*How long have you been murdering your husband?*"' She looked defiantly at the grim-faced audience.

'The depth of the emptiness of the interior world of the computer is apparent here. We will undoubtedly find ways of eliminating such revealing solecisms, but it will not be done by making computers intelligent, merely by devising better strategies for disguising their true nature, by hiding their essential emptiness.'

Several eminent professors began to leave.

'What I hope this has demonstrated is that, despite the apparently impressive aptness of the responses of ZARDOZ to an extraordinarily complex human situation, nothing meaningful made its way into the processor, which in this instance was a child but it could have been an electronic processor. Diz Baker, a processor of flesh and blood, received a mere twenty words, and some of the elements weren't even words. If you type in just a question mark, the computer will always reply: *"What do **you** think?"* "Is it all right to shoot the President?" *"What do **you** think?"* "Should I kill myself?" *"What do **you** think?"* There can be no doubt that there would be nothing meaningful in any exchange that flowed between Madeleine and a "real" ZARDOZ, not even the fact that here was a woman who found it difficult to talk about her problems with her angry husband John, because the program does not link these elements together. Nevertheless we witnessed an exchange that was apparently rich in understanding. I could have used a real computer but I chose a child to be the processor of what little information was fed into ZARDOZ because we can interrogate a child of ten, if we need to, about its knowledge of the world – although we know, of course, that a child could not understand the complex adult situation outlined by Madeleine. It seems that as we cannot interrogate, or know about, the understanding of the computer the vast majority of my colleagues in this field believe that it does contain some kind of intelligence or understanding simply because it produces apt responses. I find it hard to understand why this should be the case for computers and not for other machines which respond to patterns of input. No one, for some reason, seems anxious to invest similar properties in their washing machine or the door-bell of their house, yet it is necessary for me to produce an endlessly, and I should say needlessly, complicated demonstration to provide evidence for something that is, as we say in England, as plain as the nose on your face. But the paradox, the irony, of all this is that the computer, thoughtfully programmed, will usually perform well, but real counsellors can have off days, or simply be not much good or have dubious attitudes and commitments. I am already working on a more sophisticated version of ZARDOZ, which takes its name, incidentally, from the false god in John Boorman's film of the same name. But false divinity though it may be, I strongly believe that given time, a development of this program might be of more help to the Madeleines of this world than a foolish best friend, a too-busy doctor or a mediocre psychoanalyst.'

She looked out into the auditorium. 'In a way it's not difficult to see why we find it so easy to invest these extraordinary machines with qualities forever denied them, because it's hard to see how anything can be so rich at one level, yet so barren at another. Perhaps it was this that deceived the great mathematician Alan Turing into claiming that when it was impossible to tell the difference between the responses of a computer and a human being to a series of questions, then the computer would have passed a test that proved it was in some way fundamentally the same.'

Anne paused and looked out across the audience. 'He was wrong.'

———

BLAAAAAAAAAAAAAAAAAAAAAAAAAAAAAAAA AAAAAAAAAAAAAAAH! A scream from the horn of the car behind startled her and she was back among the gloomy drivers trapped in the terrorist-induced gridlock of the M25. The cars ahead had already moved twenty yards. Anne switched on the engine in a pointless fluster – given that the traffic would move slowly for a long time to come – and pulled away in first gear.

———

'You mentioned your mother at the end of our last session,' said David Hendrix, broaching what he expected to be a difficult subject. 'You were thirteen when it happened?'

'Yes,' said Winnicott watchfully.

'Were you with her when she died?'

'No.'

'But you knew she was ill?'

'My father told us she was sick. She was going into hospital so he couldn't very well conceal it. But when he came to see my brother and me at boarding school, he didn't say *how* sick. I didn't go to see her as often as I could have done. I could certainly have got permission, her being in hospital – but not knowing how ill she was ...' he paused, 'how seriously ill, I didn't take advantage of that. And I never knew what she went into hospital for.'

'But you did visit?'

Winnicott seemed ready to talk now, but it was like dealing with an unpredictable animal, thought Hendrix, which instead of turning on you could simply freeze you out at any moment. It was important not to give the impression of making judgements, like avoiding making any sudden movements in front of a jumpy tiger.

'Yes, several times. I remember going to see her and seeing her arms were very swollen, and afterwards mentioning it fairly casually to the matron and she said – obviously trying to reassure me – "Oh, don't worry, that's a good sign."' He looked at Hendrix. 'Well, of course, it was anything but a good sign.'

'What was she like?'

Winnicott considered this dispassionately, as if he were being asked for a reference.

'She was ... intelligent. I think she was quite a good organiser. Perhaps that's where I got my abilities from. I like to think so. She was quite a forceful woman – she could lose her temper, for instance. My father was a shy man but my mother was quite sociable ... much less inhibited as I remember and so, I suppose, you could say a better parent in the sense of being more spontaneous.'

'You think it's important to be spontaneous?'

As soon as he said it, Hendrix realised it was a crass mistake. Winnicott stared at him

'I told you before about my doubts concerning coun selling or whatever you call it. I'm still not really clear what it is, but if you want to stick me in a little box with, Example of English Middle-Class Anal Retentive stamped on the top then I have to tell you I don't much care for being reduced to a caricature.' He smiled. 'Is that spontaneous enough for you?' Hendrix cursed his stupidity, and shifted in his chair, signalling his defeated retreat.

'Sorry. My apologies.' But he did not give Winnicott time to withdraw. 'How did you learn of her death?'

'My father had sent me and my brother away on holiday.'

'And that's where you were when you heard?'

'No.'

'I'm sorry, I don't follow.'

'When we came back my father called me and my brother into the room he used as a study, if you like, though that's a grand way of putting it. And I remember thinking as we went in, "I wonder if Mum is dead", you know, in the sudden way one thinks of the impossible and you know you're never right more than one time in a million. And, of course, I *was* right.'

Hendrix still looked puzzled. 'So she died just before you returned from holiday?'

Winnicott looked straight at him.

'No. He told us about two weeks after it happened.'

Hendrix said nothing. To make any judgement would certainly bring the session to a halt.

Winnicott continued, 'No doubt you think it was wrong of my father to keep us in a state of such ignorance. Some of my father's friends thought it was unforgivable.' It was almost a dare.

234

'What do *you* think?' asked Hendrix.

Winnicott smiled. It had been a victory of sorts.

'I myself don't blame him. I think he had an extremely difficult hand to play and he wanted to keep such a dreadful piece of news from us for as long as possible.'

'How did he actually tell you?'

'You mean what words did he use?'

'Yes.'

There was a pause. 'He said, "I won't beat about the bush, boys, the fact is your mother's dead and we buried her last week – there's a glass of milk and a sticky bun for you in the kitchen."'

Hendrix's eyes widened in shock, then he realised. Winnicott laughed.

'I've already apologised once,' said Hendrix pleasantly. 'Would you like me to do so again?'

'No, it's all right. The fact is I can't really remember what he said. It was a blow and it's thirty years.'

'What *do* you remember?'

Winnicott looked out of the window. 'I remember my brother and I ...'

'How old was he?'

'He was a bit less than two years younger. We went our separate ways. He went upstairs and threw himself on the bed and sobbed and sobbed and sobbed. I went upstairs and started reading a book ... but not being able to concentrate. And I ... at one point I can remember laughing. It didn't seem like an hysterical laugh, although it may have been ... but it was definitely laughter. And I remember my father saying later, "That was a rather callous attitude." Not angry or anything. I'm not sure how you'd describe the tone. He would never criticise me very much. But if he did it was always in that tone. Mild. Sort of, "I'm not going to make a scene but I disapprove."'

'What did you say when he said that – about laughing?'

'I didn't say anything. I wasn't callous but I could see that it perhaps looked that way. I could understand why he said it, even at the time. I don't suppose I knew what was really going on. I may have thought I did but I couldn't take it in, I suppose. We all have our own way of dealing with terrible things. I discovered mine when I was very young. What can you do?'

Hendrix reluctantly brought the session to an end, feeling that Winnicott might never be so open with him again. As they parted, Winnicott nodded to a copy of *The Times* on a chair.

'I see you do the crossword.'

'Yes.' Hendrix was already late for his next client and was anxious not to get caught in conversation. Winnicott seemed not to notice his impatience.

'Have you ever heard of E13?'

It was four p.m. and Steven Grlscz was tired. As reluctant as a narcoleptic to an early rise he picked up the phone. It was answered after three rings. 'Dave Redman, please. It's Steven Grlscz.'

'I'll see if he's available.' A pause. 'He's in a meeting. Can I get him to call you back?'

Later that day Winnicott sat across from Michael McCarthy as he was attempting to explain the problems he was encountering in his submissions to the Law Commission on the reform of a 1968 Theft Act that had been written when hardly anyone had heard of credit cards. 'I mean, it's now possible to obtain goods fraudulently without deceiving a human being – you can order things direct from computers.' He was having trouble opening the peel-back Cellophane on his prawn sandwiches. 'They build these things like bloody nuclear fall-out shelters.'

'Why is that a problem?'

McCarthy looked up from his attempt to open the sandwich container. 'Because under the present law deception has to involve deceiving a person. Deceiving a machine isn't an offence.'

The sandwich container suddenly disintegrated, launching the contents across the room. McCarthy sighed. Winnicott barely noticed. He was waiting for the opportunity to pursue something that had been on his mind – the right time to deliver the favour to Healey. 'There's a matter I wanted to ask you about. A problem someone who's been of great help to me wanted advice about ... a fraud. It seems to be an awkward situation.' McCarthy looked embarrassed and Winnicott wondered if he had crossed a professional line. 'Of course if there's a problem ...'

'Ah, well, it depends,' said McCarthy, looking as if he thought it most decidedly *was* a problem. 'It would be best to keep it,' he paused, '*hypothetical* until I can see whether it might. Fire away.'

Winnicott took out the notes he had made, and after about five minutes McCarthy began to smile. 'You don't see that every day, I must say.'

'What?'

'An accountant more concerned with doing the right thing than squirming about trying to get out of their responsibilities to report crime. They are absolute bastards,' he said vehemently. 'It's taken them longer to come up with their new guidelines for reporting possible fraud than it took to build the Channel Tunnel.'

Winnicott was surprised at the extreme nature of McCarthy's loathing, sectarian in its intensity, for a group he had always seen as the model of dull respectability. 'But from what I could gather she *is* in a difficult position. Isn't that right?'

'Yes, I think it's fair enough. They've got to be careful,

but only if they want to do the right thing, and most of them are solely concerned with covering their backs and not making waves. Most of them don't give a damn about doing what's right and uncovering crime.'

'Then shouldn't we be doing everything we can to help someone who *is* concerned to do the right thing?' said Winnicott, still surprised by his irritable response.

McCarthy looked at him. 'We can stop being hypothetical. I know the company you're talking about – TLC. We've been sniffing around them for a while. But I'm afraid it's important you don't say too much to your friend. I've got a suspicious nature. It's possible this is a fishing exercise. After all, you don't *know* it's the accountant any more than you know it's his wife he's worried about. He could have made her up. TLC might realise we're on to them and this is just a ploy to find out what we know. Can you trust this person?'

'He's a serving officer in the Met.'

'But you know him well?'

'Hardly at all. He's got a good reputation, though.'

'Well, with all due respect, the same can't be said for the Met at the moment. It would be best to keep him in the dark. Tell him you're looking into it and that the situation is complex for reasons you can't reveal. It's the truth after all.'

'So what's going on at this TLC?'

McCarthy was staring at the sandwich on Winnicott's plate. 'Are you going to eat that?' Winnicott gestured at him to go ahead. 'There have been rumours about TLC going the rounds for a while. I've got someone working on collating it, but an old friend of mine is familiar with their kind of insurance work. I'd like to hear what he has to say first. By all means come to the meeting, if you want.'

The intercom buzzed.

'Yes, Lucy.'

'You're due to talk to the lawyers in five minutes.'

'Right. Thank you.'

'We'll go into the details later,' continued McCarthy, 'but we've been testing Anne Levels' new computer program. Remember that conference we went to in Canterbury? What's it called? OMERTA or something.

'NEMO, isn't it?'

'Whatever. Anyway, the IT department have been running TLC's financial transactions through it and searching for uncharacteristic variations in expected patterns. Well, to cut a long story short, its impressive increase in sales isn't so much impressive as bloody miraculous. So either the Good Lord has been made an executive director or there's something dodgy going on. That's why I've asked Howard Cornish to come and see us when he gets back from Italy. He's helped us out before. He might be able to look at what we've got and give us some idea about what they're up to.' McCarthy looked at Winnicott thoughtfully. 'The more I think about this accountant wanting to get advice from your policeman friend, the more fishy it looks. I think it would be best to proceed on the basis that this is an attempt to get information about what we know. I may well be wrong but that's how we should play it for now.'

'She might also be acting honestly. I *have* known members of the public not to be entirely frank with me,' said Winnicott. 'Nevertheless there are people who do tell the truth, often at considerable risk to themselves.'

'Of course,' replied McCarthy, realising that he had unwisely patronised his boss. Still, it was important to proceed carefully in this. 'But until we know what's going on between your policeman and his wife, I'm afraid we need to assume the worst.'

239

'I've come about the advert,' said Jane Healey, gesturing towards the door of the bookshop.

'Advert?' The man in the booth looked up. He was about fifty, short and muscular, though not in any way that spoke of the gymnasium – what her mother would have called a bruiser. His hair was white and cut short, and his expression made it clear that doubt or uncertainty had never troubled it. 'Oh. The book-keeping job.'

'Yes. The book-keeping job.'

'Um ... got any experience?'

'I'm a qualified accountant.'

'Oh,' he said. He nodded over at the piece of paper taped to the window. 'Like it says on the tin – it's only a book-keeping job.'

'I understand that. I haven't practised for a long time,' she lied. 'I did some part-time work for local businesses because it fitted in with the children. Book-keeping suits me fine.'

'Oh. Right. So, you know all about VAT?'

'I've kept in touch, more or less. It depends on the problem.'

'Did I say I had a problem?'

'Well, you're interested in how much I know about tax. It can be tricky for a small business.'

'It's not so small,' he said quickly. 'I've got another seven shops. Two in London, five around the country. You'd be doing their books as well ... *if* I hire you.'

'You've had a lot of applications, then, from qualified accountants with a knowledge of tax law? The rates *must* be good.'

He laughed. 'What if I do hire you and we don't get on?'

'Then I'll leave. I don't need the job that badly. It's just that it suits me to work around here three days a week. Is there any reason why we shouldn't get on?'

'It depends.'

'On what?'

He looked at her frankly. 'We don't sell just books here we sell ... adult books.'

'Oh,' she said flatly. 'The pornography in the basement, you mean?'

'Yes,' he said, without surprise. 'The pornography in the basement *is* what I mean. Not a problem, then?'

'No.'

'There might be another.'

'And what would that be?'

'Me.'

'You have a problem?'

'No, but *I* might be a problem for you.'

'Why?'

'I don't put up with any nonsense.'

'We've already got something in common, then, because neither do I.'

'I swear a lot. I believe in bollockings.' He said this with the unaffected openness of a Christian declaring his simple faith. 'It's the bollocking at Hat's that keeps things smooth, keeps my Jag on the road and the mortgage paid on my six-bedroom house. You see?' he said triumphantly. 'It's not such a small business. Let me show you WHAT I MEAN!' He raised his voice and looked accusingly in the direction of a pony-tailed assistant, who was just heading for the basement carrying a stack of magazines wrapped in sheets from the *Guardian*. The young man was grinning at Jane in what he clearly took to be an irresistibly attractive manner. As his boss's voice reached him, his face fell and the cockiness vanished.

'For example,' said the man menacingly, 'take that grinning pony-tailed git over by the stairs who's insulting a possible new employee who ought to be given MORE FUCKING RESPECT! I must be a fucking saint, and why? Because I let you fuckin' insult me every fucking day, Gordon. Why are you taking thirty-nine copies of the *TV* fucking *Times* downstairs? Is this a fucking joke? Then tell me, because I could do with a laugh. I need one because I have to put up with brain-dead dickheads like you. UN-BE-LIEV-ABLE!'

He switched his attention from the luckless Gordon to Jane. 'If you don't whip a horse it won't win, will it?' he said amiably. 'Well, do you think you can take me talking to them like that?'

'You can hang, draw and quarter them for all I care,' lied Jane, shaking but covering it well. 'Just don't try talking like that to me.'

An expression of appalled surprise crossed his face. 'I respect people who use their brains. I used my brain and I worked hard. That's how I've got seven shops. You've got to have intelligence. If you don't have intelligence, you're a fucking non-runner. If you don't put the effort in, you get fuck all out. These lads here, they'd do fuck all every day if I let them. I give 'em a lesson, the kind of lesson their useless bloody teachers never respected them enough to teach 'em.' He noticed Jane's reaction. 'Yeah, I respect 'em. The more I give a lad a bollocking, the more I respect him, and the more I care about teaching him to do a decent job. I feed my lads my philosophies and inspiration. They listen to what I tell them, take their bollockings, stop being the fucking losers they were when I gave them a job, then in a few years leave here, open their own place. At the end of the day you have to lead from the front. When I say "fucking move your arse, baby" they can't question it, 'cos I can always do it better.' He looked at her jauntily, as if knowing that any contradiction was implausible. 'Now the books,' he said. 'I can't be doing with the books and I can't be doing with Schedule E and that useless shitehawk Cronin at London Provincial 8 – so I won't give you any grief. If you do a proper job I can show respect. Mrs Fitzgerald, who used to do the books, she died. I always showed her respect. We got on like a house on fire. You don't rip me off, I'll show *you* respect ... you'll show *me* respect. *Are* you going to rip me off?'

'No.'

'Then the job's yours, if you want it.'

'Perhaps we should try it out for a month.'

'Suits me.'

'Fifteen pounds an hour and extra if you want advice on tax.'

'Fifteen?' he said incredulously. 'Mrs Fitz only got nine.'

'Well, when Mrs Fitzgerald gets back from the dead she can organise payment of the fine for late submission of your VAT returns.'

He looked stunned then laughed. 'I can see we're going to get along.' He looked over at a bookshelf behind Jane. 'Gordon! I told you to put the Fontana Modern Masters next to the fucking dictionaries. If you don't want to do what I ask, just fucking tell me and I'll fucking do it myself.' He turned back to Jane, smiling. 'Monday OK for you?' He held out his hand. 'Trevor Hat, by the way.'

'Ah ... Jane Percy,' she replied, having the presence of mind to use her maiden name.

Out in the street, Jane felt dazed. Her apparent coolness during the most bizarre conversation she had ever engaged in had been a product of her marriage. Geoff was a patient man whose bad temper only showed itself in trivialities. Generally calm, and always so when something important had gone wrong, he would lose his temper at not being able to find a shirt or because they were eating chicken for the third time that week. In the early years she had placated him but what had been infrequent became more regular and she eventually realised there was a connection. Nervously she began shouting back at him and to her surprise he seemed happy to accept this. Afterwards she wasn't sure what had stopped her shouting back before: fear that he'd hit her, leave the room and never come back or another act of epic and unalterable awfulness? It seemed absurd in hindsight. In time she simply refused to show that he was having any impact on her at all. An explosion about food would be met with an indifferent observation to the effect that he could make the dinner himself next time. Eventually he stopped these rants altogether, except as a kind of private joke between them. Without such practice, the conversation with Trevor Hat would have frightened the life out of her.

She told her office that she wanted to go part-time for a month, or possibly two. She didn't care how they reacted. She was a difficult-to-replace specialist who could easily get a job in twenty other firms. When it was clear that she had no intention of telling them why she wanted the time off, and indeed seemed to be daring them to protest, they simply agreed. She handed over the more straightforward projects she was working on to her junior colleagues and concentrated her efforts on the more complex few she could still deal with part-time. For a while she was going to have a secret life.

'Thank you, Lucy.'

Lucy Bradd had just dumped the last of four heavy files marked Barlow Clowes onto Winnicott's desk, having taken away eight even heavier files marked Guinness 1, 2 and 3. He thanked her again and looked down at the witness statements on his desk. Still she did not move.

'Is there anything I can do for you, Lucy?'

'There is actually, Mr Winnicott.'

'Won't you sit down?'

She sat and took a deep breath. 'I know this may

seem trivial, Mr Winnicott. It's about the water cooler.'
He began to speak but she was not to be interrupted.
'I've been to see Mr Gribben and I'm ... he wouldn't
listen.'

'What seems to be the problem?'

She stiffened with indignation.

'They've put the one on this floor next to my desk.'
She stopped, her mouth tight.

'And this is a problem because?'

'Well,' she said, with considerable feeling, 'you can
imagine. People keep coming and getting water from
it.'

He looked at her blankly. 'I see,' he said at last.

Winnicott's obvious incomprehension only annoyed
her further.

'Look, Mr Winnicott, I'm not an hysterical old
woman. I keep being interrupted. They don't just come
and get water, they meet each other. They talk. They
meet people from other departments they otherwise
wouldn't come across and they talk. I'm trying to
work.'

Winnicott was relieved. Her objections seemed
reasonable or at least comprehensible. This was not
another inscrutable problem. 'Can't it be moved
somewhere else?'

'Mr Gribben said that there *is* nowhere else.'

'Really? What about that space by the back stairs?'

'He says it would be a fire risk if it was put there.'

'How in God's name can a four-gallon bottle of water
be a fire risk?'

She sighed irritably. 'It's the cooler that's the problem,
not the water. The back stairs door ... it's a fire door.
He said fire regulations mean it can't go there.'

'There must be somewhere else.'

'He said there isn't.'

Winnicott sighed. 'Let me talk to him. I'm sure
there's a way of sorting this out amicably.'

She relaxed a little, her anger softened by half-suspicion,

'I hope so, Mr Winnicott. But I want to make it clear that I do take this very seriously.'

'Most certainly. I can see that. I understand.'

When she'd gone, he picked up the phone and dialled an internal number. A woman's voice answered.

'This is George Winnicott. I'd like to see Boyd Gribben. Is he available?'

'He's out at a meeting, Mr Winnicott.'

'I see. Tomorrow morning at ...'

'He's at a conference all day tomorrow.'

'When *is* he available?'

'There's eleven on Thursday.'

'Ten-thirty.'

'He has a meeting at ten-thirty.'

'I'd be grateful if he'd change it.'

There was a long pause. 'Of course, Mr Winnicott.'

David Hendrix regarded Anne Levels with a curiously pleasurable set of mixed emotions. He knew he was being charmed, a quality that instantly put him on alert. When speaking on the subject of charm he would always quote Camus (at least he thought it was Camus but he was too lazy to chase it up): charm can get you to say *Yes* even before you've been asked the question. He put up his defence: inquisitorial and stern.

'You're sure confidentiality won't be a problem, Anne?'

'Absolutely. Information can come into your system from NEMO but it can't go out. All I want to do is get someone who doesn't know about computers and who handles a lot of complex human problems to use the system and see if it comes up with anything of use. It may not. I can't promise this won't be a waste of your time, David.'

'I just want to be sure that my patients are protected.' David Hendrix drew in a deep breath, as if squaring up to a mild phobia. 'So, show me what it can do. But let me warn you, I'm hopeless at typing – two fingers.'

'A colleague of mine will come and set you up in a few days with a voice recognition system. You'll never need to type again if you don't want to.' Her smile was that of a siren luring innocent sailors to their doom. But what was so compelling about her charm, he decided, was that she didn't take you for a fool. She let you know she was being charming. Even more dangerous, then. But the thought of never having to type again was an effective bribe. Ah, the pleasure, he thought, of surrender to the will of another.

She gestured to the monitor. 'We use what we call microtheories to keep the mass of knowledge in NEMO in some form of order. NEMO can treat a specific set of assertions as a theory, so the sentence "It's the job of the Prime Minister to organise the running of the country" could be considered part of a microtheory on the nature of government. The major advantage of using the microtheory approach is that it allows for local consistency without requiring global consistency. Assertions within a microtheory must be consistent, but they needn't be consistent with those of another microtheory.'

'I'm sorry, you've lost me. I need an example.'

'Do you have any particular interests?'

He laughed. 'I'm ashamed to say that I've always loved horror films.'

Anne typed for a moment then turned to him. 'Ask it a question – but nothing too obscure.'

Hendrix sat next to her and began typing.

Who was Dracula?

The reply was instantaneous.

A vampire.

It was definitely not a human voice, but neither was it the toneless metallic sing-song he had been expecting from the other computer voices he had heard on the television. He typed again.

Do vampires exist?

No.

He laughed with delight.

'You see, Dracula and vampires can exist together in the microtheory in NEMO concerning Bram Stoker or horror films,' said Anne, 'but not in one of its modern scientific microtheories. So in time it'll always be able to distinguish the imaginary from the real. Ask it what will happen if Dracula drops an object made of glass.'

Hendrix typed and the reply was, again, instantaneous:

It will shatter ... break ... fragment ... smash ... splinter ... crack ... rend ... disintegrate ... crumble ...

'Oh dear,' said Anne, laughing. She typed for a few seconds and looked at him, blue eyes shining. 'Ask it something else. Something difficult.'

Hendrix regarded the computer warily. 'If it's tricky it's not going to blow up or anything? Suppose I ask it the meaning of life?'

'Go ahead.'

He typed, *What is the meaning of life?*

There was a long pause. Eventually NEMO replied.

Perhaps we could deal with that later, Mr Hendrix.

'Tell it you want an answer now.'

He typed as he was told.

There was another long pause.

I'm sorry, Mr Hendrix, I cannot give you an answer at this time.

Anne looked at him. 'It's just a more than usually complicated set of programs, David. It can't get confused. It knows things in the way that all computers know things – without knowing that it knows. It can come up with things that can amaze you with its apparent intelligence, but it's just a computer. When people talk about artificial intolligence the word to remember is *artificial*. Its ignorance is staggering. Ask it where George Washington was on the fifteenth of January 1788.'

Hendrix typed the question in slowly.

The reply was immediate: George Washington was in Valley Forge at that time, Mr Hendrix. Would you like an analysis of the importance of his leadership in holding together his troops during a period of severe hardship and the political as well as military significance of his success after the failures of Germantown and Brandywine?

Hendrix looked at her, waiting for a response.

'Ask NEMO to tell you where Washington's left leg was on the fiftcenth of January 1788.'

Hendrix, bemused, did as he was told.

There was another long pause before NEMO answered.

Perhaps we can discuss that later, Mr Hendrix.

'Tell it you want the answer now.'

Hendrix typed. There was another pause.

I do not have the answer at this particular time, Mr Hendrix.

Anne laughed. 'Just a demonstration of what NEMO is not, David. Let's try an area where it might be useful. What was the last thing you read about professionally?'

Hendrix looked across the desk. He nodded at an open book covered with a great deal of scribbling. 'That – Frank Lasch on the connection between story telling and dreams.'

She shrugged. 'Ask away.' Hendrix considered for a moment then began typing as Anne's mobile went off. He typed. *What is a story for?*

The reply was immediate – a long and complicated description of the structural problems surrounding the attempt to prevent the Leaning Tower of Pisa from falling down,

Anne switched off the phono. 'Damn!' she said.

Hendrix turned to look at her. 'What's the matter?'

She sighed. 'Just bad luck, really. I'm afraid you're talking at cross-purposes.' She was standing just behind Hendrix and leant across him, stretching to reach the keyboard. As her breast brushed against his cheek he felt an almost static charge. She stood upright and laughed. 'Have you got a dictionary – an OED?'

He went over to his bookshelf and returned with an ancient copy. She checked under S and moaned again, showing him. 'See. We use the OED as the basis for defining words for NEMO. You can spell storey as in the eighth storey of a building in two ways – storey and story. It picked up your use of the word, accessed the two spellings from the OED and related it to the last context in which it used the term.' She shut the book with a snap. 'NEMO is being used by the Department of Structural Engineering at Imperial College. For the last five years they've been trying to stop the Leaning Tower of Pisa from falling down. NEMO thought you were asking it about the storeys of the tower.'

THE STORY OF
THE TOWER

The hedgehog knows one big thing but the fox knows many small things. The human hedgehog is a visionary and everything is defined by his ideals. The twentieth century was the age of the absolutist hedgehog and his big idea – the age of men who were ready to help us towards a better world with a gas chamber or a bullet in the head. We must pray that Reynard the fox will be our hero and our king, a pensive champion whose way of thinking is diffuse, who works on many levels and is able to deal with doubt, uncertainty, complexity and flux. In the twenty-first century let our engineers be prudent and supple like the fox, let them examine, sniff, investigate. But like the fox they must, as well, be quick to strike. Prudent and decisive does it, boys and girls. Find them, these men and women, find them in the factories and in the offices; search them out in mill and forge and building site. Then beg or steal their fire.

And if the fox is *not* to be the spirit of the age? Then it will be the crocodile.

Louis Bris, *The Wisdom of Crocodiles*

Howard Cornish's mobile trilled. Normally he would let the message service take it and call back; he considered it the height of bad manners to answer his mobile in the middle of a conversation. But he was in Italy and had no intention of phoning England later and adding hugely to his already alarming bill. It was Michael McCarthy's snooty PA asking him to put back their meeting at the Fraud Secretariat by a couple of days. He would have to phone her back anyway because he had left his diary in the hotel. He put the phone back in his pocket and turned to the man waiting patiently beside him.

'Sorry about that. How long did it take to build?'

'Well, it was started on the ninth of August ...' Barton put down his wooden tray of core samples and muttered calculations, 'finished on ... the twenty-eighth of March.' He screwed up his eyes, double-checking. 'So that's a hundred and seventy-five years.'

Howard Cornish looked up at the Tower of Pisa, squinting into the sun. He turned back to Barton. 'Hard to imagine what it must be like, thinking in that way. I mean, it's incomprehensible now, sort of extinct, an idea like that. Can you imagine completing a building now begun in, what, 1825?'

Barton smiled. 'Mind you, things were different then. Building styles hardly altered between the twelfth century and the middle of the thirteenth, so you wouldn't have the problems you have now. You'd have a delicate Regency style at the bottom and a lot of exposed post-modern pipework at the top. They didn't really have styles in the Middle Ages. This your first trip?'

'Yes.' Cornish looked back at him. 'Do you know why I'm here?'

'You're assessing the risk for the insurance company.'

'That's right.' There was a brief silence. 'You were going to show me the lead weights.'

Barton led him off towards the north foot of the tower. On the way they passed two blue-jeaned, white-T-shirted men hanging from the upper storeys of the tower in slings and harnesses, easy and confident of their physical strength.

Barton saw him watching. 'They're putting the last of eighteen steel cables around the base at first-gallery level. You see, the tower won't actually fall, as such – not overbalance. It'll effectively explode at this point because this is where the leaning has caused the greatest stress in the masonry. The cables will act as a kind of corset. Combined with this.' He stopped in front of an enormous, squat, canvas-covered square. He pulled back the canvas to reveal a dull metal. 'Lead. This is the north side and it leans to the south. We're gradually loading the ground on the opposite side to equalise the pressure on the soil on this side.'

'Is it working?'

'It's not very elegant but it'll stabilise things till we decide on a permanent solution.'

Cornish stared up at the tower for almost a full minute, hearing the cries of the labourers, the distant clatter of metal on metal and feeling the sun and wind on his face.

'Are you sure there is a permanent solution? After all, they've been trying to stop the tower from falling over for eight hundred years.' Cornish smiled softly. 'And all they've ever done is made the problem worse.'

'We understand the problem better now, how complex it is.'

'They thought the same thing in 1934, didn't they? That they understood exactly what needed to be done. I believe their attempts resulted in the biggest lurch to the ground since it was built.'

Barton looked at him. A man who's done his homework, he thought. 'You're right about the 1934 attempt. I mean soil mechanics was a proper science by then. The trouble was that they thought they understood pretty much everything ... the whole story. They didn't.'

'But you understand it?'

'No, I couldn't say that. But we understand what we don't understand. What I said earlier about measuring carefully and moving slowly. We understand a lot of what's going on but not all of it. If we observe it all carefully as we intervene, then we'll know that it's working and have a good idea why. Keep to that principle: know as much as you can and don't get carried away with theories about things that are beyond you – then I don't think you can go far wrong. That's why we're more likely to succeed. The most important law of medicine is the most important law of stabilising large complex structures: first, do no harm.' He took out a cigarette and lit up. 'Let's go back to the hut. There are some drawings you should see.'

It was pleasantly cool in the site office. Barton spread out a plan like an architect's blueprint. The tower, leaning to the south, was meticulously drawn: bell-tower, galleries, steel restraining girdles and six hundred tonnes of lead weight. Beneath these were the foundations, and beneath these the striated layers of soil: silty sand over clayey silt, over upper clay, over interclay, over inter-sand, over lower clay, over sand; at depths of 3 metres, 6 metres, 10 metres, 21 metres, 25.5 metres, 27.5 metres and 40 metres.

'Right, the most likely permanent solution is to induce a controlled subsidence of the north foundations so that the whole structure tilts back to the centre by about half a degree. That'll reduce the tensions in the masonry where we've put the steel girdle by about ten per cent.'

'It all seems very straightforward,' said Cornish. 'Will it work?'

'Oh, don't worry, it'll be a long time before we actually do anything. We've been trying out a new computer system called NEMO to simulate all the different ways of stabilising the tower.' He wondered whether he should have mentioned NEMO. After three months he would have been hard pressed to say whether the computer was a help or a hindrance. It came up with useful information about as often as it talked rubbish. 'Basically there are three ways of doing it, but the method I favour at the moment is to drive a series of small tunnels through the upper clay on the north side and dig out some soil so it subsides into the space. A slow process and very carefully done.'

Cornish nodded, 'It certainly seems elegant, but so was the 1934 effort ... on paper. And this is still on paper.'

'Yes,' said Barton quickly, now fired up with enthusiasm, 'but there's a difference. Our theoretical models are better. But it's more than that. We're monitoring the effects incredibly closely and changing it all so slowly. Nobody's going to pursue a mad theory. Look, nobody understands soil,' he said, 'but I know a lot about it. We have the best computer models available, but we're not just going to rely on computers. We're going to test everything out on a site near here where the soil structure is almost identical. We're not taking chances. I can't say it too often – we'll move a hair's breadth at a time. Like the Chancellor of the Exchequer I believe it's necessary to be decisive – but not until I've had a long talk with my three wives: Prudence, Prudence and Prudence.'

Cornish laughed. 'I'd like to have a look at this site of yours.'

'Fine.' Barton began to move to the door but as he did so the computer pinged at him. It was, thought Cornish, both odd and familiar, like the sound of a doorbell coming out of an expensive loudspeaker. It was clear that Barton was pretending nothing had happened.

'What's that?' said Cornish. Barton looked slightly shifty. 'The program I was telling you about earlier … it has a sort of facility … it takes all the information we put into it and it searches all the databases it's got access to and the Internet. It's supposed to work a bit like computer brainstorming. It pings like that when it's got something to tell you. I don't use it,' he added hastily.

'Interesting. Would you mind? Just for nosiness' sake.'

'Of course,' replied Barton, hiding his reluctance. He typed, hoping to God it didn't come up with any of its more lunatic ideas. Fortunately he had switched off the voice because it got on his nerves.

Professor Barton, were you aware that your preferred method for stabilising the Tower of Pisa by the use of soil extraction was first used to stabilise the tower of St Chad in Wynbunbury, Cheshire, in 1832?

'Interesting,' said Cornish. 'Were you aware?'

'Only since my first year studying soil science at Imperial,' said Barton dismissively. 'Like I said, I don't pay much attention to this stuff. Where it's useful is in building models of collapse.' Barton pressed the escape button and the presumptuous question vanished. Then he started typing. 'I've tried every way I know to bring the tower down. Using this I've found fifty ways to do it using best current practice for stabilising buildings. I'm not going to let this happen in real life.'

Cornish looked at the screen. Over and over again, slowly, catastrophically, NEMO was causing the Leaning Tower of Pisa to fall to the ground.

'How did you feel about not being at your mother's funeral?'

Hendrix noted how expressionless Winnicott's face was and the effort that was going into keeping it that way. He was looking out of the window as if mulling over something impersonal.

'I suppose some people might rather resent not being even asked if they wanted to go to the funeral ... but I don't, again, think my father did anything dreadful. In any case, I don't think I would have wanted to go.'

'Do you mind if I ask why?'

Winnicott breathed in deeply. 'The idea that you have to get out and grieve with other people and tear your hair and tear your clothes ... which, it's a fashionable idea, I suppose, that this is somehow better than grieving in silence and grieving on your own.' He shrugged. 'I suppose you would disagree.'

'Well,' replied Hendrix cautiously, 'these seem to be extreme ways of looking at it. I mean grieving in public needn't involve anything as dramatic as you suggest. Most people, in this country anyway, admire reticence. Hair tearing is definitely frowned on.'

'What about all that nonsense over Diana?'

Hendrix laughed. 'Fair enough, but we could spend a few weeks on that one alone. From my point of view, whatever it was all about, it just proves my belief that the English are the weirdest nation on earth. But to be honest, I prefer to do my own weeping in private.'

'Do you cry a lot?'

'Hardly ever. I rather wish I could. It clearly does some people a power of good. But the tears won't come. We have more in common than you think, perhaps.'

'I can cry,' said Winnicott. 'Don't think I can't.' He was impressed by Hendrix's openness. 'Certain bars of music can make me cry almost as automatically as a peeled onion. And I cried when my dog had to be put down. But news of bereavement doesn't make me cry. Of course I don't need a psychiatrist to tell me that this is because of the news of this terrible event when I was thirteen. But you'd have thought I wouldn't be able to cry at all, wouldn't you?' Winnicott did not expect an answer to this, nor did Hendrix offer one. 'But you know,' he continued, 'I think disappointment is the ... is one of the aspects of bereavement which is not discussed. As much as anything else − sheer bloody disappointment.' Hendrix had never heard him swear before. 'You'd expected them to be there ... they should have been there, you ... they should be here now.' He looked at Hendrix. 'You know, "Why haven't they arrived?" How self-centred of them not to come, how unfeeling. How inconsiderate ...' he paused, 'not to live.' He smiled. 'I think there's a lot of that: disappointment at their lack of consideration for not living.'

'How do you think her death has affected you as an adult?'

'You mean in my relationships? Isn't that what one must always discuss?'

'It's up to you,' said Hendrix neutrally.

Winnicott considered whether or not he would continue. 'There's a point, I suppose, beyond which I won't go ... or can't go. As I told you, I can cry, I just can't cry about anything terrible. I know that. I'm not an emotional person in the sense that I might have been if my mother had lived. Perhaps I would have been more spontaneous. Who knows? Possibly not. That was the hand I was given. I remember watching a documentary when I was about fifteen about an African tribe where the women had these neck rings − they put another ring around their necks every few months or so, until after a dozen years their necks were stretched so that they were incredibly long.' He looked at Hendrix to gauge whether he knew what he was talking about.

Hendrix nodded.

'Apparently, well-meaning missionaries in the nineteenth century tried to take them off. The women suffocated. Life changes you sometimes and you can't always do anything about it. And it's dangerous to try. I suppose you can't accept that.'

'It depends. I think for certain people therapy can be harmful for the reasons you say. Obviously I'd have to find another job if I accepted it completely. The women and the rings – it's a good analogy. But the point I'd want to make is that your rings don't seem to be holding you up any more – otherwise you wouldn't be here.'

Winnicott was not obviously bothered by this. 'That's fair, I suppose, but the fact that I'm here doesn't mean that I accept   and I don't mean to be rude – that anything you say has real ...' he searched for the right word with difficulty, 'validity,' he said at last.

Hendrix again noticed the gradual increase in Winnicott's nominal aphasia.

'It's plausible that my mother's death had a huge impact on me – I'm not denying that. But if I am ... If I have some problems now it doesn't mean that that has anything to do with it. I was a policeman for twenty years and I can't tell you how often a plausible theory turned out to be completely wrong. Lots of things are plausible and wrong. Maybe it's entirely a physical problem. I haven't ruled that out and neither can you. We may be, perhaps we probably are, barking up entirely the wrong tree.' His smile was both provocative and sly.

Hendrix changed the subject. 'How does your wife feel about the way you've come to deal with things?'

'You mean, does she resent the fact that I'm not more open with my emotions?'

'I suppose so.'

'I was nearly thirty when she met me. I was pretty

much the same person I am now. And I'd say she's less emotional than I am in many ways – at least, less willing to go on about feelings in the way women are supposed to want to do all the time. She's a reserved person and I admire her reticence. Now there's an admission,' he added mockingly.

'So you get on well?'

'As I said before, we have our ups and downs like everyone else. But to be honest I'd rather not discuss her, not just because it bothers me, but because it would bother her. Her great dislike is of being exposed. She would feel it a betrayal, I think, to be talked about here.'

'Did she say anything to you to that effect?'

'I may have as little insight into myself and others as you think, but that's something I *do* understand. She does not want to be discussed. She despises people who drone on about their emotional problems.'

'So what does she think about your coming here?'

There was a long pause, during which Winnicott's expression did not change. 'She doesn't know,' he said at last.

––––––

Lucy Bradd knocked and entered Winnicott's office, followed by a tall, slightly stooped man whose eyes scanned the room with a forensic attention to detail. He gave the impression he could tell almost everything that had happened there in the recent past from a discarded cigarette, or the chewed end of the visitor's forgotten Biro, and that to shake his hand would be like going to confession after many absent years.

'How are you, Michael?' he said to McCarthy. McCarthy was clearly pleased to see him.

'Howard, let me introduce the new director of the Fraud Secretariat. George Winnicott – Howard Cornish.'

Winnicott took his hand. It was a powerful grip but

effortlessly so; he was not demonstrating anything, he was simply very strong. Cornish sat down.

'You're looking well,' said McCarthy beaming at Cornish with pleasure.

'I've just come from Pisa – looking into this attempt to stop the tower from collapsing. Fascinating stuff.'

'I've been reading about it in the papers. I went there with my father when I was a boy,' said McCarthy.

Cornish laughed. 'Well, if you want to take your own son, Michael, it might be wise to do the trip sooner rather than later.'

'Is it really in danger of collapsing?' said Winnicott.

'I hope not. But if there wasn't any risk of it falling, they wouldn't be paying me to try and find out how big that risk actually is. So,' he continued briskly, 'how can I help you?'

'We've had information about a possible fraud. Obviously at this stage I can't identify those who may be involved. There are indications that there might be some kind of collusion between insurance salesmen over large-scale projects and the actuaries calculating the figures on which the premiums have been based and ... presumably ... any underwriting of that risk by second parties.'

'I see,' said a puzzled Cornish. 'Or rather I don't really. Better give me the details.'

McCarthy glanced at Winnicott who was looking on impassively. McCarthy quickly summarised what information they had. 'Not a lot to go on, I realise,' said McCarthy when he'd finished. 'But there are questions about the probity of their dealings elsewhere which are much more substantial, and given this is more your field, what we were hoping was that you might give us an idea of the kind of fraud they might be involved in. What would *you* do in this area if you wanted to rip someone off?' Cornish breathed in and out heavily and stroked the skin on his neck, but said nothing. 'I mean, we're not asking for anything specific, just whether there could be anything in this ... give us some idea of what we could pursue. Don't feel it has to be water-tight.'

'Sort of brainstorming?' offered Cornish.

'Absolutely.'

'We're talking about oil rigs, for example – that kind of thing?'

McCarthy nodded. Cornish said nothing for a while. Then he started to speak. 'I'll have to think about this but just off the top of my head: if the person negotiating the deal is on a percentage of that deal, then obviously they'd benefit from the sale. If price is the biggest issue, you could see him conspire with the actuary who works out the chances of the oil rig being destroyed in a storm or an explosion. He could get him to produce figures which lengthened the odds and so lowered the premium ... so he gets the sale and the commission, which he splits with the actuary.'

'That sounds the kind of thing,' said McCarthy hopefully.

Cornish frowned. 'But the problem there is that you'd be ripping yourself off. I mean, if you offer people a sixty-quid deal for comprehensive insurance of their car then your initial cash intake will be massive. But once the claims come in you'll go bankrupt because the amount of money available to pay for repairing damaged cars is less than the amount it costs to actually repair them. What's the point?'

'So you think ...'

'On the other hand it's a pretty bad analogy. Cars aren't oil rigs or earthquakes. You can pretty accurately estimate the number of car crashes in a year, because there's so much data it becomes really predictable ... but how many oil rig explosions are there? I mean, you could gamble long-term on an earthquake, say, because it might never happen in your lifetime, or an oil rig might blow up tomorrow or not for twenty years. Look at Grand Prix motor racing – no fatalities in ten years then two die in one weekend.'

'So you think it's plausible,' said an eager McCarthy. Cornish drew in another deep breath.

'Possible. I don't know about plausible. 'Give me a few minutes, would you?' he said, taking out a pen and a notebook.

At this, Winnicott stood up. 'I wonder if you'd excuse me,' he said and left the room. McCarthy watched him go, worried.

Winnicott hurried past Lucy who was in a furious mood. Not only was her computer telling that all the work she had typed in the day before did not exist but a lawyer was over by the water cooler flirting noisily with one of the accountants. She barely registered Winnicott's presence. He walked carefully into the wash room, went into the toilet and locked the door with difficulty. He sat down and within ten seconds he was unconscious.

In Winnicott's office Cornish silently scribbled in his notebook, paused then scribbled again. McCarthy stood up and went over to the window. He gazed out over the City and down to the light blinking on top of the pyramid of Canary Wharf.

MICHAEL McCARTHY

The year 2000 is merely a date: the modern world began somewhere between 1962 and 1966. One day, perhaps, some prodigy will point to the precise moment, possibly to within a few minutes, when what came after was utterly different from what went before. It is, of course, almost certain that this moment has been lost; not even those who were there will have realised the significance of what it was they were a witness to. The last age, after all, began with the crucifixion of an obscure criminal in some Middle Eastern shithole. Why should its end be any more conspicuous?

Louis Bris, *The Wisdom of Crocodiles*

As a child I did not have to get used to the sight of men falling out of the sky because they had always done so from the moment I was born. So unremarkable was it that I don't have any earliest memory of when I first realised that men were falling from amazing heights, any more than you would have an earliest memory of eating or of your mother and father. For years, until now, I took these things for granted, proud that there was something unusual about my life compared to other lives; but in itself it seemed normal, what went on.

One thing I do remember as having a definite beginning was the first time I saw one of these parachutists killed. He was a novice, with thirty jumps or so, making a descent from two thousand feet. It isn't clear what happened and some of the things I recall probably did not take place. I was four years old and playing outside in a crowd of people waiting for the plane. Suddenly there was a lot of confusion, legs dispersing everywhere. Someone, I don't know whether it was my mother or my father, told me to go into the clubhouse and wait. I did as I was told. I sat on the table swinging my legs and humming to myself, but I could be wrong, it could have been another time. After a while, I've no idea how long but to me it felt like a very long time without anyone to talk to, I went out by the back door and without any particular sense of curiosity walked round to the front. People were looking towards the runway at an approaching car. No one noticed me. As I remember, it was a Fifties job in black with someone standing on a runner along the side. I stood on a coal-bunker to get a better view. I have a sense of enormous drama, of great movement, of people in shock, disturbed, craning to see, and of three men in the back with the one in the middle not like any man I've ever seen before or since. What struck me then, and now, was the floppiness of his neck, bent back and away from me and to one side so that I couldn't see his face. He lacked resilience and seemed to be attempting to flow into the man on whose shoulder he was resting. This man had shape but the dead man's shape was gone, even though there was no mark on him as far as I could see. After that I don't remember anything. Somewhere through the years, I don't know how, I got the idea that he'd been showing off to his girlfriend, intending to leave the opening to the last moment.

A few months ago, while my mother was preparing dinner for us all, I told her what I remembered of his death. She was surprised at what I'd seen but couldn't remember much herself as it was over thirty years ago. In passing, I commented on the reason he had pulled too low. She looked at me oddly and then told me the real story of what killed him.

His name was Parry Hughes and ho was married. He was an obsessive type, closed up and secretive, and had developed a fascination for calculating heights of opening, the time it took for a chute to deploy and how the one could be calculated against the other in order to give the exact lowest point at which you could pull the ripcord and land safely. His wife, also a parachutist but with only fifteen jumps, discovered what he was up to and had tried to stop him. As a result of her fearful pleas and threats he apparently relented and gave his word he would stay at home. When Saturday came, he locked her in their bedroom while she was dressing and came to the dropping zone to carry out his plan. No one knew for sure exactly what went wrong but the coroner accepted my father's likely version of events. The chances were, he thought, that Parry had simply fumbled his first attempt at pulling the ripcord and because there was no margin for error he had hit the ground while the parachute was still unfolding from his back. Later his wife found a diary filled with calculations and illegible scribbling that detailed the depth of his desire to get it right but gave nothing away about why.

I was struck by this new side to a story I had lived with all my life, touched by the locked door and fearful wife and the depth of her grief after a long and silent wait until large men in flying suits broke down the door to tell her that her husband had been killed; and Parry, overlooking the need to take himself into account, scribbling in his secret book and failing in his calculations to give a number to his clumsy hands.

My parents were both Irish, my father having come to England to join the Royal Air Force shortly after the war. My mother had the 'drop dead' attitude that Irish women often have, particularly the pretty ones, and she resolutely refused to be impressed by my father, even though impressing people, usually by attempting some dangerous and often stupid stunt, was what he enjoyed most. If you had seen her then, but hadn't heard her speak, you would have thought her a delicate English beauty, thin to the point of being consumptive. 'That one'll be dead before she's twenty,' the crones in Dublin used to prophesy, when she walked down the street. Despite this apparent fragility, she was remarkably tough even though she was often in terrible pain because of a spinal injury she'd got when roller-skating as a child. When she was bad, she'd have to lie in bed for weeks on end, and when she got up we'd ask to see how bent she was. Standing in her nightdress she would turn her back to us to demonstrate the collapsing tower of her spine and we would gawp at the way her back curved to one side by six or seven degrees. Sometimes it looked as if she'd topple over just by standing still. Her back was slowly disintegrating because of the lack of decent medical treatment. Her doctor had forbidden her, on pain of an unspecified anathema, from consulting a chiropractor, a breed regarded by the medical profession in those days as one step up from the kind of practitioners who filed their teeth to a point. In the Fifties, doctors regarded women as, in their very essence, a problem. They were inherently unhealthy in a way it seemed rarely possible to treat. Like collapsing towers, they could be propped, shored up with metal stays, their foundations reinforced but nothing fundamental could be done to treat their essential weaknesses. The pain, however, became so bad she secretly went to see a chiropractor in Bath, and I can still remember waiting for her in the Volkswagen outside the clinic feeling as if we were part of a blasphemous conspiracy, all voodoo and witchcraft.

But the sense remained with me that women were

utterly different from men in some way that I had yet to grasp. Men were muscular like my father, built for strength like posts, clear in their lines of muscle and sinew. But women were hidden, curved and blurred in their intent, bodies mysterious, soft and collapsible. Their underwear reflected this systemic instability. When I first saw my mother strapping herself into a corset in that curious shade of pink, I used to think it was unique to her because of her bad back; but one of the fascinating things about women, or at least about my mother's friends, was their carelessness in matters of dress around little boys. The result of this was that much of my childhood seemed to have been spent watching women in their late twenties wandering around in various stages of undress. Not that there was much of the essential fleshy woman on display even so. They were always encased in lacy shells, crossed by straps and buckles, bones and silver suspenders. The sense was always of something interior needing to be held in place, supported, buttressed, underwired to prevent an imminent collapse. Still, being admitted to a world from which older boys and men were excluded was freedom that I prized. There was nothing innocent about my voyeurism as I wandered through their bedrooms or sat on the floor playing with my soldiers waiting for the crossing and uncrossing of their legs; but with hindsight there also seemed to be no shame.

Things began to change when I was eight. I remember one visitor, a widow in her thirties, I suppose, whose officer husband had been killed in a flying accident in Bahrain. She had a beautiful face and would correct me if I did not put my knife and fork together on my plate when I had finished eating. At some point during her visit, as I was wandering around upstairs, I walked in through her open bedroom door looking for a toy. She was sitting cross-legged in front of the mirror. She

was naked. She was so white, so round, so uncon-
fined. I can still see the ridges of her spine descending
to the curves of her buttocks, and the hanging sideways look of her breasts. And the brown nipples,
burning me with their colour. I stood quite still. She
turned. Then, unconcerned she said, 'Hello, Michael,
are you all right, darling?' She seemed not to notice
my astonished face, wide eyes and shock. Then she
stood up and faced me. I had never seen hair on the
body of a woman before. I would have been a deal less
struck if she'd had wings. Who would have thought it?
It was so unpredictable, so black, the rest of her so
white. It was too much. I turned around and ran away.

This will never happen to my son; he's used to that
kind of thing. There are none of those astonishments
in store for him. The loss is his, I'd say, even though
he'll never have that endless nag I still feel to return to
the bedroom and the woman turning her thoughtless
head to welcome me.

The lock-out finally came one day when Bridget
Gallagher was visiting us. My parents were both bewildered and impressed by her because she would
say the first thing that came into her head, however
outrageous it might be. Although the women talked of
sex quite frequently, it was usually referential enough to
keep me slightly in the dark. I picked up lots of useful
things about sex this way, even if the satisfyingly precise
was hard to come by. Bridget didn't care for the
oblique and during her visits it was especially important to be always in earshot. On this occasion Bridget
and my mother were sitting opposite each other while
I was on the floor between them, using the sofa as a
battleground and not paying much attention because
the conversation had drifted towards a detailed
description of a lengthy shop. Still, mindful of
Bridget's tendency to sudden and dramatic changes
of topic, part of me was monitoring what was going on.

She'd been to a big department store in London and was telling my mother about her visit to the lingerie department. Ears alert, I increased the volume of my explosions to cover my newly directed interest. As usual with children, I over-acted and my mother told me off:

'Mike! Either shut up or go upstairs.'

I ignored her as I was expected to but turned the volume down. Bridget was discussing an article she'd read about a new machine that could make tights cheaply enough to replace stockings.

'I bought a pair, though they weren't that cheap. Bloody liars.' With this she stood and in one quick movement pulled her skirt around her waist.

'What do you think?' she said to my mother. 'God, they're so comfortable.'

My mouth dropped open and my eyes widened as she whirled about, her slim buttocks encased by the unfamiliar nylon and, for the times, a tiny pair of knickers.

'What do you think of the panties? Cheeky, eh?'

I was so taken aback by this that my show of indifference vanished – enough for my mother to see how transfixed I was by Bridget's exhibition of long legs and nylon-covered bum. She gestured at Bridget that I was looking, but Bridget only laughed as she pulled down her skirt.

My mother never said anything to me but after this she always shooed me out of the bedrooms of her friends and immediately distracted me if I was playing on the floor when they were visiting. And so the new freedom for women ushered in by tights, and all that they implied, signalled my ejection from the harem with its easy chat and careless immodesty. Whenever I was around, my presence was taken into account and there was no way back. In effect I had become a man. I had been expelled, and before I'd found the secret.

Maybe it's much the same for every boy. We get thrown out just as we're about to put our finger on the thing itself. Possibly that's the secret of the male gaze, why we're always looking at women. With all that gawping, all those stares, someone will be the Archimedes of the secret world of women. 'Eureka!' he will shout, the earth will move, and paradise, perhaps, will be regained.

Until this exile, my father had been a distant figure. This was not because of any manly stand-offishness with children but simply because he wasn't often there. Parachuting took him away most weekends and often he was abroad competing for weeks at a time. That year he became British champion for the first time and, one evening in September, we went off to the cinema, not to see the feature, but to watch the Pathé News which preceded it. There in black-and-white up on the screen was my father, dropping from the sky then smilingly receiving his prize from a minor aristocrat who was vaguely connected with the British Parachuting Association. How proud I was to hear that Pathé voice, fruitily congratulating him on what he'd done along with that peculiar music, which even then seemed to belong to an older, vanishing world.

Like most sports parachutists he was quite short, but he had been a wrestler before he had come to England, and on first joining the RAF had been a physical-training instructor. He was immensely muscular, his shoulders and arms particularly, and he was always striking those body-builder poses with his arms over his head to emphasise his triceps or akimbo to draw attention to his extraordinary latissimus dorsi which, when flexed, gave the impression that he had a pair of wings folded behind his back. He used to laugh at himself when he did this, while still full of admiration for his own strength and power. He enjoyed exasperating

271

my mother with these displays. She responded by mocking him and approving of him at the same time. 'You're a bloody show-off, Kevin,' she would say disdainfully. 'Bigheads, the McCarthys. Every one of them.'

Week after week I watched him fall, through high summer and into a warm autumn, waiting in front of the crowds, sometimes large, sometimes small, sharing in what it meant to be observed, drawing from the hunger for excitement – I'm not entirely sure that I can put my finger on what they got from watching men fooling about in the air with their noisy, expensive planes and their brightly coloured parachutes. But I think they were like people at a zoo: behind the bars were creatures who did not know what dread or worry was. Fear they knew, but not anxiety. My father was like an animal to them. They no more felt reproached by him than by the strength and courage of a horse. His willingness to die was admirably irrelevant. But not to me. It seems obvious now, absurd not to have noticed it before, week in, week out, loving the atmosphere, proud of the gaze of thousands watching as I walked with my father, carrying his helmet with our name printed on the front, his arms full of brightly coloured cloth, soaking it up, worshipping the admiration of the crowd the way he did, that every time I heard the engines cut and that speck begin to gather speed I was afraid that I was going to watch him die.

My father's real job with the RAF was to train and despatch paratroopers. The army had tried to do this for itself but failed. The instructors needed a combination of gentleness and discipline to handle the young troops' fear of their first jump. Fighting came naturally to these men, but not falling from a great height. To get many of them to jump required a careful understanding of the particular nature of the terror. Bullying a man into jumping, said my father, was a sure way to get him killed and yourself court-martialled.

In the early spring of the next year, two Hercules transporters left RAF Abingdon for a NATO training exercise in Italy. My Mum and I went with him because we knew an Italian parachutist from the European championships whose wife had invited us to stay in their house just outside the city. The two Hercules were based near Pisa. Each one could hold sixty paras and six instructors, but the weather was poor at first and my father took the chance early on in the first week to take me to see the city from the top of the Leaning Tower where Galileo first demonstrated the nature of fundamental forces. There my father conducted his own experiment into the nature of gravity. Someone fooling about had started him off by encouraging him to do one of his gymnastic party tricks on the edge of the tower. To their horror, and that of the paras and tourists watching, he grabbed the low wall with both hands and swung up into a handstand. The intake of breath that resulted wasn't enough and he shifted his weight on to his right shoulder and lifted his left hand clear so that he was balancing on one hand. The amazed laughter that followed egged him on and, still supported by one arm only, he lowered his chest till it almost touched his hand then pushed up until his arm was almost fully extended. He put his left hand back and, swinging his body between his arms, landed lightly back on the tower. He looked at me and I was filled with pride. Later he told me that it wasn't as dangerous as it looked, that he had balanced himself so that the only direction in which he could fall was back towards the safety of the tower.

My mum and I returned home at the end of the week. A few days later I came back from a school football match as she was sitting down to watch the six o'clock news. As the first item came up the newscaster adopted that po-faced expression and doomy voice, which always indicated that someone somewhere was about to have their world turned upside down. One of the two planes based in Pisa had gone into the side of a hill and everyone on board had been killed. The details were sketchy. My mother ran to the phone and called the base at Abingdon. Someone she knew answered it, which seemed to calm her. He had no details but promised to ring as soon as he had news. Ten minutes later the phone rang. She snatched it up.

It was Jane Briggs. Her husband had been in the other Hercules. It must have been a strange conversation, with each one longing for the other's husband to be dead. They talked briefly then cleared the lines and sat and waited. Having been afraid for him each time he jumped, I felt a curious mixture of unease and, I suppose, disbelief. It was impossible to think of him not existing. He was too confident to die. Two hours later, after some agonising false alarms, the phone rang. She picked it up. 'Yes?' She looked at me: 'He's alive.'

I was excited by the thought of my first funeral, but after six in less than a week I'd had enough. The weather was bad that month, wet as well as cold, though now I think about it, I can't remember any funeral I've ever been to where it hasn't rained. The thing about military funerals is that the men are nearly always young. The burials have run into a kind of blur of men in full-dress uniform and women in their early thirties weeping and the grave, which always surprises in the same way, the lines being so sharp and the hole so deep. I remember that cutting morning wind which seems to blow in graveyards everywhere. And, most of all, the private soldier playing the last post. You will have heard it, I suppose, in films or on television played by someone who's a master of his instrument, purified by engineers in studios. Needless to say,

274

standing in a graveyard in the cold and wet, blown by a teenager on the verge of competence with the notes flattened by the damp air and nervous breath control, the bugle produced a cracked sound which seemed to hang painfully about the young widows and sad men in uniform. I've not heard anything like it since. The squadron leader always read the same words in a dull monotone. Six times I heard it:

> They shall grow not old
> As we that are left grow old.
> Age shall not wither them
> Nor the years condemn.

There was one odd thing about the final burial. The dead man was another Irishman. His brother came across from Dublin in a uniform that most assumed was of the Irish Army. But I could see my father looking at him from time to time and there was a strange expression on his face, a kind of mild disdain. Later he told me why. The uniform was that of the IRA, illegal in his native country but not in England. It was as smart or smarter than any of the others at the funeral, with, if I remember rightly, badges of striking yellow and red. I could be wrong – it was a long time ago. Now whenever I see the balaclavas and the nailed baseball bats, I think of him with his carefully pressed best dress uniform, his upright bearing and the awkward look of a defiant adolescent who realised there might be a scene. But even though some of the others there knew what he was wearing, no one took it seriously. In 1968, all that was in the past.

For my father, and the others like him, the sandpit that they landed in was only a step away from mucking about with buckets and spades. These were men who still knew how to play. But because it was a military sport the Cold War had been fought out in parachuting long before it reached athletics or any other sport. The Americans and Russians were professionals. What they did was turn this play into work. What they did was turn it into war. It was only a few months after the Cuban Missile Crisis when we got to Germany for the Sixth World Parachuting Championship. The terror about Cuba was so great, so much a part of the air everyone breathed, that even children went to bed and lay awake dreading the end of the world, knowing that it could really happen, and at any time. All that's vanished now, even for the people who were there, as if suddenly every true believer woke up one day and all of them stopped believing in hell.

Even though things had calmed down by the time we arrived in Germany, the tensions were obvious even to a child. Competitors from the Eastern bloc were not allowed to speak to anyone from the West, and as I wandered about the enormous complex I was often eyed suspiciously by squat Russian apparatchiks with no necks. The championship was being held in Leutkirch, a small town set on the edge of a huge forest. On one side it was empty and flat, on the other the rising hills were covered in trees of a green so dark they were almost black. As night fell and the temperature dropped, the dirt-grey mist seeped down the conifers like a slow avalanche. It was in this most obscure of German towns, in this most obscure of recreations, that the idea of playfulness in sport would die. Not immediately, of course, but this was where the terminal disease began. This was where the virus took a hold.

The competition began with the team event, and after two days, with the Americans still to come, everyone in the Irish team was beside themselves at having split the favourites by taking second place behind the Russians. The team event involved all four jumping at the same time and attempting to hit a small red disc about six inches in diameter. This was at the centre of a sandpit divided by a large cross of white cloth. A top parachutist could expect to hit the red disc – a dead centre it was called – about four or five times a year. In the team event the distances of each member from the disc were added up and divided by four. The worst jump of the team from the three allowed could be discarded and the final score was based on the average of the two that remained.

We would lie on the short grass of the airfield during the endless pauses between the minutes of action, drinking incredibly cold Coca-Cola from those curvaceous bottles. Half-dozing, we'd wait for the drop. It is the *sounds* of parachuting that I think of now when I recall those days. The distant drone of aero engines slowly made its presence felt in waves, like sleep advancing on a tired child, gradually becoming a single, droning note. Searching the sky with shaded eyes, the soldiers, women, kids looked like the models for an inspirational piece of Soviet social realism. Fingers would point skywards when someone saw the plane. Then figures would fall: one, two, three, four. Then seconds later, the silence of the engines, cut before the men had jumped but oddly delayed by the slowness of the speed of sound to match the eye. Ten seconds would pass, then the parachutes would open, and, if conditions were right and the sleeve on the parachute deployed too soon, the canopy would crack like a wet towel flicked against a boy's damp skin. The coloured canopies, different for each team, produced an endless variety of electric nylon blues and greens and golds and blacks and whites, turning and swooping in the blue air. They'd line themselves up, like geese in flight, and from a distance they'd look slow and calm, but as they came in to land you'd see how fast they fell, calling aloud to get the order of landing right. Then came the swift approach; giant in size they

277

crashed into the pit, their legs outstretched, desperately trying to reach the mark with the crump of the sand as they hit, one, two, three, four, like hawks failing to retrieve a dive. Then came the judges with tapes and it was done. Back to another drink of Coke and the long and pleasantly boring wait.

The following day it was the Americans' turn to jump. Between the time they opened and the time they landed, some three and a half minutes later, it became obvious that not only was the competition already over but that the world had changed. For the style competition, because where you landed was immaterial, they had used the same single blank gore parachute that everyone used: a half globe of nylon with a panel missing, more or less depending on little more than guesswork, steered by two lines which when pulled distorted the way the air passed through the chute and allowed it to be steered with haphazard accuracy. The basic technology had barely changed in thirty years. All the competitors had gathered to see if the Americans could come up with something and at the last moment overtake the Russians. We watched as their chutes opened two thousand feet above our heads, and the numerous ways that nations have of expressing astonishment rippled across the crowd.

Instead of a parachute, they were suspended beneath what looked like hundreds of holes linked together by red and blue cloth with two panels on each side like earmuffs on a hat. They didn't turn but banked like aeroplanes, and instead of a rapid constant fall they seemed to be able to travel at will almost parallel to the ground beneath. One broke off and, impossibly, headed back into the wind that should have been driving him inescapably forward. Each new unprecedented trick brought gasps of wonder, as the Americans had known it would. They'd saved the best, or worst, till last. As they approached we could see that they were not so much hanging from this extraordinary construction as sitting in the harness like pilots in a plane. The reserve chutes, much smaller than a normal one, had been taken from their chests, where they were supposed to be, and put behind their necks as if on piggy back. They came in to land. Instead of simply riding the combination of gravity and air, they mastered it. They circled the pit above the open-mouthed watchers and seemed able to decide exactly when to come to earth. Then one by one, without effort, with none of that desperate, crashing stuff of reaching a foot towards the mark before their arse hit jarring sand at twenty miles an hour, they softly, accurately touched the ground and walked themselves to a stop. Two dead centres, and with the other two so close that even added together they were half the distance of the nearest Soviet. It was as if Achilles had produced a Gatling gun on the plains of Troy.

My father looked on entranced.

As for me, I learnt a history lesson there, that there are moments when what comes after is utterly different from what went before. In a German field, among men who played with forces more fundamental than fire, I watched Americans with flashy parachutes designed by computers meant to guide atomic missiles to Moscow or Peking exempt themselves from the whole business of slowly developing opposable thumbs and longer necks for reaching taller trees, and the endless hit-and-miss of mutant genes. For ever afterwards it gave me the sense that things could change no matter how fixed they seemed: technology could make redundant not just a skill, not just a life, but an entire world. It could do this in a couple of minutes. It could keep doing it. And my father wanted one.

Towards the end of a long day the wives and girl-friends would gather in groups to watch the last jump before the sun went down, waiting for husbands and lovers to return. They'd laugh, mocking their men while eyeing them with what I now realise was desire. The men would walk towards them, in fours or alone, their voices carrying through the still air, holding their parachutes cupped in front of them, spilling around their chests in red, white and blue, like women carrying too much washing made from brightly coloured silk. Then the men and women would split into couples and head towards their tents. Voices drifted into the gathering dark, the men teasing and the women laughing, waiting for something to happen. On the last night I simply watched them leave and turned back to watch the sun go down. As the air cooled, the hair stood up on my exposed arms as, behind me, the grey fog poured slowly through the trees. I waited for a long time, mournful, I don't know why, until I heard my mother's voice behind me.

'What are you up to?' she said gently.

'Nothing.'

'It's cold. It's time to come in.'

I stood up and we began to walk back, close but not touching.

'Can we afford it?'

'What? Oh, the parachute ... we'll have to see.'

'Will he start winning again if he gets it?'

She seemed taken aback by this and didn't answer for a moment. Then, 'I don't know, maybe. I don't know. Perhaps you should ask your father.'

'No, it's all right.'

The next day, as we walked to the prize-giving, Eichorn, the new world champion, came over to my father. 'Harper tells me you gonna buy a Para-Commander.'

'Yes, that's right. Someone's bringing it back from the States next month.'

The American nodded. 'I'll get Harper to send you

an invite to the US championship nex' July. You bring yo' PC an' I'll whip yo' ass.'

My father laughed.

'You take care, y'hear. That PC is some 'chute but it can be real mean sometimes. You saw what happen to Hampton. He mayn't be good as you are but he's still damn good.'

They talked on for a few minutes more then shook hands and parted with it clear that they were going to take each other on the following year. But Eichorn never made it. The new technology blurred the distinction between the inspired and the merely excellent. Though still the best, he was no longer indispensable. He was a helicopter pilot by training and a few months afterwards he had to stop competition parachuting for his first tour of duty in Vietnam. Later we heard he'd gone missing somewhere near Saigon during the Tet Offensive.

———

As soon as we got back to England my parents went to Barclays Bank to get a loan to buy the Para-Commander. They needed £250 to buy the whole rig, because its complexity required an entirely new system of expensive harnesses for it to be operated safely. They'd only had a bank account for six months, but they weren't naïve enough to tell the bank manager – who had to approve every loan by personal interview – what they wanted the money for; they told him it was for a car. But it was not an interview so much as an interrogation. My mother's subsequent fury at the humiliation never entirely died down. The manager seemed to regard their application as a moral affront. 'He looked down his nose at me, the creep,' she said that night. '"Can you really afford the repayments, Mrs McCarthy?"' she said, imitating the supercilious tone, the disdain. '"How dare you ask for such an amount, you common, working-class Irish person?"' He had not actually said this, it was understood, but this was what he had meant. He had calculated the repayments and their outgoings as if my mother were an idiot incapable of doing simple arithmetic. She was immensely proud of the way she handled the family accounts, and this was a grievous mortification. Worse was to come. The loan was refused.

That night my mother and father sat at the kitchen table trying to come up with the money. My father wanted to defy gravity, my mother the financial system as it puzzled its way into a new world by trying to hold onto the past with its corsets and squeezes and controls, not realising that money, too, was loosening its stays. Cash, as well, was about to torch its foundation garments. And the heat would be white, and very hot. And it would burn.

The special harness and reserve of the Para-Commander were well outside their reach but my mother scrounged through the various small savings schemes of which she was a member to find the £120 or so that they needed for the parachute alone. This was a phenomenal sum for them to find but slowly she trawled everything we had at home with a determination that made it seem unthinkable that she would fail. She buckled herself into her accounts. But more than just her pride was driving her: her desire for my father depended on feeding the visions he had. In the end it was for my father and what he meant to her that she amassed the money for the parachute from post office accounts, bits put by, the folded tenner in my father's wallet kept for emergencies and the policies taken out on us as babies for the funerals if we died. For the first time I was made aware of the heroic side of money, that my mother was a champion and that she fought for my father with what she had in her purse. Neither my brother nor I, even now, can understand how she gave the impression of having an endless supply of cash. It was difficult to understand because we had very little money. Much of my adult life has been spent with people who are good with money, both in the larger and the domestic sense, and some are tight and some are not. But while she had an exact knowledge of every penny – where it had come from, where it was, and where it was going – she used what she had so carefully hoarded to spoil us, her husband and – this, I suppose, is central – herself. There was always more, somehow, than you expected. We inhabited, all of us, a world pregnant with treats, even if it was only a cream turnover or a second bottle of Coke. It was more specific than generosity. I suppose the word I'm looking for is love.

A few weeks later, after a training exercise in California, my father brought the canopy back with him. He mastered the PC quickly and had an extraordinary ability to play off its sometimes outrageous capacity to forgive with its sudden and terrifying intolerance of the slightest mistake when used without the special equipment denied us by the manager of Barclays Bank. Even in clumsy hands it could perform wonders, but at other times using it in a way entirely suitable for other parachutes could produce a sudden and total collapse of the canopy.

He practised with it at every opportunity into a warm late autumn. All through the winter whenever the cloud base was high enough he jumped, learning its virtues and vices. As summer came in and the days lengthened, he jumped after work. I'd hear him arriving home at ten o'clock and would creep downstairs to have a cup of tea with them both and eat from his plate as he told my mother about the evening jump. Often we'd go with him and you could instantly recognise which one he was as the chutes deployed. The others would fall in their predictable descents but he would wheel and bank, turn into the wind, away from the target and back. It was rare that he was more than fifty centimetres away from the red circle and more and more consistently he'd put his foot on the dead centre once a day and sometimes twice.

In early August, a month before his trip to compete in the US championship, he was booked to jump at Biggin Hill, an RAF base where there was to be a celebration of the Battle of Britain. A crowd of two hundred thousand traffic-jammed their way onto the enormous airfield where Tannoys in all their metallic, railway-station incomprehensibility signalled the start and end of every act: Vulcans like flabby Concordes V-shaped their way across the sky; silver Electric lightnings broke the speed of sound above our heads; snatches of music from the military bands mingled with the sound of automatic blanks from a pretend assault on plasterboard citadels by men in khaki hamming it up in the centre of the field.

Half-way through the afternoon we scanned the blue sky for the Rapide; two hundred thousand faces, hands above eyes, watching for the fall. And then it came: one, two, three, four. The bodies fell, picking up speed and size. We counted them down to ten. Three of them opened; one kept falling. Thirteen, fourteen ...

'No,' my mother said, softly. Then she started to run. I stayed where I was, watching the fall. Others began to run, passing me by. It had happened before, these lengthier drops when something went wrong. Still he kept falling. There was a movement of arms, a twist of his body; the stop.

My father was dead.

Few deaths, I imagine, are so abrupt and absolute, yet give the man who dies such time to consider the relationship between the awful mass of the world to which he is falling and the mysterious fundamental force pulling him to his most sudden death. There are many horrible ways for people to die: death by fire, by water or by slow disease. But what is so terrible about these deaths is the pain and suffering that accompany an end that is the logical result of what is killing them. The inhalation of water, the burning of skin, the wasting of a body is dreadful, in itself to be avoided. But for my father, and for my father's son, the free fall was the point. I know that it served him right. By now having taken the plunge so many more times than him, I know that men were not made for falling, to be without weight, and that there can be no complaints for what was freely chosen. But even now I ask myself what was responsible for his death. Animal spirits? Class? The new technology? All of these, certainly. But in the end it was the banking policies of the age that killed him. Money that broke him. The squeeze on credit robbed me of my dad. He fell to earth because of economics.

It's over thirty years ago but it still surprises me how walking past a church tower or some pillared monument can take me back; still watching him balanced precisely on his hands in the tall and leaning distance of the Tower of Pisa; or how, early in the morning, just between waking and sleeping, the sound of the central heating coming on becomes the intermittent drone of a Rapide, and I can see the faces turned upward into the sun and the wide expanse of short grass moved by the wind.

And my father, falling.

SECRET VOICES

You may be familiar with Kant's remark that out of the crooked timber of humanity no straight thing was ever made. But what if, instead of a lament, we treat this merely as an observation? It would follow that perfection for human beings is an irrelevance, something that would break or split. Abolish notions of the straight, the level, the vertical and rectilinear and understand that perfectionism is a blasphemy against the human; idealism is the enemy of life. Elegance, said Einstein, is for tailors. Perfection for human beings is deadly or banal: it ends in a gulag; or a Barbie doll.

Louis Bris, *The Wisdom of Crocodiles*

Winnicott tried to open his eyes. He was desperate to stay asleep but sure that he had to get up for an important appointment. He forced his eyes open but once he saw the tiny room with its white walls and bright light he panicked. Was he awake? Where is this? It is the toilet on the third floor he told himself. How long he had been unconscious? He waited for a few moments and then got up slowly, unlocked the door and came out into the washroom. He looked at himself: white, gaunt, haunted, the bright light thinning the hair on his head.

His stomach heaved, then his chest. Something surged into his throat as if it were alive. He staggered back against the wall, cried out in terror and began to speak: '*You're going to have to let me tell them,*' said the woman's voice. *'I'm sorry, but this is not the kind of thing I can keep to myself any more. I know the ...'* The voice stopped, trying to find the right word, frustrated as it struggled to do so. *' ... design . . end ... consequence ... the **meaning** of life.'*

It was gone. He stood there for five minutes staring at his reflection in the mirror. He looked like a man of eighty. He tried using his fingers as a comb, pushing and scrabbling and rubbing his hair into a presentable state.

Slowly he walked out of the washroom and past Lucy, still huddled at her desk with the boy from the IT department. He swallowed hard and went back into his office.

There was a brief pause and then McCarthy spoke. 'Howard just had a thought ... we waited for you.'

How long?

Cornish began to talk enthusiastically. 'I was just thinking it through. I mean, obviously the point is not to get caught – to bury whatever you've done so deeply no one could ever really find out what you'd been up to. The thing is, when you're dealing with large sums to insure an oil rig, say, and it explodes, OK, there are advantages to that. You could make big money on a commission because there's a lot of money involved. But it also means that when whoever you've deceived has got to pay out – what? – three thousand million pounds, they take a damned good look at the way the contract was arrived at before they pay up. If you've screwed the figures they'll find it. OK, you could take the risk that an oil rig won't explode. But there's a better way – and I don't think there's much chance of getting caught.'

A mobile trilled. Gasping with irritation, Cornish opened his briefcase and switched it off. The interruption had put him off his stride.

'Sorry,' he said. 'Where was I? Right. No one would believe you if you calculated unrealistic odds, but with the kind of money involved here you only need to shave a few per cent to undercut your rivals by enormous sums, but you get the commission on the whole lot. That's if it's just an assessor and actuary fraud. Anyway ...' his face creased under the effort, like an explorer confronted with the choice of a dozen paths, 'let's keep it simple. An actuary can calculate the odds in different ways perfectly legitimately. I mean, it's just a form of gambling. You can use – within limits – the figures optimistically or pessimistically. There are different figures you can use particularly when the data is limited – there's not much in the way of experience to go on when it comes to really big disasters. So ... all you do is consistently interpret the odds at a realistic but always optimistic level. Your calculations show the rig is less likely to blow up than other actuaries' more pessimistic calculations.'

'Wouldn't it be obvious that you'd always done that?' said McCarthy.

Cornish seemed deflated and said nothing for a moment. 'No, think about it,' he said. 'They might suspect ... *would* suspect. But what could they prove? That's the issue, isn't it, for you? You've got to prove a guilty intent. That's right?'

McCarthy nodded.

'How are you going to prove that – if all the figures are realistic. I mean prove it in a court of law.' He laughed. 'So, first the disaster's got to happen – and it might not – then they've got to find the figures are a bit odd. They probably will – but they might not either. Then you've got to prove beyond reasonable doubt that they did this with the intent to defraud.' He grunted. 'I'll have to think about it.' He stood up. 'I'll be in touch.' He was about to move to the door when he stopped and said to McCarthy, 'You know, if you were clever and it was the right kind of risk, maybe, you could even avoid suspicion when they checked you. I mean, what *I'd* do is throw in a few unusually pessimistic figures as well, and some middling ones. You'd still be able to come out optimistic – unrealistically so in the end. But if you camouflaged it well enough it wouldn't even be suspicious. After all, the calculation could even be right – actuaries make guesses. We're not talking about certainty here, just probabilities.' He smiled. 'This is beginning to make my head spin. I'll talk to you.' He looked over at Winnicott, white and vacant. 'Nice to have met you, Mr Winnicott.'

'I'll show you out, Howard,' said McCarthy and followed after him.

Later that afternoon Winnicott was in his office distractedly attempting to solve E13. He couldn't settle to work. He was tense and bewildered at what was happening to him, but unable to think calmly, so it was better not to think at all for the moment. *It's probably the blow to the head. Thirteen letters after E in the alphabet is R. You came back too quickly. ER stands for Elizabeth Regina. Queen Elizabeth has fourteen letters. You need a holiday. Remember to check the postal district E13. Can't remember it. Why can't I? Just wait and it will stop. A few more days. If it happens again ...*

Lucy walked in and put several papers on his desk.

'Thank you, Lucy,' he said without looking up, hoping she would take it as a signal not to interrupt.

'Pat Shepherd rang to cancel your meeting with Boyd Gribben.'

Winnicott sighed with irritation. It was the second cancellation.

'She was very apologetic.'

'Please make another one,' said Winnicott, almost inaudible with exhaustion. Then irritation flared up in him. 'And you can make it as clear as you like that I don't want to hear this a third time.'

She was pleased at this robust response, and left the office full of enthusiasm for the phone call ahead.

Geoff Healey was in a bad temper. Roache sat on the other side of the office listening to the radio. It was Virgin. Healey knew this not because he was a frequent listener to commercial radio but because of a deep-seated insecurity on the part of the DJs. They knew the audience *loved* Virgin Radio, but they seemed convinced that most of the listeners were dreadfully afflicted by a medical condition that gave them the memories of goldfish. If not reminded every five seconds that they were, in fact, *already* tuned in to their favourite radio station, their endlessly amnesiac congregation would forget and might at any time twiddle the dial and tragically vanish in search of the beloved station they were, in fact, already listening to. Healey was about to tell Roache to switch it off when a brief commercial for the news at mid-day interrupted the prattle and endless songs by Phil Collins, an artist for whom Healey had long harboured a deep loathing. To his surprise, the second most important item – the lead being an exclusive on whether or not the station's owner was really having sex with one of the Spice Girls – concerned the fact that the new Governor of the Bank of England was about to announce his first decision on interest rates. 'What will Charley decide?' asked the DJ chummily. 'Will it be up – or will it be down? Find out the good or bad news for your credit card at twelve today. Virgin – first with all the news that matters.'

Healey's mobile rang. 'Switch that bloody thing off,'

he said to Roache as he picked it up. 'Healey speaking.'

'Geoff, it's Snowy here. Look, we've just had a call from a woman who lived in the flat opposite Maria Vaughan. She says she saw her outside in the street two days after she disappeared. She was with a man and they were having a big row.'

'What's her number?'

'Seven. Same block. Phone number ...'

Two hours later, Healey and Roache were back at the station going through the statement they'd been given by Maria Vaughan's neighbour, and file checking for anyone who might answer the description of the man she'd been arguing with in the street; but there was no denying it could have been Steven Grlscz.

'Do you want me to recheck the dates with Grlscz? See what he's got to say for himself?'

'No.'

Roache was surprised. 'You're just going to put him straight on an identity parade?'

'I want to think about it. The problem is that the woman didn't get all that good a look, whatever she says. The description of the man is pretty vague and she only caught a few seconds of the row they were having. More to the point, she didn't see Maria's face. She just recognised her voice and that it looked like her from the back.'

Roache looked at him slyly. 'Did you notice who else fitted the description she gave us?'

Healey realised he was being teased. 'It wasn't much of a description, was it?'

Roache smiled. 'No, it wasn't – but even so. I mean, after all, it could have been a description of me, but it couldn't have been one of you. Still can't think who else it could be?'

'No.'

'George Winnicott.'

'You're kidding?'

'No. Look at it. About six foot, dark hair, between thirty-five and forty-five, long, thin, face, well-dressed.' Roache smirked. 'Makes you think.'

This was alarming. Healey was sure Winnicott couldn't have been involved. It was impossible. But then a flicker of doubt. It's never *entirely* impossible. Of course it was nonsense. All this could do was alienate Winnicott when he might need him on his side to keep his wife out of trouble. On the other hand, Roache was right. The description *did* fit him. He couldn't just ignore it, could he? What if he was involved? Failing to look into it when it had been brought to his attention would be wrong – pure and simple. He sighed and looked at Roache. 'So what you're suggesting is that I bring in the former Head of the Anti-Terrorist Squad, now Director of the Fraud Secretariat, and stick him in a line-up just in case he might have done away with his goddaughter?'

'There are loads of photos of Winnicott around. Why don't we just show her a dozen different pictures of slim, tall, dark-haired men and put one of him in it. Simple. We could stick in one of Vaughan's psychiatrist as well – what's his name? Hendrix. He fits the description pretty well, too. Nine times out of ten the murderer is well known to the victim. In fact, why don't we put Hendrix in the line-up?' Roache smiled unpleasantly. 'Nobody will kick up a fuss if we annoy a psychiatrist or whatever the bloody hell he calls himself.'

It was with a mixture of the deepest trepidation and an emotion she could not identify that Jane Healey walked down from Holborn tube towards Trevor Hat's bookshop to begin her new career in pornography. She arrived just before nine-thirty and was spotted by a young man of twenty-odd with short hair and a bad complexion. He opened the door for her deferentially. Hat was on the other side of the shop looking out of the window with Gordon and another young man of twenty-five or so, neatly dressed in a green Lacoste T-shirt and a pair of sharply creased trousers. Hat was passing judgement on the women walking past the shop.

'That one on the left has got a sweet little bottom but, dear oh dear, look at the one on the right. Last time I saw a mouth like that it had a hook in it. Look at her nose – it's like a cormorant.' He shouted at her, merely for the benefit of the others because the glass was thick. 'Hey, darling, how much do you charge to haunt a house, then?' The others smirked. The boy standing next to Jane shuffled awkwardly. 'Uh ... boss,' he said at last.

Hat turned round. 'Ah, Mrs Percy, good to see you. Let me introduce my lads. Lads, this is our new book-keeper, Mrs Percy. You will be courteous to her because she is going to ensure you all get paid on time and that shitehawk Cronin gets off my back. Any one of them gives you any cheek, Mrs Percy, just say the word. I'll put his lippy arse through the blender.' The three looked uncomfortable, as if they suspected the threat was not metaphorical. 'The one next to you is Kevin.' Kevin nodded shyly. 'The smart one here is Neil, and you're already an intimate of Gordon's, eh?' He leered at the uneasy-looking Gordon. 'Right then, your office. If you'd step this way.' He headed for the stairs. Jane followed, her stomach plunging as if in a lift.

He talked over his shoulder at her as he went down the wide stairs. 'I forgot to mention that the office is through the other side of the basement, so you'll have to come back and forth sometimes when the customers are in. That won't bother you?'

'No,' she said, as they reached the floor. It was L-shaped, with magazines on floor-to-ceiling shelves completely covering the walls and with another smaller rack in the middle of the room facing both ways. There were an assortment of videotapes in glass cabinets down the stairwell, but she'd only taken in two of the covers, one of a woman vainly attempting to get an erection whose head was the size of a lampshade into her mouth and another of two women, fully clothed, wrestling. He unlocked a door in the side of the room. It was a small, sparsely furnished office with natural light coming from a thick pavement window in the ceiling. He took her through the various ledgers for the next half hour, maintaining a quiet, even gentle, tone.

'Do you want to discuss the tax matters?'

'Oh ... not just now. Get settled in and we'll talk about it at the end of the week. Friday's OK, is it?'

'Yes. Fine.'

Kevin walked through the door. 'There's a secretary on the phone. Says the managing director of Electric Blue wants a word.'

Hat looked up thoughtfully from a ledger. 'Tell him to fuck off,' he said pleasantly. Jane noticed that Kevin showed no surprise at this and quickly left.

'The washroom's in there, by the way,' he said, gesturing at what looked like a broom cupboard.

'Won't my coming and going frighten your customers?'

'It depends what you were thinking of doing to them, I suppose. What did you have in mind?'

'When I came down here by accident once ...'

'Yeah, Gordon told me you were in here buying. We give a staff discount,' he said. 'More than generous.'

'The customers who saw me looked a bit put off. Ashamed, I suppose.'

'Well, you won't need to come in and out that often,

and they don't look up much when they start on the magazines. Half of them are in a world of their own. Clear as mud now, is it?' he said, nodding at the books on the table.

'It might take a little while. Your Mrs Fitzgerald seems to have had her own system. I'm sure I'll manage.'

'Great! Best be off. God knows what those sponge-brains are up to. Call me if you need anything. I'll get Kevin to bring you a coffee.'

'Thank you.'

He went out, leaving the door ajar. As he reached the top of the stairs she heard him bellowing at Gordon for not having the initiative to open the shop. She shut the door, deciding that whatever it was she was doing here could wait, and turned to the accounts.

After an hour she revised her opinion of the difficulty of dealing with Trevor Hat's financial affairs. Her predecessor had devised an entirely eccentric way of tracking the financial doings of the business. Jane was used to dealing with the most complicated forms of accounting, but whatever Mrs Fitzgerald had been up to was still opaque. She had devised a system that only nodded in the direction of conventional ways of accounting.

'Keeping busy?' Hat put his head around the door, letting in the sound of customers from the next room.

'This is going to take a while, I'm afraid.'

'I'm sure you'll sort it out. Did you get your coffee?'

'Ah.' She realised as she expressed hesitancy that someone was going to collect one of Hat's bollockings. Her decision to lie was pre-empted by Hat shouting over his shoulder for Kevin, who appeared with an appalled look on his face.

'Anything wrong, Trevor?'

'I told you,' said Hat softly, 'to bring Mrs Percy a cup of coffee and you didn't do it, did you, Kevin?'

'No, Trevor.'

'Why was that, Kevin? Why did you deliberately disobey a direct instruction from the person who pays your wages? Why do you insult me every fucking moment of the fucking day?'

'Sorry, Trevor.'

'Don't tell me you're sorry. Don't insult me again, boy. How old are you? Well?'

'Nineteen.'

'Nineteen ...' he said and repeated it, ' ... nineteen ...' as if he could barely believe the existence of such a number. 'You're nineteen and you're insulting me every fucking day.' His voice changed down a gear.

'Give me the knife, Kevin.'

'What?' said the startled boy.

'Give me the knife.'

'What knife, Trevor?'

Hat looked at him, mystified. 'You're telling me that you've decided to be nineteen and to insult Trevor Hat every day of your working life and you haven't got a knife?'

'No, Trevor.'

'Then I forgive you.'

'What?'

'I forgive you, and I forgive you because you've got diminished responsibility. You must've been starved of oxygen at birth ... WELL?' he screamed.

'Yes, Trevor.'

Trevor grabbed him by the front of his shirt and slammed him against the wall. 'Now go and get Mrs Percy a cup of coffee. Do you take milk, Mrs Percy?' he said, through gritted teeth.

'A little, please,' said Jane. She had no idea what else to do other than act as if nothing unusual were happening.

'And do you take sugar?'

'One, thank you.'

'There you are, then, Kevin. A cup of coffee with a little milk and one spoonful of sugar. Do you think you can manage that?'

'Yes, Trevor.'

'Because if you can't you only have to tell me, Kevin.'

'Yes, Trevor,' said Kevin, wild-eyed with horror. Hat seemed to feel that Kevin had fallen sufficiently far down whatever gradient of humiliation he felt appropriate and let go of his shirt. He reached behind the boy's skinny back and shoved him towards the door. He turned to Jane. 'I'm sorry about that.'

'I thought you were going to disembowel him.'

'Not that,' he said, impatient. 'I'm sorry about the coffee.'

'Well, it wasn't that important.'

Hat breathed in with an air of injured hauteur. 'This is a service industry. My customers come to me for one reason. I'm not joking. It's the service. They can get harder stuff in Soho. Give me five minutes and twenty pounds and I'll be back with things it'd sicken you to look at. And I could exchange it for ten pound a throw. The real thing, even in Soho, the home of the rip-off. But my shop is always full and theirs aren't. It's always full upstairs because I give them what they want up there: good books, interesting books, I read them myself, at a good price. And down here I give them what they want as well. They don't want to be ashamed. I see them coming out of a nasty sex shop doorway in Soho like little rabbits. They go in ashamed and they come out even more ashamed than when they went in. Would you go to Marks & Spencer if you were ashamed to go in when you could go somewhere else and not be ashamed?'

'I don't suppose so.'

'Of course you wouldn't. But when they come into Hat's, they come into a proper bookstore with good books on display. So they're not ashamed to come in and go out. My ambition used to be to make this place the Marks & Spencer of adult erotica. Not any more. *They* forgot the customer is king. At Hat's the customer is *always* king. I'll give them total quality fucking management. At Hat's we don't rip 'em off, we don't charge 'em a quid for two baking potatoes wrapped up in a bit of foam and clingfilm. That's when the rot set in at Marks & Sparks. I let my customers look at the magazines, let them see what they're buying so they won't be disappointed when they get home and they'll come back to Hat's and buy again. Repeat business, a customer base, that's what it's all about. You want to see some real retail management? I'm not putting you on, you just keep your eyes open.'

Keeping her eyes open, however, was exactly what she intended to do. In practice it was not that easy. Attempting to reconstruct Mrs Fitzgerald's peculiar ways of thinking about the world of numbers involved too much time.

At the end of the day she would often browse around the bookshelves upstairs, a part of Hat's business that returned a solid profit as far as she could tell from the badly-kept ledgers. Despite the usually interesting selections, she was not really looking at the books. She moved around the shelves for ten minutes or so watching the men as they went down and came up from the basement. Despite several of these vigils, she'd failed to work out what they had in common. Certainly it was not their appearance. Some were badly dressed in cheap suits with cheap briefcases in which to hide their purchases; and they had poor haircuts and worn skin with a clear sense of defeat about them. Others were young, good-looking and even stylishly dressed. There were at least as many men in their twenties and thirties as there were the middle-aged types she had expected. Oddly, there were few men over fifty. Sometimes there were women accompanied by men; on rare occasions a woman came on her own.

In general, however, the unexpected difficulty involved in sorting out the tangled accounts meant that she had to concentrate on the work she was being paid for and opportunities to observe the men in the next room were rare, though she had no clear idea what she was looking for anyway. Trevor's three assistants weren't going to be of much help: whenever she tried to question them they either went blank or just parroted what she took to be Trevor's opinions.

'They're all gonks,' said Neil, with total contempt, 'ugly bastards who can't get a real woman. I'm sorry I have to look at their ugly mugs all day.' Gordon joined in the disapproval. 'Thank Christ they've usually got their disgusting noses in one of the mags. What a bunch of wankers.'

She realised that Neil's dismissal was partly for her benefit, that he was anxious to disassociate himself in her eyes from the men next door. Why this might be so puzzled her, but she began to suspect that he was not just being chirpy, he was chatting her up in a mild way. She was aware, for example, that when she bent forward to pick up the cup of coffee that he, rather than Kevin, now usually brought her, he would always try to look down the front of her blouse. Perhaps, she thought, it was just habit; he'd probably done the same to Mrs Fitzgerald, who had been in her mid-sixties when she died. Now that she looked at him he was quite a handsome boy. In his early twenties with a moustache, a wispy, unconvincing attempt to appear older. He dressed carefully but his shirts, always worn outside his trousers and always immaculately pressed, were horribly ornate. His hair was cut too severely, with a kind of circular fringe that did nothing for his best feature: his dark brown eyes.

As it turned out, Gordon had definitely not borrowed his opinions about the shop's customers from
Trevor, or at least had not borrowed them in the right
way. One Friday evening about three weeks after she'd
started at Hat's she had stayed behind to start looking
over Trevor's tax affairs. She had left the door open
and could see Gordon sitting behind the tall desk in
the bookshop overseeing the customers. They were
two deep, sometimes three, because it was the weekend and, presumably, this was the way many of them
wound down from the rigours of the previous five
days. She moved closer to the door to spy on them. It
was so crowded that a few stood forlornly in the middle
of the room unable to reach the magazines because of
the wall of men in front of them blocking their access.
They just stood there, looking at the covers that now
mocked them. They became increasingly awkward, as
if not doing what they had come to and yet being so
close to doing it made them painfully aware of the
indignity they were inflicting on themselves. A place
at the wall was clearly precious and not to be given up
unless a place nearer to where they wanted to go could
be swapped for the space they already occupied. A
kind of dance emerged in which those at the wall
would swap with one another in such a way as to keep
out those behind them who had nothing to offer in
return for a place. The intense overcrowding seemed
to clarify something she had begun to notice as she
walked up and down between the two floors and
peeked from behind her door. There was some kind of
search going on. When it was crowded, the men had to
start wherever a space was available – say, the section
devoted to women with large breasts, or leather and
rubber wear. They would then move around the room,
sometimes missing out a section in which they had no
interest, but generally scanning the whole collection.
Each magazine was examined quickly, but with great

care. So careful were they that if they missed a page, they would go back and check it. There were therefore few quick visits. It became clear after she saw them going through this intricate ritual on so many occasions that a specific search was going on, as if on a previous visit they had left an object of immense value in one of the magazines: money, a letter of significance or incriminating evidence. There was no contact between the customers, no one said anything or acknowledged the presence of another except in the peculiar shuffle, like bees signalling the presence of water to the hive, that indicated they wanted to swap places. The men trapped behind would try to take advantage of their movement but would usually be frustrated. Those at the wall seemed as disciplined at holding the line as Roman soldiers in a phalanx. These were professionals.

'Come on, gentlemen,' sneered Gordon loudly, 'make your selections – this isn't a library.' But it *was*, thought Jane, it was like a reference library in an ancient university packed with scholars searching for a reference whose source was on the tip of their tongue. And it was the quiet of dedication, desperate though it was, that Gordon had brutalised. As he spoke there was an almost universal start, as of rabbits at an unfamiliar noise. Immediately the room began to break up. Some grabbed books and rushed to buy, but the ones he had scared most left immediately, looking away from him as if anxious that he should not remember them. Suddenly Trevor thundered down the stairs, Kevin at his back.

'I want you,' said Trevor, clearly angry. He grabbed Gordon by the elbow and pulled him towards Jane's office, so swiftly that she barely had time to sit down.

Trevor marched in dragging the white-faced Gordon behind him. He pushed him to the other wall. 'Sorry, Mrs Percy, but this pony-tailed bastard is trying to

destroy my business and I want to know why. Well?'
he yelled at Gordon.

'What have I done?' wailed the desperate Gordon

'UN-BE-LIEV-ABLE!' screamed Trevor. 'Are you
fucking stupid, or what? No one ever – EVER! – tells
my customers to hurry up. Do you savvy? Do you?'

'Yes, Trevor,' said Gordon, shaking his head to
underline his total surrender.

'This is a *real* shop, dickhead, and I don't want you
turning it into a sleazy porn outfit run by fucking
pimps who think it's smart to turn their customers
over by ripping them off and treating them with contempt. Is that what you're trying to do? Because if you
are, you know where the fucking door is.' Gordon
started to speak but Trevor seemed to regard his ability not to drop dead on the spot as a deliberately
provocative act of outrageous insubordination. 'Don't
insult me!' screamed Trevor. 'Get out!'

Gordon, now gopher-eyed with terror, fled, melting
around the formidable figure of his boss without oblig-
ing him to move. When he had gone Jane, appalled but
now secure that Hat would not speak to her in this
way, felt it safe enough to point out how crowded the
basement had been. Trevor's reply was calm and
polite. 'Don't think I haven't tried to explain. I try to
give these boys the benefits of my philosophy, but they
never listen. It drives me crazy. I learned to stop using
my wide-boy routines with the customers years ago.
On my own I might add – I didn't have anyone to
inspire me.' This was said with a mixture of indignation and loss. 'But I tell them every day: your
customer is king. He may also be a miserable little
wanker but if he wasn't you wouldn't have a job. But
does it go in? No.'

'But surely it *was* too crowded,' said Jane, perplexed at his obvious concern over customers he
always spoke of with unmitigated contempt. 'And

302

they weren't buying much. He only said it wasn't a library.'

'Oh,' said Trevor with distaste, 'that's what he said, was it? Lippy bastard.'

'You didn't know?'

He looked at her with tolerant condescension. 'It doesn't matter what he said. I knew everything I needed to know by a trail of gonks coming out of the basement instead of a trail of gonks going down – the way it should be on a Friday at six forty-five. It was like the retreat from fucking Moscow up there. There were ... what? ... fifteen customers out of there in two and a half minutes. I lost eighty or ninety quid because of that bird-brained pillock Gordon.'

'But they weren't buying anything, most of them,' she said, bewildered.

He breathed out heavily in exasperation. 'Look, you're supposed to be an expert with numbers. I've got it all worked out. I did it years ago. I timed the gonks for a week, y' know, to find out how long an average customer took to buy a mag. Put it this way, for every twenty minutes browsing, they buy one mag. I've brought the buying time down over the years – it used to be more like twenty-seven minutes. Anyway, the more twenty-minute periods you pack into a day the more you sell. And you don't sell magazines by frightening the gonks or making them feel ashamed. Would you buy your clothes at a shop where they made you feel ashamed? Would you go back? I know, I already asked you before.'

'They look ashamed to me,' she said.

'Of course they're ashamed. So they bloody should be – but it's my job to make 'em feel as good about being here as I can. Then they'll buy more.'

'Like Marks & Spencer.'

'You may laugh,' he said quietly, 'but it's just the same. They don't care about their customers at Marks

& Spencer. If they *cared*, they'd all be social workers or have buggered off to Calcutta to join up with Mother Teresa's mob. If they really cared about their customers they wouldn't rip them off just because there are enough dickbrains wandering around the aisles without the sense to realise that a pound for two baking potatoes wrapped in cling film and foam is fucking daylight robbery. What they care about is their customers' money. But they forgot that people aren't totally stupid even when they're being led by the dick, like here. People get fed up of being taken for granted. Marks & Spencer thought that just because some of their customers were stupid enough to want to pay fifty pence for a fucking potato, then fuck 'em, that's what we'll do. And look what happened. Hero to fucking zero in a couple of years. So we treat our customers with respect even if the dodgy little creeps don't deserve it. Only M & S don't have to put up with gits like Gordon.' He paused and when he spoke again it was in a mildly inquisitive tone as if the previous ten minutes had been utterly erased from his memory. 'How's it going with the books?'

'These figures are peculiar,' said Jane. 'I can't make them out yet.'

Trevor sucked his teeth and wiped his hands over his scalp. 'Bloody hell, don't tell me old Ma Fitzgerald had her fingers in the till. It'd destroy my faith in human nature.'

'Really.'

'You think I don't have any?' said Trevor. 'I know you think I'm just a lowlife with a porn shop and a bad temper,' he winked at her, 'but I'm not all bad.'

'Perhaps I should ask Gordon what *he* thinks.'

Trevor laughed and turned to go then changed his mind and turned back. 'You don't think she *was* ripping me off, do you?'

'I don't know. I've got no evidence either way. I just can't work out how she got to some of these figures. I will though.'

Trevor sighed. 'Well, let me know when you've got something definite. I'd like to talk to you about the tax next week, if that's OK.'

'Of course.'

He opened the door and went out, bumping into the unfortunate Kevin as he did so. For one moment it looked as if Trevor was going to eviscerate him with his bare hands.

'Why are you so fucking clumsy? What's the matter with you? Last night you tried to set fire to me with a match and now you keep walking into me. Do you think I work a hundred hours a week for you to walk into me? Do you?'

'No, Trevor.'

The trio of Gordon, Neil, and Kevin seemed more or less permanent, but to be fully staffed the shop needed five or even six to run the shifts involved in being open for sixteen hours a day, and though this was Trevor's base he also had to keep an eye on his other shops. He filled the gaps with several OAP cronies, who were familiar with the routines and who were treated with respect, and a collection of casuals who barely lasted the week. Even if they were capable, they were endlessly scapegoated for everything that went wrong and most got fed up or were kicked out. One, Martin, a pale-looking seventeen-year-old, had been the butt of a particularly unpleasant outburst for having given the wrong change to a customer who had protested to Trevor. Martin, who was usually given the menial tasks of tidying the shelves, had been told to man the till when Gordon had called in sick. Trevor had ignored his attempts to refuse. When the customer had gone he turned on the terrified boy and demanded an explanation. Martin started to cry, which hadn't bothered Trevor at all. When he admitted that he could not read nor add up, Trevor changed his attitude immediately.

He's as arbitrary as a tribal god, thought Jane, when Kevin told her the story next day.

Trevor assigned Gordon, who had dropped out after a year of university, to teach Martin to read. Every evening for twenty minutes after closing, Trevor would restack and tidy the rows of magazines and sweep the floor while a reluctant Gordon would instruct the puzzled Martin in the storage room with the door open so Trevor could check that his generosity was not being taken advantage of. This was a matter about which he was deeply vigilant.

Trevor would call over his shoulder to the attendant Kevin while he kept an ear open on the lesson.

'BIG ONES!' he would shout to Kevin. 'OVER 40.'

'See ... the train ... John.'

'See the train, *Janet*,' corrected the reluctant Gordon.

'See ... the train ... Janet.'

'A-CUP HONEYS! COME ON, KEVIN. FUCKING WAKE UP!'

'See ... the snow ... Janet,' misread Martin.

'See the snow, *John* ,' corrected Gordon again.

'RUSTLER! PENTHOUSE! Quickly. QUICKLY! WHEN I ASK FOR SOMETHING I WANT IT AND I WANT IT NOW!'

When the terrified Kevin scurried over with whatever magazines he had called for, Trevor spoke softly to him as if he was in bewildered pain whose terrible effects he was stoically attempting to control. 'When I want something, Kevin, I want it ... and if you don't want to give it to me you know where the fucking door is. Do you UNDERSTAND?'

'Yes, Trevor.'

'See the train in the snow, Janet ... says John.'

'Good.'

'I like snow ... Janet ... I like trains.' Martin, realising from Gordon's expression that he had made a mistake, looked miserable.

Gordon sighed. 'It's "I like snow, *John*. I like trains",' he intoned wearily.

'I like snow ... John ... I like trains.'

A fractal is a pattern in which the overall pattern can be found repeated in miniature within that pattern; and within that miniature version yet another smaller version of the pattern can be found. Unless you are told the scale of what you're looking at, it is impossible to tell the difference between a photograph of a rocky desert landscape and another of a microscopic particle of dust. The list of known fractal systems in nature is long and growing rapidly: coastlines, clouds, feathers, forest fires, mountains, sneezes, the universe, broccoli, the heart, the lungs, the nervous system. In effect there is no more complexity in the shape of all the galaxies than there is in the shape of a cauliflower. There are no sub-plots in this natural world; in the story of the fractal universe everything is as important as everything else. Another fractal structure is the snowflake. As water cools, ice crystals form, binding the water molecules in an open lattice of puckered layers. At some temperatures, the snowflake that is formed is made of long hexagonal needles. At other temperatures, the snowflake grows in plates, resulting in fern-like crystals and dendrites. And the more humid, the more feathery the crystals will appear. This might help to explain why it is that since the first snowflake fell, quite a long time ago now, not one of them has been the same.

On platform two of Marylebone Station, a new sleek diesel, turbocharged, gently hums to itself. Inside the carriage it is clean, the seats spacious and comfortable, with lumbar supports adequate to the buttressing of many aching commuter backs. This train will leave on time. Only a few years ago, you would have had to endure the smell of damp, a heater dispersing a benzene-scented too-hot air, decaying coverings to the seats and frequent cancellations because the diesels were too old to work.

The station itself has had a face-lift, too. Once a decaying reminder of Victorian ambition allowed to lapse, it now has marbled floors, and quiet machines to keep them free of dirt, monitors to give you information that is up-to-date. There are no kiosks selling dried-up sausage rolls in Cellophane grown brittle through being kept for many hours in glass and stainless steel; now there are food halls, carefully lit and carefully designed, with the shop assistants and the food to match. Papaya, Class I Mauritius, the chewiest of breads, exotic-flavoured drinks; and coffee: latte, mocha, with a twist or double fun, and neat, attractive people serving them.

Waiting for his train to leave, George Winnicott sits in his comfortable seat looking pale and distant. This train has been the subject of much mockery. Three weeks into their winter start the snow had fallen. Within hours the pride of British Rail – free of delay, incompetence and grime – had stopped, defeated by a December fall barely thicker than a dusting of sugar on a cake. It was the wrong kind of snow, they said, for England: not only rare, unique. The wrong snow, the wrong snow, endlessly repeated in the press, in sniggering asides, weary exchanges, tired, cynical, full of hysterical contempt. A legend.

The Inuit have twenty words for snow, or is it forty or a hundred? At any rate, we know it's quite a lot. They also have a word for the wrong kind. I don't know what it is, but I bet they have one; and also I bet they wouldn't laugh at a bright train stalled by the unpredictability of matted crystals formed at minus 32°F on minute particles of dust locked in a chaos of pyramids and prisms and stars, and each one different as a fingerprint, each one wrong. It's easy to see why Eskimos would have a lot of words for snow, harder to see why we have only one.

A few seconds before the train was due to leave, the sliding doors gasped open and a woman entered. She had been following Winnicott for forty minutes. In her anxiety not to be spotted, she had made a mistake in letting him get too far ahead and had lost sight of him as he boarded the train. She had intended to take the carriage behind him. She sat down quickly, her heart thumping. At first she did not notice the admiring glances from the two men across from her, both of them scanning the attractive face and the curve of her breasts. She gave them a brief, disdainful look.

Trying to ease his aching back into his comfortable seat, Winnicott began to feel an upsurge in his throat, as if something soft was on the move in his larynx. He barely had time to reach the toilet and lock the door. The dreadful cry as he stared into the mirror was muffled by the revving of the engine as the train left the station.

The woman kept her eyes on the door of the toilets for the next fifteen minutes until he returned to his seat looking horribly ill. She was feeling only one thing:

I.

I hate.

I hate you.

It was six o'clock on a Thursday evening and in his comfortable consulting rooms David Hendrix listened with considerable alarm to George Winnicott. He had phoned him earlier that morning in an unusually agitated state and asked to see him as soon as possible.

'Can I ask why you didn't tell me about this the first time it happened?'

'I couldn't ...' Winnicott's voice trailed away. 'I didn't want to face what it meant, I suppose. I thought ... I don't know.'

'And as far as you know, your wife is the only other person who has heard this voice, after your collapse at the school.'

'As far as I know. Obviously the teacher heard it – but other than that no one has said anything to me.'

'Would they be likely to?'

'I don't think so. But it's not the sort of thing you can really ask people, is it? Just after one of the collapses my deputy came into my office and clearly thought he had heard my secretary in there. I suppose he must have heard the voice. Since then I've got used to the signs, and I've always been on my own when it's happened.'

'And this voice always says the same thing?'

'Yes.' Winnicott looked miserable and ashamed. 'It always talks about a secret and that I'm going to have to tell it.'

There was another long pause before Hendrix spoke again. 'It's important that you're honest with me. Do you know what this secret might be?'

Winnicott stared at Hendrix – it was a desperate look from a man who was now too afraid to be evasive. 'I have absolutely no idea.'

'So if I understand correctly, your wife heard the voice before you were yourself aware of it?'

'Yes.'

'Why didn't she say anything to you?'

Winnicott shifted uncomfortably in his chair as if in real physical distress. *This kind of thing is agony for you*, thought Hendrix.

'It's not ...' He rubbed his hand along his chin as if wiping away a stain. 'I haven't been entirely straight with you. Things haven't been particularly good between us for a while. I'm not sure why, if you were going to ask. These things seem to happen, don't they? You just find yourselves not talking. You suddenly find you don't get on. And you don't know how it happened, but it has. I suppose she didn't tell me because she's been worried about what's happened between us. This was just one more thing to make her anxious. So she just put it out of her mind. It was just one of those things ... pretend it didn't happen.' He looked across at Hendrix again and smiled. It was as wintry a smile as Hendrix had ever seen.

'You see, however badly we're getting along, we have a lot in common, my wife and I.'

Hendrix felt a rush of pity for the man sitting in front of him.

'Harry Stack Sullivan calls it selective inattention – the unconscious censorship of information likely to lead to an increase in anxiety.'

'It's nice to know one's failings have a name,' Winnicott said.

Hendrix was silent – the rebuke had been well-deserved.

'What now?' said Winnicott after a while.

Hendrix sighed. 'I'm not sure. Although there is one thing we must do.'

Winnicott looked at him, anxious and hopeful.

'You must go back to your doctor. I'll write to him. It's important that you're checked out thoroughly – and I mean thoroughly.'

The phone rang on his desk. 'Yes?'

'There's a policeman wants to talk to you,' said his receptionist. 'A Sergeant Roache.'

The cramped and airless room used for identity parades looked like a recording studio fallen on hard times. A window took up the upper half of one wall and behind the window there was only black. Roache stood beside a woman dressed in clothes that looked as if they had come from a charity shop, and not recently. The door opened and in came Inspector Healey, smiling affably. 'Thank you for coming at such short notice.'

The woman seemed anxious. 'Does this mean you've found Maria?'

'Oh,' said Healey evasively, 'no, no sign of her at all. There are a few other reasons why we need to go through this at this stage. It won't take long.' He went over to an intercom on the wall and pressed a button. 'OK, Des, send them in.'

Immediately a fierce light went on in the space over-looked by the window in the wall. It was so bright and so uniformly applied across the room that there was no shadow anywhere, as if some overachieving football hooligan had stolen a floodlight from a premiership football pitch and switched it on in their front room.

'It's all right,' said Roache reassuringly. 'When they come in they won't be able to see or hear you.' A door opened in the brightly lit room and a line of men made their way along the far wall looking as if they had been allowed out into the noon sun after several months in darkened solitary confinement. 'I have to be formal here.' He cleared his throat. 'Please take a careful look at the men in front of you. Take as long as you require. If there is someone here you recognise, then loudly and clearly speak the number you will see on the wall just above their heads. I have to make it clear to you that the person you saw may or may not be here.'

The woman looked anxiously at the line of men. What if she thought she saw him in the line-up and was mistaken? What if she wasn't sure? Should she say so, or keep silent? What was the right thing to do if you were almost sure but not absolutely sure? There was a bleached look about them as if they were a collection of albinos who had tried to disguise their lack of colour by dyeing their hair black. They all looked uneasy, as if each had something important to hide. She found herself wondering if by an astonishing coincidence every one of the randomly chosen people at an identity parade had actually committed a serious criminal offence.

'Take your time,' said Healey. She walked to the window and began scanning the ten men. Both policemen watched her carefully to see where she paused. The first time she stopped it was to look at a tall, slightly drawn man in his thirties: Maria Vaughan's boyfriend, Steven Grlscz. There was a long pause. 'Can I see him more closely?' she said. Healey spoke into the intercom. 'Number five, please step forward to the black line.'

Healey watched Grlscz carefully. His expression was not the look of a guilty man, it was the look of a man who was appalled at what was happening to him but unable to think what he should do. Healey felt an unaccustomed stab of guilt: what must it be like to have lost someone you loved, someone you had rescued from a life of relentless misery, only to find that she had vanished and now you were standing in a police station at an identity parade and you were the one they wanted a closer look at? Healey also felt bad because when they had talked at the flat, Grlscz had been lean already; but now he was verging on gaunt. It was the same look Healey had seen in his brother two months after his wife had died.

Grlscz stood about three feet in front of the others and waited in his solitary, over-lit purgatory. Only this particular purgatory, thought Healey, could end in hell as well as heaven. Still the woman looked. Roache began to smile with satisfaction.

'He can step back now,' she said at last. The smile left Roache's face as Healey spoke into the intercom. Steven Grlscz moved back into line. The woman walked on but did not pause again until the last man. After a moment's hesitation she turned to Healey. 'Number ten.'

'Number ten, please step forward to the black line.'

David Hendrix looked as if he had been struck a hard blow to the face. He moved towards the line fearfully, as if approaching the edge of a vertiginous cliff. There was another pause, not as long as the first then she turned to the policemen. 'I'm sorry. They have similar kinds of faces but I don't think so.'

'But there's a possibility?' urged Roache sharply.

'Sergeant Roache!' said Healey sternly. Roache realised what he'd done and looked as if he wanted to swear loudly. But before he could apologise, the woman let rip her own confusion and annoyance.

'If we're talking about possibilities, Sergeant, you've got the kind of face I saw in the street that night.' She felt as if she had let Maria down and resented that feeling. She looked at him angrily. 'There's a *possibility* it was you.'

Healey smiled placatingly. 'I wonder if you could just give us a few more minutes. There are some photographs I'd like you to look at. It won't take long.' Healey gestured towards the door and as he did so caught sight of a terrified Hendrix still standing at the black marker. He had clearly decided that he was about to be arrested for murder, given that he had been left standing in front for twice as long as the man further down the line. Healey pressed the intercom. 'Um ... step back number ten,' he muttered apologetically. 'That will be all gentlemen.'

Sitting at the computer in Healey's office the woman finished scanning a succession of twenty faces. She scrolled back to one of the earlier ones.

'Him,' she said, unreassuringly uncertain.

Both men were shocked. It was a photograph of George Winnicott.

The woman was puzzled by the intensity of their reaction until she realised what she'd done. 'No, I don't mean he *was* the man in the street that night. I mean it could have been him. He's got the same shape of face as the others. Other than that ...'

'Obviously we have rules about leading questions,' said Healey. 'I have to be careful here. Can you definitely identify this as a photograph of the man you saw in the street the night you last saw Maria Vaughan?'

The woman sagged. 'I can't be sure. It could have been him.'

———

Out in the street Steven Grlscz was feeling unwell. The police had told him very little about the reasons for the identity parade, only that someone had seen Maria arguing with a man several days after her disappearance. Whoever had seen the argument had obviously not been certain it was him or he would not be free now. But how could they have been certain? Maria Vaughan had been dead for two days when the witness claimed to have seen her. He had almost been picked out at an identity parade as having had a violent row with a woman who had vanished and whom he had claimed not to have seen for weeks before that disappearance. This would have made him a proven liar and a probable murderer. And yet the argument had never happened. It was not ironic. It was *appalling*.

———

Healey and Roache sat drinking coffee and mulling over what they'd witnessed.

'I'd say that got us precisely fucking nowhere,' said Roache resentfully.

'Perhaps. But it's all we've got. I think we're probably flogging a dead horse with Steven Grlscz but, reliable or not, she fingered him first. It's all we've got. If Maria Vaughan is dead, then as the person closest to her he's statistically the most likely. Not that I want to encourage your lack of objectivity as regards Grlscz, but there's something not quite right there. I'm probably wrong.'

'I don't like him,' said Roache.

'You don't like anybody.'

Roache shrugged. 'Well, if you want me to shake his tree and see what falls out I'm only too happy.'

Healey looked at him thoughtfully. 'Tree-shaking is not required. If it should prove necessary I'll fill out an application for a warrant detailing the legally appropriate measures. How does that sound?' He sighed. 'I wonder if we should ask the information technology people whether there's any point in using that new computer of theirs. What's it called – NORMA?'

'OMEN,' corrected Roache smugly. 'I wouldn't bother.' He gestured at the grey box in the corner. 'I lost four days' work when that useless pile of crap crashed on me last week. I'd backed it up and everything. The IT department did fuck all about it. Computers are a complete waste of fucking time.'

GOOD NEWS FOR ROMANTIC LOVE FROM THE BANK OF ENGLAND AND ALAN GREENSPAN OF THE UNITED STATES FEDERAL RESERVE

The biggest and most complex challenge for any man or woman is to choose a mate and, having chosen well, demonstrate that they have the brains to keep them. There's an old saying, 'When poverty knocks at the door, love flies out the window.' When the Monetary Policy Committee at the Bank of England decides to raise or lower interest rates they are actually raising or lowering the level of anxiety in society about its financial future so that behaviour will change. Imagine by how much a rise will cause devotion to leak out of the window, or by how much a fall will cause an increase in expressions of tenderness behind the bedroom door. Perhaps to make the point that economics is about emotions we should just get the Bank of England to declare that the MPC has announced a half a per cent fall in love, or a quarter per cent rise in anxiety.

Louis Bris, *The Wisdom of Crocodiles*

Tessa Nancarrow sat up in bed, the elaborate break-fast her husband had prepared in front of her.

'Don't you want any jam on it?' he said as she took a delicate bite.

She brought the toast back to the plate. 'I'm being a bit careful,' she said, smiling apologetically. 'I had some chocolate cake when I was in town yesterday. I couldn't resist.'

'Why should you?' he said, exasperated. 'I don't know why you're always on a diet these days anyway. There's nothing wrong with your weight.'

'Exactly,' she said cheerfully. 'I just want to keep it that way.' She laughed nervously. 'It's all right for you, you eat like a horse and never put on an ounce. Some of us aren't that lucky.' He watched her as she slowly nibbled at the toast.

They heard the clatter of the letterbox.

'Aren't you going to get that?' she said.

'I suppose so.' Allan Nancarrow stood up, trying unsuccessfully to restrain a sigh of deep frustration. 'Eat up.'

He went downstairs. After about ten seconds she got up, went to the top of the stairs and looked down into the hall. He had picked up the mail and gone into his study. Going back into the bedroom she poured most of the tea into a small hand-basin in the corner of the room, broke off a crust of the toast, put it on her plate and hid the rest in the wastepaper bin beside the bed under a pile of multi-coloured tissues. Then she went back on to the landing. There was still no sign of him. Returning to the bedroom again, she took a large pat of butter from the dish with the knife, wiped it off with a tissue and added that also to the others in the bin. Then she got back into bed.

Down in his study Allan Nancarrow was not, at least for the present, worrying about his wife's diet. For the moment he was contemplating the good news. The letter he was holding was telling him that his lender was pleased to inform him of a reduction in his repayments due to a recent fall in interest rates announced by the Bank of England. But there was not just one piece of good news. In the other letters there was more. And it was all the same good news. The accumulation of good news meant that next month all that Allan Nancarrow would have to repay to the people who had sent him all this good news was £34,462.48. With luck there would be another cut, and the Bank of England's policies on interest rates might mean that in the following month he would have to repay even less.

Forty-five minutes into their meeting about the poor relationship between the police and the lawyers at the FS it was clear to Winnicott that he had encountered Boyd Gribben on a number of previous occasions. Sometimes he had been wearing a skirt, at others instead of being well over six foot he had been barely five foot seven. He had been twenty-four, forty-three, and on another occasion he had talked to him the day before he retired. What persisted throughout these many incarnations was the endless set of gestures: there was the pursed lip over the clasped hands to signal at once a deep thoughtfulness about an opinion being put to them of a kind which invariably led, after much deep thought, to an unequivocal defence of things being done exactly as they were before. There was also the smile with the head cocked to one side to indicate that they, too, had once taken a position very similar to the one they were listening to but which they had come to see was untenable, given the particular circumstances in which they found themselves, although they retained a considerable sympathy with that position and that perhaps it was time to look at it again before settling on things rather as they had been.

There were familiar sighs, specimen grunts, exemplary lamentations, object-lesson frowns and habitual murmurs. As a response to every suggestion, or even implication, regarding the poor state of the relationship between the seconded police and the lawyers and accountants, all of Gribben's looks and noises expressed qualified agreement mitigated by condescension. Every idea put to him he had already considered. And not just the idea's three-lane highways, its no speed limit autobahns: there was no byway of the idea he had not explored, no path along which he had not ridden, no tributary down which he had not sailed. There was no track, footway, flyover or alley that had been unvisited by Boyd Gribben in his search for a solution to the problems being put to him. Winnicott was almost impressed that Gribben had failed to concede anything of even the most minor kind throughout the entire meeting. It suggested a pure spirit, since no one with any real strategic sense would dream of being so uncompromising in refusing to accept any suggestion whatsoever from their new boss. There was no time to deal with this now so Winnicott asked him to put something in writing. 'There is one other thing, Boyd,' said Winnicott.

Gribben looked at him attentively.

'The water cooler next to Lucy's work area.' He paused. 'It's causing a few problems.'

'In what way?' said Gribben, eyebrows raised.

'It's become a meeting place. She finds it distracting. I wonder if it would be possible to find somewhere else to put it.'

Gribben opened his mouth to dissent then changed his mind. He smiled softly. 'Let me have a look at it and I'll see what can be done.' He stood up and gave an apologetic frown as if he had overstayed his welcome in his anxiety to discuss these matters with Winnicott. 'I know you have a meeting – I won't keep you.' Gribben walked to the door and then turned, all casual afterthought. 'Lucy is, of course, a very experienced secretary. But I have to say that she can be a little inflexible. I've tried to build a real team among the admin staff, and the others are very open to new ideas.' He waited to see whether Winnicott would respond. He smiled as if it were a painful duty to point this out. 'Her contract is coming up for renewal next month. Perhaps you'd like to give it some thought. Of course, Director, it's up to you.'

He left and Winnicott sighed as he began to see how the business with the water cooler would proceed. Gribben would make delaying the removal of the cooler a matter of principle. He would drag his feet endlessly in the hope that Winnicott would give up, or that while he was attempting to shift him about this he would not have the time or energy to trouble him about other more significant matters. He had seen these victories by delay many times: the person with the troublesome notion got bored or became exhausted, or it got lost among more pressing matters, or they were promoted, or left, or died, or something else. What really made him dislike Gribben was not the drag on efficiency that such people represented, it was the way he had dealt with Lucy. Gribben had not even bothered to be smarmy with her in the way he was with anyone who had power. He could sense Gribben's dismissal in the deep sense of affront that animated Lucy whenever she touched on the water cooler. It was not indifference she felt from him but contempt and malice. He was going to teach her a lesson out of spite.

———

'Well, I can't think of anything better, Eddy. If *you* can then please feel free.'

Eddy Haynes sighed and looked down at his feet as if the excuse he needed might be found on his shoes.

Hendrix took another sip from his glass of room-temperature white wine and grimaced. Haynes looked up again.

'You know what I think about hypnosis and multiple personalities.'

'I didn't say he had multiple personalities, there's just one.'

'Look, I've got a lot more experience of this kind of thing than you ...'

'That's why I want your help – I just can't seem to get the hang of putting them under.'

' ... and I can tell you on the basis of that long experience that once you start down that road these kind of patients can produce an endless series of personalities. It's like pulling fucking rabbits out of a hat with some of them.'

'But—'

'Look, David, I agree it's a weird phenomenon, but in the end it's not usually worth the trouble, for you or the patient. Anyway, half the time they're making it up.'

Haynes glanced over at a young woman sitting on a high stool talking to a friend. 'Look at that,' he said. 'Tell me, David, she's wearing a mini-skirt and the mini-skirt has a slit up one side. What's that *about*? What did she say to herself this morning when she chose that dress?'

'It's a skirt.'

'Don't be such a fucking pedant. I mean, there are two things that basically separate men from women: one is the ability to have children, and the other is the ability to say to yourself in the morning, "I'm going to decide to have every man I meet today think about having sex with me." You just don't have that power, do you? But *they* do.'

Hendrix thought about taking another sip of the wine but decided against it. 'This wine is disgusting. Look, Eddy, as a favour, all right?'

Haynes sighed. 'You're a bloody pest, did anyone ever tell you that?'

'No.'

'Well, you are. OK, I'll do it.' There was a brief pause while Haynes again considered the legs of the young woman in the split skirt and lamented that the days when a woman of that age would stir at his presence were gone. He was beginning to understand with a greater degree of sympathy why one of his delusional patients was convinced that he was slowly disappearing. *I'm starting to know what you're going on about, old son,* he thought. Miss Thunderthighs over there couldn't see him at all. He came out of this melancholy reverie and turned back to Hendrix. 'As it happens, I did have an interesting case a few years ago ... could really have led to something – a man in his early thirties who thought he was turning into a monster who needed to feed on human blood.'

Hendrix rolled his eyes.

'No, it wasn't as deranged as it sounds. This guy's alter ego was almost exactly the same as his ego – same thoughtful, likeable personality. Intelligent. Had a very good job. At least that's what he said but he was clearly very prosperous – this wasn't a nutter having noisy conversations with little green men. I'm not even sure it was a multiple personality thing. He was deeply alarmed by his growing conviction that he needed human blood.'

'As you would be,' laughed Hendrix.

'Absolutely. But the really interesting thing is why he needed the blood. It wasn't the blood as such. He was convinced that he would starve to death if he didn't have the blood of women who were happy. Women who were in love with him.'

'Interesting,' said Hendrix, intrigued.

'You can say that again,' replied Haynes regretfully. 'He didn't go in for any supernatural nonsense. He had this incredibly complicated explanation, you know, a rational scientific explanation for why he was like this. He claimed that except for this one thing, and the fact that he had to remember to breathe all the time, he was exactly like everyone else. The odd thing is, I tried putting him under once and he actually did stop breathing. I was a bit spooked at the time but according to Mac Fowler there's a medical condition, Pike's Syndrome ...' he paused, 'or was it Park's Disorder? Anyway, it's a real medical condition – pretty rare but he'd come across a couple of cases.' Haynes looked wistful for a moment. 'The really interesting thing was that this patient was genuinely concerned about his moral position. Because, of course, he knew it would be wrong to kill someone just to preserve his own life.' He shook his head and sighed.

'So what happened?'

'The fucker didn't turn up for his fourth session.'

'So that was it?'

'Was it hell. This was too important to leave it like that. I tried phoning but the number he'd given me was disconnected. Then I went to the address on his records, but it turned out to be a dry cleaner's in Kentish Town.'

'So why do you think he did a runner?'

Haynes grunted. 'My guess is that it just went away. To be honest, he seemed too well balanced to have snakes in his boots. Except for this idea of needing happy blood, that was what made him so unusual. He was incredibly convincing. You just didn't feel you were talking to a nutter.'

'God, if your patients could hear the way you talk about them.'

'Well, they can't.'

'You don't think his vanishing might have had more sinister implications?'

'No – definitely not. Well, reasonably definitely.' They both laughed. 'The point is that he wasn't a sociopath. On the contrary, I'd say he had a highly developed sense of what other people were like.'

'So why the fake name and address? I have to say I find that pretty sinister.'

'I don't see why. I'd have done the same in his position. He realised the implications of what he was thinking, and he was worried I might turn him in to the police.'

'When in fact all you really wanted to do was turn him into a career.'

'Hah, bloody, hah.'

Hendrix signalled to the waiter to bring them the bill. Then a thought struck him. He took out a notebook and began writing.

'Look,' said Haynes, 'I don't want what I've just told you turning up in some psychiatric journal. It's mine.'

'It's got nothing to do with your bloodsucking liberal psychopath.' He put the notebook down on the table. 'That,' said Hendrix triumphantly, 'is the solution to what I've been told is the most difficult crossword clue ever devised – E13.'

Haynes snorted with derision. 'I'm better than you are at crosswords, and I'm not much good.'

'Look at this, then.' He showed him the page proudly. 'There's the E. The thirteenth letter of the alphabet after E is R. So that gives you ER. ER is an abbreviation for Emergency Room. Emergency Room has thirteen letters. The answer to E13 is Emergency Room.'

Haynes looked at the page for a moment. 'No, it isn't.'

'Why?'

'Because if that were the answer and the number thirteen actually *does* refer to the number of letters in the solution, then the clue would have to be E 9, 4. In case you hadn't noticed, Emergency Room is two words, not one. Let's face it, David, if this is the most difficult crossword clue in the world you've got fuck all chance of solving it.' He looked over at the bar impatiently. 'Where's that bloody waiter got to?'

Less than twenty-four hours later, Eddy Haynes and David Hendrix sat looking at a pale man lying on a green Dralon-covered recliner. His eyes were closed and he was breathing slowly as if in the middle of a restful afternoon nap.

Haynes looked at David Hendrix and nodded.

'What is your name?' asked Hendrix.

'George Winnicott.'

'Where do you live?'

'Harrow-on-the-Hill.'

'And what is your job?'

'I am the director of the Fraud Secretariat.'

'Do you remember collapsing on several occasions in the last few months?'

'Yes.'

'Do you remember a woman speaking to you after these collapses?'

'Yes.'

'What did she say?'

'She told me I would have to tell a secret.'

'Do you know what this secret is?'

'No.'

There was a pause and Hendrix, who was feeling increasingly foolish about the whole idea, looked at Haynes. Haynes shrugged.

'You've no idea at all?'

'No,' said Winnicott calmly. 'Except that it's the most important secret in the history of the universe.'

Both the analysts looked stunned – not only by the

claim but by the matter-of-fact way it was delivered. Recovering first, Hendrix whispered to Haynes, 'What do I do now?'

'Call the demon out and see if she can back it up. This I've got to hear.'

'I would like to speak to the woman who talked to you.'

There was a pause of about thirty seconds during which Winnicott's breathing grew deeper and deeper. Hendrix was about to ask the question again when Winnicott spoke. Except that the voice was not Winnicott's. It had a strange, slightly blurred quality to it, like a recorded voice slowed down in the replaying. But it was clearly the voice of a woman.

'Yes, Mr Hendrix, how can I help you?'

The analysts said nothing, not only because they were surprised but also because they were afraid.

'What's the matter, Mr Hendrix? Cat got your tongue?'

Hendrix looked at Haynes for help, but he was equally startled. He whispered to Hendrix, 'Ask for a name.'

'Who are you?'

'My name is ... Jean Smith,' said the voice. There was a long pause, then Winnicott smiled. It was a pleasant, friendly smile, but it unnerved Hendrix because it was nothing like any expression he had ever seen on Winnicott's face. 'And so we can get to the point, why don't you ask me where I come from.' She laughed.

'Where *do* you come from?'

There was another laugh. It was a delightful sound – teasing, yet full of warmth and generosity. 'I come from Mars.'

With that Winnicott pulled himself upright and stared at the two astonished men, alarmed at the expression on their faces. 'What's happened? What's going on?' The voice was querulous and fearful. It was Winnicott's own.

Trevor Hat was a grotesque chauvinist – as he had demonstrated during Jane Healey's first minute as one of his employees – but he gave no sign of this when talking to Jane. It was not that he declined to condescend to her, but that when he did so it was because he thought she was middle-class or didn't have enough experience of life – a quality he set great store by, especially his own – and not because she was a woman. She had the feeling that along with his curiosity about her intelligence there was a complete lack of curiosity about her as a woman. Unlike Neil, who was always trying to look up her skirt, Trevor Hat clearly didn't think of her as someone it would make sense to think of as a sexual object – either with a nice bum or a nose like a cormorant. It was not that she wanted him to look down her blouse, but an acknowledgement of the fact of her physical existence as an object of desire would have been – but it was hard to say what it would have been.

Neil was a mild nuisance, but without his clumsy ogling she would have felt even more threatened by the pictures in the album. She had begun to feel rebuked by them. She hated feeling this because it didn't seem fair that it should be so.

Without Neil to look at her she would, she knew, have believed that Geoff coveted those women with their cheerful smiles and open legs because their desire was so direct. They must have been sexy or he would not have collected them so carefully, and they would not have gone to the trouble of sending in their photographs. Magazines would not have been created for them, and many thousands of men would not have bought them. Without Neil's compulsive glare it would have been easy to have become demoralised, to think that they were a substitute for something she lacked. That was what she felt at times: an asexual accountant in young middle age with an estranged husband who collected pornographic pictures of women who were certainly no better looking than her. It didn't make sense. It didn't add up.

Dressing in the morning became a tricky business. On the one hand she had decided before going to Hat's that she would lose weight and exercise more, but on the other the relentless nature of Neil's ogling was not something she wanted to encourage.

Nevertheless, she had found this interest in her of rather deeper importance than she liked to acknowledge, although acknowledge it she did. And though she did not in any way want to encourage him to see her as a possible target for his sexual interest, she had to admit that she resented Hat's refusal to see her as in any way desirable. She did not find him especially attractive but there was an incongruous dignity to the stern face that was enhanced, if anything, by the beak-like broken nose. The choice of blouse, the length of skirt, the height of heels, the colour of nails became bound up with these paradoxical demands. She had always been reasonably careful with clothes, but now sometimes found herself changing them in the morning after she had dressed, something she had never done before. A sudden impulse to frustrate Neil's eyes or ignore her irritation about Trevor Hat's inability to look at her at all would lead to wearing a brown, pleated, lengthy A-line skirt, followed by a refusal to let the way she looked be dictated by either of them. Then she'd change into a straight skirt ending just above the knee but feel that this had not readily solved the problem; whatever choice you made it was dictated by the eyes of men, what they did, what they did not do. It was an illusion to think you could please yourself.

At first the realisation that however she dressed was a reaction one way or the other came as a shock, and this feeling pursued her the following Friday. She had been working late in town on the previous day because there had been a minor emergency at her real place of work. Both her children were staying with friends and because she had finished so late she decided to stay the night in town. She needed a couple of new bras and took the next morning to get this chore over with. But what had previously been merely an effort because she was so hard to fit was now fraught with a complexity made worse by an article she had read in the *Independent* magazine the previous week which outlined the emergence of the new Gossard Superbra. The journalist had described it in breathless terms as a reinvention of the Wonderbra, as if it were one of those technologies that cause a sudden leap in our grasp of what is attainable. It had achieved sell-out status in a few weeks in the way normally associated with the latest toy just before Christmas.

She stood in the lingerie department in Selfridges and saw it with new eyes. No longer was it merely a random collection of underwear: now it seemed like an avant-garde exhibition of desire behind which lay a reckless individual inventiveness. It was a retrospective of an artistic life racked with changes, loss of form, sudden resurgences; the classical, the abstract and the surreal hounded each other in a riotous and inconsistent clash of styles. Like some brilliant work of abstract art these garments seemed to describe nothing you could relate to anything in particular, but yet were rooted in something that was everywhere. But those who had mounted this astonishing sight had made one mistake, she thought. To give the exhibition a shape, a unifying theme, it needed a naked woman suspended, untouchable, above it all.

'Can I help you?' The voice was friendly.

'I'm looking for a bra – well, more than one, actually.'

'Let me show you over here.' The assistant, about the same age as Jane, led the way towards what she could only think of as a column hung with the beautifully preserved skins of exotic, endangered species. 'These new French ones are very pretty.' She gestured at a collection of gauzy constructions in a delicate powder blue. 'Call me if you need any help.'

Jane spent five minutes choosing a few to try on and went over to the woman who was standing at a discreet distance. As she did so she noticed a half-mannequin display of the Superbra. With its overtly complex construction, its solidity, it seemed to belong to a species only distantly related to some of the moth-like designs she had just been looking at. A before-and-after picture of a woman in a black dress testified, however, to its efficacy. Jane pointed. 'Could I try one of those?'

The assistant grimaced. 'Actually,' she said apologetically, 'I don't know if you can. The demand for them has been incredible, hasn't it, Suzy?' She gestured to the assistant next to her who nodded in concerned agreement. 'It was worse after a big article in one of the magazines last week. Did you see it?'

'No,' lied Jane.

'You'd think we were giving them away.'

'We've only got a few sizes left and not many of those,' said Suzy, 'and we aren't getting any more for two months. They're completely overwhelmed, the factory. What size are you, madam?'

'34B.'

Suzy sighed, as if to prepare Jane for disappointment, and vanished into a store room.

'Why is it so popular?' asked Jane, making conversation while they waited. The assistant laughed. It was an unexpectedly deep sound, a rich noise that made you like her immediately. 'It can make a new woman out of you. Really.' Then she laughed again, this time Jane with her.

'I could do with being made a new woman of,' said Jane. 'Especially for sixteen ninety-nine.'

Suzy emerged clutching a small box. 'The last one,' she said conspiratorially, as if it were a wartime treat beyond the grasp of ration books.

Jane tried on the other two first. One fitted well enough but when she tried on the second she wondered if she'd put it on incorrectly. It seemed to have been constructed for a different purpose, the inner lining, perhaps, of a jacket designed for someone with a severe disability. Then she tried on the Superbra. Turning to look in the mirror, she laughed. My God! she thought. She was an entirely different shape. Pushed up and in, it was as if a skilled surgeon with a pornographic mind had performed an operation on her. She pulled back the curtain and stepped out into the corridor to look at it in the full-length mirror. The assistant was taking clothes from a rack. She smiled and her pleasure was clearly genuine. 'Amazing,' she said chattily, 'isn't it?'

'I look like Jane Russell.'

'It does that with some people,' said the assistant. 'I don't know why. It must depend on the shape you are as well as the cup size.'

'I can't go out like this. The people at work will think I've had an operation.'

'Oh, it's not that dramatic,' said the assistant, sensing a lost sale. 'It just takes a bit of time to get used to it.'

'I'm not sure I want to.'

'It looks really nice ... and it's going to be weeks before we get any new ones in. Look on it as an investment — you could probably sell it on the black market.'

Jane gave in and bought it. As she wandered through the other departments in the store she wondered why she had. The difference in her appearance would be so obvious that people who knew her would certainly notice and someone would be bound to comment, or think it if they didn't say it. There would be presumptions. At Hat's it was impossible to say what the reaction might be. She was on the top floor when she went to the ladies' room and did something she had never done before: she put on an item of clothing conscious of the desire it might provoke. As she came out of the cubicle and looked in the mirror she very nearly went back and changed again. She told herself that while she noticed the difference no one else would, at least in town. This was not so, however. The combination of the bra and a previously innocuous sweater resulted in a sight that was blatantly orotic. She was about to cross a line that previously she had barely approached.

Because the Powder Room, as it was archly called, was on the top floor, she had to make her way down to the exit via numerous escalators. They were arranged in a criss-cross fashion so that those going down could be viewed by customers going up. In the couple of minutes it took, Jane entered a world where she was not only visible in an entirely different way, but where others were newly visible to her. It became apparent not only in the way men stared at her, but also in the way they tried not to. On the escalator the pattern was pretty much the same: the bored distraction of shopping husbands, the sudden look at Jane's chest, her face, the shameful lowering of eyes, and then, as they came parallel, a sideways furtive glance. Some men, the cocky ones, simply stared. In the street and in the various shops the strategies were different, depending on how close she was to them. Some would pretend to look across her at the other side of the street, but gave themselves away by the sudden dip of eyes as they swivelled across her breasts like headlights to an

333

advancing car at night. She became profoundly aware of the ubiquitous gaze of men. Jane and the men were locked in an endlessly repeated game, like tennis players beating out an infinite variety of moves with just a bat, a ball, a net, a bit of grass.

After a couple of hours of being panned and scanned she'd had enough, but it was then she realised that she had missed something. Ogled by a man in his late twenties in a shoe shop she stared straight back at him. He immediately became furtive and ashamed. It was the look of the men who'd been driven out of Hat's basement by Gordon's sneers. Outside she continued doing this. Some brazened it out but most were cowed. Made bolder by her success, the tube ride home was another lesson in the numerous ways that men had developed to look without being seen to do so. Even the ones she stared down kept on trying different tacks: over their papers as they turned the page, scratching the back of their heads while glancing in her direction, interested looks around at scenery they must have seen a thousand times before. *And all for sixteen ninety-nine.*

When she got home she went upstairs and looked at herself in the full-length mirror, trying to grasp what they'd all been looking at. 'I don't think so,' she said to herself, and taking off the bra placed it in a bottom drawer under a pile of clothes she seldom wore. She heard her mobile ring and rushed downstairs to get it out of her bag. It was Scott Wexler, the company solicitor, an unlikeable man she had been forced to consult about the problems with TLC. Michael McCarthy, the Deputy Director of the Fraud Secretariat, wanted to meet her at the end of the month.

———

McCarthy and Winnicott were sitting in Sally Brett's office on the top floor along with four of the other senior managers: Elmwood, the chief accountant; Trish Maxwell, the legal director, whose waist-length hair, parted in the centre, gave her the appearance of a middle-aged hippie who had been forced to dress up in a navy blue jacket for a family wedding; and McKinnon, Maxwell's deputy. Finally there was Boyd Gribben. The meeting had got off to a bad start after Brett had announced the news, with all the heartiness of a games mistress announcing the winning of a hockey cup, that the Attorney General was about to back the Fraud Secretariat publicly and reject any idea of allowing the CPS to take them over. McKinnon had been unwise enough to compare this to the kind of support traditionally shown to football managers by their chairman immediately before they were sacked. Brett was Victorian in her lack of amusement, staring balefully at the now pale McKinnon. There was a long silence. 'You've all had an agenda sent to you,' said Brett finally. Taking her eyes off the hapless McKinnon, she looked around the room. Gribben, who had thrown his agenda into the bin as soon as it had arrived, looked at her with vacant interest: there was only the absence of a view concerning the question of not possessing an agenda. Agendalessness, his expression said, was an experience utterly unknown to him. McCarthy was thinking about Winnicott. *He looks so ill, so grey.*

The meeting launched into a long and bad-tempered exchange about their conviction rate. Winnicott's attention began to wander: *E13 ... Enlightenment is a word beginning with E and which has thirteen letters. So what? What district is E13 in London? Plaistow? Look it up in the A-Z.* He tried to pay attention to what the others were saying. They were arguing about the jury system now.

'... Come on, John. It's not that simple. Abandoning the jury system on the grounds that the world of crime is too complicated for ordinary people to understand is a big step. The implication ...'

'... The world *is* too complicated for ordinary people ... I mean, I'm sorry ... that's just a fact. Me too. I'm not being a snob here. I still don't understand the difference between the Bosnian Serbs and Croatian Bosnians or whatever in God's name is going on over there. Until two years ago I thought Montenegro was somewhere in South America ...'

'I really disagree most emphatically. The whole princi-ple of our judicial system is that a defendant should be judged by his peers ... if justice can't be understood by non-specialists then it's a pretty frighten—'

'Peers! Exactly – exactly that. Louis Bris doesn't have any peers among TV repairmen or personal assis-tants or teachers or journalists. His peers are financial people. My dad used to do all his own car repairs until ten years ago. Now, what with fuel injection and chips instead of simple old carburettors, he hasn't got a clue. Pretty well everyone is going to be an expert in what-ever it is they earn their living at, and they're going to know bugger all about anything else. We know more and more collectively and less and less individually – these days outside of their speciality, everyone's a couch potato. I know highly intelligent, literate people who've never heard of Alan Greenspan. The most powerful economist ... no, pretty much one of the most powerful *men* on earth, and they don't give a toss who he is and that he runs the economy of the world. Welcome to the new Dark Ages.'

'Please,' said Brett irritably, looking down at the piece of paper on her lap.

'Next on the agenda ... shouldn't take long,' she added with emphasis, 'Allan Nancarrow's appeal against our use of DTI evidence in the TLC case.' She looked up at Trish Maxwell. 'This is yours obviously ... a quick summary.'

Trish searched for a moment in her briefcase and brought out a black plastic folder. 'The defence submission to the judge basically accuses us of deliberately allowing the DTI to question him first, make him answer self-incriminating questions which can be used in court, and then taking over the prosecution to get round his legal rights.'

There was a pause. Winnicott coughed apologetically. 'And are we?'

'Sorry?'

'Is that ... what we're doing?'

Trish looked over at Brett. 'Well,' she said, 'your predecessor was ... um ... enthusiastic about improving the conviction rate, and he was anxious to pursue this as a general strategy. I think the view of the rest of us ...' she looked around the room with a collegiate expression on her face, ' ... was that this was perhaps cynical and likely to backfire. I think that's fair.'

There were nods of agreement.

'It certainly wasn't the case this time,' continued Trish. 'We're entitled to use that evidence. We'll see whether the judge agrees on Monday.'

'Right then. Next item on the agenda,' said Brett briskly. She looked over at Gribben. 'This is your area, Boyd. Perhaps you'd like to take us through it. Quickly.'

Gribben's expression barely changed as he strained to look at McKinnon's agenda. McKinnon casually allowed his hand to fall over the page.

'Ah ... um ... well, obviously it's a difficult area.'

'Really?' said Brett, puzzled.

'Well ... not difficult exactly.' He looked at his colleagues who were enjoying his increasing panic like connoisseurs of encounters between Christians and lions. 'What's the word I'm looking for?'

'*Easy?*' suggested McKinnon helpfully.

Brett's face darkened. 'Perhaps, David, you'd like to give Boyd a temporary loan of your agenda.'

Gribben took the proffered piece of paper.

'Given the complexity involved,' said Brett sourly, 'perhaps you'd like to postpone the question of whether we lease these cold water dispensers until next week?'

'One – two – three.' Eddy Haynes nodded that Winnicott was under and Hendrix shifted the pause button on the tape recorder.

'The last time we talked you claimed to be from Mars.'

She laughed. 'I'm sorry. I was joking, of course.'

'Of course,' said Hendrix, looking at Haynes.

'I come from a planet much further away.'

There was a brief pause and a further exchange of looks.

'And this planet is?'

'I told you, much further away.'

'Still, it would be helpful if you could be exact.'

'I can't imagine why. There isn't any way in which you could verify any claim I made, however specific I was.'

'Tell me about your name.'

'Jean Smith is an alias.'

'I thought perhaps it might be. Will you tell me your real name?'

'No, I don't think so – and for the same reason. What are you writing, Eddy?'

'Just making notes.'

'Are you recording our conversations?'

'Yes. Is that a problem?'

'No.'

'What are you doing here?'

'I'm an observer, if you like.'

'Observing what?'

'Money. I'm an economist.'

'I see. Where does George Winnicott fit into this?'

There was a laugh, again charming, and mocking. 'Everyone needs somewhere to live.'

'So,' said Hendrix, 'this is an Invasion of the Body Snatchers we're talking about?'

'Not really. I haven't taken over control of his mind or anything. I'm occupying part of his nervous system. Sharing it, if you like.'

'Like a parasite?'

There was a short silence and when she spoke again her voice was apprehensive. 'As it turns out, I'm afraid that's more accurate than I would wish it to be. The theory is that my presence should be completely ... neutral. I would share Winnicott's perceptions but not in any way affect him. He would not be aware of me.'

Haynes was writing furiously. 'And ... what you're saying is that you *are* affecting him.'

'I think so – I'm not certain.'

'Can you explain?'

'I have no way of knowing for sure. I don't know if Mr Winnicott's collapses are caused by my presence or if they are the result of a breakdown in his health which has driven me, as it were, to the surface. It ought not to be possible for me to speak to him. But it became possible during the brief periods in which he was recovering from his state of unconsciousness.'

'So, you have no explanation for these events?'

'I told you, I'm not sure.'

'This is difficult to accept.'

'Yes, I imagine it would be.'

'I'd like to ask you more about why you're here. You say you're an economist?'

'Yes.' She smiled. 'The ultimate visiting fellow-ship.'

'Why?'

'Because this is the most interesting place in the universe.'

'Really?' said Hendrix. 'That's very flattering.'

'That depends on how you look at it.'

'What do you mean?'

'It's going to be difficult to explain.'

'I see. Is that because we have a lower intelligence than you?'

She laughed. 'No, of course not. It will be difficult to explain because a considerable degree of effort has gone into ensuring that I should *not* explain.'

'This is the secret you've been talking to Winnicott about?'

There was a long pause, and when she finally replied the voice was deeply troubled, even afraid.

'Yes.'

'But you won't tell us what this secret is?'

'I can't tell you. What I know about you ...' another troubled pause, 'makes it very difficult to decide the right thing to do. The view has always been that you should never be told and that everything possible should be done to prevent you knowing. That's why I've been given a post-hypnotic treatment that prevents me telling you anything directly.'

Haynes was taking notes furiously.

'So,' said Hendrix finally, 'you're an alien economist who possesses a secret so terrible about human existence that it can never be told.'

There was a short silence. When she spoke, her voice was cold and angry. 'Your summary does you credit, Mr Hendrix.'

'Why have you made yourself known at this time?'

'What? What?' Winnicott sat upright, calling out in panic.

Haynes spent a few minutes talking to Winnicott checking that he had emerged completely from the hypnosis. Flustered at first after emerging so suddenly from the trance, he seemed to have benefited from the experience of being hypnotised. There was more

340

colour in his face. He was only mildly curious about what they had discovered and seemed happy to accept that while they had begun to get somewhere with the hypnosis it had been inconclusive so far. Hendrix gave him no details of what had been said. After Winnicott had left Hendrix returned to find that Haynes was relaxing in the recliner.

'You never had much of a way with the ladies, did you, David? Now we may never discover the meaning of life.'

'What do you make of all that, Eddy?'

Haynes sniffed dismissively. 'Well, I've come across a delusion like it once before.' He smiled slyly. 'That was when I still thought that studying multiple personalities wasn't a complete waste of fucking time. Anyway, this patient was a minor clerk at the DSS, but he also had an alter ego who was called – what was it? – Rogor, Destroyer of the Universe. He was biding his time until it was the right moment to unleash his power on an unsuspecting world which would then learn the true nature of his awesome might. He actually spoke like that as well.'

'And your diagnosis was?'

'A classic example of personality inflation. This was a young, ineffectual and unsuccessful man with a history of mental breakdowns, relatively mild, which suggested the possibility that he might develop full-blown schizophrenia. Rogor was an attempt by his unconscious to compensate for his crippling sense of inferiority in the real world by regressing to a primitive fantasy of apocalyptic power.'

Hendrix grunted dismissively. 'I don't see the similarities, frankly. Winnicott is in his early forties and has had a considerable amount of success. Head of the Anti-Terrorist Squad, director of ... what's it called? ... the Fraud whatever. High-powered stuff. He may be deeply repressed but then so are three-quarters of British males.'

341

'I know all that, but this is just how it looks from the outside. He might *feel* completely powerless, he might think he's not up to the job I mean he may not be conscious of this necessarily. But we've both had any number of apparently successful patients who think they're frauds and that one day the world is going to find them out and see them as they really are. This new job of Winnicott's sounds like a recipe for psychological disaster for someone who secretly thinks like that. Look at all the flak there was over that bloke Bris. I've read your notes – my guess is that you're dealing with a personality with an unusually strong ego that's held back all the other stuff for years. I've seen it before, many times, and so have you – that's what most mid-life crises are, after all, the cracks appearing in a personality that can't take the strain of keeping up a front.'

'I think you're being a bit smug. Do you want a drink?'

'Whisky.' Hendrix got up and went over to a drawer and took out a bottle of Tesco's own brand. 'Haven't you got any single malt?'

'No. I don't drink whisky. I keep this for visitors.' He poured the whisky into a tumbler then poured a brandy for himself. 'Cheers.'

They both drank silently for a moment.

'I grant that this is more complex than I've made out—'

'Of course it is,' interrupted Hendrix. 'This voice isn't the voice of a regression into a primitive fantasy of absolute power.'

'Isn't it? The voice is telling you that it's in possession of an enormous secret of fundamental significance. It's still a fantasy of absolute power.'

'No, it isn't. The voice makes it clear that her powers are limited – someone else has control over her and she can't reveal what she knows.'

'OK, I don't mind admitting this is more complex. I'm not disagreeing. I'm talking about the underlying meaning here. The fantasy has to be plausible to maintain itself. Rogor the Destroyer was always able to act, according to itself, whenever it wanted. When I asked it why it didn't just destroy the world it would laugh and say that it was waiting until the time was right, that there were reasons of which I knew nothing. It pretty simple-minded stuff, as excuses go, but it was good enough for the patient. Winnicott's unconscious has created a character who knows an immense secret. Information is power here. It's obviously acceptable to his unconscious state that there are limits on his other powers and this is a way of protecting itself from actually having to deliver on its claim. Rogor doesn't want to attempt to destroy the world because he will obviously fail and so reveal his true inadequacy – and in a more complex way Smith knows *The Great Secret* but has found a reason why she – or he – can never reveal it. If it was revealed it would show that there *was* no great secret. It would only demonstrate that in reality Winnicott finds aspects of his life incomprehensible.' He put down the empty glass on the floor. 'Must dash.' He stood up and went to the door. 'By the way, I heard a good one the other day. An English teacher goes to a Freudian for analysis and he lies down on the couch. So for the next hour he pours out his heart and all the time the analyst says nothing. Then the hour's up and the English teacher stops. There's a pause as the analyst looks at his notes and then he leans over to the patient and says, "I wonder if I could ask your advice." The patient is a bit surprised about this but says that he'll do whatever he can. So the analyst says, "To be honest, grammar has never been my strong point. Do you spell *fruit cake* with a hyphen?"' Haynes burst into laughter. He looked at Hendrix who was staring at him unmoved. 'Well, *I* thought it was funny.'

Hendrix considered this for a moment. 'Perhaps it's the way you tell them.'

Haynes grimaced.

'I've made another appointment with Winnicott for Friday at six. Can you come?'

'I'm supposed to be at a meeting – but I can shift it. I'll be honest with you ... could be an interesting case. As delusions go, this could be worth following.'

'He's a human being, not an interesting delusion,' said Hendrix mildly.

Haynes groaned. 'God, David, you can be so pious sometimes.'

Hendrix looked at him, his eyes filled with a parody of gentle hurt. 'Eddy, I forgive you for that.'

'Why do you think it's a woman's voice? I have to admit when I heard it first I was spooked a bit.'

Hendrix acknowledged that he had felt the same. 'It was strange, wasn't it? It's hard to resist your basic instincts sometimes – to think of ghosts and possession. But that it's a woman's voice, it doesn't surprise me all that much. This is someone who's repressed his feminine side, if you like, to an extreme degree. The world for Winnicott is a place where you can only think your way through to an answer. Life is to be ordered and planned and controlled. He's uncomfortable with emotions and intuitions.'

'We're English. Aren't we all?'

'But I suspect that at heart Winnicott is an unusually emotional and intuitive person, perhaps to an extreme degree. That's why he's over-compensated by repressing this aspect of himself so deeply.'

'Why an economist?' he laughed. 'You never think of things like that, do you? That if there's life out in the stars they'll have to have boring jobs as well.'

'I suppose it depends on whether or not you see economics as boring.'

'Sorry, but I'm just not that interested.'

344

'If someone said the same thing about novels or classical music you'd think they were just plain ignorant, wouldn't you? Perhaps you should *get* interested.'

Haynes looked at him with friendly malice. 'How's it going with E13?'

———

Howard Cornish sat at his desk miserably re-reading a report from the chairman of the international committee in charge of supervising the engineering work on the Leaning Tower of Pisa. Professor Barton, it was clear, had been sidelined, despite all the reassurances he had been given. There had been a significant majority on the committee who'd refused to accept his plan. It was clear there was much politics involved, and many professional rivalries. These were all hidden in plausible objections. Without unambiguous scientific evidence that would stand up in court there was no way in which Cornish could intervene without paying a substantial penalty for withdrawing cover. Since the moment he had signed the agreement, the feeling had been growing that deciding to support the underwriting of the project had been the biggest mistake of his professional life. Now the unease had begun to solidify into a hard lump in his stomach. If the tower fell, he would fall with it.

———

Georgina Beatty of the Relationship Guidance Council looked across her desk at the petite forty-year-old woman sitting miserably opposite her. 'So, Mrs Nancarrow, if I can sum up, your husband is attentive to you, you find it easy to talk to one another, and he doesn't want you to be on a diet.'

'That's right,' she said nervously.

'Do you think he resents the cost?' asked Georgina, desperate for any clue, anything that might persuade the woman to open up. 'All those low-calorie frozen meals, they can be quite expensive.'

Tessa thought carefully about this. 'No,' she said at last. 'I don't think so.'

'What seems to be the problem, then?' said the woman, with rather more irritation in her voice than her relationships management supervisor would care to have heard. Tessa sat in uncomfortable silence.

'If you don't tell us what the problem is, Mrs Nancarrow,' said the woman softly, suddenly aware of the woman's misery, 'how can we help you?'

'I can't say,' said Tessa, quietly. 'I don't know how to tell you.'

'You needn't be embarrassed with me. I'm trained in these matters. There's very little I haven't heard.'

Tessa looked up, her eyes without hope. For three weeks they had been treading the same ground. Then the woman thought of something. 'Look, Mrs Nancarrow, could you come back next week at the same time? I might be able to help. I can't promise anything but it might be worth a try.'

Tessa was cheered by her optimistic tone and agreed.

When she left, the counsellor reached for her diary, found a number, dialled and waited. After three trills there was an answer. 'Machine Intelligence Ltd. How can I help you?'

'Can I speak to Anne Levels, please?'

———

When she got home later that night, Anne sat down and reviewed the phone call with mixed feelings. The Relationship Guidance Council was an organisation with problems and its new director had been brought in to do something about a succession of humiliating scandals. These improprieties ranged from one of its counsellors being imprisoned for writing poison pen-letters to her lover's wife, to a probationary sentence for a senior executive who had molested a teenage girl who had come to the centre he managed for advice. Although these discrepant punishments seemed to reflect as badly on the judicial system as they did on the moral culture of the Council, these events, and others like them, had severely damaged its reputation with the public and threatened its funding from the government.

The DSS was extremely interested in NEMO and putting heavy pressure on the Council to cooperate with Anne as she began the first trials. After years of ruinously expensive debugging, the DSS's own computers could now survey how much it was costing the Treasury to support the increasing price of people's inability to put up with whatever it was they used to put up with before the simplification and destigmatisation of divorce. There was nothing short of fiscal horror that such a humane and apparently straightforward reform of the law should ease the tax-payer into funding an ever-increasing pool of layabout teenage boys and family-deserting, middle-aged men. Hands were being wrung at the opportunity costs involved: an incalculable loss of investment in jobs, schools and hospitals; funds diverted from avant-garde theatrical productions and British films that no one wanted to see. There was the extra expenditure on police to combat the alarming growth in delinquent youths free of fatherly restraint; the rising cost of drugs and beds for adults pining for their long-lost dads or crippled by a sour relationship with their deserted mums.

Given that the most recent figures provided by the DSS to the Treasury suggested that the annual cost to the public purse of marital breakdown was five billion pounds, they now took the view that irrespective of its repressions, hatreds and Oedipal yearnings the nuclear family was wonderfully cheap to run. Married love besmirched was costing the British tax-payer £416,066,667 every month or – to put it another way – people not being able to get on was costing £13,698, 630 every day; that's £570,776.20 every hour of the day and night. That's 68.4 pence per day for each working person, or £249.66 per year. If you are married, both working, and likely to continue putting up with whatever the others are not putting up with for another year, over the next twelve months your household will pay £499.32. This is the price of love gone sour. Everything can be turned into money, every given or ungiven kiss. Currency conversion is always taking place and one day some accountant of commitment will look at figures in a book and tell us how much misery or happiness there is. Legal. Tender.

The DSS was deeply sceptical about the Council's ability to produce counsellors of sufficient quality and training to make much difference to the problem. A computer that could offer consistent, monitorable advice of a high quality and that could analyse the data it had itself collected struck the DSS as well worth exploring, despite Anne's warning that it might be a long time before it would be capable of the things they hoped for. Yet again she found it almost impossible to restrain this overwhelming desire of otherwise hard-headed people to invest impossibly premature hopes in her impressive but unmysterious machines.

Outside, sitting in his car, Steven Grlscz watched her flat for another ten minutes before driving away.

———

'How did you get here?' asked Hendrix. It was six o'clock and he was in his office with Eddy Haynes and the hypnotised Winnicott, lying on the recliner with his eyes closed, was talking in the warmly feminine tones of Jean Smith. Smith was still claiming to be from another world.

'It's very important that I say nothing that might give you any clues as to our technology. Again, you couldn't possibly verify it so there's no point in any case. I know you think that Winnicott is some kind of lunatic who thinks he's a little green woman. You're wrong but you'll just have to take my word for it.'

'Very well. *Why* are you here?'

Smith paused as if weighing up whether or not she was going to answer. 'There are fifteen civilisations in the known universe. They are remarkably similar in many respects. Most of them are about the same age, a recorded history of about a million years or so. Technologically speaking, they are all at a broadly similar level. No one can account for this uniformity, though, believe me, a great deal of effort and huge amounts of my government's money have been spent trying to unlock this particular secret. There are only two societies that have developed in any significantly different way. One is extinct, but because their true name is awkward to pronounce, and because I can't think of anything better at the moment, I'll call them the Vanguard. Most civilisations are clustered around a comparatively small island of cosmic intelligence. The Vanguard is a much older civilisation and their planet is very far from this island, which is why it took so long to find them. They have a recorded history of nearly two million years. Their existence was discovered five hundred years ago by . . .' she searched for a suitable name, 'let's call them the Illyrians. They kept their discovery a secret from the rest of us because the Vanguard had left behind a record of their history and science in a code form that proved impossible to crack. Or at least impossible to crack for two hundred years. When they finally did so, they discovered that the Vanguard had deliberately left their secrets in such an elaborate code because they were concerned that a less technologically advanced society than theirs would be massively destabilised by discovering so much new information. The Vanguard reasoned that only a sophisticated society could uncover the code in which all this information was stored, and that cracking it was a form of proof that they had obtained the necessary level of scientific attainment for the information to be of little value in a practical sense.'

'I'm sorry,' said Hendrix, finding it increasingly difficult to hide his surprise at what he was hearing. 'I don't follow you exactly.'

'The Vanguard wanted to leave a record of themselves, of what they'd achieved – but they didn't want to leave it just lying about in case the race who discovered it didn't have the means of absorbing such enormous amounts of information. The purpose of the code was to ensure that whoever was intelligent enough to crack it was advanced enough to be at a similar level of technological sophistication. It was meant to be an historical record – no, more than that – they didn't want everything they had been, everything they *were*, all they had known and felt and discovered just to vanish as if they had never existed. I don't know ... an obituary, perhaps.' She stopped. 'At any rate it wasn't supposed to be a source of economic and technological power.'

'That seems very sensible.'

Smith sighed irritably. 'It would have been but for the fact that the premise was completely wrong. It ensured that the Illyrians were close enough to understand most of the science they found but unable to absorb the social and economic changes they brought about. It was as if the early Italian Renaissance had discovered a way of gaining access to the second Industrial Revolution. Vanguard science and culture descended on the Illyrians like a disease, disrupting it at every level, whether it was in making vast numbers redundant from their jobs or altering entirely their way of relating to sex. Within a hundred years, the Illyrians had collapsed into barbarism. When the rest of us finally found out what was going on ... in violation of every known agreement on matters of this kind,' she added indignantly, 'we sealed off their planet as if it were a medieval plague village.'

Haynes was writing furiously. Smith paused for him to catch up.

Hendrix felt that he was no longer in control of events. Somehow he had allowed the patient to run things. The patient was giving him information to enlighten him rather than for him to make a diagnosis which would help the patient. He wondered if this unease was due to a proper concern that the patient's unconscious creation was running away with not one but two analysts, or simply hurt vanity that this was a matter of immense importance in the understanding of mental breakdown and which, he suspected, he lacked the intellectual weight to comprehend adequately. He did not feel in control because he was not in control.

Smith sighed. 'I'm feeling very tired. I can only talk to you a little longer.'

'What caused the Vanguard to become extinct?'

Smith laughed, again a pleasant and even musical sound. 'That's a very good question. In fact it's really the most important question of all. When we went to their planet we found that although they were massively different in many ways from every civilisation we have so far encountered, they were also very similar in that they were obsessed by the same question that had been on our minds as well: how do civilisations come to an end?'

'And did they have an answer?'

'If they'd had an answer then presumably they wouldn't have become extinct.'

'Not necessarily,' replied Hendrix, feeling a measure of control seep back. 'It's entirely possible to

351

understand the nature of a problem but not be able to do anything about it.'

Smith laughed again. 'I stand corrected. But they didn't know, and this implied something very worrying for us. If a civilisation as far advanced as the Vanguard had been helpless to understand the forces of decline it didn't bode too well for our own, believe me, concerted efforts to understand how societies decline and fall. Sociology is a much-derided field on Earth, but to us the sociologist is,' she smiled, teasing, 'next to the economist, the most highly regarded of all the specialists. We believed that it was only by understanding great social change that we could prevent catastrophe. You must remember that all the civilisations we knew about, with the exception of the Vanguard – and one other – were at roughly the same level of development. And we had one other thing in common – we realised that we were going into an apparently irreversible decline, and had no idea why.' There was a long pause.

'You said there was one other civilisation that was entirely different.'

Smith smiled. 'Surely you've guessed, Mr Hendrix.' And with that she began to breathe more and more deeply.

Winnicott opened his eyes and looked at the two men watching him. 'I feel bloody awful. Could I have a glass of water?'

THE GLASS CASE

There has been a gradual demotion of mankind
since the Renaissance. We are no longer at the
centre of things, literally or figuratively. We
live in the light of a minor star in an obscure
galaxy in a backwater of the universe. We are
merely animals which share 99% of our DNA
with a creature that gibbers, eats bananas and
spends its days in the trees. In the great scheme
we are insignificant. But what if this is wrong?
What if there is no life among the stars but
here? What if in the unimportant variations
that make up the difference between a genius
and a dunce, there lies the very summit of
everything?

Our every deed, no matter how squalid, would
make the cosmos hold its breath.

Louis Bris, *The Wisdom of Crocodiles*

On the first and second Friday of every month,
Trevor Hat opened the bookshop half an hour later
than usual for what he described as staff training. This
consisted of ten minutes of bollockings for whatever
blasphemies had been committed against his philosophy and which had not been discovered at the time
they had been committed. Sometimes this was followed by a few minutes of praise for anything he
considered had strayed out of the cretinous norm
usually his lot to have to tolerate.

'I believe in the carrot and stick approach, Jane ... a

small carrot and a fucking big stick. It's the bollockings that make this place pay. Bollockings have paid for my house and a flat in Spain and an off-roader the size of a fucking cathedral.'

Whatever time remained was devoted to Trevor's outlining of his philosophy of life. A mixture of vanity publishing and public service announcement, Trevor enjoyed explaining his convictions to his staff while at the same time attempting to inspire them with the belief that by following his philosophy and having the courage to accept the bollockings they, too, could have a detached house, a flat in Spain and an off-roader the size of a cathedral. 'I used my brain and worked hard … so I got somewhere. You've got to have intelligence; if you don't have intelligence you're a fucking non-runner. But you've got to work hard. If you don't put any effort in, you get fuck all out …'

The basement was deserted because the training sessions were conducted upstairs where there was more room. It felt empty in the way that a football stadium without an imminent game felt empty. The arena lacked atmosphere in direct proportion to the intensity of its weekly epiphany. Whenever there were customers here, and it was nearly always full, there was a palpable tension. First there was the excitement attached to any crowded selling place: a market, a bazaar; second the mixture of desire and shame, of furtiveness, hope and curiosity. And there was another quality Jane couldn't place, a kind of frenzy.

She started to look through the magazines. Within ten minutes she had examined twelve or thirteen. Within each there was hardly any variation. The girls of *Escort* (Liza, Samantha, Paula, Jane) were bright and perky and cheerfully unashamed, pretty variations of the girl-next-door. The girls of *Penthouse* (Astrid, Janine, Patricia, Jo) were softly focused unreachables who looked away into the distance as if they dreamed

354

of men as unreal as themselves. In *Rustler* they were lewd, pretty girls-next-door willing to display their inner genitalia, in *Model Girls* they were as unreachably beautiful as the girls of *Penthouse* but just as lewd as the girls in *Rustler*. The girls of *Mayfair* were not lewd, but were more unreachable than the girls of *Escort*, although not as unreachable as the girls of *Penthouse*. In turn the girls of *Playboy* were so unattainable, so curved and narrow, so enigmatic in their secret knowledge of what they knew, so impossible to sully with ordinary lust, that they seemed to belong to another species from the models in *Groupies* whose lack of reticence extended to the fact that they seemed determined to introduce you to their uterus, liver and lungs. They were like sects, these magazines: there were pornographic Shakers, obscene Adventists, indecent Catholics, smutty Huguenots, debauched Episcopalians and lascivious Copts. There were the same alliances of view, the same disdains, the same tiny but essential disagreements on a point of faith. *Blue Book* had stories of ecstatic lust, orgies, lesbianism and zipless fucks; *Playboy* had fiction by the great and good, by Borges, Cheever, Updike, Kundera.

The men arranged about the room, facing the shelves with the others waiting for their turn behind, reminded Jane of worshippers: apostate Buddhists and Jesuits and Ashkenazim at a wailing wall, after a strange and unsatisfactory god. Their frenzy was the frenzy of the Golden Calf.

' 'Scuse me.'

Jane looked up from her copy of *Real Wives*. 'I was just looking,' she said and was pleased at how little embarrassment she felt.

'I didn't think you'd approve,' said Trevor Hat.

'What makes you think I do?'

'It pays your wages,' he said, unconcerned.

'I suppose you're right.' Her flat admission caught

him out and he couldn't think of a reply. She went back to flicking through the magazine. 'Do you like this kind of thing?' she asked after a brief pause during which he began to put cash in the till.

He stopped and considered for a moment, refusing to be guilty.

'It's all right, I suppose. It's like working in a sweet shop – only instead of Mars Bars and Twixes and Crunchies and Bounties and all that, it's big tits, small tits, solos, duos – they sound like chocolates don't they, Duos? – rubber, leather, readers' wives ...'

She interrupted. 'Why do you think they do it, these readers' wives?'

'They like the idea of all those men tossing off over them, I suppose. I'll tell you,' he said, with greater enthusiasm now that he had the chance to change the topic to business. 'We can't get enough of 'em. The wives, any home-made stuff – it practically walks out of the shop. That mag up there – *Over 40* – out the door in thirty-six hours, the lot. Nobody wants to buy *Playboy* any more – it barely earns its place on the shelves.'

She looked up at a magazine with a picture of a heavily endowed half-naked woman on the cover.

'So,' she said, 'magazines with big breasts are the most popular.'

Trevor looked at her, mystified. Then he realised her mistake. 'Oh, no, it's not over forty inches, it's over forty ... y'know ... over forty years of age.'

A stab of grief passed through her as she reached up and took one from the top shelf. Again there was the endless variety: plump, tall, short, large bums and small breasts, happy smiles, lewd poses on beds from MFI or John Lewis; women who looked thirty and immaculate; women who would not see fifty-five again.

'Do you think they'd publish my photograph in

here?' she said in a flat, cold tone that in his astonishment he did not pick up. He said nothing then looked at her suspiciously. 'You're winding me up.'

'Why do the customers buy them and not *Playboy*?'

Trevor looked up from the till and smiled knowingly at her. She felt suddenly that she didn't want to hear the answer. 'Search me,' he said, and went back to counting out his float.

She put back the magazine. 'I'd better get on with my work.' She walked into the office, and closed the door behind her.

'Trevor!' shouted Gordon, from the top of the stairs.

'What?'

'Minogue's on the phone.'

'Toll him to fuck off,' he said calmly, and carried on filling the till.

Later the same day, just before six, Jane sat in the office worrying about the meeting the following day with the Fraud Secretariat. Despite her preoccupation, she was conscious of Neil, who was supposed to be cashing up, nervously looking at her legs. She wondered whether this had been done to her by lots of men, but more skilfully, or whether her recent experience with the Superbra had simply made her more aware that, by and large, men were perpetually going through an endless optical grazing of the women around them. It followed that many women (most women, *all* women?) were constantly striving to be grazed upon in turn. If not, then why lipstick, underwired bras and sheer tights? Why not the scrubbed face and a pair of loose trousers? Why not a chador? What were mini-skirts *for*?

Neil was certainly thinking about it, though not in any hidden way. The awkward fashion in which he dropped things and picked them up, or craned his neck unnecessarily to reach for things easily within his grasp brought a childish quality to his attempts to ogle her. What was it that was reducing him to this? She felt amused, bewildered, and then a sensation both warm and not exactly pleasant started to spread inside her stomach. A frightening, even sickening, daring seized her. She shifted in her seat, pushing herself forward and crossed her legs so that her skirt rose almost half-way up her thighs.

For the next ten minutes she hardly moved except to push her skirt higher. All the time she was acutely conscious of the young man's gaze. During that time he only looked directly at her legs on five or six occasions, and then only for a few seconds, ten at most. But she could feel throughout that he was thinking of nothing else. After a few minutes the warmth in her stomach had spread to the middle of her chest. She looked at him only once during the ten minutes. His eyes moved away quickly.

She inched forward once more taking her skirt so high along her thighs so that he could see the change in colour of her tights to the deeper black at the top of her legs. A sudden belief in her absolute power took hold of her, a mixture of revenge and mischief. 'All right, Neil. If you have to keep looking up my skirt let's get it over with.' She stood up. He looked at her, startled, as she took two steps back, reached down for the hem of her skirt and in one swift move pulled it up around her waist.

He went white then red, and stood up as if he had been struck. Close to tears he turned and left. She was shaken, for all the cool she displayed to the boy, by an uncanny mixture of malice, daring, meanness, power, and pity for the look of terror on his face.

As she pulled down her skirt she was shaking. She went into the washroom and put down the wooden lid of the toilet and sat for five minutes. Then she stood up and looked at herself in the cracked full-length mirror: a middle-aged woman whose best asset was her legs – not plain, attractive enough if she took the trouble with lipstick, powder, spray. There were a million like her and yet, vibrating in her stomach like a tuning fork, she could feel his fear, his compulsion, his desire and shame, but above all the driven nature of it all. It was something you had, an inheritance that was nothing to do with being beautiful – a terrible, irresistible gift. Slowly she reached down and lifted her skirt a second time. But something of what she had seen in his desperate look was with her still and she saw herself through his eyes. How long her legs seemed, how hidden. The gauzy nylon seemed to pull the eye from the knee to the hidden upper thigh, to the secret inner thigh; and then the sudden shock of white between her legs, drawing attention to itself all the more by being underneath the fine transparency. *Yes,* she thought. *Yes, I see.* The surge in her stomach returned. It was not a surge of desire for Neil, but of the desire to be desired. And it was different from the desire to touch and be touched. She looked for a moment longer, then pulled her skirt down to her knees and went back to finish her work.

The offices of Laird, Colbourne and Cantrell, accountants, were in a sound nineteenth-century building clearly influenced by Pugin, although not as ornate. A too aggressive recent cleaning, the subject of litigation, had caused some damage to the stone and given the gargoyles a slightly blurred quality and a disconcertingly contradictory appearance, at once satanic and mellow. Inside it was quiet because the walls and the carpet were thick, and also because of George Winnicott.

In April 1993, £400 million pounds worth of damage had been caused to the Baltic Exchange by a thousand-pound IRA bomb contained in a lorry parked next to the building. In response Winnicott had devised a drastic plan to ring the City with permanently armed roadblocks, a security wall that had removed most of the traffic from the streets of the Square Mile. As a result, respiratory infections had fallen dramatically, and seven people who would otherwise have been knocked down and killed were instead working at their desks, oblivious to their debt to the silver lining of extreme Irish Nationalism and George Winnicott, former head of the Anti-Terrorist Squad.

For the moment Winnicott sat in a large office gazing mystified at the arched Gothic window facing out onto Gutter Street. 'Why is the floor half-way up the window?'

McCarthy, who had been thinking about the coming interview, looked up. 'Oh, that. When they refurbished this place it was supposed to be offices for the new futures and options exchange markets. They couldn't refurbish these old buildings internally with the same dimensions because the kind of computerised screen trading that had come with the Big Bang needed miles of cabling and lots of air-conditioning. It all has to go in between the floors, and there was so much of it that they had to push the floors upwards. Then the market crashed and no one wanted a place like this until Laird's got it for a song. Makes you feel queasy, doesn't it? As if the inside is slipping.'

The door opened and a middle-aged woman walked in followed by a sleek-looking younger man. She was dressed smartly: a simple black Jaeger jacket and a checked skirt from Marks & Spencer, the shortest of the three lengths they offered. The man exuded confidence of a not entirely convincing kind, while the woman seemed apprehensive. The introductions began. The smart man, Wexler, was a solicitor who clearly knew McCarthy quite well. Wexler turned to the woman beside him. 'This is Jane Healey.'

They sat down.

'If you don't mind my asking, Scott,' said McCarthy pleasantly to Wexler, 'why are *you* here? Mrs Healey asked to see us after she resigned from her post as TLC's auditor. Why would she need the company solicitor present?'

Wexler leant back in his chair. 'As you'll see, Mrs Healey's position is a difficult one. They always are in these circumstances. She simply felt my advice might be useful.'

Jane Healey looked at Wexler and her eyes filled with dislike. 'Perhaps I'd better explain the background,' she said quickly, her nervousness now mitigated by her obvious annoyance at Wexler.

For the next ten minutes she laid out her eighteen month relationship with TLC. She did not touch on any problems, merely setting out the company business and her responsibility for auditing the accounts.

As soon as she finished, Wexler spoke. 'In my view, it would be best if this interview were to take place on a section-two basis.'

'Why?' asked McCarthy.

'You know as well as I do that a resigning auditor is in an extraordinarily difficult position legally. An auditor's primary duty is towards his or her client, and reporting fraud or *possible* fraud,' he emphasised the word dramatically, 'without the prior permission of the client is a violation of professional ethics and in breach of the civil law.'

'Has there been a fraud?' said McCarthy innocently.

'If you were to interview Mrs Healey under section two then it would no longer be legally dangerous for her -- and for this company -- to discuss the matter with you. She would be under an obligation to answer your questions and the duty of client care would not apply.'

'I'm sorry, Scott, there's no question of us doing that.'

'I don't see why.'

'Very simple. Until now we had no reason to view TLC as anything more than a reputable Insurance group. We still don't have a reason, and until you give us evidence to the contrary I can't give you an order under section two.' He looked straight at Jane. 'It's not the case that you're worried you yourself might be implicated in any way?'

Wexler protested as if personally offended. 'There's absolutely no question of any wrongdoing on our ... Mrs Healey's part. Absolutely none.'

'No,' she interrupted softly. 'I'm not implicated in any way.'

'You still want to talk to us?'

'Yes, although I'm afraid you might find this a little frustrating. I'm an auditor, not a fraud investigator.'

'Of course,' said McCarthy. 'When did you become concerned about TLC?'

'Well, after about eight months I talked to the management team.'

'Anyone in particular?' asked McCarthy casually.

She paused for a moment. Winnicott had seen this a thousand times: the moment when someone has to overcome the unpleasant sensation of getting other people into trouble.

'Allan Nancarrow, mostly.'

McCarthy finished writing.

'I'm not saying he was involved in anything,' she said sharply.

'Of course not.'

'I pointed out to them that they needed to exercise more thorough controls in some areas.'

'So, you were suspicious that there was ... wrongdoing?'

'No.' She was much more at ease now and clearly glad to be talking. 'I'm an accountant, Mr McCarthy, not a policeman. It was just bad practice. It never occurred to me that people would be involved in something criminal – an auditor doesn't go looking for fraud. That isn't my job.'

'What did Mr Nancarrow say when you confronted him?'

'I didn't confront him. He said he'd look into it.'

'And did he?'

'Apparently. When I returned to TLC a few weeks later they'd obviously made an effort to at least look as if they'd changed some of their practices. Certainly I didn't see the salesmen wandering in and out of the assessment section. Except once.'

She was evidently hoping to be drawn out, but McCarthy said nothing.

'I saw one of the salesmen walk up to the assessment section and take out a security card – the section was supposed to be secure so you had to have one of those credit card things to get in. If he'd just gone in, I don't suppose I would have even noticed – they'd been so much better about staying out. I'd have put it down to one lapse. But when he saw me, he looked startled, put the card in his pocket and tried to pretend he wasn't going in.' She stopped again, clearly wondering if, now that she was saying it aloud to the FS, it sounded insubstantial. 'Of course what drew my attention after he covered it up so badly was the security card. Why did he still have one?'

McCarthy said nothing for a moment, concentrating on making notes. 'My impression is that something else made you feel this business over the salesman and the assessment office was important – is that right?'

'Yes. The oil and gas side of the business was outselling its rivals by half as much again.'

'Good salesmanship?'

'Possibly – but the differences are too great for that, surely? And another thing. Their financial records were extremely complicated, and I couldn't see why.

There was no obvious reason, in terms of accountancy practice, why that should be so.'

'What did Mr Nancarrow say to that?'

'He said that the accountancy staff were very old-fashioned.'

'What did you say?'

'Well, they didn't seem to be hiding anything. All the figures added up for tax purposes – certainly the Revenue weren't worried.'

'Then what was the problem?'

'No one could give me a plausible reason for the way the accounts were structured. Nancarrow's explanation about old-fashioned accounting methods was complete rubbish.'

'But the figures checked out?'

'Yes. But I started doing some reading up – the Americans and Australians have a much more determined view of these things.'

'Aren't we straying outside your remit, Mrs Healey?' said Wexler who seemed to have abandoned the pretence that he was representing her interests rather than those of her employer.

'No, we're not,' she said.

She really dislikes Wexler, thought Winnicott.

'In one report by an Australian forensic auditor,' she looked at both McCarthy and Winnicott, 'that's someone who specialises in finding fraud ...' she trailed off. 'I'm sorry – teaching you to suck eggs.'

'Not at all. Please go on, Mrs Healey.'

'Well,' she continued, 'there was one case, a very sophisticated Revenue fraud, where in order to throw any investigator off the trail, they didn't just make it very complicated, they built in what he called audit breakers – devices that were designed to make it impossible to follow the movement of funds. The intention was to use these very complicated structures to make the fraudulent transactions undetectable.

They didn't go into as much detail as I would've liked. But one of the features of the fraud was what they called a pseudo-audit-breaker.'

McCarthy laughed. 'Now that's one even I've never heard of.' As he had intended, she was pleased with this.

'They were used to exhaust the investigators by pulling them down into transactions that were extremely and unnecessarily complicated, but which turned out to be legitimate. It would take weeks sometimes to find out that what looked suspicious was actually quite proper. And they'd vary them. Sometimes there would even be mistakes that meant the fraudsters lost money or paid too much tax. When they were confronted they just admitted they should do things differently or that it was the way they'd always done it. Accounts just have to be true and fair, they don't have to be ... entirely in line with current accounting practice.'

'And you think that the unnecessary complication of transactions at TLC might have been put down to these pseudo-audit-breakers?'

'You can't answer that, Mrs Healey,' said an annoyed Wexler. He looked at McCarthy, his eyes full of aggression. 'You know as well as I do, Michael, that we're in a cleft stick here. If you want to pursue this further then the whole thing will have to be done formally. Given that, it seems to me that we should end the interview at this point, don't you agree?' He stood up, smiling and dismissive. McCarthy did nothing, but Jane Healey reluctantly got to her feet. 'Of course, Michael, if anything substantial comes to light and we're legally able to pass it on then we'll get in touch.'

'I thought Mrs Healey had resigned,' said McCarthy pleasantly.

'Yes,' replied Wexler sourly.

'She hasn't been replaced by another auditor from this firm, has she?'

'No, of course not,' said Wexler stiffly.

McCarthy smiled again. 'Then I don't suppose there's much chance of anything substantial coming to light then, is there?'

Wexler did not respond and was not expected to. Jane Healey held out her hand to McCarthy. She turned to Winnicott, but as she did so a look of alarm crossed her face.

'Is anything the matter, Mr Winnicott?'

Wexler, Healey and McCarthy looked at Winnicott. He'd gone white. He stood up quickly to reassure everyone watching him that he was in fact full of energy. 'I wonder if I could trouble you ...' He looked at Wexler, who stared at him blankly then realised what he wanted. They said a further round of good-byes, then Wexler led him down to a discreet-looking door.

'I'll wait for you in the lobby,' said McCarthy. He was about to ask Winnicott if he felt ill, but decided this would be unwelcome. He turned and walked towards the lift.

Winnicott rushed inside the toilets and leant against the wall, staring into the expensive smoked-glass mirror that took up most of another. Then he felt something pushing inside his chest. He stared, horrified, then began to speak. '*I want them to know,*' said the woman's voice, determined but slurred like a slow tape-recording. '*You're going to have to let me tell them why people are so ...*' the voice struggled, searching, ' *... irregular ... jagged ... asymmetric ... rough ... disproportionate ... uneven ... bumpy ...* **strange.**'

Steven Grlscz walked out of the flats and waited at the kerb for a taxi. Within two minutes he'd flagged one down. 'Soho Square,' he said, and was about to get in when someone appeared at his side. It was the policeman, Roache, smiling pleasantly. Grlscz's heart mislaid a beat.

'It's all right, Mr Grlscz,' he said laddishly. 'I'm going your way. I'll drop you off.' He gestured towards a blue Mondeo.

Roache brought Grlscz up to Healey's office, chatting amiably as they climbed the stairs. 'The thing about identity parades is that there's always an element of luck involved. The Russians have a saying, I'm told.' He paused, delight and malice in his eyes. '"He lies like an eyewitness."' He sighed as if in regretful fellow feeling. 'In my experience, juries set a lot of store by a positive identification. But you know, Mr Grlscz, sometimes at night when I can't sleep, well, I worry. I worry about miscarriages of justice.'

By now they had arrived at a glass-paned door. Roache knocked and opened it, showing Grlscz through.

Healey was behind a desk. 'Please sit down, Mr Grlscz,' he said.

'Am I under arrest?' asked Grlscz softly.

'It depends.'

'I don't understand.'

'I *could* arrest you ...'

'Then arrest me,' interrupted Grlscz. This was the indignation of a man who'd had enough of being cooperative. A man who had been, perhaps, afraid or confused and intimidated by what was happening to him, but who had finally, indignantly and with cause, had enough.

Healey continued, placatingly. 'But I'd rather not. If I arrest you, then everything is a matter of record. Things are written down. Conversations are taped. It all gets very formal, very solid. And I'd rather just sort it out, ask a few questions and get some answers. And if – as I expect – it all makes sense, then it's as if it had never happened and you can forget about it.'

367

'Why did I have to empty my pockets when I came in?'

Healey looked mournfully at the small pile of Grlscz's personal effects lying on the table between them.

'Yes. I'm sorry about that. It was a misunderstanding. They shouldn't have taken them from you. My apologies.' He gestured for Grlscz to take them back and watched him as he replaced the various keys, wallet and notebook in his jacket.

'If this is just a chat,' said Grlscz, 'then I'd rather it was just between the two of us.'

Roache looked at him resentfully.

'Of course,' said Healey, all accommodation. He nodded to Roache, who sauntered out as if he'd been going to leave anyway.

'He's a cocky little sod, your colleague,' said Grlscz, deciding that some expression of a genuinely held irritation would be appropriate.

Healey did not react. 'You had a card in your wallet ...'

'You looked in my wallet?'

'I shouldn't have, I admit. But it seemed simpler than going through the business of arresting you.' He held out his hands in a gesture that said: It's up to you.

Grlscz laughed.

Healey smiled as if they were co-conspirators in a game. 'You had two cards in your wallet. Both in your name.'

'Yes.'

'One of the cards is a business card and the phone number on it is in the phone book as well.' He held up a small cream-coloured card, very simple, with just a name and number printed on it. 'The phone number on this card. It's unlisted.'

'So?'

'Well, maybe it's just me but I found it odd. Small

but odd. At first. So I called up and got your phone records for the unlisted number.'

Grlscz said nothing but he looked shocked.

'Now the phone records are very interesting because you've had the unlisted number for eighteen months, and yet you've never made a call on it. I'd call that odd.'

Healey watched Grlscz. He had the numb look of someone who had been caught out, was considering lying then thought better of it. There was a long pause as Healey watched him run through all the ways that whatever he was trying to explain might look less damaging than it probably would be.

'It was a way of picking up women,' he said at last.

Healey did not say anything, forcing Grlscz to continue.

'If I see ...' He stopped awkwardly and corrected himself. 'In the past when I saw a woman I found attractive sometimes I used to give her my card.' He stopped.

'And you waited for them to call?'

'Yes.'

'You didn't say anything to them?'

He winced as if experiencing a minor pain. Another awkward pause. 'I used to tell them it was something I would never normally do.'

Healey nodded. 'OK, I can see that, but what about the private number?'

'I didn't use it for anything else.'

'Why?'

'So that I would always know whoever was calling me – well, *why* they were calling.'

'I don't understand. Explain.'

Grlscz looked down at the floor as if he truly felt the miserable nature of his self-exposure. 'Sometimes, often, I would pick up the phone and there would be just silence. I suppose they felt ashamed for some reason ... married, whatever.' He looked Healey directly in the eye as if he was now ready just to face up squarely and honestly to what he was telling him. 'The reason I never used it for anything else, why I never made any calls myself, was so that I could say ...' He looked away again.

Throughout his twenty-year career Healey had seen many respectable people mortified by having to tell a complete stranger about something shameful they had done, but there was an acute quality about the man in front of him as if what he was feeling was not only shame at being caught out, but also had a precise awareness of why, and exactly why, it was shameful. 'Whenever they were silent and I could tell they were going to ring off, all I had to do was say, "It's you, isn't it?"' He looked back at Healey again. 'And, of course, it always was.'

Healey thought about this and admitted that while he was disdainful of the nature of the insight he had just been offered, he was also impressed. It was like reading about a terrible laser-guided anti-personnel weapon in the Sunday papers against which there was no defence. 'It's strange,' said Grlscz. 'I was never exactly proud of it but saying it aloud it seems ...'

'Sinister?' suggested Healey, mocking.

Grlscz took the point that he was not going to be allowed off the hook. He acknowledged the rebuke. 'Cheap, I was going to say.'

'Perhaps we could agree on sinister *and* cheap,' said Healey, unrelenting.

'Fair enough. Would you believe me if I told you I stopped doing it after I met Maria?'

'Are you going to tell me that?'

Grlscz looked at him directly again. 'Yes.'

Healey looked down at the list of calls made to Grlscz during the eighteen months. He wondered how many lives it would be possible to destroy if he rang these numbers; he felt a surge of resentment against the devices that had made a record for ever of what might have been only a moment's temptation. If he decided that Steven Grlscz had been involved in the disappearance of Maria Vaughan and was not the admirable saviour of a broken woman everyone said he was, then he would have to ring these people. Hidden lives would come out, no distinction being made between the treacherous user of a faithful husband and the woman momentarily tempted by the flattery of a handsome man who had acted on an impulsive longing to know her better. He had no stomach for this.

'Fortunately for you, the number spies at British Telecom bear you out. No calls during the last six months.'

Grlscz decided it was dangerous to play the penitent for too long. It was time to draw a line between the business of the phone calls and anything more serious. 'It was just a shoddy pick-up routine. I haven't done any-thing illegal, I've just confessed to behaving badly.' He smiled. 'Perhaps you've missed your vocation.'

Healey smiled back but his expression was difficult to read.

'I don't think so, Mr Grlscz. A priest helps a sinner to tell the truth so that he can be saved; a policeman so that he can get him into trouble.'

'And *am* I in trouble?'

Healey said nothing, then picked up a passport which was lying on top of Maria Vaughan's file.

'I couldn't help noticing in your personal posses-sions that you had your passport with you.' He looked at Grlscz pleasantly. 'Going somewhere?'

'I was going to Barclays in Soho Square. I was open-ing a bank account. I'd forgotten I had it with me.' He reached out to take it but Healey put it back on the file out of his reach.

371

'I'd like to keep it if you don't mind.'

'I *do* mind.'

'I'd like to keep it all the same.' Healey's expression communicated with unambiguous eloquence that it would be very much better for Grlscz if he cooperated in this matter.

Grlscz sat back.

Healey sat back also. 'Tea?'

Grlscz laughed. 'Not good cop, bad cop?'

'Not at all. Polite cop.'

When Steven Grlscz got home, feeling as if he'd been worked over with a truncheon and a telephone directory, he checked his answering machine. There was one message. He pressed play. 'Hi, Steven, this is Alison ... Alison Cross. Sorry it's taken so long to get back to you. I liked the proposal very much but I'm afraid the others were less easy to convince. We all have to agree about something like this so for the moment we'll have to pass. Sorry.'

George Winnicott, hypnotised, was lying on the recliner in Hendrix's consulting rooms with his eyes closed, breathing deeply and evenly.

'Why didn't the same terrible collapse happen as it did to the ...' Hendrix checked his notes, 'the people who originally discovered the Vanguard?'

'We kept it secret. Very few people were allowed to come into contact with their records and anyone who did so had to agree to what was effectively permanent exile from their own communities. Once they went to the surface of the planet they had to agree that they would stay there – never leave.'

'But they could pass on information, couldn't they, and wasn't that the problem?'

'It would have been, if they'd been allowed to pass on what they discovered there. But they weren't.'

'So what was the point of doing this?'

'They were there to find something that we knew was there from research the Illyrians had uncovered. The Vanguard had also been profoundly worried about their own decline. They'd been trying to find a solution.'

'And they failed.'

'Of course. But if we could find out more about that failure, then we could avoid the same mistake. Knowing where *not* to look would have been invaluable. Our survival was at stake. We had to take the risk. And, besides, who can resist the apple of knowledge?' Sho laughed. 'It isn't human.'

'I take it you found what you were looking for.'

'Yes.' She paused for a moment. 'I'm not sure what you'd call it – a theory of extinction, perhaps. There's a great history of things dying out in the universe ... ninety-nine point nine per cent of all the creatures and plants that have ever lived are now extinct. The Vanguard believed they had uncovered a pattern that we had missed. To put it simply, our view had been that complex living systems, whether they were a species of plant or a civilisation, went into decline when something happened that put a great strain on the social and economic or biological order. Any system can adapt to a certain amount of change but if this change is too radical, the plant, the animal or the civilisation simply can't cope and it collapses. It seemed obvious, common sense, and the evidence seemed to back it up. We thought we knew how it happened but not what we could do about it. The Vanguard showed us that we were wrong.' There was a short pause.

Winnicott sat upright and looked at them. 'I wonder if I could have a glass of water. I'm very thirsty.'

Both analysts looked at him in surprise. Winnicott

was looking at them and smiling. But he was speaking in the woman's voice. There was a brief pause.

'I'm afraid I've only got tap water.'

'Tap water would be wonderful,' she replied, amused. Already it was impossible to think of the person sitting across from them as a man. The way they were being teased was immensely alluring: the tone of voice suggested the presence of a wonderful quality which you entirely lacked yourself but deeply wanted to share in. They were both disturbed when Winnicott crossed his legs because the gesture was entirely womanly. There was nothing parodic about what they were watching – this was not an impersonation, however skilful. Winnicott's face had relaxed into an expression at once sweet and strong. There was a warmth and ease with the physical world that was entirely absent in Winnicott. His eyelashes seemed to have grown, although this could not possibly have been the case. Both men were disconcerted by what they were witnessing. On the one hand they were sitting across from an emotionally restricted middle-aged man in the throes of a serious mental breakdown and with a five o'clock shadow falling across his pale cheeks; on the other, they were in the company of a woman who knew, without question or conceit, that she was an object of desire. And both men were uncomfortably aware that if this woman took a liking to you, you would be given something you had always wanted and never had.

Hendrix left the room, leaving Eddy Haynes on his own. He felt an unaccustomed emotion it took him a moment to recognise: he was starting to panic. She noticed this and smiled, as if secretly flattered by the anxiety of an adolescent's confused desire. But clearly she could not resist. She looked directly at Haynes and, after a pause, winked at him. She laughed at his confusion and for the first time since he was seventeen, Haynes blushed at being teased by a woman.

Hendrix returned and handed her the glass of water.

'Thank you.' She took a long drink then put the glass on the table. 'What was I saying?'

'Um ... extinction,' said Haynes at last.

'Oh, yes. My memory, it's slipping a lot these days. Anyway, the Vanguard had realised that matters were more complex than that. The onset of rapid change was a crucial first step but it wasn't this that usually caused extinction. It was what happened when things began to return to normal after the period of rapid change had worked itself out. They claimed that it was the return to something like the previous state of affairs that usually proved too much for the organism. It was as if having had the strength to overcome a major change in the environment – a series of bad winters for a type of plant, the social changes brought about by too much economic change in a society – they were unable to adapt to yet another change, even if that change was a return to normality, to the familiar. In terms of behaviour, for want of a better term, it was still one more drain on their ability to adapt. Going back to the way things used to be, to ways that had formed their very nature was the last straw.' She stopped and waited for them to ask a question.

Haynes spoke first. 'But why was this so important? I mean, I understand the point but it's just a refinement, isn't it? Most periods of major change are followed by a return to normality. OK, so it's the last bit that kills you off. It seems pretty academic to me.'

'Yes,' she said, thoughtfully, 'academic is quite a good word under the circumstances. Understandably you're looking at this in human terms.' She looked out of the window. 'The thing is, it's only in human terms that it isn't quite so significant.' There was another pause and she frowned. 'Life in the rest of the universe is

375

quite different from life here. Even though the Vanguard were different in many ways, in one essential way they were exactly like the people who sent me here ... exactly like me.'

Even from across the room they could hear her breathing become laboured and her language halting. 'Everywhere else in the universe, everything changes very slowly indeed compared to here. It took ...' She was clearly in increasing discomfort now.

'Are you all right?'

She held up her hand impatiently. 'Let me finish. It took human civilisation barely five thousand years to go from the first writing to the invention of the computer. Everywhere else as far as we know – and this was true of the Vanguard as well – the same process has taken approximately two hundred thousand years. Everywhere else life changes much more slowly than here. Gradual change is normal everywhere else ...' She stopped, breathing heavily and clearly in pain.

'We should stop now.'

'Let me finish, please.'

Both men had stood up but the determined tone of her voice made them hesitate.

'Please.'

They sat down, uncertainly.

'Until we discovered your existence it was an absolute given with all of us that intelligent life moved slowly, that gradual change was a feature of all known societies. When rapid change did occur the results were always catastrophic. We presumed that without an ability to progress in a relatively ordered way ...' she stopped again as if struggling to be clear, ' ... a primitive society that changes too rapidly will simply disintegrate. They always have – always.' She held up her hand again and waited for the pain to subside. She said nothing for nearly five minutes, but as Hendrix was about to end the session, she began again, this time more in control. 'The problem we had was because of the slow rate of change. Because things moved slowly we couldn't easily see the shape of things at all ... Everything took place over such a long period of time we couldn't see the underlying trends clearly, it was all buried. The Vanguard knew that sooner or later something would happen which was going to disrupt their way of life. By your standards a serious change in social trends could happen in a few years ... For five thousand years most cultures on earth regarded the question of whether women were the equal of men with either indifference or hostility. What did it take to change that? At the start of this century even most women didn't believe they should have the vote. And now? It's nearly ten years after the fall of the most powerful, and most hated, English prime minister for two hundred years. A woman. The same process took the Vanguard nearly two thousand years of undramatic gradual drift. By the time women were the equals of men, no one even noticed it had happened. But it was all so slow, they couldn't understand the causes of the change.'

'Why does it matter? It all sounds admirable,' said Hendrix, perplexed.

Smith was exasperated. 'You can't see trends when they move so slowly. More to the point, you can't understand them – and if you can't understand them how are you to change the trends you can't see that are destroying you? They started to realise that they were going into decline – fewer ideas, less drive – but it took a thousand years for them even to suspect that something odd was going on, that they were wearing down in some way.' She looked up at them, revealing a desperation that they must grasp what she was saying. 'Do you see?'

Hendrix looked at Haynes then back at Smith. He nodded.

'So that's why you came here. We're different – as a race we change more quickly so you can observe and understand how complex societies change ... that's what you're saying.'

She sat back and closed her eyes.

It was Haynes who spoke next. He realised that his feelings of protectiveness had been aroused by her obvious discomfort. He was also aware that while he would have been concerned for Winnicott as a middle-aged male, it was clear that he now felt protective as he would have done for a woman in distress. Nevertheless he could not stop himself. 'Are you sure you're all right?'

She opened her eyes and stared at him.

'Stop fussing. I can assure you I'm not made of glass.' The impatience, and it was a female impatience at being condescended to, was absolutely clear.

His irritation was out before he could stop it. 'What *are* you made of, then?'

Despite the pain, she laughed. 'I'm sorry to disappoint you, *Eddy*,' and she emphasised his name in a way that was both flirtatious and dismissive, 'but the real Jean Smith isn't green and I don't have tentacles. I'd cause a stir if I walked down Oxford Street, but not much of one. And there are other differences, of course. Where I come from I'm considered rather plain because I have large breasts and a small bum.'

As was intended, this startled them and she laughed again. Once more they were struck by the sound – rich, good-humoured and deep. She was so sexy. Yet she was a man, and a not particularly good-looking one at that.

'If you're a woman why have you taken up ...' he paused, searching for the right word, ' ... residence in a man?'

'It was a mistake, in a way. It's far too complicated to explain. In any case, I'm not willing to. And even if I did, you wouldn't believe me.'

'You could try.'

'No.'

Haynes looked at Hendrix with an I-told-you-so triumphalism.

'Could you tell us a little more about the differences between ... well, us and you?'

She looked at him mockingly. 'Do you mean men and women, or aliens and humans?'

Hendrix laughed. 'I may not know all that much about men and women, but I see *them* all the time. Why are we useful to you if we're so different?'

She looked at him for a moment and Hendrix began to wonder if he had offended her. But then she began to speak briskly, as if addressing a business meeting. Hendrix noticed that the painful interludes seemed to have stopped.

'What you must understand is that you *are* like us – only much more so. While there seems to be a universal inevitability to personal, social and tribal conflict, mankind has these qualities in what I can only describe as terrifying abundance. War does exist elsewhere, but it's rare and on nothing like the scale that's common here; social disintegration takes place but over much vaster time scales. We have about the same level of artistic diversity as you ... but our equivalent of, I don't know, the Impressionists would have been the dominant style of work for a thousand years before something else came along ... slowly. There are no overnight sensations where I come from. We *evolve* everything and we evolve slowly. There is no word for *revolution* or *fashion* in any culture except on Earth.' She gasped as if she barely knew where to begin. 'For goodness' sake, there are six thousand languages in the known universe and all but sixteen of them are spoken here.' She looked at them intently. 'Now do you see?'

Haynes was scribbling in his notebook as if his life depended on it. 'Not really.'

'None of us can understand how such hyperactivity is sustainable. It shouldn't be.'

'Why are we so different? Do you know?'

She started to go very pale. 'That's the secret. It really is the most important secret in the entire history of all living things.' She closed her eyes and grimaced. 'And now we must stop because it hurts too much.'

A few minutes later Hendrix returned from seeing Winnicott to the door. Haynes was pouring himself a drink.

'This is brilliant!' said Haynes excitedly.

Hendrix looked at him. 'I thought you took the view that multiple personalities were a waste of time.'

Haynes sighed impatiently. 'All right, I was wrong. Happy now? You *do* realise what we've got here, don't you?'

Hendrix looked at Haynes. 'I think so. A patient suffering from a serious delusion to the effect that he's been taken over by an alien woman from another planet.'

'Don't be such a smartarse. What a wonderful delusion. It's so brilliant. I've never come across anything like it in the literature – nothing. It's so complex, so clever. It's so ...'

'Convincing?' offered Hendrix.

Haynes laughed. 'Yeah ... you, too.'

'Alarmingly so. I take it you won't be mentioning in the lecture tour – the one I can already see you're planning in that greedy little mind of yours – the fact that you only have to listen to that voice for a couple of minutes and you're completely won over. It's almost impossible not to be carried away.' Hendrix looked at Haynes slyly. 'I'd say she's taken a shine to you.'

'You're very amusing.'

'I'd say you've taken a bit of a shine to her as well.'

'Fuck off.'

'Look, Eddy, as an analyst of many years' experience,

I can recognise the signs ... you know ... when the patient-and-doctor relationship crosses the line. I'd have to advise you that it could never work. You're an unattractive middle-aged man ... and so is she.'

Hendrix giggled.

'Ha, bloody, ha,' said Haynes, smiling, but ill-at-ease with the joke.

Hendrix did not notice that he'd made Haynes uncomfortable. He stared out of the window thoughtfully. 'I agree with you that this is a fascinating delusion. But what I find most disturbing is that voice – not the voice but the personality speaking through it.' He shook his head, bewildered. 'It's so incredibly *female*.'

'How about a drink?'

Hendrix stood up and went over to the cabinet.

'How are you getting on with that crossword clue?'

Hendrix did not rise to the bait but Eddy Haynes was not a man to give up easily.

'Whenever I contemplate my growing spare tyre ...'

'Tyre*s*,' pointed out Hendrix.

' ... or consider my declining abilities to cause a ripple of sexual excitement when I enter a room full of women ...'

'When did you *ever* do that?'

' ... all I have to do is think of the two little words of nine and four letters that make up Emergency Room, and I don't mind telling you, it brings a little rainbow into my life.'

'I think,' said Hendrix, 'that on the matter of E13 I might be on the verge of a breakthrough.'

THE DARK FIGURE
DOES LUNCH

The total amount of deception in a marriage, or
a financial centre, or a nation state, is an index
of confusion and ignorance about the nature of
the soul of man. The more ignorant and confused
people are about their nature and their heart's
desires, the easier they are to deceive and, more
than this, the more likely they are to deceive
themselves. The financial regulator is a
policeman of the heart.

Louis Bris, *The Wisdom of Crocodiles*

The room where Justice Arthur was about deliver
his judgment on the arguments put to him by Allan
Nancarrow's defence was a disappointment to George
Winnicott. With its subdued, recessed strip lights and
stretches of blond wood it reminded him of a register
office. It seemed to him unbecoming to the seriousness
of the law, its management of ruin and reprieve. The
judge was examining a thick file. No one but
Nancarrow looked at him directly. All three defence
lawyers were quite still as if waiting like athletes for a
starting gun. Only Nancarrow moved, his hands flut-
tering in slight gestures of anxiety. He was a tall, gaunt
man, sagging in his seat as if the air had been let out of
him. Nancarrow slowly turned his head towards
Winnicott and their eyes met briefly.

... Oh, shit. Oh, shit. Oh, shit. I'm in trouble now.

Oh, shit. Oh, God. Oh, shit. Oh, God. I didn't mean it, let me go. I won't do it again. I won't. Help me. You look like a nice man ...

What's she going to say? What'll she do? She's lying. I can tell, because they're telling me, they're telling me on a need to know. I get told. You know those messages from Mars for schizos, nutters, lunatics ... I get messages but I'm not deranged. They don't give me kill-your-first-born summonses, shoot-the-President commands ... there's no babble or static, it's always clear as day. *She doesn't love you any more, that's what they say. Don't send me to prison ... let me off instead. I ask her all the time. What's the matter, sweetheart? Take my hand. She always does and tells me it will be all right and takes my hand and tells me not to fret.*

... This is Mars on the blower ... Venus returning your call. *The bitch is lying through her teeth ... and there isn't anybody else – it's you. She doesn't want your mouth on hers, your hand upon her breasts ...*

I need an even break, m'lud ... another chance ... a gift. They're always coming through the door those gifts for free ... the funny thing is all the prizes that they offer you I really need: a toaster, a compact disc, a holiday in the sun. How do they know, you ask yourself, that's what I need? You throw them in the bins those prizes you would get for turning up ...

I kiss her lips, she doesn't close her eyes ... the voices point this out to me. *It's gone ... it's gone ... it's gone ... it isn't coming back. The stroke, the kiss, the reassuring fuck ... it's only done to keep you off the scent.* I picked some up this morning off the mat: a set of crystal glasses, somewhere to live for free, a television set, something for nothing for a change. I want to be let off. I know that it's a lot to ask. I won't say anything. I'll never breathe a word. I'd do the same for you ... I would ... I'd ...

383

Winnicott's eyes snapped open as the judge began to speak.

'It is natural that there should be a relationship between DTI investigations and those of the Fraud Secretariat, but it is not a close one. The DTI deals with civil matters such as bankruptcy – the Fraud Secretariat investigates and prosecutes crime. Their connection is, as it were, one of coincidence. If the DTI uncovers a crime while clarifying a civil matter this does not make those who uncover the crime a part of the criminal legal process. It is for others to investigate any criminal offence that results from their inquiries. It is the contention of the defence that the Fraud Secretariat have colluded illegally with inspectors of the DTI. Their argument is that knowing Mr Nancarrow had no right to silence while being investigated by the DTI during a civil inspection, the Fraud Secretariat arranged with the DTI that they should continue with this civil investigation long after it was clear it was a criminal matter in order that they could use the answers given by Mr Nancarrow against him in a criminal proceeding. The defence request me to set aside this evidence.'

He stopped again and searched his papers. Nancarrow sat upright, tense. The lawyers for the prosecution were gripped by alarm, their tension showing in the curve of their backs, the way one of them held his disposable biro as if it were the slim neck of a feckless lover.

The judge continued. 'I refuse the submission by the defence.'

Nancarrow did not move – but everything he was feeling agitated the room like some terrible tuning fork, vibrating misery and loss. There was no longer any difference in the private and the public world for him; the judge's words were collapsing his borders, edges and margins, his brinks and boundaries, his deepest shame and loss exposed to view in the form of prison clothes, the locked door and the absence for ever of her touch. He was reducing to nothing in a terrifying mutual collapse of everything. The voice of doom for Nancarrow was a mulling voice, a puzzling out and thinking voice, an introspective, absent of malice, weighing in the balance and found wanting voice. The defendant was being unravelled by eight hundred years of precedents, judgments and appeals, of justice, injustice, truth and lies ... You will be taken from here to a place ... It's a fit up! ... Order in the court! ... Let right be done ... Has she fragrance? ... I submit ... Are you suggesting the police? ... I find these sentences to be unsafe ...

'The erosion of the right to silence is a grave matter,' continued the judge. 'But it seems to me that this right exists to protect the weak, the inarticulate and the suggestible from having to answer questions in the strange and hostile environment of a police station. As such, this general right to silence must be upheld. However, these protections are less obviously needed to protect those likely to be witnesses in a serious fraud investigation, who will usually be intelligent, sophisticated, self-confident and articulate. They will usually be accompanied by lawyers, giving evidence by prior appointment in an environment not so foreign to them. I cannot see that a right designed to protect the vulnerable and the weak should become the means by which the strong and the ruthless are protected in their attempts to prey upon the vulnerable and the weak.'

Nancarrow was now quite still, immobile as a stump. The judge sat upright and breathed out deeply as if he were pulling himself together for the final round in a physically bruising contest. This was a man who felt the danger of his power, drawing on courage to make a break with the past and who feared the

385

consequences of being wrong. 'By seeking to modify such a central feature of our judicial system as the right to silence, I realise I will have dismayed many who will fear I have embarked here today on a slippery slope, that to limit these rights for a strictly defined group is but the first step to limiting them in such a way for everyone. My reply is that I can very well understand these concerns. But the purpose of the law is to preserve order, to ensure that right be done. The financial world as we see it now is very far from that susceptible to common understanding, and the superior cunning that is needed to understand such complexity and manipulate it to criminal ends can be very cunning indeed. Fraud is a modern crime – one might even say *the* modern crime – difficult, often impenetrable even to the brightest and best. Yet those with the power to control this complicated world can do damage to us all far beyond the most extravagant robbery.

'The late Robert Maxwell used the law for many years to intimidate those who rightfully sought to expose the business practices he employed to plunder the savings of the weak and vulnerable pensioners who were dependent on his company for their livelihoods. How can this be right? Whether eroding the right to silence is a mistake I cannot know for certain, but what I am certain of is that we cannot rely upon precedent to manage those things which are unprecedented.'

The judge nodded to the clerk of the court and gathering together his papers, packed them into his briefcase. There was a strangely loud snap as he shut the locks. Nancarrow started as if at the sound of a pistol shot.

'All rise!'

The judge stood up and in a few seconds had gone.

'Are you all right?' said McCarthy to Winnicott, who looked as if he were about to faint.

'Yes, oh yes. Fine.'

'I'm going for lunch at the Owl Café, want to join me?'

'Oh, thank you ... that would be nice.'

The Owl Café on Elgiva Street, was not the kind of restaurant Winnicott had been expecting. It was a caff: tea or instant; bacon, eggs, chips and beans. 'You don't mind, do you?' said McCarthy, noticing Winnicott's expression.

'Not at all. I'm a little surprised. I wouldn't have thought this was your kind of place at all.'

'I just fancied egg and chips for a change.'

The waitress arrived. McCarthy turned to her and began to order. Winnicott looked around at the customers: bike messengers and labourers who were refurbishing a restaurant on the other side of the road.

'Do you want anything?' asked McCarthy.

Winnicott looked back at the waitress who was staring at him with silent bad temper. She clearly regarded speaking to the customers as an unnecessary addition to her already burdensome duties.

'Oh ... just tea for me.'

'Are you all right? You don't seem well.'

'Ah ... no ... not too bad.' Normally he would not have said anything and he could not account for bringing up such a personal matter. 'It's ... today, it's the anniversary of my mother's death.'

'Ah. I'm sorry. A year ago?'

'Oh, no. She died when I was thirteen.'

McCarthy smiled. 'It's a melancholy thing to have in common but my father died when I was fourteen. How did she die?'

'Cancer. And you?'

'An accident.'

387

The waitress arrived with two cups of tea whose greyness had nothing to do with Earl's. When McCarthy began to speak it was, he recognised, with a new ease.

'I was looking for some statistics the other day and I came across an OECD report on world trade. It had the numbers for the amounts exported by the world's economies and the amounts imported. Obviously they should balance, give or take a bit for human error. But it turns out that one hundred billion dollars more was paid to people world-wide than was received by them. Now unless we're doing an awful lot of trade with outer space ... Think of it, a hundred billion dollars in saved paperwork.' He laughed gently. 'The Dark Figure. No wonder it's dark.'

Winnicott looked at McCarthy, his eyes widening.

'The Dark Figure?'

'Oh, it just describes the amount of unreported fraud there is in the economy. We don't know how large the figure for fraud actually is, hence the Dark Figure.'

'I see,' said Winnicott, his voice tired and puzzled. 'Shouldn't we do some research ... ?' His voice trailed away.

'No real point. It's not called dark for nothing. You can never know how much fraud there is.'

'Exactly, no, but you could get a clearer idea.'

'I mean it – it's impossible. The thing about fraud is that you can manipulate the victim's perception of the crime. Taking risks, that's what capitalism is all about. An investor or a Name at Lloyd's, think about it ... how are they to know that the best risks have been siphoned into their dealer's own account or that the reinsurance business has been given to a firm owned by the underwriter? They don't have to lose anything, they just fail to make as much money as they would have done if they hadn't been defrauded. Insider dealing usually goes unnoticed by everyone except the conspirators. Why do you think we never catch anyone, not seriously anyway, for insider trading? I mean, you can't rob a bank legitimately, can you? But you can use good judgement to buy shares about to rise in value. Sixty per cent of all shares rise in value before a takeover – so what's that? Good judgement or insider trading?' He gestured to the waitress to bring him another cup, then looked back at Winnicott who seemed not so much pale as ashen.

The waitress brought the tea and, as she left, McCarthy grimaced to see half the cup sluicing around in the saucer. McCarthy sighed. 'You have to look at it this way, things are the way they are. Unemployed single mothers who persistently fiddle their gas meters go to prison and their children get put into care, persistent insider traders who fiddle ten million just have to pay the money back – OK, and with a hefty fine. They probably won't get caught in any case. But if you did catch them more often, really produced an atmosphere of fear in the City of London – all that would happen is that a wall of money would head out of the City to someplace people weren't worrying whether they were about to be woken up in the middle of the night and carted off to prison. And if that happened, your single mother can kiss goodbye to a rise in her benefit when she comes out of chokey and the chance of a job for her teenage eldest.' He leant back, depressed. 'I mean, the judge is right about protecting the weak and all that. Nobody wants to see those in a position of power or trust get away with defrauding people. But he's only right up to a point. Zero tolerance for fraud would be a disaster for every man, woman and child on the planet. What the Fraud Secretariat is *for* ...' he shook his head as if to clear it, ' ... is to serve as a warning to the waverers who are thinking of swindling some widow of her savings but lack the courage, for want of a better word, to go through with it – and to be someone to blame so that when a scandal breaks from time to time and Something Must De Donc, thon there's a regulator to be thrown to the wolves. Brett, *you*, the entire Fraud Secretariat if necessary. You can't stop fraud because it's what people *do*. I don't just mean money. People lie all the time about everything ... wives, husbands, children, colleagues ... good people ... honest people ... and mostly it's what they don't say that's the biggest lie of all. You don't get to the bottom of people, do you?' He laughed though he wasn't amused. 'De maximus non curat lex.'

Winnicott smiled. 'I'm sorry, I'm only an ex-policeman ... my Latin isn't up to much.'

McCarthy felt a growing affection for the strange man in front of him. 'For the greatest things, the law provides no remedy.' He raised his dripping tea cup and gestured towards Winnicott with a weary smile. 'Here's a toast to our shadowy employer. Be upstanding for the Dark Figure.'

There was a long silence while McCarthy finished the last of his egg and chips. When he had cleared the plate, he sat back. 'I shan't want that for another year, but I enjoyed it.'

———

Outside in the street, the long-haired woman watched Winnicott pay and get up to leave. She moved back into the recess of the doorway from which she had been watching him throughout lunch. As he came into the street she felt her hatred of him move in her chest like a living thing. As he was about to turn the corner of the street, he stopped and looked down the alley, his face pale and haunted. She felt a kind of joy flowing through her: his fear seemed to connect with her, to shoot through every part of her like an injected drug connecting with the very nerve endings in her brain, filling her with an exultant rush. She waited for a minute, partly to let him get far enough ahead and partly to allow her racing heart to slow, then began to follow him.

As Jane Healey walked back from a business lunch to Laird, Colbourne and Cantrell, the heel of her shoe snapped, almost tipping her into the road. She hobbled into the nearest shoe shop, furious because she had bought them only a few weeks earlier. She tried on a pair of flat-heeled moccasins. The manageress, in passing, commented sympathetically on the poor standard of workmanship of the broken, though not inexpensive, shoe. Jane bought the first pair she tried on and left. Standing outside, she breathed in and out deeply, as if trying to control a sharp pain. The manageress was one of the women whose picture Geoff had cut out of a magazine and put in his photograph album.

She spent the rest of the afternoon trying, and failing, to concentrate on an audit into a foundry that had gone into receivership leaving complicated debts of over a million pounds. Eventually she stopped and went for a walk. She had recognised the woman because her picture had appeared four or five times, covering, she guessed, a ten-year period. She was older than her last picture, which must have been taken in her late forties, by about five years. Eventually Jane went back to the office. Although this was functionally pointless, it was necessary: the senior partner had been dropping hints about her returning full-time. It was hard to justify staying at Hat's: it was interesting and she had undoubtedly learnt something, but the notion that there might be a satisfactory answer to the problem that had caused her to take the job had slowly dissipated. She realised, with amused shock, that as a result she had something in common with the men who came to Hat's shop – a vague but still powerful sense that there was an ultimately satisfying discovery to be made there, along with an equally vague sense that they were wrong.

The next day Jane waited outside the shoe shop from a quarter to five. At a quarter past six, the manageress came out and started to lock the door. Jane stood behind her silently. The woman turned and started.

'Oh! You gave me a fright, I'm afraid we're closed.'

'I don't want to buy shoes,' said Jane, pleasurably surprised by the steeliness in her voice.

'You're the woman with the broken high heel.'

'That's right. I want to talk to you.'

'I don't understand,' said the woman, alarmed by Jane's tone. 'What about?'

Jane reached into the pocket of her jacket and produced one of the pictures from the album. It had been taken in a wood on a warm summer day. The manageress, with a wide-mouthed cheerful smile, was sitting on a fallen tree stump with her skirt pulled around her waist and her legs apart. The woman's face fell, her mouth opening slightly in alarm.

Jane noticed the reaction and also how much she enjoyed the woman's fear.

'Why don't we go inside?'

Again Jane found it odd being inside an empty shop. The ranks of shoes had all been tidied for the next day. Empty and immaculately tidy, the place had a sombre, unlived-in air as if this was the mausoleum of a wealthy eccentric obsessed with ensuring an adequate supply of footwear in the next life.

The woman stared at her, sullen, frightened and unsure.

'Why did you do this?' asked Jane.

'It's none of your business.'

'Do you want me to send a copy to your employers?'

To her surprise the woman laughed, an uneasy

barking sound. 'If I was worried about what people think do you really imagine ... ?' She breathed out dismissively. 'Whoever you are, you've got a lot to learn about blackmail.'

Jane was shocked. For the first time in her life she realised that there was some vicious quality inside her, and that it had not been created by grief, betrayal or confusion; these things had merely uncovered it. There was a sudden change in her grasp of what kind of person she was, as if complicated tunnel-work for a long time improperly buttressed had collapsed with a crash of falling props and masonry and dust. But it was not only shame she felt, but also a kind of wonder that after all this time there should be something so staggeringly new to uncover about herself. There was also, buried further under her dismay and surprise, a pride in her ability to call on something ruthless, but as yet this was unacknowledged and the easiest emotion to feel was remorse.

'I'm sorry.'

The woman sat down and crossed her legs, as if to signal her relaxed control of the situation. She could see that whatever danger there was had passed. 'What do you want?'

'I wanted to know why you did it.'

'Why?'

At first Jane thought of leaving. The woman was clearly not going to be frightened into telling her anything, and the last thing she wanted was to be in her debt. To have an explanation given out of pity would be unbearable, yet this was an opportunity she would not get again.

'I found this ...' she gestured at the photograph, ' ... after my husband died.' She felt shocked by the lie, almost superstitious.

The reaction from the woman was so quick it would have been easy to miss. Jane did not: a flash of pride so intense that not even her instant shuttering of it could prevent the momentary leak.

An intense loathing heated Jane's stomach excusing any shame she had felt at having threatened her. She turned and started to leave, a move which caused the woman to panic. Her apparent indifference to being exposed seemed to collapse as she saw the furious decisiveness with which Jane walked to the door.

'Wait!' There was a desperate note in her voice. 'It's not what you think.'

It was this curious assertion, not the pleading note in her voice, that caused Jane to turn round.

'Well?'

'I swear I didn't know your husband.'

The woman misread Jane's uncomprehending look as scepticism. 'It was nothing like that. I didn't meet them. Really.'

Jane said nothing because she did not know what to say.

The silence obliged the woman to say more. 'I didn't know your husband,' she finished lamely.

'Do you still do it – pose for these pictures?'

'No,' she said softly.

'Why not?'

'Why do you think?'

Jane looked at her. In her mid-fifties, carefully made-up, she was plumper now than in her photographs, but her face was still thin and her hair still unusually short. She was still attractive. Neil would look at her. There were many women in the magazines, younger and older, who were less desirable.

Instinctively the woman reacted to Jane's appraising eye, and she began to hold herself in, raise her chin, melt imperceptibly into a more attractive pose. It suddenly struck Jane that the woman was seducing her. But it was not sexual, at least not in any way that she could easily grasp. For a moment, like a breeze passing over her, she could feel what this woman wanted. Something in her came alive on being watched – something ghostly pulling at Jane from the crossed line of her legs, the curved division between her breasts and the dilating of her pupils. Jane felt the same alluring undertow as the searching men in Trevor Hat's basement. The woman wanted Jane's acknowledgement that she possessed this power. Then it was gone.

Jane was tempted to say nothing, to take revenge by denying her what she so clearly longed for, but her newly discovered ruthlessness applied even to her own vanity. She wanted to see just how far the woman would go.

'You're still very good-looking.' Jane could see that the coldness in her voice carried great weight, that the compliment rang truer for seeming to be forced out of her. She watched the woman's flush of pleasure, and it was all she could do not to slap her face.

The woman sighed, a mixture of relief and a kind of self-regarding embarrassment. The reassurance from Jane began to soften her and she looked up almost sorrowfully as Jane turned back to the door.

'I'd like to pose in a glass case, where people could see me, but no one would be able to touch me. I'd like the power. But I suppose that's selfish.'

The lame appeal of her last words might have touched Jane at another time, but she'd had enough of the woman. She opened the door and left.

———

Jean Smith said patiently, 'But I've told you before, I'm collecting information, that's my job, it's what I'm paid for. Winnicott is suffering these episodes because something has caused his interior world and mine to become mixed. Think of it as interference. I'm collecting evidence in the same way that an anthropologist would. I'm an economic anthropologist if you like, only instead of collecting stories about a man with one sandal and a missing sword, I collect ones about economics and fraud.' She sighed, exasperated, as if considering how to describe the idea of yellow to a blind man or the ocean to someone who had never seen a lake. 'Where I come from the great figures of economics are regarded in the way that you look on Shakespeare or Michelangelo. Economists are mobbed at airports, their private lives reported on in the papers, teenage girls weep into their pillows because their love is forever unrequited. No one on my planet would dream of reading an interview with an *actor*.' She gasped with mock irritation. 'I mean, what *for*?'

Hendrix and Haynes laughed, as they were meant to.

'Now you're teasing us,' said Hendrix.

'Am I? What happens in the Bank of England matters. Once your greatest works of art were about kings. Charley Varadi is your king. Alan Greenspan is your emperor. And yet you're bored by them. And what *do* you read about? Rubbish. Actors and food and gardening. Rubbish! Where I come from people understand that what they do with their money is one of the central ways to grasp what they are. You don't teach your children to recite the times table any more, but we do. Only what we get them to learn by heart is that the economy is the sum of all human desires expressed in goods and services; or that disappointment is the origin of every price increase. But *you*,' she gasped with disgust, 'even your farmers don't understand there's a law of supply and demand and that they have to obey it. We wouldn't let a child out on his own who had the understanding of economics of the average graduate on this ignorant lump of rock.' She looked at both men who were startled by her sudden vehemence. 'You don't know anything either, do you? Admit it, both of you, you couldn't tell a monetary theory from an underconsumption theory if you had a gun to your head. And what really makes me mad is that you're not ashamed.'

'I'm sorry,' said Haynes unapologetically. 'I'm just not all that interested in economics.'

She stared at him coldly. '*Get* interested,' she said menacingly. 'Listen to me. People do not buy fridges just to keep their milk from going off; they do not buy cars just to get from A to B; they do not buy pensions just to ensure a provided-for old age. The fridge preserves the purity of milk in daily remembrance of your mother's breast. The automobile is horse-power, your clutching for the potency of the stallion; the pension is a plan to ease the horror of your death by dreams of cruising to Miami or the Cyclades. You do not just buy fridges or cars or pension plans, but absolute love, a permanent erection, and defeat of death.' She looked at them as if she were a patient parent reaching the end of her tether. 'One of our ten-year-olds who didn't know this off by rote would be given a bloody good thrashing.'

Haynes was clearly nettled at being baited in this way. 'So – your civilisation is so much more advanced than ours that you still physically abuse children,' he said, covering his annoyance, thought Hendrix, with an unconvincing smirk.

'Spare the rod and spoil the child, Eddy. Over thousands of years we have accumulated overwhelming evidence that a clip on the ear never hurt anyone.'

'I wonder if—'

'Sorry for interrupting,' said Hendrix, 'but I think we're being distracted. Why did you choose Mr Winnicott? He's not an economist.'

'You're misinformed, Mr Hendrix. George Winnicott is studying for an economics degree at the Open University.'

'I didn't know.'

'He seems,' said Smith, 'to be a secretive fellow. But that wasn't why I chose him, although it was a factor. His new job at the Fraud Secretariat seemed to me to offer a unique opportunity to research what it is I came here to do. Confusion is my speciality – distraction and bewilderment. Fraud is a measure of how uncertain people are. The more confused the easier it is to cheat them. Find out about lies and you have a measure of distraction and bewilderment. *That's* why I chose Winnicott.' She could see Hendrix and Haynes being tolerant of her fantasy and this infuriated her. 'You don't want to face the fact that all your pet theories about the world are wrong, do you?' She sighed irritably. 'And you think *I'm* deluded.'

'So,' said Hendrix, changing the subject before the session became too bad-tempered, 'the post-hypnotic block implanted in you is preventing you from telling us this extraordinary secret, and whenever you try to do so it causes you serious physical pain?'

'Is that your summing-up-the-patient's-delusion voice? It's very good,' she said irritably. '*So* soothing.'

Hendrix had decided it would be best and would give him greater control in the therapeutic situation if he responded to the delusional persona as neutrally as he could. Despite the grumpiness of today's session Winnicott's alter ego was a seductive one and he was at a loss for the right way to deal with it other than to limit his reactions in every way possible. Unfortunately Smith seemed to have seen through his strategy almost immediately. She had responded, in general, by teasing him at every opportunity.

'Thank you,' he replied flatly. 'Is my summary correct?'

'Yes.'

'Do you have any suggestions as to how we should proceed?'

Hendrix and Haynes had debated whether or not

they should confront the question of The Big Secret. Hendrix had finally decided they should broach it directly. Knowing that the usual response among delusional patients to such confrontation was that they would clam up altogether, Haynes had pleaded with Hendrix to continue exploring what seemed for the patient to be the uncontroversial subject of her role as alien economist. Hendrix had testily reminded Haynes that his prime concern was the good of the patient and not the good of Haynes's career. Despite a subsequent apology for his bluntness, their relationship was still in cool-politeness mode. The two men watched closely as Smith considered. For the first time during the session she looked hesitant.

'You could try hypnotising me – get round it that way.'

'But we've already hypnotised you. That's why we're talking now.'

Smith sighed irritably. 'I mean hypnotise *me* – Jean Smith.'

There was a brief pause. Hendrix looked at Haynes. He could almost see his brain scanning the literature for a precedent. After thirty seconds it was clear he hadn't found one.

'Well?' said Smith, impatient.

'Um,' began Haynes, 'I ... I don't see why not.'

'You're sure about this?' whispered Hendrix.

Haynes nodded, stood up and went to sit beside Smith. After a couple of minutes of soft talking he was ready. 'Now, I'm going to count down from three and when I've finished you will be able to tell us anything you wish to without feeling pain.' He paused.

Her breathing was shallow as if in the early stages of a night's sleep.

'Three, two, one.'

He walked back to the sofa and sat next to Hendrix. 'Well, this is either going to be one of the high points of modern delusional analysis or a spectacular anti-climax ... if you can have such a thing.' He gestured that it was now Hendrix's turn.

'Are you comfortable?' asked Hendrix.

'Yes.'

'Do you think you're ready to tell us what you discovered?'

'I think so.' She began to breathe more deeply, and they waited for nearly a minute before she spoke again. 'The researchers on the home planet of the Vanguard discovered that they had been conducting an experiment, one that under normal circumstances they would have regarded as deeply unethical. They justified it to themselves on the basis of necessity. They had become convinced that their own decline would reach a critical point in less than five thousand years, at which point it would begin to accelerate rapidly. They had to find some answers so they began a series of experiments on a planet where life was at an extremely primitive stage ... reptiles, small mammals. They were skilled geneticists and in effect they began to create a new life form. It took far longer than they had anticipated and the experiments failed many times. But after five hundred years they had a breakthrough, and within another two hundred the experiment seemed about to produce results when a virus wiped out nearly all of their specimens. Their results were poor, it was hugely expensive and the political will to continue was lost as their dying culture began to turn in on itself. The experiment was abandoned and the scientists went home. Within four hundred years the most advanced civilisation ever known had disintegrated completely. Within a thousand years, the last of them was dead. It was five hundred thousand years before the Illyrians discovered them again.'

She stopped for several minutes as if brooding over what she had said.

'When we discovered records of the experiment and what it was meant to achieve we felt it was vital to find the planet and see if there were more details of what they'd been doing. It was clear that the scientists involved felt they were onto something. At any rate, we couldn't afford to ignore it and fortunately we found out where they had been conducting the experiment. It was a long way, even for us and so horribly expensive that we had to do an enormous amount of lobbying to get the finance for an expedition. Finally, it was done and we arrived.' She smiled. 'You can imagine our surprise when we came to Earth and found that the mixture of mammal and reptile manufactured by the Vanguard half a million years before had risen to become the dominant species on the planet. We thought there might be evidence that could be of use. But what we found beggared imagination. Nothing could have prepared us for the astonishing variety of life we found here. There is nothing like this planet anywhere in the universe.' She opened her eyes and looked at the two men. 'The reason why, of all the intelligent creatures throughout the universe, mankind alone has maintained such a powerful belief in a divine creator is really quite simple. You *were* created.' She closed her eyes again. 'And the Lord God formed man of the dust of the ground, and breathed into his nostrils the breath of life, and man became a living soul.'

Neither of the two men said anything, but as he got over his shock, Haynes began scribbling in his notebook. As they confessed to one another later, each felt that they were listening to the truth – so absolute was the conviction, so deep and sincere the sadness with which the patient told her story.

'So,' said Haynes, 'I just want to be clear. You're saying the human race was manufactured as an experiment in survival?'

401

She sat upright, with a look of alarm. Both men stared at her, wondering what she was going to say next.

'No, I'm sorry, that's not it at all,' she said. The familiar grimace of pain was mixed with a look of dread. 'You were manufactured as an experiment in extinction.'

———

'Right, then?' It was a Friday, Jane's last day at Trevor Hat's bookshop. He had received the news that she was leaving with complete indifference, interested only in whether or not she had finished sorting out the books. She had promised that she would do so and had arranged to go through them with him before she left.

Trevor looked at Jane morosely as he came into the small office. He sat down, a watchful grimness daring her to make him blanch at bad news. 'Was old Mrs Fitzgerald ripping me off?'

'No. In the end it turned out to be a series of ... eccentricities. There are bits and pieces of good accountancy practice here left over from years ago but she had her own way of doing things. Unfortunately she wasn't just idiosyncratic, she was hopeless. I mean, Trevor, not being able to add up is a bit of a liability for a book-keeper. Look at this.'

She passed over one of Mrs Fitzgerald's ledgers. In her immaculate handwriting it seemed a model of old-fashioned fastidiousness and attention to detail. It had always given Trevor immense confidence to see her fill in row after row of figures in her spidery italic.

'This is called a transposition,' said Jane, pointing towards a minor total of £879.12. 'This is telling you you're short. It often happens. It's divisible by ninety-nine – nearly all these errors are. What she's done is recorded £888 at this end of the transaction for these copies of *Debbie Does Dallas*, but only £8.88 at this end. As a result the sum of £879.12 seems to be missing. Only it's not.' She looked at him, shaking her head. 'There are lots of blunders like this. There's practically every mistake I've ever come across plus a few that are entirely new. Look at this ...'

'Yeah, all right, I get the point. She was a fucking menace. How much am I down?'

'Well, that's the strange thing. There are loads of errors here. But they more or less cancel each other out. You're poorer by £447.58 , that's all. God knows how.'

'How much?' he said, indignantly.

'Look, I didn't want to worry you so I didn't say anything. At one point I couldn't account for nearly seventeen thousand. Consider yourself lucky.'

'Bloody hell.'

Jane stood up and took her coat from behind the door. 'In future hire someone who knows what they're doing.'

Neil put his head round the door. 'It's the phone ... that git Carver from the British Board of Film Classification. He's whining about us selling un-certificated tapes. Y'know, *Transvestite Apartment Wrestling*.'

'I want to talk to him. Tell him to wait.'

Neil vanished. Jane had finished putting on her coat. He looked at her.

'So ... you're leaving.'

'Yes.'

'Right, then.' He went back to looking at the ledgers. She knew he was doing it deliberately to taunt her but she was mildly put out at the loss of the pleasure of refusing his entreaties for her to stay. 'Well,' she said after a pause, 'it's been an education, Trevor.'

'Of course it has,' he said without looking up. 'See you.'

She turned to leave but as she walked out of the door he called out, 'Get what you were looking for?'

She stopped. 'Not really,' she replied.

'Who does?' he said.

'Is that another example of your philosophy of life?'

'Definitely.'

She started up the stairs and as she got to the top floor she heard him bellow, 'NEIL!'

Neil, looking perplexed and gratifyingly alarmed at seeing her leaving so early, rushed past her towards the stairs. As Jane left the shop for the last time she heard Trevor call to Neil, 'Is that Carver still on the phone?'

'Yes, Trevor.'

'On second thoughts, tell him to fuck off.'

———

Like some vast Leviathan of sound, thunder rolled up the Chess Valley, dying as it came to the moor that jutted into Maltby like an arrowhead. The cloud base was low, a thousand feet, thought Healey, but it looked lower, dirt grey like pavement snow a few days old. The wind was bitterly cold and a fine but heavy drizzle soaked everything. Getting wetter, Healey moved miserably from stall to stall. He had dropped off his two children at his house and had vanished before they even got to the door. The train back to London had been postponed for at least an hour because of a bomb scare. To kill time he'd gone to the moor for the town's annual fete. By now it was late afternoon and the light had almost gone, but more people than he would have thought likely were wandering coldly around the exhibits which ringed the field in an historical order meant to demonstrate the continuity of the town's small-scale industrial and agricultural past. He found himself standing in front of a pig. It was not an ordinary pig because no one had reared it commercially for more than a hundred years although it had once been the source of the area's wealth. 'It's living archaeology,' said the sour-looking man who fronted the stall. 'Today's pig, well, it converts low-grade food into muscle five times as quick, resists disease – these things are buggers for foot rot – and they're a lot bulkier in the places you get your meat from.'

'I suppose these taste better, though,' said Healey, looking at the pig.

Cold and wet and fed up himself, the man looked at him as if seeing him properly for the first time. Healey felt his loathing, arbitrary and intense. 'Not really,' said the man and turned into the stall to get out of the rain.

The first wave spread through him like a red stain on a white cloth. He felt bad, the way only a cold, wet skin and too long living with an unpleasant truth can make you feel. And though millions were miserable for many reasons – lack of food, lack of love, lack of peace – no one on the blue planet was feeling the breadth and depth of his original shame in such an acute way. Some physicists believe the universe has no boundary; some biologists think there is no life among the stars but here; and if they're right then Geoffrey Healey, standing in this market town, wet and cold and tired, became the centre of something unimaginably old. Gist of reptile, essence of snake, Healey's inheritance swept up the cold and stony field along with the ripple of thunder and the rain, laying him to waste and then leaving him behind, changed, newborn, shocked. A few more seconds and he would have broken. Luck, perhaps, or something else (the wife, the kids) saved him from the early morning walker finding the locked car in an isolated place. This is the door we did not open; this is the path down which we did not go. Opportunity is not alone in knocking once.

Healey made his way to the station, where normal service had been resumed, and in the hour and fifteen minutes it took to get home, his personality came back, reasserting itself around what had been left on the moor. He opened the front door, concentrating on getting the stiff key out of the lock while the serpentine big bang still echoed around in his bones.

When he got inside there were three letters waiting. Two of them were identical. They were from Barclays Bank, financially randy identical twins imploring him to surrender to their unquenchable lust to lend him money. He threw them in the bin, then opened the third. The Abbey National Building Society was pleased to announce that his variable mortgage rate was to be lowered by one quarter of a per cent. The phone rang next to his bed and Healey picked it up. 'Hello,' he said. There was a pause before he heard a voice he did not recognise.

'Geoff?'

'Yes.' He wondered who the woman could be.

'It's Jane. I ... thought you might have come in when you dropped the boys back today.'

'Oh, I had to get back. You sound different. Is everything all right?'

'Yes. Everything seems to have been sorted out over TLC – at least from my point of view. The FS have been very good. At work they're pretending nothing happened. Thank you for your help. I really appreciate it.'

There was an odd note in her voice still, as if she were anxious, but more than that, the disdain had vanished.

'Well,' he said lamely. 'I'm glad I could be of use.'

'You were,' she said. 'Look, I wonder if we could meet. Would you mind?'

HEALEY'S
SECOND NUN'S TALE

Every life has its magic door, its hidden threshold. If by accident or through a rash desire to understand yourself you should uncover that door and decide to enter, you should pause for a moment and consider. It is only in books that the hero endures to the end and is saved. In real life, for every man or woman with one hand on the glittering prize and the other on the unreliable thank you speech, there are courageous multitudes dying of thirst in the desert who will be dead by four o'clock, but have plenty of time to watch the vultures of failure circling above them in the air. Mostly heroes die, mostly champions fail. Some of these losers manage to stumble back, returning with who knows what. Not a magic sword but a disfiguring scar or a sliver of ice in their hearts put there by an evil queen to burn them up until the day they die. What's done cannot be undone.

Play it safe is my advice. If you find an unexpected entrance to another world, brick it up and then forget about it.

Louis Bris, *The Wisdom of Crocodiles*

'HEALEY ... COME HERE!' The priest was shouting at a boy of about fourteen, lounging with his hands in his pockets on a low wall that fenced off the square of Tarmac from the rest of the school.

The boy started to walk slowly towards him.

'Quickly ... and take your hands out of your pockets!'

The boy moved faster but only by a margin small enough to demonstrate that he had not deliberately disobeyed. The priest considered the ways in which he would teach the boy a lesson, and as he approached, he noticed that he could make him have his hair cut on Wednesday when the barber came. An Italian barber without any talent beyond speed and cheapness, he was known to the boys, delighting in the geographical inaccuracy, as the Butcher of Seville. So disfiguring were his haircuts that even the least vain preferred to spend their own money on a cut in one of the hairdressers on the Cowley Road. The general length of the boys' hair in the school was the result of an evolutionary battle between what they felt they could get away with when they paid for the haircuts themselves and what the man standing over Geoffrey Healey could plausibly reject and so send them to be shaved by the Italian.

The line the boys pushed did not consist of the meeting point between his tolerance and their ambitions, but a line defined by the relationship between him and the world of the late 1960s going about its business beyond the high wall that surrounded the school. Like a communist empire of watchtowers and state police and heavy punishments for dissent, the priests' attempts to keep this world at bay seemed entirely successful: everywhere could be seen the signs of post-war austerity, from the glossy but drab paint on the walls to the poorly cut 1950s school uniforms. But it was not working. Seeping between the odd crack, something in the air invisibly worked to change the notion of what was acceptable. The boys were allowed an hour of television a day – an advance on a year ago from two, carefully vetted, hours a week. The important day was Thursday when the school acculturated itself with *Top of the Pops* and *The Man from U.N.C.L.E.* The priests, even if they only watched the news or the occasional documentary on Lourdes, unwittingly absorbed the propaganda for a hairier skull in everything they watched: even the television newscasters had hair touching their ears, even the paraplegic and his helpers at Our Lady's shrine shadowed the hair of Jagger, Hendrix and the Mothers of Invention.

'Next time I call your name, you jump. D'ye hear me?'

'Yes, Father.' Healey stared sullenly ahead.

'There's a pile of laundry-bags up in the main building next to the refectory. Take them round to the convent.'

The boy was astonished by this command. In over four years he had never been sent into the small convent that abutted the school and which fed it and washed its clothes. Neither had he heard of any boy who'd been sent there. He started to walk up to the main building, then turned.

'How do I get in ... to the convent?'

The priest sighed irritably. 'Into Junction Road, first right and ring the doorbell marked "Convent". Even you shouldn't find that too difficult.' Smirking, he walked off.

The boy watched after him, flicked a V-sign at his retreating back and turned on his way, still wondering at the task he had been set. Five minutes later, carrying four heavy laundry bags, all with the names of different priests printed on the outside, he stepped up to a door with CONVENT. RING. written on it. He pressed the bell. Almost immediately a nun opened the door.

'Yes?' she said pleasantly.

'Father Corrigan told me to bring these around to you, Sister.'

'Ah,' she smiled, 'that's very kind.'

'There are another two loads,' he said.

She did not seem to notice the sullen tone. 'Right you are. You run off now and I'll be here when you come back. I'll take these.'

Walking back up to the main building Geoff thought about this odd meeting. He recognised the nun's voice but he had never seen her before. For the past year he had been a dinner server. This was a highly prized job because the dinner servers took the food from the kitchens and distributed it to the rest of the school. It allowed them to wield great influence at all levels because they determined, within limits, the size of servings. Extra portions for friends and people with influence meant that the job was a means of controlling a powerful black economy within the school. Chips and sausages were as stable a currency as a pre-war pound backed with solid gold.

Although vast amounts of food came out of the kitchens and vast amounts of soiled dishes went back, no one ever saw the nuns who cooked the meals which fed the school and allowed Geoff and the other servers to wield such economic power. The synapse of this exchange between the nuns and the servers was a huge cylinder, a drum with a sheet of wood running vertically through the middle like a wooden curtain so that you couldn't see through to the other side. The servers turned the drum once, knocked on the dividing wall as a signal and whatever they sent across would be whisked away. Occasionally they would need to talk to the nuns on the other side to pass over or hear simple instructions, but there was nothing to indicate who it was that fed and cleaned them, other than the muffled disembodied voice he had just recognised. This was the way it had always been. But now the school was to close. The local council wanted it to become a comprehensive and to be mixed; but while the priests had no real objections to the first condition of change, they refused to teach girls. A female future was beyond either what they understood or wished to understand. To teach women would change everything. This was not a mistake, however regrettable the lack of egalitarianism. They were misguided, but they were not wrong.

The council had insisted and, rather than bend, the priests had decided to close the school down and withdraw to their stronger bastions in Liverpool and London, where they were less reliant on government grants to stay open. The news had thrilled Geoff, a minion watching the collapse of an empire it had seemed impossible to dent.

When he returned with the laundry bags a second time, the smiling nun was waiting for him. And again when he returned with the final load.

'That's the lot, Sister,' he said flatly.

She smiled, again not seeming to have heard the lack of grace in his voice. 'Thank you. And what's your name?'

'Geoffrey Healey,' he replied, as reluctant as Rumplestiltskin.

'Come in, Geoffrey. Have a drink for your trouble.' He was surprised at how nervous he felt, and wished he had made an excuse to avoid going into the convent, but it was too late now. The nun led him into the large kitchen with which he had had so much blind dealing during the last year. Around a large wooden table in the centre of the kitchen sat six nuns enveloped in black and with the contrasting white veil, all looking at him with expressions of anticipation and pleasure. The nun who'd invited him in sat him down at the head of the table while another fetched him a glass of diluted orange juice and a currant bun.

'This is Geoffrey Healey.'

He smiled weakly at them.

'Hello, Geoffrey, how are you?' they chorused.

'Fine, thank you,' said Geoff.

'Weren't you at St Matthew's when Sister Grace was the headmistress?' said one of the oldest nuns.

At the mention of her name Geoffrey's stomach turned over violently. 'Yes,' he said.

'God bless her soul,' said the nun sadly. 'You must have been very sad to hear that she died.'

He did not say anything and they took his silence for consent. 'Well, I'm sure you pray for her, Geoffrey. She was a good woman.'

'How's your knee, Geoffrey?' said one, who seemed to be in her forties, although the tight headpiece and the extreme paleness of her skin made it difficult to guess her age with any certainty.

'Oh, fine now,' he said for lack of anything else to say, although it was not entirely true.

'You had a nasty fall, Geoffrey,' said another one. 'It was bad luck to snap a ligament at your age.'

'And you such a fine runner. We were very proud you did so well for the school. What was it you won, now?'

'I didn't win, I came second,' he said, with a mixture of pride and embarrassment.

'Ah, but you were much younger now, weren't you, than those other boys?'

Geoff was obliged to admit that his second place in the All England Under 15s 200 metres had been against much older opposition.

'You're still under treatment, though, aren't you, Geoffrey?'

'Oh, twice a month at the Nuffield.'

'Will you be able to run again, now?'

'Oh, yes. But ... not as fast ... probably not.'

'That's a great shame, Geoffrey. But you mustn't be

unhappy about it. God has great plans for you. Doesn't he, Sisters?'

They all agreed, smiling at his embarrassment, that God indeed had plans for Geoffrey Healey. They seemed to know an extraordinary amount about him, not only what had happened to him recently, but also since he had come to the school, a small, frightened, fat boy of ten. They were a benign Stasi, a beneficent KGB who only wrote down nice things about you and wished you well. They could call up events in his life that he had long forgotten. And this interest was not confined to him. He was questioned sweetly but carefully about other boys, what they were doing or not doing, whether they had been in more trouble or less, how they were taking a father's death, a mother's illness.

'You've grown in the last year, I'd say, Geoffrey,' commented the nun who'd invited him in.

'Oh,' said Geoff, astonished, 'you've seen me before.'

'No,' she said simply. 'We've seen none of you. I can tell you've grown because your trousers are half-way up your legs.' They laughed at him and he felt annoyance, but not much.

Gradually, without fuss, they ceased to focus on him and Geoff listened to them as they talked, joking about this, complaining about that. They were particularly indignant about a recent ban on Catholic civil rights marches in Northern Ireland.

'All that Gerry Fitt is saying is that Catholics in Derry should have the same rights as someone in Doncaster. It's a disgrace in this day and age.'

'That O'Neill is a great hypocrite, Sister. All he's after doing is stalling for time until the Labour government falls and the Conservatives get back in.'

'Well, he won't have to wait long, will he?'

'Direct rule from Westminster is what's needed.

413

That's the only solution. O'Neill will never give anything away. He'll have to be forced, that's all there is to it.'

Bored, he gradually floated into the background, drinking his synthetic juice and eating his currant bun, with the sun streaming through the window, and the nuns talking. For a while his sourness ceased to taint everything he felt. Sullen and cynical as he was, he liked them. There was something about them and the way they were with him and with each other that he had never experienced before.

It was a distant sound but everyone in the room heard the shrill clatter of the school bell summoning the school to evening prayers. He stood up, thanked them and said goodbye.

'God bless you.'

'God bless.'

'God bless,' they called after him, as the nun led him out through the cool corridors and into the world outside. He stepped down into the street and looked back.

'Pray for us, Geoffrey,' she said, and shut the door.

It was the last time he would ever enter the convent, but it had not been the first.

———

It had happened a year earlier during the Feast of the Assumption, when Ginky and Biffo Guareschi, twins in the fourth form who were as fat as they were violent, had decided it was time they found out what was on the other side of the drum – this was mostly out of nosiness, but partly because they wanted to know if there was anything worth stealing, given that they made most of their money from the other boys by selling everything from slide rules to *Playboy* magazine at half the price charged by W.H. Smith. This was an arrangement that had its problems, given that Smith's

414

took part on an involuntary strictly non-profit basis. The twins had recently had several narrow escapes, which meant they had decided it might be wise to develop alternative suppliers. Too large to fit into the drum themselves they had bullied Geoff into going in on their behalf. Geoff was deeply unwilling. If found, he would be beaten and possibly expelled. But more than this was the chance that he might encounter his old tormentor from St Matthew's primary, Sister Grace. St Matthew's supplied boys who had passed their 11-plus to the secondary school. Sister Grace was a member of the order that served the needs of the priests and boys of the Catholic grammar school, but she was one of three trained teachers whose salaries helped maintain the convent. She had become ill, however, and had stopped teaching for a year and was now living at the convent until she recovered. Nevertheless, the Guareschi twins were an unpleasant pair and Geoff knew that he had every chance of getting away with going into the convent while the nuns were at High Mass, but absolutely no chance of getting away from the twins.

The three hid until all the boys had been herded across the road to the local church, and gave the nuns ten minutes to follow. The nuns always waited until the boys were settled, then crept up into the balcony at the back where they could see but not be seen.

Once the three boys were sure the school was deserted, they went into the refectory, the Guaraeschis shoved Geoff into the drum and turned it round. As the drum revolved, he felt he was not just entering another world but going back in time to the point of greatest dread in his life. He found himself staring into a kitchen. There was nothing homely about the place. It was an industrial workshop for the daily preparation of hundreds of meals. There were vast ovens and dishwashers and stacks of plates in metal cages, huge towers of china, stained as old teeth. There was a loud thump on the wooden divider, 'Come on, you useless spaz, we haven't got all fucking day.'

Slowly, as reluctant as the first soldier over the top, Geoff eased himself out. He listened: it was as silent as if it had been empty for years. He started to walk towards the kitchen door, feeling more secure. Outside the kitchen was a hallway, and on the other side a room as large as the kitchen full of enormous washing-machines for the boys' laundry. To his left was a flight of stairs. And still the absolute silence. Mass would take another hour at least, and in any case the nuns waited up in the balcony for the school to leave, as fearful of the male gaze as a breed of rare penguins who had been hunted to the point of extinction by adolescent boys. More confident now, he started up the stairs, but half-way up he felt a surge of old panic and stopped for a full minute before the reassuring silence and a growing curiosity drove him on. He wanted to see where these mysterious women lived whose disembodied voices he had known for almost three years. And also he wanted something deeper, something alarming and unclear – a kind of revenge on the monster who had terrified him for so long. To stand where she slept, perhaps, maybe even to steal from her room, and puzzle her and have power over her because she would never know. He had pilfered things from Smith's for the Guareschi twins; now he would take something for himself. His heart raced at such a daring thought, at the possibility after all these years of a measure of retribution. He kept walking, the smell of old vegetable-water receding as he made his way to the top of the stairs.

On the landing, everything was now on a human scale and very simple. It was not like someone's home, but neither was it like the regimented deadness of his dormitory, which slept one hundred and eighty boys, a hangar filled with steel beds and floored with brown lino. This place was austere but still human. People lived here; they were not lodged or barracked. Off this landing there were eight doors, all shut. He felt the sudden urge to run but he did not move. Neither did he dare to turn the handle on the nearest door. He could lie to the twins, having already been here so long, but something kept him there. Very slowly he put his hand on the doorknob. He waited. Then he turned it. Stopped. Waited. Then turned again. He opened the door onto a small bedroom, plain, hospital neat. There were some photographs on the bedside table – a father, a mother, a sister, perhaps – a missal, and on the wall a print of Jesus with His sacred heart exposed for all the world to see his suffering. He did not go in. Shutting the door, he went to the next room, which was much the same – few possessions but enough to make it clear that this was not her room. Finally there was only one door left on this floor and a washroom next to it. He was getting nervous about the time. There was another staircase leading upwards but he did not have the nerve to go any further. Opposite the next door was a deep alcove full of brooms and buckets, and a canvas-bagged Hoover almost hidden in the gloom. He turned the handle of the next door and opened it slowly. He stood still. It was her room. And she was asleep in the bed.

He knew she was asleep because she did not move but he could not have accounted for how he knew it was Sister Grace: her head was almost buried under the blanket and she was turned away from him. He felt nothing, only a stunned sensation, not fear at all. But when she started to shift uneasily, the terror swept though him as if his blood had been charged with electricity. He did not have the presence of mind to shut the door but he was able to step back into the alcove whose deep shadows swallowed him up, so that

417

unless you looked directly into it he could not be seen. Frozen, he waited as she sat up, swung her legs to the floor and began looking for her slippers. She stood up and saw that her door was open. She seemed to shrug this off as of no significance. Picking up a plain washing-bag, she made her way to the door with the familiar, dread beauty as if she moved on silent wheels. Coming into the corridor she turned, without looking at the dark alcove, and turned into the washroom.

She flicked a switch and the room was illuminated by a fierce fluorescent light. It had a tiled floor, several hand-basins and a butler's sink set low so that it could be easily stepped into. As she turned on both taps and it swiftly began to fill, he looked at her, for the first time seeing all of her face and head. The face was the same, though paler, still pinched and angry – or, rather, with a kind of anger in repose, as if her fury slept just below the skin ready to surge, like a flash flood sweeping all before it. Her hair was cut very short, shorter than his, and she was wearing a long white shift that fell to the floor and also covered her arms. As she stood and patiently watched the basin fill, she swayed like an invalid who had been standing too long. She turned off the taps, reached into the small bag and took out a small bar of Camay. She undid the top buttons on the shift and, reaching to her thighs, pulled it over her head then hung it on a hook by the basin. In this way the thirteen-year-old Geoffrey Healey saw a naked woman for the first time. Then the subcutaneous anger seemed to ebb like one of those sea creatures whose colour changes as you watch and there was only a pale woman, so pale that she seemed to soften, and an expression came over her he had never seen before, except in a cartoon he had seen on television about the Snow Queen who stole a boy from his true love by causing a splinter of ice to enter his heart through his eye. He had stopped breathing as he looked at her as she stood waiting patiently for the basin to fill. The skin below her neck was white, almost like paper. But there was something that made him feel sick to his stomach, mesmerised and frightened. Her breasts, untouched by pregnancy, were round and high for a woman of her age. The nipples were small and pointed and a colour he had never seen before, an intense but soft pink. Her belly was curved but it did not sag, and below was the most astonishing, terrifying shock of all: a mass of blackest hair, almost alive in its blackness, luxuriant and thicker by far than the short fine hair on her head. It reached up to her lower belly and down to her thighs, covering her like some wrap or mantle.

She bent to the basin, and began to wash herself. This was not done gently at first but with a need to get this over with. She almost punished her face as she rubbed. She rinsed and then began to wash under her arms – more of the thick, black, living hair. Then it was her breasts – but she took more care with them as if they were tender and needed a delicacy that only pain could force on her. The pink nipples became hard as the water cooled over them, but the soft flesh moulded and shaped itself to her touch like another living thing. Quickly she washed along her stomach curve then down to her pubic hair. The black hair and white of her hand seemed to merge as she washed below, between and behind.

In his shadow cave Geoffrey Healey watched as she parted the lips of her so very private parts, the soft skin, almost as pink as her nipples, and then the flash of a deeper red more terrifying than anything since the dreadful beatings he had endured from her. He felt sick, as if he would die with the rush and tenor of his beating heart.

Now cleansed, she took a towel, and began to dry

herself, again rough on her face but soft on her breasts, then rougher again between her legs. Dry now, she reached for the white shift and, facing the hidden boy, raised it above her head – allowing him one last stretching look at round and pink and black – and then it fell to her feet.

She sighed pleasurably, as if refreshed from her illness, for sick she must have been to be in bed at such a time. Then she put on her slippers, came out onto the landing, turned to her room and closed the door behind her.

Geoff stood and waited. He felt his heart begin to slow, then surge again. Fear was what he felt, the terrible impact of a few moments in which everything was utterly changed and could never be the same again. Something was lost and something dreadful that he could never understand was found. He did not move until the sound of a car horn outside brought him back. Taking one slow, terrified step at a time he made it to the top of the stairs. Then he bolted, racing down and almost falling, through the kitchen, clambering into the drum and banging on the wooden wall in desperation.

'Where the fuck have you been?' said Ginky furiously.

Then the drum was turned and he was back once more in the world of men.

THE CRUEL MADNESS
OF LOVE

The trouble with villains in books and films is
that they are held to possess the one quality
genuinely worth having: clarity. They always
know, these monsters, exactly what they
want: money, power, sex, revenge. I blame
Shakespeare for this rubbish: the origin of evil
is confusion.

Louis Bris, *The Wisdom of Crocodiles*

As Michael McCarthy approached Lucy Bradd she
was looking irritably at a group of secretaries
standing over by a water-cooler chatting. In fact, he
noted, it was more than irritability: blind loathing and
absolute hatred would have been closer. McCarthy
passed her desk and signalled that he wanted to see
Winnicott. Barely taking her eyes from the women at
the water-cooler, she nodded and he went through the
open door, knocking as he did so.

Winnicott was looking down at his desk in the
slightly dazed manner of someone who had just been
sick. *He looks dreadful*, thought McCarthy. Winnicott
looked up. 'I just thought I'd bring you up to speed on
the Nancarrow case. Not that it'll take long.'

'Don't tell me he's confessed and named every one
of his ...' The good-humoured but tired expression on

Winnicott's face was replaced by one of frustration as he failed to find the word he was looking for. ' ... you know, people who criminals are in league with.' McCarthy looked blank for a moment.

'Associates? Companions?'

' ... accomplices,' said Winnicott with relief.

'No such luck. He's refusing to say a word. And I mean not a word. He's gone silent. He's also lost a lot of weight. Two or three stone, I'd say.'

'The punishment is the process.'

'Sorry?' said McCarthy.

'One of our policemen said it when I first came here. Um ...' He screwed up his face, frustrated at not being able to remember. 'Sergeant Stowell,' he said at last. 'He said that for a respectable person with a position in society, just being accused was enough to ruin their life. His view was that we should charge more people – that would discourage the others like them from putting their fingers in the till. Looks as if he has a point if Nancarrow is in such a bad state.'

McCarthy sniffed. 'Perhaps – but he might be swinging the lead.'

'I don't understand.'

McCarthy laughed bitterly. 'As a copper used to prosecuting less socially advantaged members of the public, you may not have come across some of the more unusual ways of evading consequences which obtain in the upperworld. During the Guinness trials, the case against Roger Seelig was dropped on the grounds of suicidal depression and breakdown – only for him to be seen a few months later terrifying the yokels by driving his Porsche like Toad of Toad Hall through the leafy lanes of Oxfordshire. Then there was Ernest Saunders. His medically well-attested case of Alzheimer's was miraculously cured on his release, a spontaneous remission hitherto unknown to medical science.'

Winnicott stretched his aching back. 'What do you suggest doing about Nancarrow?'

'He's out on bail, so I think we should keep building the case and let him stew. Once we've got enough evidence I have the feeling he'll change his tune. The real question is whether he was acting in concert with the rest of the senior managers at TLC or if he was off on a frolic of his own. Perhaps you'd like to review it before we have another go at him. You're the man with the experience of dealing with awkward customers.' McCarthy wondered whether to bring up the matter that was really on his mind. 'The thing is, this case is pretty important. Unless we feel a couple of high-profile collars successfully in the next year or two, we could all be spending more time with our families. We need TLC and Nancarrow – and we need them badly.'

There was a brief silence.

'I see. I'll have a careful look at the Nancarrow case when I get back. I'm going into hospital on Wednesday so it may have to wait until next week.'

'Ah,' replied McCarthy. 'Right. I hope they find whatever it is – if you know what I mean.'

'I'm sure you'll manage without me quite happily, but if you need to contact me, I'll be leaving my ward number with Lucy.'

McCarthy nodded. There was another silence. 'She seemed upset, Lucy. Not like her – she's generally one of the sweetest-natured people I know. Perhaps ...' He trailed off, not knowing quite where he was going with this.

'She's upset about Boyd Gribben.'

'Ah.'

'What do you think of Gribben?'

'As I said before, I strongly disapprove of what he's been doing with these short-term contracts. If people aren't any good at their jobs then you get rid of them – short-term contracts aren't, in my opinion, about

423

flexibility, they're about control. They're about making people compliant. When I hear Gribben talking about team-building I start wondering who's next for a sandbagging. Other than that, I don't have much to do with him.'

'Well,' said Winnicott, 'I'll have to see what can be done.'

After McCarthy had left, Winnicott took a document out of the top drawer of his desk and spent a few minutes reading it. Having done so, he signed it, then called in Lucy. He asked her to prepare several documents for his return from hospital then handed her the piece of paper he had just signed. She was surprised that it had her name written at the top.

'It's the renewal of your contract,' he said. 'I hope you don't mind but I thought it would be convenient if I extended it up to your retirement.'

'But that's five years away. We're only supposed to have two-year contracts.' She looked at him, bewildered. 'Does Mr Gribben know about this?'

Winnicott looked thoughtful for a moment. 'No doubt the legal department will, in the fullness of time, inform our head of personnel. What you have in your hand is a binding legal document.' He offered her the pen he was holding. 'Or at least it will be once you've signed it.'

Martin Beck swore under his breath as the morning staff meeting came to an end with a reminder from the headmistress that because of the renewed bombing campaign on the mainland there would be a practice bomb drill at an unspecified time during the week. This was greeted by all concerned with carefully suppressed irritation, not because of any scepticism concerning the likelihood of the men of violence deciding to launch an attack on a girls' grammar school in Berkshire ('*You can't be too careful"* might

424

easily have been the school's motto), but because these time-consuming exercises were usually instigated immediately before lunch so that the drill would not detract from time at the blackboard.

Martin was also mildly depressed at his failure to be taken seriously by Anne Levels. It wasn't love, he knew, but desire, and desire did not mean just sex. That was what made being with Anne so frustrating. It was the blouses that did it. There was always this gaping mouth between the third and fourth buttons, so that when she turned to one side you could catch sight of the curve of her breast. It was a kind of erotic grief, because he knew, although maybe he was wrong, that he was never going to be allowed. He wanted her, but he was not going to get her. He was going to miss out and the grief was so intense because he had an idea of what he was missing – he was the not quite-talented-enough player who was going to sit out the final on the bench.

As he went towards the central staircase, he passed the wooden bays that fronted the staff room. There it was in the space reserved for him: a Cellophane bag and inside it something white and soft. The bag was pulled around it tight with the excess formed into a column at the top so that it looked like an upside down mushroom.

Standing on the stairs looking at the plastic bag, he was held back by a strong sense that this was better left unopened. Eventually he reached up and took it down to look at it more closely. Even before he had done so he could see that the soft white contents consisted of a sanitary towel. Without realising, he had stopped breathing. The towel was stained with red and flecked with solids. It was not the deep red of coagulated menstrual blood but the red of coloured ink, and the solids were of dried leaves from the trees outside: deep golds and reds and the palest yellows, with some leaves

425

brown and skeletal to the point of the most delicate disintegration.

He put it back and went for a walk around the grounds. When he returned, he looked at it again. The lack of any clear point to this message – for it was obviously that – made him decide to go and see Alice Winnicott. It was a decision he would come to regret.

———

A cowboy went to San Francisco with his black cat, which he left at a friend's house while he went to buy a new suit. Dressed in his brand new suit he came back to the cat, called it by name and tried to pat it. The cat would have nothing to do with him in his new coat and hat, and hissed and spat at him. Coaxing the cat was of no avail, so the cowboy went away and put his old suit on again and the cat immediately showed its wild joy on seeing its master as it thought he ought to look.

The friendly nurse put the card she had been reading back in her top pocket. She smiled. 'All right, Mr Winnicott, you've got to try and remember it and tell the same story back to the doctor tomorrow.' She stood up. 'I'll just take your temperature.'

That night, bored and ill at ease in the ward, he tried to work on E13. In the past few weeks he had almost given up, but he thought that he would have one last try while he was in hospital where there would be more time and fewer distractions. He had even brought his palmtop dictionary and thesaurus. But he found it difficult to focus and his attention kept wandering as he tried to ignore the strange sweet smell of incontinence and disinfectant. He tried to concentrate. E. E. E. E. E was the common nickname for the drug Ecstasy. What were the synonyms of ecstasy? One of them might have thirteen letters. He typed ecstasy into the palmtop: Bliss. Transport. Rapture. Joy. Happiness.

Delight. Enjoyment. He tried playing with variations of these. Bliss gave him Blissfulness – but that was only twelve letters. And besides the answer had to be complex; there had to be much more to it than that. He would know it when he saw it.

That night he dreamt the Dark Figure was sitting on his chest dressed in a cowboy suit leaning over him with the face of a black cat. He began whispering to him: *Inert. Insensible. Insensate. Unintelligible. Incomprehensible. Incoherent. Inchoate.* Then the Dark Figure raised his huge black body up into the air as if he were a snake about to strike and screamed at the top of his voice: 'SENSELESS!'

―――――

The following day mostly consisted of hanging about in a pale green smock. It was string-tied at the back as if designed for maximum humiliation, revealing a line of spine and buttock where the hemmed material did not meet. He felt exposed every time he shifted his position as he sat in the various waiting rooms. It was like wearing a skirt – the inconvenience of it, the sense of never being able to relax in case you revealed something private. Why *did* women wear something like this all the time when they didn't have to?

He drank various liquids throughout the day whose metallic origins could not be disguised by sugar. Machines on angled arms were buzzingly passed over and under him from groin to head and back again, clicking and grinding like sharp teeth.

'Right, Mr Winnicott, I want you to repeat the story the nurse read to you yesterday as exactly as you can.'

'The one about the dog?' There was an awkward pause. 'I mean the one about the cat.'

'That's the one.'

Winnicott cleared his throat as if for a recitation and began. 'A man came to town to buy a suit and he brought his black cat with him but left it with a friend. When he returned wearing his new clothes, the black cat did not recognise him and wouldn't go near him and began to attack him. The man tried to reassure the cat that he was the same person he had always been and tried to pat the cat but the distressed animal would not let him near. The cat was very angry. So the man went and changed back into his old clothes ... he was a cowboy ... and the cat ... and the black cat ...'

He stopped. The doctor made a note on his pad in the way of an examiner marking someone down for a clumsy three-point turn or a feeble spelling mistake.

'Who is the heir to the throne?' asked the doctor, as if nothing unusual had happened.

'Prince Charles.'

'Repeat the number: 743825.'

'743258.'

'And this one: 249281.'

'248189.'

'Who was the Prime Minister during the Second World War?'

' ... Um ... not Baldwin ... it's gone.'

'What does piscatorial mean?'

'Appertaining to a fish.'

'Where do you live?'

'Harrow-on-the-Hill.'

'On the paper in front of you would you draw a map from the centre of the town to your house.'

A furious and anxious Howard Cornish paced up and down in his office as he talked into his mobile. 'Mr Ginelli, you assured me that this was the safest way of stabilising the Tower and that John Barton's suggestions were too radical. This report makes it clear that removing the lead weights and replacing them with cables was directly responsible for a lurch of ...' he looked down at the thick report in front of him, '... 1.5 millimetres to the south. That's the equivalent of one year's movement in a single night. I want to know what you intend to do.'

As chairman of the international committee responsible for the work on the tower, Ginelli was already a weary, harassed man when the call had come from the furious Cornish. Caught in the crossfire of endless disagreements about the right course of action, he had taken the blame on every side for the most thankless task of his life. If Cornish were to propose withdrawing the underwriting for the stabilisation of the tower, the effect on the already crumbling confidence in the committee would be catastrophic.

'We are already putting a further three hundred tonnes of lead ingots on the north side to halt the movement,' he said. 'We know that will work for the present time, until we consider what is to be done next.'

'And what *are* you going to do next?'

Ginelli sighed. 'In the light of events and some further investigations we have invited Mr Barton to resubmit his plan to manage a controlled subsidence on the north side by means of soil extraction.'

'Can you assure me that this time the decision will be taken on strictly scientific grounds?'

Ginelli bridled. 'I can assure you without any contradiction, Mr Cornish, that the committee has made its decisions *only* on such grounds – and at all times.'

'I hope so, Mr Ginelli. But the position is this – if you do nothing, the tower will fall. If you do the wrong thing, as has just been so impressively demonstrated, then it will fall even more quickly. So it follows that we have to be decisive, and it also follows that we have to be careful. My advice – and this advice is the best available, *I* can assure you, given everything at stake here – is that Barton's plan has been meticulous in its preparation and has the best chance of working, not least because he has made it clear that he will proceed with extreme caution—'

'Are you accusing us of being reckless, Mr Cornish?' interrupted Ginelli.

'*I'm* not accusing the committee of anything, Mr Ginelli. I'm looking at an independent report that states the committee was overly influenced by the local government of Pisa concerned about the loss of tourist revenue caused by the closure of the tower, and that insufficient consideration was given to Barton's plan for reasons which were not as scientifically objective as you suggest.'

'You talk,' said an exasperated Ginelli, 'as if it was perfectly clear what was the best thing to do. It's *never* been clear what should be done about the tower.'

'I appreciate the difficulties, but a great deal of money is at stake. Given that doing nothing is not an option, I suggest it's time that the person who everyone I've talked to says is the best man for the job is allowed to get on with it. If he's not, let me make it clear that the consequences will be serious.'

There was a defeated silence on the line. 'Mr Cornish, I am an admirer of Mr Barton – indeed, I supported his plan, but there was a vote and others eminent in the field did not. If he's allowed to go ahead with this he may well be remembered as the genius who solved the riddle of the Leaning Tower. But you should consider that he may also be remembered as the man who finally brought it crashing to the ground.'

———

Although it was dangerous with Healey still hovering, Grlscz could not afford to delay any longer. The decision about Anne Levels was made. Despite his fear of being spotted lurking outside her flat he felt he had no choice, but he was careful to avoid hanging around for hours on the off-chance. It seemed reasonable to wait until the end of the working week. He needed to tempt her into striking up a conversation with him. If Healey kept after him, she might learn about Maria. It would reassure her, make him seem less sinister, if she had been the one to approach him.

Friday night was a washout because she stayed in. He left at nine, fearing to stay longer. That meant he was obliged to return next morning.

The next day he arrived at ten-thirty, deciding to stay no more than an hour. At eleven, she came out of the flat and walked to the tube. She went shopping in Oxford Street and had lunch at the New World, a restaurant he had eaten at himself and which was famous for its dim sum as well as having the most foul tempered waiters in Chinatown – no mean feat, he thought, given the competition. He found he could safely watch the exit to the restaurant from the other side of the narrow road because of the rank of phone boxes stationed there. In deference to their location in Chinatown, a plastic pagoda roof had been stuck on each of them. Despite being virtually glass on three sides, the panes in his had become so encrusted with postcard-sized adverts for prostitutes that it had been transformed into the perfect place from which to spy on the world outside. Without any danger of being seen, he could peep through the cracks between the cards like an archer in a castle keep. He passed the wait by looking through the services on offer. Most were conventional enough – Voluptuous Australian; Big Breasted Maid – but others were less so. The most expensively produced card of all, professionally type-set on a pale gold background, was fascinating in its pitch: '*Les Girls is a co-operative of professional working girls whose aim is to provide a high standard of personal services in accordance with client needs delivered in a healthy and mutually respectful environment. In House or Visiting.*'

431

There followed two telephone numbers and an Internet address. There was a footnote which he found both unsettling and oddly poignant: "*Kissing Service Available.*" He felt a kind of kinship with the women who were behind this new deal, with their insight into the way respect and tenderness could be transformed into a thing you could touch. Anything, it seemed, could be rendered into cash.

He became so wrapped up in mulling this over that he almost missed Anne's exit from the restaurant. Berating himself for such dangerous self-indulgence, he followed her onto the Charing Cross Road and down to Trafalgar Square where she turned towards the National Gallery. Following at a distance, he arrived in time to see her enter an exhibition on the etching techniques of Rembrandt. He quickly bought a sketchpad and pencil in the museum shop, then followed her into the exhibition. The layout of the room with its numerous separating screens meant that for the first time since the lecture in Canterbury he was able to observe her closely. She wore a tailored suit which accentuated her voluptuous figure and heels which, he felt, were slightly too high given that she was tall already. He wondered if she was self-conscious about her weight and wore the heels to appear thinner. He studied her face as she walked around the room. Just below the left-hand corner of her mouth she had a raised mole, large and a beautiful creamy-brown colour. Most striking, however, was her intense concentration as she examined the etchings. This was someone, he thought, who knew how to look.

Finally she left the exhibition and went into the main rooms of the gallery. Following, he took out his sketchpad. Wherever she settled to look at a painting he would sit down as close as possible, but not too close, and draw her. After a while several people noticed what he was doing, although he was careful to

432

be discreet. Fascinated, only half hiding their interest, they scanned between the man on the bench and the woman he was drawing. As he knew they would be, the watchers were less careful of alerting Anne and in time she started to glance at him. Whenever she did so he was always looking in another direction, as if still copying from the paintings on the walls. The watchers grew bolder as the picture emerged and commented to each other on the way in which he had caught her looks. When she moved on to the next gallery so did he and, gradually, some of the watchers. By now it was clear to her what was happening and Grlscz noticed her confusion, the half-conscious way she tried to strike a more interesting pose as she looked at a painting to which she could no longer give real attention. He also noticed she was holding in her tummy. The watchers became more overt in their open examination of her, like bystanders at a lifeclass. He watched the way her eyelashes moved hesitantly, the slight, unconscious parting of her lips as her breathing quickened and the way the colour rose along her throat, darkening the skin of her neck and face. He stood up and was gone.

She turned in time to catch his retreating back, but stopped herself from going after him. The proof that this was not a pick-up, that an impulse beyond desire had obliged him to follow her, made her doubt the rights she had in what he'd made. And maybe, implausibly, she was wrong; maybe he was drawing someone else; or worse, that the truth about her he had put down on paper was better left alone.

'He was drawing a picture of you, you know.'

Startled, Anne turned, and was faced by a middle-aged couple smiling at her. She feigned surprise. 'Oh ... really?'

'It was very good,' said the man.

'Yes,' the wife agreed. 'It was just like you, and he did it so quickly.'

'It was the spitting image of you.'

Anne smiled as if mildly disappointed: what had easily come could be easily let go. 'A pity I didn't get to see it, though I'm not sure if I'd really want to.'

'You should ask to look at it,' said the man. 'It was really like you.'

'Oh well, he's gone now,' she said with regret and moved off in the direction of the man with the sketchpad. They looked after her, still smiling.

She found herself looking for him, while also pretending to herself that she was not. There was no sign of him in the next gallery, nor in the one after that. He was gone. She turned, partly sorry she had missed him and partly relieved. And then there he was, three rooms away, about to disappear down a wide spiral staircase. She immediately followed, all sense of relief vanishing as soon as he reappeared. He was about fifty yards ahead of her, and by the time she reached the bottom of the stairs he had gone again. Either he had walked out into the crowded street and would now be lost, or had gone into the museum shop directly across from her.

The rush to follow him had left her breathless, though she had not run at any stage. With one eye on the door of the shop, she searched her bag and for a blue inhaler and squirted it twice into her mouth. Almost immediately the sandy rasp in her chest eased. She walked into the shop but could not see him, although there were many displays which might have hidden him. As she turned into the annexe of the shop she saw the black sketchpad. It was lying on a table next to a display of glossy art books. She looked around but couldn't see him. She looked at the sketchpad for some time, reached out to touch it, then lost her nerve. She turned to leave, then changed her mind and, decisive at last, picked it up. The first drawing was a quick sketch of 'The Man With the Golden

Helmet', which so impressed her that she almost forgot about her own picture. The second was a nude, with carefully drawn labia which made her heart pulse. And finally her own picture. Her eyes widened as she looked.

'Excuse me.'

Anne nearly dropped the book.

'It's mine. I'm always losing the damn thing.' He clearly thought she was merely a good citizen and she quickly recovered herself. She was puzzled, and a little put out, that he did not seem to recognise her.

'Um ... look ...' She laughed, acknowledging her own embarrassment.

He watched her with polite interest.

'Were you ... Some people told me you were drawing me in the gallery back there.'

'Yes, I was,' he said.

'Can I see it?'

'You mean see it again,' he replied, smiling.

'If you like,' she said, smiling and looking him straight in the eye, refusing to be mocked.

He examined her face as she studied her portrait, watching the tiny movements of her eyes and lips as she absorbed the care and attention with which he had put her down on paper.

'It's ...'

'Beautiful?'

She laughed, the colour again flushing along her throat and face. 'No, I don't mean that.'

'So you don't think it's any good?'

'No, I don't mean that either. It's very ... impressive. I just don't think I look, well, this good.'

'Several people said it looked exactly like you.'

'I'm not beautiful,' she said, staring directly at him, daring him to flatter her.

'They didn't say you were beautiful, they said it looked exactly like you.'

435

She smiled at being teased.

'Keep it,' he said.

'I couldn't.'

'All right then.' He reached out to take it but she pulled it away. They both laughed. 'On one condition.'

She looked at him coolly, gaining a measure of control. 'Yes?'

'I've been given two tickets to a showing here next Tuesday at six. It should be interesting.'

'And?' she said, unwilling to make it too easy for him.

'I wondered if you might like to come.'

'What's it a preview of?'

'It's an exhibition of fakes.'

She laughed. 'OK, I'll see you then ... here at the shop. I have to go.'

'What's your name?'

'Anne Levels.'

'Steven Grlscz.'

She looked puzzled for a moment, then her eyes opened wide. 'You're not the one who writes about stress?'

'Yes,' he said, looking surprised.

'I've read your work. It's fascinating. What an amazing coincidence.'

Steven agreed that it was, indeed, an amazing coincidence.

'I sent you an invitation to come to a lecture I gave in January.'

Now it was his turn. 'The computer woman. I should have recognised ... I know your reputation, of course.' He looked awkward. 'Now I'm embarrassed. But I swear I only got the invite just before I had to go away. I gave it to a friend who went along. He was very impressed. But bad manners – I should have written.'

She waved her hands, brushing away the apology. 'Look, I have to go.'

They shook hands and both smiled at the slight awkwardness of the gesture. Then she turned and walked towards the exit.

He watched after her until his attention was caught by a couple in their thirties. The woman was reading a heavy art book, when her lover or husband came up behind her. He leant into her gently and with his left hand touched her almost imperceptibly on the side of her breast. Grlscz saw that the man barely realised what he was doing. She smiled, but delicately. It was not a sexual gesture, or if it was, it was desire rooted in the deepest, simplest tenderness. Then the man turned away to look at the bookshelves. Grlscz took out his diary and made a careful note.

———

The existence of fakes certainly raised a lot of questions, thought Grlscz, most of them not very interesting; but the organisers of the exhibition, entitled FAKE?, had been too anxious to avoid a number of accusations, mostly that of being philistines. In doing so they had pleased the reviewers but disappointed him. The former approved of the museum for not satisfying the general distrust of the art world by its refusal to present the forger as the craftily successful version of the child-of-three or the monkey-let-loose-with-paintbrush whose efforts were universally held to ridicule the pretensions of artists and the assertions of critics. Grlscz grew bored in the end by the playful nature of the exhibition, the arch tone indicated by the question mark that followed the title.

But he was particularly taken with a van Meegeren fake 'Vermeer'. The forger was smart. This was no copy but an attempt to invent a hypothetical Vermeer style from the missing years of his career from which nothing much remained. In doing so he had avoided the difficulties of a direct comparison of form and style. Successful enough to have fooled the experts of the 1930s, he managed to sell "Christ and the Adulteress" to Hermann Goering. This dangerous act of cheek backfired when, after the war, van Meegeren was obliged to own up to his forgery as the only means of establishing that he was not a collaborator, a confession so ironic that Grlscz laughed and in doing so attracted Anne's attention.

She had arrived at six exactly and in the five minutes' reacquaintance that followed it was clear that this punctuality was a sign of confidence. She had no fear of seeming too keen or any need to test his patience. Without formally agreeing to, they had slowly drifted apart. She was examining a nearby exhibit on the Cottingley Fairies when she heard his dry laugh and watched him, intrigued, as he became lost in thought.

What had Goering felt before this painting? wondered Grlscz. Nothing but the pride of ownership, perhaps. Many would find it comforting to think so. What if, on looking at the slightly balding, thick-lipped Christ bestowing both life and dignity upon the kneeling woman it tearfully changed his sense of what it meant to hate and to forgive? Dabbing his flabby cheeks, Jews were still gassed, collaborators shot, but sometimes, perhaps, an erring secretary remained unshouted-at, a malign subordinate found himself shunted to the Russian front rather than signing warrants of execution in a Polish town. And if he had discovered it was fake? Certainly he would have dried his eyes. But what was the status of those tears? Did a revision of the heart take place, rooting out the modest change in his idea of what it meant to behave badly? And even if it did, the secretary remained unbullied, the executions were still undone, the body was still frozen in a ditch somewhere along the road to Stalingrad.

Every owner of a discovered fake, he thought, and everyone who looked at it believing it was not must subsequently account for being moved. That there was a difference between the forger and the artist and what they made, he was sure, but what perplexed him was not only where to draw the line, but what kind of line it should be. Sincerity would seem to be the key. The artist had to mean it; in order to be beautiful it must be true. Fraudulence was what the forger painted with – for money or revenge or just for kicks. He filled the aching human need for things we shouldn't want, like status, or which don't exist, like magic. Hence Goering and his "Vermeer", and mermaids made of monkeys spliced to fish. It seemed clear enough; it's all a question of intent. But status and magic are the stuff of art. How many painters got money for art which pleased Renaissance gangsters whose only interest was to celebrate their ownership? How many Masters did the same, fooling their patrons with the truth but still got paid? Da Vinci painting a fat Italian banker's tart makes something amazing, only for four hundred years of reverence and an unnameable price to turn it into a special kind of forgery. How many gimcrack deceptions followed the salty tracks of Goering's tears and moved their gulls in ways that could not be erased by ridicule or shame at being conned? At the root of it all, magic: the perverse alchemy of the human heart trumping up something genuine from something counterfeit, generating something fraudulent from something true. *No wonder I'm so fucking desperate*, thought Grlscz.

Anne joined him and asked why he had been laughing while looking at the fake Vermeer, and he explained as they walked around the rest of the exhibits. They stopped here and there, discussing or looking in silence at the curiosities. She listened as it became clear that his was more than just a passing interest in forgeries.

'Does it really matter?' she asked. 'I mean, auction houses and investors have such an interest in what's genuine for one reason: money. This is all good fun,' she said, gesturing around the room, 'but if you collect borderline cases in anything and present them with enough glee and exclude whatever contradicts it, then of course it seems to call everything into question. My mother used to do that whenever she wanted to demoralise me for one reason or another. She'd list all the things in me that were spiteful, or selfish, or whatever quality in me she felt ought to be brought to my attention, and she'd make me feel that's what I was. I mean, she was good at it, she only used what was true. They were real instances of my genuine spite or self-ishness, but she could spin an entire personality out of two or three examples. Sorry, you don't want to know about my mother.'

Oh, but I do, he thought.

Without either issuing an invitation they found themselves outside the museum looking for somewhere decent to eat, finally deciding on the Café des Amis in St Martin's Lane.

During the walk and the first drink he learnt the basic facts: where she was born, brought up, her age, that she was divorced. They quickly moved on to jobs. 'So,' she said, 'what are you working on now?'

He sighed with genuine irritation. 'I'm trying to solve a real pig,' he said, with feeling. 'Do you know much about tomography?'

'Nothing really ... to do with computerised X-rays, isn't it?'

'I've been hired to sort out a ... well, it's a bit more than a problem. I'm a consultant for a company which has been working for years on a three-dimensional X-ray system – Tomography by Unitary Particle Computerisation, TUPC for short ... more popularly held to stand for: Totally Useless Pile of Crap.'

He kept it short since he was keen to avoid talking too much about work until he knew her better, and she was equally ready to drop the subject.

The food arrived and Anne began with the appetite of someone who hadn't eaten all day. He was nervous and started to talk about the exhibition to cover up the fact that he was barely touching his food. She picked up readily on what he had to say. 'I mean, it's all about things that can't be reproduced ... and I was thinking that exact copies are second nature to what I do. You know, I wonder if there's something important about that, I mean ... revealing about the difference between what computers are in their nature and what people are like. I was just ...' She paused and he sensed a mind grappling with something tricky and taking pleasure from doing so. She smiled. 'OK, imagine a perfect forger. He can copy everything you could observe – brushwork, ways of seeing light, signatures, everything; right canvas, right chemically constituted paints and the right ways of ageing them exactly. Then you get it examined by the perfect critic and get a perfect scientist to go along. Everything they trust to help them discover if a painting is a forgery is copied perfectly, so nothing observable distinguishes real from fake. Even if the forger tells them which is which, they'll just have to take his word for it. But then, of course, even the forger can't tell. So tell me – is it real or is it fake?'

He felt it would be wise to engage with this, that she wanted a challenge. This, he thought, is what interests this woman. 'So what?' he said. 'I can't see it matters. If it's as perfect as you say then it means the same thing. Anyway it's not as interesting as you think it is.' He smiled to signal he thought exactly the opposite. He could see she was pleased by this insulting line; it meant he felt at ease with her. Having let this sink in, he continued. 'It's too easy to get lost in impossible

441

hypotheses. There's a saying where I come from, "If Uncle Bob had tits he'd be your Auntie."' They both laughed and he let it settle before catching one of the waiters as he passed. 'Could I have some water?'

'Actually, it isn't an impossible hypothesis,' she said. 'It's going to happen, and quite soon too, and everyone will be able to have one.'

'How?' he said, disbelieving.

'They'll be perfect copies, and I mean perfect right down to the depths of the troughs caused by the distances between the bristles in the brush; but there won't be a forger, just an imaging system breaking down everything in the original into numbers and feeding it into a computer. Then, maybe, it will just etch the lot on to a metal sheet, or use laser printers or another process we haven't thought of yet. At any rate, the number's up, authenticity is on the way out.'

'Good,' he said. 'All this obsession with status will have to go. I can hardly wait.'

'I wouldn't start celebrating yet. Paradoxically enough, authenticity is going to be the next big thing.'

'Go on then,' he said, intrigued.

'Now that everyone can afford compact discs, the purists, the audiophiles, have invented something called the envelope of sound. According to them there's a space around sounds that digital recording just chops out. If you were to record the conversation we're having now on a compact disc our voices would be very clear ... but all those other little micro-sounds that creep in around our voices, that give them life ... depth, they'll disappear. For them, the pure listener, a person who loves the sound of a piano or a violin or a human voice, will absolutely be able to identify the absence of that envelope. CD is a way of playing sounds, not music. Tape or vinyl reproduce the world in the envelope of sound, digital recording just turns it into code.'

442

'Does it exist, this envelope?'

'Only if you believe in souls.'

They talked on and drank two glasses of brandy each. Then he took her home.

They stood on the steps outside her flat, facing each other.

'Give me your hand,' he said. She held it up slowly until he reached for it with friendly impatience, hooking a finger in one of his own. 'I'd like you to come to my flat and have dinner with me.'

'All right.'

'Tomorrow.'

'All right.'

'Eight?'

'Eight it is.'

He let her hand fall and gave her his card. She bent her head down to put it in her handbag and as she looked up, he moved towards her. It was so fluid and graceful a movement that by the time she was aware of it he was kissing her. She enjoyed the kiss, the way his lips touched hers. Then she stopped thinking and began to give way. It was not just his touch but the intensity of his concentration. It was as if he were measuring her with his lips and in the careful touch of his hand on her waist. He felt the tip of her tongue flick briefly, barely, into his mouth, and then she ended it. There was an awkwardness in the way she suddenly pulled back. He felt she was worried, but it did not seem to be about him. Separating herself with a reassuring smile, she moved up a step towards the stained glass door. They regarded each other with pleasure.

'Goodnight,' she said, affection already in her voice.

———

'Three, two, one. The tape is running.' Gary Epper pressed the record button and spoke into a microphone.

'This is departmental conference number one on the preliminary results of NEMO's interview with subject A417: a middle-aged woman suffering severe marital difficulties.' Epper looked around nervously. 'This is NEMO's analysis of her problem, as well as his ... its ... suggested course of action. These were not given to the subject on the day and will not be given to her before being scrutinised by the Relationship Guidance Council. In my view they are unlikely to be sent to the Council.'

There was a general stirring of interest at this and Anne, irritable after an early morning flight from Edinburgh, asked why.

'Well,' said Epper, 'NEMO's told her to run away from home.'

'What?' replied Anne, even more irritably.

Epper became flustered.

'Well?' said Anne, impatient and anxious to find out what he meant.

He grabbed at some papers beside him and dropped them. 'Bugger!' he said through clenched teeth. As three of his colleagues knelt down to help him, two clashed heads with a hollow sound that made everyone but Anne wince.

'For goodness sake, get on with it!' she said, stonily. Epper took a deep breath and started to hand round the papers as the two wounded scientists sat down, both looking at her sulkily. As the papers went swiftly round the room, Anne felt guilty. *You're turning into a bully.*

'Why is NEMO advising her to leave home?' she said, in a tone that tried to make peace with the nervous Epper.

'Well,' said Epper, still unhinged. 'It ... uh ... says that her husband is trying to poison her.'

There was a silence as half the scientists looked at Anne and the other half looked at the wall opposite. Anne sighed with disappointment.

Epper continued, his tone ingratiating. 'As you know better than I do, the mnemonic chaining codes can be very difficult to trace because there are so many blind alleys involved, but I'm pretty confident that its overall conclusion, at least in terms of the advice to leave home, is derived from the ABUSE expert system we tried to set up for Strathclyde Social Services in 1986.' He turned to those in the room who were newer to the department. 'We'd been asked to devise an expert system to cope with women suffering physical abuse from their husbands, and children suffering sexual abuse. It was a success as a system but, unfortunately, the social workers refused to use it.'

'Why?' asked someone.

Anne interrupted. 'They said that the notion of "expertise" in child and wife abuse decision-making was "totally suspect", as one of them put it. Perhaps we could go into this later if anyone's interested.'

'Right,' said Epper quickly. 'Well, if you look at page one of the paper I've given you you'll see I've printed out the rule it seems to have used – there are about four hundred and fifty in the knowledge base altogether.'

There was a rustling of papers and a request for another copy from someone who had contrived to lose the one he had been given in the two minutes since he'd been given it. They all looked attentively at the sheet on which the rule was written as follows:

IF THE CONDITION OF SUBJECT IS [UNHAPPY]
<-> 7
    AND THE TYPE OF [UNHAPPY] IS [MARITAL]
    AND THE TYPE OF {[UNHAPPY] [MARITAL]}
       IS EXTREME [PHYSICAL DAMAGE] <-> 8
THEN there is suggestive evidence that the
subject should leave marital dwelling.

'What do the numbers seven and eight mean?' asked someone.

Epper looked almost simperingly at Anne and replied. 'Anne had the idea to grade levels of unhappiness or violence on a scale of 1–10. The social services were dismissive, very, at the time, but in practice it worked well. I understand it's the only bit of the system they still use.'

He smiled at Anne and she felt ashamed that she had forced a man of Epper's ability to behave towards her in such an ingratiating way. *You can be a real cow sometimes*, she thought to herself. Then she looked more carefully at the paper and saw the bizarre nature of the reasoning. 'Where, in God's name, did it get the idea she was being poisoned from?'

'I checked it out,' said Epper, 'and there's nothing in what she said to NEMO during the interview, or in any of the other records we inputted, to possibly justify that inference.'

Anne became intrigued. 'What can it mean?'

'Well,' said Epper, the light in his eye gleaming with the hope of redemption, 'I think I know.'

'Well?' she said, and her mouth was open like a toddler's hungry for a late meal.

'At one point NEMO accessed the DORIS system.' He explained quickly because not everyone was familiar with all the systems at NEMO's disposal. 'DORIS is a collection of script-like representations called MOPS, TOPS, TAUS, META-MOPS ...' He was halted by an urgent look from Anne. 'Uh ... that's not very important at the moment. To cut a long story short they're used to break down all the quotations in the Oxford Dictionary of Quotations.'

Anne interrupted, torn between her desire to get on and her desire to hammer home her most abiding obsession after NEMO. 'Let's get it straight, these aren't the quotations or even a formal representation of the lines quoted. They're just ...' she cast around for the right way of explaining herself, ' ... diagrams. Imagine a diagrammatic representation of, say, the concepts in the Gettysburg address.' She looked back at Epper, urging him again to get on with it.

'Well,' continued Epper, 'it seems to have searched through the program in several directions at once, and three of them met up. One of them was food, the other was love, and the third was unhappiness. It ended up with a quote from Tennyson. It's printed on page two.' There was a quick rustle and they collectively pored over what was written there:

1 HONEY: (has-property) edible
2 POISON. (has-property) sickness
3 LOVE: (has-property) food.
4 Absence, imperative [cause] {love}: (has-property) insane, wicked [honey; poison]

'This is a diagrammatic representation of the quotation printed below,' said Epper, the gleam now a shine. They all looked down as one and read:

And most of all would I flee from the cruel madness of love –
The honey of poison-flowers and all the measureless ill.

'Not quite the same, is it?' said someone.

'Fascinating,' breathed Anne at last. 'Why did it search food?'

'She talked about that a lot,' said Epper. 'It seems she was always dieting, and he was always cooking for her, preparing her meals, always worried she wasn't eating enough. "It was a real sore point between us" as she put it.'

'Fascinating,' said Anne again. 'She's unhappy. He

loves her because he's worried about her appetite. Love can make people unhappy. Love is a kind of food, therefore he is poisoning her because he is always feeding her in a way that makes her unhappy. Poison is fatal, therefore she must leave home. Strange,' she said, smiling, 'but not much help to Mrs Nan— the woman. An interesting failure.'

'Are you talking about me or the program?' said Epper, smiling. Anne laughed, and he noticed the movement of her breasts, languid as if she were not wearing a bra. Deep down something stirred in him, as desire and resentment began to weave together.

The bell had just gone at Maybes Grammar School for Girls and floods of teenage girls were rushing up and down the school's stairwell, a huge tower that stood slightly apart from the main building to which it was linked at each floor. At the end of each period upwards of six hundred noisy girls flushed through its numerous flights, generating the raucously echoing din that caused it to be known as the Tower of Babel. Martin Beck, English teacher and the frustrated lover of Anne Levels, was walking down to Alice Winnicott's office and had been caught in one of these A-line skirted spates. Even the weediest of the girls lurched about the stairway under the weight of schoolbags that looked large and angular enough to contain half a dozen breeze blocks. Perhaps that's what they were and he had stumbled across a new form of female self-punishment to displace the eating disorder. Certainly whenever he was clattered by one, which he frequently was, it felt as if he'd been hit by an object solid enough to be used in the construction of a garage or a bathroom extension. He considered the long-term effects. It was possible that in the future all women would lean slightly to one side, that skinny girls would fall over more often in the twenty-first century and no one would ever know that it was caused by the disinvention of the school desk.

Escaping to the second floor, he approached Alice Winnicott's office. Martin considered her an intelligent but unlikeable woman. They had not got on particularly well even before the parents' evening when her husband had collapsed, but after this her attitude to him seemed to have soured even further. Possibly he was being over-sensitive because everyone knew that her husband was seriously ill and in hospital. Maybe she was like this with everybody because she was worried. But he didn't think so. He had wavered in his initial decision to go and see her for nearly a week because he was reluctant to admit that consulting her was a form of subservience. It wasn't altogether a good thing to be on Alice Winnicott's bad side. He knocked on her door and went in. She was staring out of the window. Slowly she turned towards him.

'What can I do for you?' She had clearly seen the bag he was holding and registered its contents. 'Oh. Where did that come from?'

He put it on the table in front of her. She winced in a way that was both delicate and calculated.

'I think you should look inside.'

'Must I?'

'It's not quite what you think.'

She opened it without any further show of distaste and looked at it carefully and thoughtfully.

'I found it in my bay outside the staff room.'

'Ah,' she said in a tone that made it plain that all was now clear to her, 'that does make a difference.'

'To what?'

'Do I have to spell it out?'

'Yes, I think you probably do.'

'This is a girls' school.' She looked at him patronisingly. 'You are an attractive young man.' She gestured as if to say, "Obviously you know the rest."

'Isn't it more usual to leave an apple?'

'That's girls for you. They're hysterical creatures and if you start taking them too seriously they'll run away with you. Ignore it. Leave it to me to sort out.'

He was not willing to be fobbed off. 'What about the ink and the leaves?'

'Be thankful for small mercies. I am.' She looked at him dismissively. 'There's often less to things than meets the eye, wouldn't you say?'

'As it happens, yes I would, but not in this case.'

He reached to pick up the bag, but she swiftly placed it her desk drawer.

'I'd like it back, if you don't mind,' he said.

She looked at him calmly. 'I'm afraid this must be considered my responsibility now. But are you sure you want me to look into this? I can't think what you expect to find.'

He was surprised by her attitude. Normally she would have seized the opportunity this gave for one of the interrogations at which she excelled.

'I want to know what it's about.'

'Even if it's *about* anything, I don't know what makes you think it isn't going to be decidedly unpleasant. Girls can be sordid sometimes. I've seen things you'd hardly believe.'

'Really?'

The disdain in his voice clearly offended her and there was genuine anger in her reply. 'There's always one of two things wrong with men teaching in girls' schools, I find, and in your case it's the way you sentimentalise women. You came here expecting some kind of refuge. You think that women are nicer, kinder, and that you'll find something here you think you lack. Well, they're not, and you won't.'

450

Not bad, he thought. 'What's the other thing?'

She picked up a pen and began to write. Her voice changed tone from malice to disdain. 'What do you think?'

Closing the door behind him he said to himself, 'Idiot!' and went down to the book cupboard to collect thirty copies of *Kes*.

In her office Alice Winnicott was staring out of the window again, having already forgotten Martin Beck.

After three dates, the dinner at his flat, a meal at a restaurant and a visit to the theatre, Anne seemed to have decided Steven was to be trusted. To his surprise, the daring implied by her seeking him out in the museum and accepting his invitation so quickly was not altogether as strong in her as he'd hoped. She had turned out to be a cautious woman, reserved even. While not evasive about her past, his careful questions were only answered up to a point. This might be either a difficulty or an opportunity.

The invitation to pick her up at her flat before going out to dinner with her friends was clearly an act of social acclimatisation. A good sign, like being taken home to Mum for tea. He had arrived on time but she had not finished drying her hair.

While she was in the bedroom, he looked around the living room. It was untidy, although not remarkably so. Two pairs of shoes lay on the floor as well as the previous Sunday's papers, and two dirty mugs on a side-table. He went over to the window and examined her bookcase carefully. There was some nineteenth-century fiction – Dickens, Eliot – then nothing until early Greene; some European fiction – Mann, Kundera – *The Hip and Thigh Diet*; an American paperback of *Paradise Lost* that looked as if it had never been read; a Fontana Modern Masters on Jung and another on

Auden; the collected essays of Malcolm Muggeridge; and a former library book: *The Man with the Golden Gun*, which was also a first edition. He looked inside two, the diet book and *Paradise Lost*, noting that the name inside each was the same. He took out a small black diary from his inside pocket and made a few notes.

He looked over his shoulder. She was standing in the doorway; her hair was dry but she was still in her dressing-gown. 'Writing about me?' she said, nodding at the book.

'An idea for work. If I don't write them down straight away ...'

She pointed her index finger at the books. 'What do you think?' she said.

He took up the challenge. 'Well read, certainly, but slightly ashamed of being conventional – but not ashamed enough to do much about it.' He looked at the bookcase again. 'Someone dishonest, but not in a very imaginative way and not to any great extent.' He pulled out the Fleming and opened it. 'On the other hand, this is a first edition, so maybe I'm underestimating them. Or should that be overestimating? Someone who likes to sneer, who thinks they're less easily fooled than other people.'

'Anything else?' Her voice was flat.

'Yes.' He paused, looking at her directly. 'They have a big bum.'

She laughed, realising that he knew the books were not hers. 'If there's anything that interests you, take it. They're not mine. They were in the flat when I rented it.'

'Conventionally that means they're not yours to give.'

'They said they were coming back for them, but they never did. That was two years ago. Most of my stuff is in store.'

She turned and went to finish dressing. Steven continued looking around the room. On a large table by the far wall lay piles of thick scientific textbooks. Two of them, *Artificial Intelligence and Language* and *Cognitive Technologies*, had been written by Anne herself. He made a note of the titles. Behind the tallest stack of books he found a bonsai tree. At first, never having been close to one before, he thought that it must be artificial, so striking was its manikin perfection: gnarled, twisted and ancient. Even the tiny size of what looked like a yew could not diminish the feeling of mass wrought by years of patient growth. This is a tree, he thought; not a toy, a clever act of miniaturisation, a trivial but patient act of manipulation. It was an old tree.

'It was my grandfather's,' she said, again appearing silently, now dressed in a green evening dress and vivid mustard jacket. The colours were slightly too strong for each other; they didn't clash but neither did the combination work. 'He brought it back from Japan fifty years ago. It was already over a hundred years old when it was given to him.'

'It's extraordinary.'

She looked over at the table on which he had placed a bottle of champagne. 'Celebrating?'

'Yes. I've got a new contract with the Wellcome Foundation.'

She smiled. How pleased was she, he wondered. It looked as if she felt genuinely glad at his news. This was a measure of something.

'So, tell me about it.' She went over to the sideboard and took out two tumblers. 'Sorry they're not proper champagne glasses.' By now he had taken off the foil and popped the cork. 'Well?'

'I've been working for a while now on stress – on the way it affects the body.'

'Like ulcers?'

453

'Yes, though it's beginning to look as if ulcers are caused by bacteria rather than stress ... but that's life I suppose. Anyway, there's a lot of work to be done, putting all the research on stress together. I've persuaded them that there's more to be gained by examining what we already know more carefully than by doing more new investigations.'

As he had hoped, her eyes lit up, and for the next half-hour she questioned him non-stop. She spent the next hour delightedly answering questions about her own ideas. Their views were almost identical.

'Funny, isn't it?' she said finally, 'that we should see things in the same way.'

'Yes,' he agreed. 'It is extraordinary.' He paused, started to speak, then stopped.

'What?' she said.

'I shouldn't ask.'

She smiled but it was not clear why.

She's a tricky one, this, he thought.

'If you don't ask, I can't say no.' She laughed sweetly. 'You *do* want something?'

He laughed. 'Yes, I do. But only in the disinterested pursuit of knowledge.'

'Spit it out.'

'This machine of yours, I don't suppose you could ask it to do some searching for me, looking for things on stress ... on anything related.'

She didn't say anything at first and he wondered if he had offended her, that this was like asking to borrow money. But she was only thinking whether she could really be of help. 'I can try. We'll need to spend a few hours setting out the search parameters. Just don't be disappointed if it comes up with nothing. But I can tell you it's neither powerful enough nor consistent enough to be comprehensive. We've got a lot of medical databases linked in but ... well, the point is, don't expect too much. The research I was telling you about ... the paper on slugs and how their secretions thin the blood. Well, it was a bit of a fluke to be honest. We'll get there one day, but don't get your hopes up.' She looked at her watch and groaned. 'We *must* go.'

———

They were having dinner at a floating restaurant with friends of hers. He was anxious because he knew that Martin Beck would be there. She had responded easily enough to his careful probing about Beck. He had been a casual date who had become a good friend. It was a black tie occasion, a fund-raiser for a hospital where one of Anne's friends worked. Unreassuringly, Beck was rather good-looking. Steven could easily see why Anne would enjoy his company since he was amusing and easy to talk to, but it was also easy to see why she did not view him romantically. From what he had already gathered about her – and no new lover could have been more attentive – he sensed Beck was simply not her type. He was not intense enough for her. On the other hand, that women's taste in men was difficult to read at the best of times was revealed by the woman Beck had brought with him, Karen. Attractive, stunning, beautiful, none of these words could describe her. The problem lay, he felt, in the degree of workmanship involved in her appearance. The short black dress accentuated the aerobicised figure which lacked even the slightest curve along the tummy, the most touching of all the soft arcs of the female body, he thought, yet the one displayed, if ever, with the most regret. Her face was flawless, like an artefact. What such a woman saw in Beck was an intriguing mystery.

Still, he found Anne's friends easy to relax with and he was at his most amusing. The conversation drifted comfortably and when they got on to the subject of names someone pointed out that of the eight people there, four had surnames of eastern European origin.

Steven's was the most unusual and he wrote it down for them on a napkin: GRLSCZ.

'How do you say it again?' asked one of the other women around the table.

'GRILSH,' he replied.

'I wouldn't have had a clue how to pronounce it if I hadn't heard it first,' said Karen, leaning towards him with a lascivious enthusiasm she made no attempt to disguise either to Beck or Anne.

'It's Bulgarian,' said Steven. 'The shortages over there are so bad you even have to queue for vowels.'

As well as playing the part of the amusing new boyfriend, Steven had been keeping an eye on the other diners. At one of the tables close by sat a couple in early middle age. They did not talk much and it was always the woman who began any conversation. Steven saw that she was eavesdropping on a heated exchange between a much younger couple behind her, while the husband stared into the distance. Still lost in thought, Steven saw him gently stroke his wife's index finger, just two or three times. She smiled, as if reminded of a familiar and deep-seated pleasure. She loves this man very much, thought Steven. Still looking at the couple, Steven gently stroked the top of Anne's hand, leaving his just barely in contact. Feeling his touch, Anne turned to look at him, watching his distracted gaze. She was about to speak when Karen leant forward, deliberately addressing him with her cleavage.

'So, Steven ... tell me about how you met Anne. Drawing her picture! So romantic, or was it just a clever routine?'

He looked at Anne and smiled softly. 'It was just a clever routine.'

But it did not work. Anne's hand had barely a fraction of a millimetre to disengage, but the coldness with which she did so made it seem as if she had wrenched herself free.

There was a sudden flurry of movement among the waiters as they started to move quickly around the tables, filling every glass with wine. At the far end of the room, standing self-importantly beside the guests of honour, stood a fat toast-master whose red face was only a few shades lighter than his absurdly tiny formal jacket. As the waiters hurried about their refills, one of them accidentally shoved Anne's chair as he rushed to finish serving the table. She turned, eyes flashing, but the waiter had gone. She turned back to the table with a murderous expression on her face.

The toastmaster stuck his chest out like a fat pigeon and began to speak. 'Ladies and gentlemen and honoured guests,' he bawled, 'please raise your glasses in honour of our patron, the Duchess of Montrose. Pray be upstanding.'

The room, fuelled by an excess of alcohol and too-rich food, scraped noisily to its feet like an exhausted, drugged leviathan, drowning out the remainder of the toast.

Later in the car park Anne's temper did not improve when her old, or as she described it, classic BMW refused to start. They walked to Leicester Square tube with Steven making efforts to keep the conversation going without making it too obvious he was doing so. He did not expect to lift her bad mood, but to prevent it catching fire. It was late and the station was full of people going home from a night in town. The air was thick with the heavy scent of booze on people's breath, so strong it was like an unwelcome kiss. The screechy voices of young men echoed down the tiled corridors – an exuberance that might, or might not, be laced with paranoid violence. It added unease to her coldness. They waited in silence for the train and when it came he stepped through the sliding doors with her. She looked at him as if he had walked uninvited through her front door.

'I thought it might be best if I came with you.' He nodded in the direction of four men laughing and shouting at the far end of the carriage.

She gave a dispiritingly ghostly smile of thanks. 'I do this journey all the time on my own.'

There was an awkward beat, not least because he had expected her to relent a little at his concern. Caught out by this, and having to move quickly to get off the train, he moved to kiss her. It was merely a gentle attempt to touch her lips, but she turned her head, offering him only her cheek and instantly pulling away.

'Mind the doors,' came the driver's voice over the intercom, his boredom apparent even through the distant crackle of the clapped-out speaker.

Steven stepped outside, and as the doors closed he called out, 'I'll ring you tomorrow.'

She smiled with all the warmth of a January sun.

He walked along the platform as the train took her away, wondering how the evening had disintegrated so very badly.

———

After shaving the next morning, Grlscz looked at himself in the mirror, searching his reflection. He smiled. It was a warm smile, seeming to mock the intensity of his self-absorption, as if catching himself in an act of vanity he had the grace to find himself faintly ridiculous. It faded to a watchful blankness. A phone rang and he was instantly alert and moving. It was not the phone in his living room and he felt a stab of disappointment that it could not be Anne. He ran up the stairs and was at the door of the spare bedroom by the beginning of the third beat and answering it before the fourth.

'Hello,' he said softly.

There was no reply but someone was there; the hesitancy, the awkwardness, the shame emerging in the imperceptibly faint breath. He waited.

'It's you, isn't it?' he said, his voice generous, kind, longing.

But there was only silence in reply. Then the buzzy drone as it went dead.

———

Martin Beck looked at Nick Gau through the window of the history book room. Gau was in his early forties and must once have been beautiful. Time, his dishevelled clothes and what he proudly referred to as his fast-food and malt whisky gut, had eroded his looks, although from time to time in a good light and after a proper night's sleep his lost bloom would return briefly. The general effect was that of an over-the-hill angel dressed by Oxfam and fed by Burger King. He was loathed by most of the women on the staff because he treated the things that were important to them with aggressive indifference. This dislike invariably boiled over during the termly ritual of report-writing.

Report-writing at Mabey's had nothing to do with an attempt to fix a moment of time in the intellectual and emotional growth of a developing human being in all their flux and fractal roar. Anything but. Martin had once been the unwitting cause of gasps and pursed lips in the staffroom when he had written that one girl was *"lazy, and she had better start doing some work or she will fail her exams"*. This had been amended by the head of the sixth form to read *"she should be more rigorous in her approach and pay closer attention to her texts"*. In this way the possibility of disturbance – parents might complain, questions might be asked – could be eliminated by language which sought to eradicate itself even as the sentence was being read. Ideally, nothing should emerge from a Mabey's report. Each one aspired to a set of self-annihilating symmetries drained of every quark of sense, a bliss of utter meaninglessness. A friend of Martin's had recently

459

come home after working in Japan for many years. The Japanese, he said, were mad, but it was only now, returning after all this time, that he realised the English were even more deranged. The Japanese had at least acknowledged their violence, hatred, and disdain by making life possible through the world of ritual. The English were stranger than the Japanese, he said, because they acknowledged none of it. Martin thought he was wrong in at least one respect. Like a Japanese tea ceremony, a Mabey's report was intended to create a moment of absolute stillness, of total self-abnegating purity in which all disorders, fragments, paradox, all the howl and crash of life, were to be eliminated by total attention to pure form.

Despite the disapproval of his own failure at report writing, it was nothing compared to Gau's first attempt. These reports were legendary because he had written them using green ink. The sheer fury of Emma Caxton, who was responsible for the sixth-form reports, seemed rooted in her notion of the sacrilegious; she was affronted in a way that only the notion of profanity could explain. Martin was with Gau when she came to tell him to do the reports again. 'It's green,' she kept saying, 'it's green,' in the tone one would normally hear the words "rape" or "incest" or "massacre". She seethed as if real flesh were burning. The intensity of her anger was obvious and she spoke to him with the studied determination of someone controlling physical pain. Yet it was as if she were muzzled, but by what Martin couldn't think. He put it down at the time to her cowardice, since Gau was not a new-girl teacher straight out of college who could be easily traumatised by sharp words. It was only months later that he began to understand that her inability to let her anger flow was not due to lack of courage, nor did this inability stop at Gau, nor was it confined to Emma; none of these women in late middle age knew how to be angry with a man.

Interestingly, it was only the women over fifty that Gau treated in this way. But there was nothing timid about these women. They did not suffer from doubt or low self-esteem and within their departments they were as ferocious and arbitrary as robber barons; but when dealing with men something was missing, or was present, which confounded them like Antony's spirit before Caesar's. For Gau it had become an addictive semi-spectator sport, like bear-baiting. He didn't care what tethered them but he trusted it as if it were a chain hammered into the ground by a steel spike.

Martin opened the door and went in. Gau was sitting on the window-sill at the furthest point in the room from a fifth-former, a girl of about fifteen. She was an extraordinarily beautiful child with a delicate bone structure, enormous eyes and a strong, athletic body.

'Ah, Martin, come and have some Earl Grey.'

'Have I interrupted?'

'Not at all.' He looked at the girl and smiled. 'Emily was just about to leave. You've got some poor third-formers to go and oppress, haven't you, my dear?'

She got up, leaving the full cup of tea on the table next to her, and said, 'Thank you, Mr Gau.' Gau waved to her without looking as he filled a kettle from a large jug which had written on it: "Not to be removed from the chemistry lab". Speaking over his shoulder he said, 'I hear you've been visited by the curse. I must say, at twenty-nine you're a bit of a late developer.'

'So it's out.'

'Indeed it is. By the end of break you'll be the talk of the staff room.'

'How come?'

'You surprise me. I mean, what a mixture of the unspeakable, the shameful and, hush, the sexual! Such an opportunity for a lifting of eyebrows, a lowering of voices and the shaking of heads. In our neck of

461

the woods sorry stuff like this passes for scandal. They think all their birthdays have come together.'

Martin looked at him as he brought the tea. 'Is it sorry stuff?'

Gau looked at him, disdainful and mocking. 'She didn't even drop the real thing in your bag as her little act of spite. Typical bloody Mabey's girl. I mean, if you're going to do something like that at least do it properly. I'd have admired that; it would have shown some balls.'

'Maybe it wasn't an act of spite.'

This delighted him. 'It's not your birthday, is it? My dear fellow, you should have said, I'd have baked a cake. I suppose you think the red ink and ... what was it?'

'Leaves,' said Martin quietly.

'Leaves ... dear God. So there's a message in the entrails, is there?'

'Yes, I think there probably is.'

'And what would it be?'

'I don't know. You're so sure of yourself, you tell me.'

'You're barking up the wrong tree, old son. Forget symbolism and psychology. Biology, that's the answer. Women are complicated creatures. I don't mean emotionally complicated or any of that, I mean physically complicated. They're an endless succession of tubes and tunnels, exits and entrances, causeways and cul-de-sacs, obstructions and blind alleys. And the chemicals that serve them! My God! Endless secretions and discharges and hormones. Half an ounce of FSH could poison a small city. It's a factory in there and it doesn't really work – it's always on strike or dumping things illegally into the river.' He took out a cigarette from a packet of ten Benson and Hedges on the table, lit up and blew out the first lungful in a long, extravagant breath.

'Women are like Third World countries that buy these complicated tractors that can do amazing things but no one knows how to fix when they go wrong – which they do all the time because they're too complicated. No infrastructure, that's the trouble with emerging nations, and that's the trouble with women. What they need is experts, professionals, specialists. Instead, all they've got is you and me.' He took another long drag at his cigarette. 'Look, they have to go to well woman clinics even when there's nothing wrong with them. And you know what? They always find something. A well woman? Take it from me, old son, there's no such thing.' He took a deep swig from his mug. 'God, I feel sorry for them,' he said breezily. 'Don't bother looking for an elaborate explanation for your little present. With all that lot going on inside them, it's no wonder they're all so fucking crazy.'

———

Grlscz had thought carefully about how he would make up with Anne. He was alarmed at the unfairness of her response, its obvious irrationality. He had done nothing to encourage Karen. In the end he decided it would be no bad thing if he allowed his sense of unfairness to emerge. If she wanted a fight, he saw no alternative. This, in turn, made him wary. Being spontaneous was dangerous. There was an alarming pleasure in indignation. Letting himself go was always a temptation, like an athlete resisting a plate of chips, or a Mars Bar, or an extra hour in bed.

To his relief, she phoned two days later and invited him over. When he arrived, he could tell she had decided she had gone too far, and the distance between them consisted solely of her uncertainty as to how she could let it go without the loss of too much dignity. While she was in the kitchen making tea he came up behind her and put his arms around her waist, kissing the back of her neck. He felt her relax then stiffen again, but as he looked at her sideways on, with his head over her shoulder, he could see that she was mocking herself.

'Oh, Steven,' she said, mimicking Karen's breathily sexy voice, 'if I hadn't read your name, I'd never know how to pronounce it.'

'And what was I supposed to do, refuse to talk to her?'

'You could have taken your eyes off her cleavage for five seconds.'

An expression of mock confusion settled over his face. 'What cleavage?'

She laughed as she pretended to turn her head away from him, covering her face with her long black hair.

'I was incredibly embarrassed, as it happens. I had visions of Martin asking me to step outside.'

'Martin?' The note of friendly derision in her response settled any lingering concern about Beck's status.

'I said I was embarrassed, I didn't say I was worried.'

'Ooooh! You're going to have to show me your gold-medallion collection, Tiger.' Now she was making fun of him. A good sign.

'I don't have a gold-medallion collection,' he said. 'But I do have some etchings I'm pretty anxious for you to look at.'

She turned round and kissed him with an intensity that surprised him, her body pushing into him. Her tongue touched his lips again, and, for a moment, he felt just the tip inside his mouth. She was exploring the edge of some high dive. But she wasn't ready yet for the vertiginous leap, the loss of control, the surrender to a fundamental force. Slowly she eased herself back. He could feel it leaving her in the touch of her lips, the movement of her arm, the way she relaxed her body, the force of her breath upon his face. This was all right, he thought, this would do.

She went over to her briefcase and brought out a file. She was smiling. 'This is to say I'm sorry for being such a bad-tempered madam.' There were two papers. 'Have a look – it's all right.'

He sat down and began to read. The first was a report from the *Lancet*, dated 1951, on the growth patterns of children in two German orphanages just after the war. The second was much more recent: *Neonatal Intensive Care for Low Birth Weight Infants: Miami 1986.*

He read for twenty minutes then looked up at her. She could see how grateful he was, and was touched. He was clearly excited by what he had read. 'Thanks,' he said. 'This could be of immense help.'

'Don't thank me, thank NEMO. Would you like to?'

She went over to her computer and began typing. After a couple of minutes she turned back to him. 'Come on.' He walked over to her and she put a headset on him. 'Just talk normally.'

'How do you thank a computer?'

'Don't bother. We haven't got round to teaching it about gratitude yet.'

'What shall I say?'

'Ask it for advice about your love life.'

'What?' He felt uneasy about this.

'It's programmed to behave as an analyst. It's one of our trickiest research areas but we've learned a lot from doing it. And, of course, there's funding for it. Always a good reason to pursue a research field, in my view. The program's a bit of a mess at the moment, we're doing a major rethink, but it can be good fun.'

'What shall I say?'

'*Do* you have any problems with your love life?' she said, laughing.

'My love life is perfect.'

'Then we'll just have to pretend.'

She typed for a few seconds and then looked at him. 'NEMO's got a voice but it's not patched up to work here, so it'll just answer on the screen. Tell it your name.'

'My name is Steven Grlscz.'

I'm sorry, could you repeat your name.

'My name is Steven Smith.'

How may I help you, Steven?

He looked at Anne.

'Tell it you're unhappy,' she whispered.

'I'm unhappy.'

Why are you unhappy, Steven?

'Nobody loves me.'

She giggled and again he was struck by the musical sound of her voice when she laughed.

Why do you think nobody loves you, Steven?

She leant close to his ear and he could feel the warmth of her breath. 'Tell it, because I'm too good to be true.'

This sent a spasm of alarm through him. But she was, he thought, too subtle to mean it. It was a joke which meant she felt at ease with him. Or perhaps not. Make the best of it, he thought.

'I'm too good to be true,' he said.

Why are you too good to be true?

'Ask Anne Levels.'

Tell me about Anne Levels.

'She's bad-tempered and unkind.'

Anne laughed. Good.

Why is she unkind, Steven?

'I don't know. But everybody says so.'

She laughed again and hit his shoulder. Even better.

Are you thinking of anyone in particular?

'Not really. Just one or two people who know her well.'

She brushed an imaginary speck of dust from her

bosom and said softly in his ear, 'I think I feel a headache coming on.'

Steven, tell me more about what *you* think of Anne Levels.

He looked her directly in the eye and put the palm of his hand around the side of her breast so delicately she could barely feel it. 'The smell of her breath is like apples and her lips are like a thread of scarlet. And there is no flaw in her.'

Steven began laughing and she groaned: they had both noticed NEMO's reply simultaneously.

Tell me about Anne Levels' floor.

She sighed. 'As you can see, NEMO has its limitations,' She stroked his face. 'Unlike you, it isn't perfect.'

There it was again – the affection and the reservation.

'Is that what you think?'

'Absolutely.'

'Not a very likeable quality.'

She pouted apologetically. 'Don't worry, I'm only joking. Don't take everything I say so seriously.'

'If you insist,' he said, mocking himself.

Martin Beck was working on Anne's car and thinking. He enjoyed listening to Gau but he did not like him, and he liked him even less after the conversation they'd had the afternoon they'd talked about the sanitary towel. He was thinking about what Gau had said about women. Although Martin was capable of the deepest affection he was not a man of extremes, but he was uncomfortably aware that he was finding it difficult to avoid thinking about Anne more or less all the time. His relationship with Karen was little more than a not-very-close friendship with sex included, and he was surprised it had lasted so long. He didn't even

467

find her all that sexually attractive. He couldn't understand why he didn't. It seemed perverse not to find someone who so exactly fitted the modern conventions of what was gorgeous not to be all that exciting. He liked looking at her naked body but that was the greatest pleasure by far. Her breasts practically pointed at the sky and her stomach was six-pack flat, her legs and buttocks taut. Perhaps that was the problem. That was the current ideal for women, even among women: a boy with big tits. And he didn't much care for it.

There was nothing boyish about Anne. He laughed as soon as he thought it: she was all woman. There were no straight lines on her. The way her little tummy bulged slightly beneath her clothes was almost as maddening as the way her breasts seemed to be in a permanent state of movement, twin sirens calling innocent men onto the rocks of frustrated desire. And what Karen wanted from him was a mystery, given that what she clearly *did* want was someone as utterly unlike him as it was possible to be. It went back to what Gau had been saying about how unfathomable women could be. He had never thought about the differences between men and women much before because he had never needed to, and in any case he had moved from teenager to man at a time when that kind of thinking was regarded as reactionary. He certainly liked being around women. He had been elbowed by his girlfriends about as often as he had elbowed them, and when he had been the elbower he had shown, he thought, rather more consideration for their feelings than had generally been shown to him as elbowee. Anne liked him, he knew, but he felt she did not take him seriously. Why not? he wondered. He was at least as good-looking as Steven Thingy. He was as educated, as interested in her and her work. He made her laugh and he had read in innumerable women's magazines how that was supposed to be a great aphrodisiac. Presumably that was bollocks like almost everything else you read in them. Sighing, he finished off adjusting the timing chain, shut the bonnet with a bad-tempered bang and went inside to clean up.

As he went through her front door, she looked up from her magazine expectantly. 'What's the verdict?' she asked.

'It'll be all right for now, but basically the engine's buggered,' he replied grumpily. 'Classic cars are all very well but it needs about three thousand quid spent on it.' He looked at her pointedly. 'I did warn you when you bought it.'

She smiled at him sweetly. 'Some people don't like their friends to say I told you so – but it's a quality in you I've always admired.'

He went to the bathroom, washed his hands and decided that a certain amount of careful probing might make things clearer. He was pretty confident that Anne had no real sense that he was smitten. Perhaps that was the problem. Maybe he wasn't intense enough. He came out of the bathroom.

'So, how's the great love affair going?'

'What?' she said, not looking up from an article on the means by which her pout could be perfected by applying Rouge Pulp, whatever that was, to the centre of her lips then working outwards.

'You and Steven,' he said.

She looked at him, puzzled. 'Why?'

'Because I've just done about two hundred pounds worth of work on your car and the least you can do is talk to me.'

Sighing extravagantly she put the magazine down. 'Actually it's going very well.' She paused for a moment as if considering something she had not thought about explicitly before. 'He's so … *attentive*.'

'You mean he opens the car door for you and helps you on with your coat?'

Her eyes narrowed. 'Yes, that's exactly what I mean.'

'All right, I'm sorry. Attentive in what way?'

She began to wonder why he was asking, but answered anyway, just in case he was becoming more interested in her than she wanted him to be.

'He's attentive because he really listens. And I mean *really* listens. I mean, you know the usual agreement between couples – I'll let you bore me about your day at the office if you'll let me bore you. Ten minutes each of: *oh dear, how awful, he didn't, did he?* All that.' She paused again. 'But Steven listens. He's so curious. You can feel his absolute attention on you. You feel the focus. He listens to everything I say as if it were always incredibly important.'

'That doesn't bother you, that kind of intensity?' he said, hoping that a hint might make her find this off-putting rather than thrilling.

She thought about this for a moment. 'No,' she said with absolute finality. 'These days if you really want someone to listen to you carefully, you have to lie on a couch and pay them fifty pounds an hour.'

'He sounds perfect.'

He missed the microscopic widening of her eyes as this sonared its way into the depths. She laughed, awkward. 'You know, he *is* difficult to read. I mean, he's …' She searched but failed to find the exact word. 'I don't really understand him all that well … I don't get a sense of what's going on inside.'

'I thought women liked men with a bit of mystery about them.'

She laughed. 'Not really, only the kind of mystery where you know the answer. Now that I think about it, he's attentive to everything. He watches people.'

'You mean he gawps at girls?' This sounded usefully dubious.

'No, nothing like that. He watches people, carefully.

470

You know how we met, him drawing my picture? Well, he's a bit like that all the time. You get the sense that he's drawing in his head.' She laughed. 'And he writes things in little black books.'

This was more like it. Perhaps she was, after all, just a little dissatisfied. Even though she was mocking her uncertainties, there was, he thought, an edge to them.

She had been about to tell him what she had seen Steven doing on the night they had all had dinner together on the boat. At one point in the evening he had been distracted and she had watched him as he looked around the room. He seemed to fix upon an older couple at a table nearby. After a minute or two the man, looking out of the window at the wharfside conversions drifting past, reached over and, without looking, gently stroked his wife's hand. Anne was about to ask him why he was so interested in the couple when one of Beck's friends distracted her. As she was talking to him, she felt Steven's index finger slowly caress her hand. Startled, she turned to him, but Karen interrupted him and he looked away. She had worried about it for several days. Had he copied them? Or had seeing them merely reminded him to touch her tenderly? Or was it just coincidence? And then she realised what Beck was up to. She felt a stab of guilt at talking about Steven in this way, and remembering the touch of his hand now seemed trivial and neurotic. It felt like bad faith. 'It just goes to show that maybe what my mother said about me was right.'

'And what was that?'

'She used to say that I was never satisfied.' She smiled at him but the edge in the smile was a warning to drop the subject. 'There's a little something for you on the dresser.'

He looked and saw a carefully wrapped parcel. He walked over and opened it. Inside was a copy of

Orwell's *1984*. A first edition. He was astonished at her generosity and for a moment didn't say anything.

'It's to say thank you for all the work you've done on the car,' she said, pleased at how touched he was.

'Well, what can I say but *thank you* back. It must have cost a fortune.'

'That's all right,' she said, going back to the magazine, 'but if you hadn't kept going on about how it was a mistake to buy the car in the first place I would have spent even more.'

―――――

They had been to Martin Beck's flat for dinner and were walking to the tube when Steven realised he was failing to make ground with Anne. Somewhere along the way, despite the warmth she felt for him, the desire, the affection, he had stalled. A terrible surge of fear flooded through his stomach then began to die away. It was vital not to give in to the endless unease always at the back of his mind. He reassured himself that everything was in place; it was a question of watching and picking up any clue as to what was present in him, or what he lacked, then acting on it. Be patient, he told himself, feeling her affection for him in the close grip of her arm in his. Be patient.

Arm in arm he could feel, nevertheless, Anne's sense of intrigue at the elaborate balance of pleasures his personality seemed to offer her. He stopped her and they kissed. Again he felt the pleasure she took in his touch and in touching him: those extraordinary kisses and the occasional soft invasion of her tongue. And yet for all that there was nothing lukewarm in her touch, there was always a point when her passion receded, always the careful, discreet pulling back, the contracting of the pupils, the merest turn of the body, a tensing of the muscles along the inside of her arm. It was everywhere and nowhere and yet her affection and desire for him were also present in the very

472

actions that were telling him he was here but not there. Where was it? How was it done? How could it be so clear yet so impossible to pin down?

They had walked to a quiet row of houses parallel to the Harlesden Road to avoid the late night emergence from the local pubs. They stopped kissing and began to walk, but as they passed behind the Saracen's Head, three men stepped out of an alley that connected the two roads. He guided her to the other side, feeling how tense she was.

'It's OK, don't worry,' he said. The three crossed in front of them and he was obliged to stop in front of a man well over six feet tall and about fifteen stone. The casual clothes he wore were fairly expensive, not Lacoste but pretty close. The second man, much younger and smaller though still heavier than Steven, wore the traditional uniform of cropped hair, Crombie, Ben Sherman and Doc Martens. The third, a tall and elegantly dressed black man, stood some distance behind the others. Incongruously, he was carrying an ancient Tesco's carrier bag.

'Lend us a fiver,' said the big man amiably.

'Why?' said Steven.

'Give it to him,' whispered Anne. He could feel her terror, and tried to gauge the proportion of fear for herself against fear for him.

'Yes, go on, give it to him,' mocked the smaller man, with great bonhomie.

'Why do you want it?' said Steven, a touch more aggressively.

The big man looked at him, more affronted than surprised. 'I need a cup of tea.'

'We're dying for a cup,' said the smaller man.

Steven looked at him directly for the first time. 'You want five pounds as well?'

'Yes. Yes, I do. But I prefer coffee. Nes-caf-e.' He said each syllable as if it were a separate word. 'Only decaffeinated, mind. I can't sleep if it isn't decaffeinated. Can I?' He looked over at his friend.

'Five pounds seems rather a lot,' said Steven, as if this really were a negotiation. 'I mean, you're a long way from the Savoy out here.'

'What's it to you, pal?'

Steven turned back to the big man. 'It's ten pounds to me, and I'm not your pal.'

Anne pulled away from him and opened her handbag. Clumsily she pulled out about thirty pounds. 'Take this,' she said, fear shaking her voice and body. 'Just leave us alone.'

The big man reached over to take it, grabbing her painfully by the wrist. Steven moved towards him but the other two shifted themselves in a slight but clear gesture of menace. Steven stopped as if his initial aggression had vanished with the realisation that they were not just after money. He reached into his pocket. They looked at him, interested in what pointless ritual of appeasement he would choose. He took out seventy pounds which the short man received with the bored automatism of a check-out girl; then he offered his watch, a Rolex, and his credit cards. All were taken in the same spirit.

'What do you want?' said Steven.

'Anything you give us we can take,' said the elegant black man, revealing that he was the leader. He took out a Polaroid camera from the carrier bag. He pointed it at Steven and blinded him with the flash. He waited patiently for the picture to emerge. 'I love watching them develop,' he said pleasantly, then explained, 'We take one photo before … and one after.'

Steven looked lost and then made as if to rescue Anne from the grip of the large thug holding her. He had hardly begun to move when the skinhead produced a Stanley knife from his Crombie jacket. Given that there were three of them it was hardly necessary, serving only as a sharp symbol of Steven's impotence. Again they watched him silently. Steven, looking feeble, said nothing. Then the black leader spoke. 'As it happens, we can make a deal.' He waited as a sudden wary hope came into both Anne and Steven's eyes. He paused. 'Give us your wife.'

'What do you mean?' said Steven.

'Simple,' said the leader. 'Just give her to us. Then you can walk away.'

Horror and grief spread through Anne as she looked at Steven. She realised that he was, with the most intense and appalled reluctance, considering what he was being offered. He clearly wanted to refuse heroically, but the words would not come. She lowered her eyes.

'We're going to take her anyway,' said the leader reasonably. 'This way one of you is saved.'

Steven said nothing. Anne spoke softly – a terrible sound. 'Go on, Steven.'

The leader nodded to the skinhead. 'Take him down to the Rec and keep him there till I send ... Bartholomew.' The other two laughed at his invention and the skinhead gestured mockingly with his free hand for Steven to go ahead.

Anne watched him as he walked on but he did not look at her until he was about ten yards away. Her face was white with fear and grief as the skinhead posed her for the Polaroid he was about to take, gentle as a school photographer with a timid child. In the brief burst of light from the camera, standing under a broken lamp-post it occurred to Steven that he had never seen anyone so alone, so abandoned.

'Don't worry, old son ...' The skinhead moved close to him, letting his guard down for the first time since he had pulled the knife from his jacket. Steven grabbed the man's wrist with his right hand and smashed the heel of his left upwards into his elbow. It broke with a loud crack. He screamed and kept on screaming as Steven turned to face the other two. As he walked towards them the big man stepped up to meet him, pulling out a hammer which he fumbled and dropped. He paused for a moment, as if mystified by his clumsiness. As he bent to pick it up, the toe of Steven's shoe caught him just behind his left ear. He was only stunned though and staggered towards Steven waving the hammer erratically at his head. As he lashed at him, Steven grabbed his wrist in one hand and pulled him over to the edge of the path. In one fluid move he took hold of the back of his head and smashed it down onto a low garden wall. Less than eight seconds had passed between the first blow and the second.

The big man was unconscious. The skinhead with the broken elbow had stopped screaming and was kneeling on the road, white with shock. 'Oh. Oh. Oh,' he kept repeating. Steven walked over to Anne, and pulled her out of the way. The leader stood as if completely unable to believe this turn of events. He stared at Steven like a small boy before a playground bully. He started to speak but Steven stepped between him and Anne, obscuring the blow he struck from her astonished gaze. When he turned back to her, the man was on his knees retching like an animal choking on a sharp bone. Carefully Steven opened the man's immaculate coat and dipped into the inside pocket. He took out a wallet and his own watch, money and credit cards. He checked them, replaced the wallet then turned to Anne.

'Are you all right?' he asked, pulling her gently towards the end of the road.

She stopped, forcing him to turn to look at her. She stared at him, then her shoulders started shaking and her face creased into a grimace all the more terrible because there were no tears.

He held her in his arms but he was clearly worried. 'We have to go now.'

She said nothing more as they walked to the Harlesden Road and hired a mini-cab from some scabby cabinette. They drove out of the decayed terraces of Harlesden in a death-trap Nissan helmed by a bewildered Moroccan who seemed uncertain as to the difference between left and right. Steven listened to the increasing rasp of Anne's breathing until it became so loud he searched her handbag for the inhaler. As always there was the immediate response, the easing of that curious sound as if two files were rubbing together deep inside her chest. They arrived at her flat, he got her key out of her bag and in a few minutes she was sitting opposite him drinking the brandy he had poured for her.

'I thought you were going to leave me.'

'I'm sorry ... the knife,' he said quietly.

She put the glass down and gestured for him to sit beside her. Before he realised what was happening she was kissing him but it was different from the delicate touch he was used to. She forced her mouth onto his, pushing him back and pulling at his shirt. She stood up and clumsily unzipped her skirt. Failing, she gave it several hefty tugs, freed it, and the skirt fell to the ground. Watching him, she took off her shoes then rolled off her tights and knickers in one quick movement. He did nothing. She waited, still looking intently at him, her pubic mound a deep black against the white skin. She took off her blouse and bra, and stood naked in front of him. It was always an astonishing moment for Steven, even a moving one. How unprepared he always was for the first occasion, for the sight of the thin or heavy waist, the particular way the breasts hung, large or small, and never exactly what he expected. She turned and moved towards the bedroom.

He watched her buttocks, large but muscular beneath the subcutaneous fat, stretching and shifting as she walked. He followed as she switched on the dimmest light and gestured to him to undress. He avoided her gaze as he gathered his thoughts, and when he looked up she was resting on the double bed with her back against the wall. Her legs were splayed, one on the bed, the other on the floor, and there was a curious smile on her face, a smile of welcome mixed with intense sexual excitement. It took him aback, struck by its sweetness and incongruity. There was a moment of silence as he looked into her eyes, between her legs, then back at her again. Her expression darkened and he noticed again the faint half-flush of red growing along her neck.

He sat beside her and took her breasts in his hands. He was surprised at how heavy they were. Reaching up, she put her arms around his neck and pulled him down to kiss him. She unzipped his trousers and he pulled them off, almost falling over in his eagerness. She slipped her hand over his penis, her fingers outlining his erection beneath his shorts. To his surprise, she pulled him over with real force and pushed him on to his back. Without pausing she climbed astride him, immediately pressed herself down and then he was inside her. She pushed up and down on him faster and faster as if taken over. Her hand moved between her legs and then she came. And as she came, she began to cry, huge racking sobs beating out of her as if she would break. Amazed, he waited for the weeping to stop. He did not say anything but held her hand. Then her breathing slowed, and in two minutes she was asleep.

Half an hour later, when he was sure he would not disturb her, he walked over to the window and looked out over the city. That a man could have a capacity for extreme violence was in no sense, he knew, an attractive quality to most women. But that a man could have such a capacity, call on it in defence of himself and of the woman he loved, yet show he was unhappy that she had witnessed this dangerous aspect of his personality, was more than all but a very few women could resist. This was the terrible paradox he could always exploit given the opportunity: the need for predictable men, providing men, for caring men who were also unpredictable, dark, and with a sharp pair of teeth.

She moved in her sleep, and most of the sheet fell to the floor leaving her uncovered. Across the years he'd developed a deep affection for the shape of women. The endless variations on a simple theme seemed to emphasise the lack of uniformity. There was something in the contours that was pleasing to the hand, flesh and bone creating something that was neither soft nor hard. At first when he'd discovered he'd acquired this taste he had considered it unimportant. But between the necessary sex, women could feel that his touch was charged by admiration, which made them feel safe when they were in his arms. Producing an erection was something they felt that anyone could do; it followed inevitably from the way things were. His thoughtful touch was something else again: it spoke of a quality particular to them, an exploration of the difference between the perfect shape implicit in the common skeleton and the variations that emerged in thighs too large, bottoms too big, uncleavaged breasts or hair that failed in manageability or shine.

The fact that you could borrow and graft emotions in this way gave him an insight that subsequently saved his skin. He realised that he'd been living on borrowed time, not quite grasping what was required of him if he was to stay alive.

Some sportsmen are like that: for years they battle on in fitfully successful mediocrity until a point arrives when suddenly everything seems clear and then they play as if they'd been possessed by someone else. Steven learnt to fuel his perjuries with whatever he discovered he genuinely meant. Sometimes there wasn't much but, to his great relief, homeopathic doses of sincerity would often do.

She woke up.

After they had finished making love for the second time, he fell asleep without meaning to. For a long time, resting sideways on one arm, smoking and watching over him she hardly moved at all. After a while he shifted to his side and she looked thoughtfully at his cock. It lay across his belly still swollen beyond its resting state but now it seemed most natural of all somewhere between soft and hard, the first quite ugly in a pleasant sort of way and the second always catching you unawares no matter how often seen. She continued to watch in the dim light, barely conscious of the too rapid movement of his stomach and his ribs. After a long time she fell asleep.

The next morning Steven lay in Anne's bed, dozing but trying not to fall asleep. Every time his eyes closed fully there was a brief pause, then they were forced slightly open so that a fraction of the whites showed through between the lids. They would hold for a short while then descend, his breathing growing heavier with his eyes until they closed and were jerked a quarter open again. In the distance he was conscious of her voice. She was part-singing, part-humming a hymn from another room. He tried to use the sound of her voice as a measure of how deeply he could allow himself to sleep, but was frustrated by her intermittent silences. Eventually the singing became so unreliable that he forced himself awake, sighing reluctantly, for he was very tired. Eyes open, he listened to the pleasant, womanly sound of her voice. He stood up and walked over in the direction from which it came.

''Tis the gift to be simple, 'tis the gift to be free,' she sang softly as Steven walked towards the half-open bathroom door. 'Hmmm, hmmm in the valley of love and delight.' She stopped and he heard the swish of water. She began again in a higher key. 'Da da da dum we shan't be ashamed … hmmm hmmm hmmm … turning, turning we come round right.'

He could see her now through the doorway. She had her back to him and she was wearing a tank top and a pair of white cotton knickers. Her right foot was planted firmly on the wooden floor but her left was resting on the edge of the wash-basin full of soapy water. She was shaving between her legs. Every now and then she would rinse the safety razor in the basin, leaving behind white foam threaded with the black of her pubic hair. Humming a few bars of the hymn, she would stop, rinse then resume. He watched her, drawn to the intensity of her concentration, the odd changes in register of the song, and the contrast of her white skin, pulled taut in strange combinations of sinew and muscle by her stance, and her hair, which fell in straight soft lines, brushing the top of her raised thigh every time she moved.

'Come in, if you're coming,' she said quietly.

As Steven opened the door and walked in, she lowered her leg from the basin and raised the other. She pumped foam from a can of shaving cream onto the palm of her hand and carefully wiped it over the inside of her right thigh. She took the razor again, rinsed it in the creamy water, then handed it to him. He took it and bent his head so that he could see what he was doing. He wet the razor again and began his first stroke across the skin of her inner thigh. The hair was thick, even low down, and very black. The razor was sharp and flowed easily enough along the tight skin, culling the hair with a barely noticeable pull. He continued with immense care and concentration, the slight tension he felt in her body easing as she felt more confident of his careful touch. Her cotton knickers were daubed with the synthetic white of the foam, and as he proceeded they began to darken as the water was absorbed by the dry unbleached cotton, revealing in part the outline of the double ridge of skin beneath. She tensed again as he brought the razor to the edge of the skin hidden by the cotton but he proceeded with ever greater care, and she relaxed. Finally, he stood up straight and taking the face cloth dabbed at the foam that remained. When he had finished, she brought her foot down. 'Take off your shirt.'

He looked at her, puzzled, then began unbuttoning. As he took it off she squeezed more foam into her hand. 'Turn round.' She spread the foam along his shoulders. He heard the blade being rinsed then the sharp pull on his skin as she started. His firm muscles made it easy and in two minutes she was finished, despite the slow speed of her strokes.

There was an intense pleasure to be had shaving someone else, the smoothing of something rough, the removal of something coarse. It was like making some-thing new, a powerful reclamation. She wiped him clean, enjoying the touch of her fingers along the mus-cular body that had so surprised her the night before, the waist so slim, like a woman's, the chest so big, like that of an animal, a bull, a horse. Along the ridge of his shoulders two or three pinpricks of blood seeped like beads of water condensing on a cold glass.

Turning around, he kissed her, and she smiled as his fingers failed to slip under the wet elastic covering her labia. Pulling back she slipped a long fingernail between the wet elastic and her skin and pulled it away, allowing him to drag the cotton to one side. She felt the air cold on her exposed wet skin, then his hand covering her. For five minutes he did nothing but kiss her face, cheeks, lips, eyebrows, ears, chin, allowing the warmth of his hand to seep through every nerve until her breathing quickened, the skin flushed along her throat and cheeks and she was squeezing his hand so hard between her legs it began to hurt.

Tom Clavell was a worried man. He was not just worried about one or two things at work. He was structurally worried, fundamentally ill-at-ease, because like so many people earning over forty thousand a year he did not realise that being permanently anxious was what he was being paid for. He also did not realise that worry doesn't understand about clocking off. Worry is a workaholic. Worry is a body-snatcher. It had been a gradual process, so gradual that he did not even realise it. He was like that frog in the pan of water – if you put it in the pan when the water is cold and turn the heat up very slowly, it won't even notice it's being boiled alive. Knowing a thing or two about worry himself, Steven Grlscz was trying to get Clavell to fund an extension of his contract by the promise of an easy prize.

'I'm right about this. I'm sure.'

'If it was as easy as you say everyone would be doing it,' said Clavell, dubiously.

'Come on. This isn't about research, it's about putting two and two together. The problem's crept up on everyone and now it's just part of the air we breathe.'

Clavell was softening.

'You know as well as I do that there's too much new research and not enough attempt to put together what we already know. I bet you somewhere out there there's a cure for cancer – or baldness or weight loss or whatever.' He paused for effect. 'The cure for cancer would be worth a fair bit.'

483

Clavell grunted. 'Not as much as a pill that stopped people from getting fat. Why a database on stress?'

'Because there's a fair bit of research, but people aren't really grasping the implications of what's being found. Scientists, doctors, they're used to the physical world, things you can measure. They don't believe that emotions exist in the way a table exists. They like to buy solid machines to deal with solid diseases. Intervention here isn't about expensive machines.'

'We *make* expensive machines. In this business people hate consultants – they like to see things they can touch for their money. You can't touch good advice.'

'You can if you package it properly.'

'OK, give me an example.'

'Fair enough.' Grlscz reached into his briefcase and pulled out a sheaf of notes, laying them on the table in front of Clavell. They were the research findings Anne had found for him using NEMO. 'Right.' He pointed at a pair of graphs, the drab typography declaring their age. 'This is Widdowson in the *Lancet* in 1951. It comes from research done in two orphanages in Germany just after the war.' He pointed at the first graph. 'This orphanage was run by a Fräulein Grun – a happy woman, warm, kind. The other was run by Fräulein Schwarz – sour, critical, hostile. They were run by the same government department. Conditions – heating, food and so on – were virtually identical. You know what the Germans are like, everything standardised and all detailed down to the yearly amount of milk for each child. They weighed and measured them every month. Look, the growth rate of the children under Grun was twice that under Schwarz.' Grlscz put a third graph on the table. 'In time, the nice Fräulein Grun moved on and nasty Fräulein Schwarz came to replace her. See. The growth rate of the children starts to fall dramatically. They were still eating the same amount of food. Here are the records.'

Clavell grunted, sceptical. 'There could have been an infection or one of a hundred things.'

'Possibly. But look at this second line. These children – four of them – were growing at a faster rate even than the kids brought up by nice Fräulein Grun.' He paused.

'And?'

'It turns out that Schwarz wasn't entirely heartless. These four were her special favourites. She brought them from her old orphanage.' He turned back to the first set of graphs and pointed to a dotted line on the graph. 'There they are, the four of them. Growing at twice the rate of the others.'

'This is all a bit neat, isn't it? Always makes me dubious.'

'I'll keep my eye out for something less persuasive.'

'It's pretty ancient.'

'That's my point. What's that got to do with anything? It's solid research and it's been lost, forgotten. If we can put it together with all the other good work that's been forgotten ...' He gestured to signal the endless possibilities.

'I'll need more.'

'Look at this.' Grlscz laid the second of NEMO's documents on the table. 'Miami, 1986, premature baby unit. This is ... Field and Schanberg. They noticed that the babies were fretted over and pampered and treated with care – love even.'

'Very scientific.'

'Anyway, attention was poured over these babies. They also noticed there was one thing the nurses weren't doing. So, based on their work with rats, they did this three times a day to half the babies for fifteen minutes. Not only did they grow fifty per cent faster, they were released earlier and years later were healthier than the control group. What was it?'

'I give up.'

'They just stroked them – stroked their skin for fifteen minutes, three times a day. For all the tender loving care, the nurses hardly ever picked them up.' Grlscz handed Clavell two closely typed pages. 'These are Purcell's calculations of how much money stroking underweight babies could save every year. That's just in the USA alone.'

Clavell looked straight at the bottom line. 'A billion dollars?'

'The figures are rough but it's there or thereabouts. It's based on a federal report from 1987.' Grlscz carefully checked in his notes. It was important to throw as much dull science into the ring as possible. 'Here it is: *Neonatal Intensive Care for Low Birth Weight Infants: Costs and Effectiveness. Health and Technology Case Study 38.*'

Clavell looked through the numbers for several minutes. 'Let me think about it,' he said at last. 'We'd better be going.'

———

There is a point in the morning when the office machine begins to hum. Something, an adequate supply of caffeine, a sufficient amount of chat, a quota of procrastinations, of wool-gatherings having been filled, when the machine begins to work: the telephones are quiet, the interruptions easily recovered from, and for forty-five minutes to an hour things actually get done. Discovering how it begins and how it ends will make some theorist of these organisational machines a greater shaker of the world than Marx, Einstein or Ford, because it's not the manifesto or the university or the factory that is the beating heart of the world: whatever the prophets of teleworking say, everything that matters now happens in the office.

Anne had not heard from David Hendrix since Gary Epper had installed the voice-activated software. She suspected that Hendrix had taken her at her word when she reassured him that he was not expected to deliver anything if he wasn't happy with NEMO. She decided it was time to give him a call. The guilty tone of his voice when she identified herself confirmed her suspicions.

'I'm terribly sorry, Anne, but I'm afraid there have been a series of patient crises here. I'm working on getting the voice thing used to my speech but I just haven't had the time to give it the attention it deserves.' The apologies over with, he delivered a reminder: 'I warned you it might be a while.'

She considered taking it back while she had the chance, but there was no great loss in leaving it with him for a few weeks. 'No, not at all. I'll give you a ring in a few weeks and let's see how it's working out then.' They exchanged a few social pleasantries and she rang off.

When he put the phone down Hendrix was moderately relieved that Anne had left the computer with him. He had not been entirely straight with her. He was well advanced with the speech software and it had turned out to be extremely useful. Already it was about ninety per cent accurate, which meant that it was already twice as accurate as his own typing. He had started putting all his patient notes through the system and it was saving him a great deal of time. But as for doing anything that would be useful to Anne Levels, he hadn't got round to it yet. His initial reluctance about confidentiality and a general suspicion that computers could store information all over the place where anyone who understood these occult devices could get at it had returned. He stared at it. It was damn useful, though. It was then that he had the idea. Hendrix sat in front of NEMO and contemplated the pointlessness, the *childishness*, of what he was thinking of doing. It was a pointless, childish act of fraud.

'Nemo,' he said at last.

Yes, Mr Hendrix.

'Can you solve crossword puzzles?'

Anne, back at work and blind to the quiet business beyond PAs, typists, secretaries and clerks, sat behind her expensive desk, devising a bid and balancing the personalities to put it into operation: leaders, supporters, innovators, blockers; an attempt to get task A done with cost B. The phone rang. She picked it up. 'Levels.'

'It's David Elwes here. That stupid girl in reception has sent a call for you down to us. It's a Mrs Beatty from some relationship council or other. Nothing wrong between you and the significant other, I trust, but if you want to tell me all about it over dinner you know I'm here for you, Anne.'

'In your dreams.'

He laughed; there was a click and a short pause.

'Hello, Anne Levels.'

'Oh, Dr Levels, it's Georgina Beatty here.' She paused oddly, as if she had forgotten why she had telephoned.

'Is there a problem, Mrs Beatty?'

There was a sudden collapse in the woman's voice. 'Yes, it's Mrs Nancarrow. She's been murdered.'

'Murdered!'

'Yes. By her husband.'

'Good God!'

'The terrible man – he poisoned her.'

For a moment it was as if the world had gone silent.

'Oh God, how awful.'

'The police would like a statement from you.'

'What? Yes. Of course.'

'I thought I should tell you what they were phoning about.'

488

'Yes. Thank you.' She paused. 'When did it happen?'

'Well, I learnt about it this morning, but apparently it took place last night. He poisoned her and then he hanged himself from a tree at the bottom of their garden.'

'Why? Why would he do that?'

'I feel as if we let her down,' said Mrs Beatty, and Anne could feel her begging for absolution.

'Of course you didn't,' she said dutifully. 'How could you possibly have known?'

'I suppose so, but I still feel we should have done something.'

Anne ignored the attempt to ensnare her. 'Do you know why he killed her?'

'No. There was no note. One of his neighbours saw him hanging from an apple tree in the garden the next morning.'

Again Mrs Beatty delicately tried to implicate Anne, but she quickly got off the phone and flicked on her office intercom. 'Sonia?'

'Yes.'

'Get everyone involved in the NEMO project in here in twenty minutes.'

'Mr Hewitt's on a course.'

'Then get him off it ... please.'

'Right.'

Anne pushed the small of her back into the inbuilt lumbar support of her executive chair, a feature only allowed those in the officed classes. She sat still for about five minutes then swung out a workstation and was soon lost in another search for the origin of NEMO's terrible prophecy.

Returning late and tired from a long, unsatisfactory meeting spent trying to persuade Clavell and two of his partners to fund his research into stress, Steven opened the door and called out to Anne. There was no response. He headed for the dining room, then heard the slicing rasp of knife on wood. He turned to the kitchen and found her preparing a meal with her back to him, not having heard him come in.

'Hello.'

'Oh, hi,' she said, without expression. He walked up behind her and slid his hand under her arm, barely touching the side of her breast. It was not meant as a gesture of desire but one of unconscious intimacy and tenderness.

'Stop it!' she shouted, and pulled away.

He stepped back as if she had struck him. 'What's the matter?'

'Nothing's the matter. I just don't like you mauling me all the time, that's all.'

'What do you mean?' The shock on his face was plain as she turned round, dark-faced, to look at him.

'You're always touching me, like I was ... I don't want you grabbing me, OK? How do you like it?' Her hand shot out, reaching for his crotch. Whether she had intended to touch him or not he moved back involuntarily. She looked at him, eyes pin bright with anger.

'I didn't think I was ... I'm sorry. I won't do it again.' He turned and started to walk away. Had he reacted as angrily as her bad temper deserved, she knew she would have become even more foul-tempered. But seeing the hurt on his face, the quiet words warmed by mortification, all her malice drained away. 'Steven.'

He stopped, waited then turned.

'I'm sorry. I didn't mean it.'

'Then it's a pity you said it.' His voice was soft but there was a coldness in his voice she had never heard before.

'I didn't mean it, honestly. I shouldn't have said it. I was taking something out on you. I'm sorry.'

His expression did not change, nor did he move away.

She sighed. 'It's been a bad day at work. I shouldn't have taken it out on you. I'm very sorry.'

She walked over to put her arms around him.

He held back at first. He was disturbed by the virulence of the emotion that had assaulted him and was unsure what to do, and frightened. 'That's all right.' He held the back of her head in the palm of his hand, then gently pulled away, going over to the kitchen table to pick up the *Evening Standard.* He sat down and began reading. She returned, subdued and thankful to have got away so lightly with her exhibition. Underneath her shame she was, unconsciously, forming a new geography of his tolerance to her capacity for unpleasantness. He could not allow this.

'Martin wants to go to dinner,' she said, knowing that the silence must be neutrally filled to ease any remaining bruise.

'Oh ... I don't think I can be sure of making it this week. Saturday I've got to have dinner with Tom Clavell and his wife. You as well, of course. I forgot to mention it. If you want to.'

'Sure. Martin was angling for next week anyway. Friday.'

'Fine ... anywhere in ...' He stopped suddenly, sighing as if both angry and weary. 'Actually, could we not do this?'

She turned, alarmed. 'What?'

'Look, it's an old fault of mine. I accept apologies when I'm still angry with someone. I can't do it this quickly. I'm still annoyed. You can't say a thing like that and then just say sorry. Do you see?'

She did not say anything.

'So I'm going to go and read the paper for half an hour ... only I won't be reading it, I'll be thinking very unpleasant things about you broadly equivalent in

491

offensiveness to what you've just said about me.' He stood. 'Then I'll come back and we'll see how it goes from there.'

———

Forty minutes later the door to the bedroom opened and Anne came in contrite yet confident. 'Hey, your thirty minutes are up.'

He continued to read his paper. She waited.

'I was wondering,' he said, still not looking at her, 'whether I should make you suffer for another fifteen minutes or so.'

'I don't need to suffer. I'm really sorry.' She climbed over the bed, assuring herself by the look in his eyes that he was ready for this. She pulled the paper out of his hand, threw it on the floor and sat astride him. 'Perhaps you should punish me,' she said flirtatiously.

'What did you have in mind?' he said, smiling despite himself.

'Oh, I could write out fifty times, "I must not be such a poisonous bitch".'

They both laughed and she said softly, 'I can be ... poisonous sometimes.'

'Well,' he said slowly, and with a hint of malice in his voice, 'I like a woman with a few character flaws.'

'Oh, really?' she said, poking him in the ribs. 'And why's that?'

'It makes them less easy to disappoint.'

'Oh, I wouldn't say that,' she replied. 'And what are your serious character flaws?'

'For one thing I'm generous to a fault.'

'Is that right?'

'Well, I've forgiven you, haven't I?'

She leant back on his knees laughing, allowing her skirt to ride up her legs. She started to undo the buttons on her white blouse but as he went to help, she pulled back. In one movement she pulled off the blouse and threw it on to the floor. She was wearing a coffee-coloured La Perla bodice, whose sexiness resided in its lack of transparency and its absurdly expensive cut. The cups supporting her breasts rejected the emancipated fashion of moulding themselves to her natural figure. The bodice described an hypothesis of a female shape that was in small but significant ways not possible at all: the tailored waist was too small for the exaggerated way it flattened the ribcage and forced the breasts into an unnatural curve, the cleavage so compressed and the upper breast so swollen. Objectively it was as decorous as a 1950s bathing suit: its expense lay in the skill by which it committed its act of erotic aggression on her body while remaining comfortable to wear. She stood up and undid her skirt, stepped out of it, went to the end of the bed and lay down on her side, elbow bent, resting her head on her hand. One leg, her left, lay flat on the bed, her right was bent. He watched. She stretched, then looking him straight in the eye, reached her right hand between her legs. One of the three poppers that fastened the bodice snapped open, distorting the complex engineering of forces that held her body in place, squeezing her labia to the centre, and pushing up the black hair and pink skin. She licked one of her fingers and gently rubbed the skin protruding through the hole she had made, then pulled at another popper. It came free reluctantly, the distortion pulling at the bodice, changing the dynamic of forces around buttocks, midriff, breasts, freeing one side of her labia and pulling painfully at the other. Lowering her eyes, she released the last one, slowly easing the flap towards her stomach, restoring an equilibrium to her body once again. Her hand, fingers splayed, pushed through her lips. He undid his trousers quickly, pulling out his erection painfully. He grimaced and though she might have smiled at another time, there was no warmth in the way she looked at him. He moved towards her

493

face, meaning to kiss her, but she bent her head as he knelt clumsily on the bed and, despite the awkward angle, took his penis in her mouth. His back arched, one hand went between her legs, the other pulled at the carapace around her breasts so that he could feel the contrast of white skin, erect nipple, and the viscose, silk and elastin mix that held her in. She saw a rage of indecision sweep through him. She shifted her head back, her pupils dilated, and said, 'You don't know where to begin, do you?'

An hour later they were lying in each other's arms, neither having spoken for ten minutes. The intense animal release that had becalmed her for a while was receding and she was looking around the room idly, feeling like talking again.

'What's in the parcel over there?' she said, nodding at a carefully wrapped package leaning against the mirror. 'Is it a present for me?'

He said nothing.

'Is it a present for somebody else?'

'Serve you bloody well right if it was.'

She got off the bed, walked over to the mirror and touched the package, then without ceremony she tore away the brown paper. There were three expensively framed copies of the Rembrandt etchings from the exhibition at the National Gallery where they had first met. She examined them carefully. 'You're very good,' she said without turning her head. 'These are wonderful copies.' She looked back at him and smiled, meaning to be light-hearted. 'I can see I'll have to keep my chequebook away from you.' She saw the barely perceptible look of disappointment on his face and felt a warm embarrassment begin along her neck and cheeks.

He seemed to think better of his own reaction and smiled softly.

494

'I really like them,' she said, relieved that she had recovered herself.

How clumsy people are ... and how dangerous it makes them, thought Steven.

They made love again and afterwards he lay next to her as she dozed, considering the strange rebound of intimacy from a row made up. Why was it that after a fight things sometimes seemed better between people? How was the air cleared, and of what? Or was it ever cleared at all? A few months before, he had come across a line by Thornton Wilder: *'Wrapped in forgiveness and understanding it sinks into the heart like a stone'.* He was astonished that someone he did not know could express what he was feeling so exactly, had crystallised it so that it was only when he read it that he realised precisely what he had been feeling for years. Why, he thought with bitter frustration, were people always so *contrary*? Carefully sliding her head from his arm to the pillow he got up and, as he dressed, looked at her sleeping face. The hidden life of lovers was constructed as much as anything of the fights you didn't have, according to agenda printed on paper that had been devoured. It could be stored away, he knew, wherever such things are kept, comatose until revived by the presence of others of these hoarded resentments. There seemed to be a critical mass involved, he thought; given sufficient numbers they felt obliged to organise a great escape. After a while it was like a German prison camp in there: forged papers, searches, tunnels under the wire; and some ambitious madman attempting to make a break by building an aeroplane from bits of string and wood. In the past this had never been more than a minor problem because there wasn't long enough. Now the relationships took more time and, as each increased in length, the greater the opportunity to store up these unacknowledged disaffections.

He went to the kitchen, poured himself a glass of water and switched on the television in time to catch the news. It was coming to the end of an item on interest rates. House prices were rising and old fears of aerated money were resurfacing. There were calls for the Monetary Policy Committee of the Bank of England to increase rates. But there were also calls from business for another cut. Increase the rate and stop inflation but run the risk of slowing growth. Cut the rate and aid recovery but watch recovery become a boom. Be prudent. Do nothing. Worse than either, perhaps. Or better. What you did or what you didn't do. It all mattered, all of it, all of the time.

He heard her clattering about between the bedroom and the bathroom for a few minutes and then the noise stopped. She was so quiet it attracted his attention. He turned around. She was standing in the doorway watching him. 'I love you,' she said. Her open gaze was impossible to meet. 'Aren't you going to say anything?' Her voice was low, and slightly mocking.

He looked genuinely shaken.

'I should have been at Martin's two and a half hours ago.' He looked at her but he didn't say anything and she realised he was too deeply affected to speak. She was pleased.

'Don't bother to give him my regards,' said Steven, not taking his eyes from hers. 'I know it's none of my business but what do you see in him?'

'I like him. He's quite funny, you have to admit. I suppose I feel ...' She frowned.

'Sorry for him?' suggested Steven.

'Why should I feel sorry for him? He's good-looking ... lots of women fancy him. Why shouldn't they?'

'I see now,' he said, teasing. 'Lots of women like him and he dotes on you. How flattering.'

'Does he?'

'Oh, please.'

She laughed.

'That good-looking one, what's her name?'

'Karen, as if you don't remember.'

'What does Karen see in him?'

'Maybe *she* feels sorry for him.'

'I doubt it. She didn't strike me as the merciful kind.'

'I understand it's a side effect of using sunbeds,' she said. 'They weaken your pity. Scientists are concerned.' She went back into the kitchen, calling out to him over her shoulder. 'To be honest I think she's about to leave him. She was dropping hints the last time I talked to her.'

'If she needs somewhere to stay, she could come and borrow my sofa bed.'

She came back in carrying her handbag. 'I'll bet,' she said, smiling. 'Anyway, nearly all the women I know are dropping hints about leaving their husbands or lovers. It ought to be an organised sport, like football, with rules and a special kit.'

She kissed him warmly but with no trace of the hunger that was such a feature of the way she touched him now and which she had originally fought to restrain. How calm she felt now, and satisfied. 'I'll go now.'

'Don't.'

'I have to.' She was firm and he could see that she was not to be argued with. She kissed his cheek and went out into the hall. He followed her and helped her into her coat. He was still in a state of shock at what Anne had said. She seemed to have forgotten all about it until she looked him in the eyes, held his gaze, then left.

Epper knocked on the side of the open office door and Anne looked up with a vacant expression that suggested her mind was still on what she was doing.

'Have you got some time, Anne?'

'Not really,' she said, with neither kindness nor irritation. 'I'm a modern woman. I have it all. Except for one thing, Gary, and that's time. I'm timeless.'

'It's NEMO ... important. We've found something about Tessa Nancarrow.'

'I thought you showed me everything,' she said, alarmed.

'It turns out we didn't.'

She put aside what she had been working on. 'You'd better sit down.' Epper was conscious of being watched as he came in and shut the door behind him. He felt like a shoal of fish being radar-scanned by one of those Russian trawlers with a seventy-mile net.

'You know we've been working over at the Tavistock Clinic on techniques for getting people to talk about things they ...' he paused, 'don't want to talk about.'

'Yes.'

'Well, I picked up on some research they'd been kicking around about the psychology of confession. Basically, they found there was a much greater willingness on the patient's behalf to tell their counsellors really difficult things about themselves if they'd already told someone else, a friend or a priest or whatever.'

'It makes sense,' said Anne, meaning to be encouraging, but he misunderstood and thought she was unimpressed. The undertow of his mixed feelings about Anne – desire and admiration – swirled with the added salt of repressed resentment and fear. He was afraid of Anne because she held him in her hands. He was on a three-year contract and it was soon to expire. Nothing had been said about its renewal. In fact, it had not occurred to her that he would worry in any way, let alone so deeply, about the contract because it had never crossed her mind not to renew it. She had assumed he realised this. But in this one respect, Anne was behind the times. Her irreplaceability had insulated her. He was right to fear the new emperors and their absolute power of life and death over work. She would have been horrified to know how anxious he was, an unease that was to a greater or lesser extent continuous. As soon as a new contract was signed, the sense of security began to diminish as the date for its renewal approached. The worry graph for millions in the time to come will look like an alarming ECG, the teeth of a saw, a lightning bolt, a mountain range of peaks and troughs leading into the distance as far as the eye can see.

Epper continued coldly. 'I set up an extra program so that whenever it reached a blocking point of this kind NEMO would offer the patient the confessional. It would assure them that whatever they said was totally confidential. NEMO wouldn't know what they'd said and no one could get access to it without their permission. I've been working on making it watertight but it's only experimental.'

Anne looked nonplussed. 'But what's the point if you can't get access without permission?'

'It's very simple. You persuade them to confess by offering them a situation where they're comfortable about telling their secret, but once they've told it, you've broken down a major barrier, so that if you ask them to tell you the same secret in the main program the following week, they're much more likely to do so. The thing is, I'd decided that in order to be truthful about the confidentiality of this "confessional" I'd have to set it up so that it wiped out the answers immediately after it responded to them. But I haven't done that yet.'

'What's this got to do with Tessa Nancarrow?'

Epper took a deep breath. 'She got into it by mistake.'

'What?' Anne was appalled, and all thought of being

kind to Epper fled. 'You left NEMO linked up to an experimental program? For God's sake, Gary, what on earth were you thinking of?'

'It was a chance in ten thousand ... more than that. She just happened to reply to one question from NEMO in a particular way which connected her up with CONFESSOR. I'm sorry. I didn't think it could happen. Anyway,' he said, hurrying past the apology, 'it's all worked out for the best because what she told it, well, it's pretty amazing.'

Anne's annoyance was overcome, as Epper had hoped, by her curiosity. 'Show me,' she said. Epper stood up and went over to the work-station and swung it into the room so that they could both see it. He started typing, talking at the same time.

'I did a lot of work on managing silences, particularly on not prompting people too soon. That psychiatrist, David Hendrix, I went to see about installing NEMO was very helpful there ... he gave me a lot of suggestions about leaving big gaps after questions so that you'd force people to respond, things like that. Otherwise CONFESSOR is pretty rough – it's early days.'

'Let's see, shall we,' she said, impatiently. He typed into the terminal for a few moments. The screen filled with the last testament of Tessa Nancarrow.

{[Silence: [At one minute prompt with question]]}
Confessor: What do you want to tell me, Mrs Nancarrow?
Mrs Nancarrow: It's very hard to talk about.
Confessor: Why is it hard to talk about?
Mrs Nancarrow: (silence) [one minute]
Confessor: Why is it hard to talk about, Mrs Nancarrow?
Mrs Nancarrow: (silence) [one minute]

Confessor: Why is it hard to talk about, Tessa?

Mrs Nancarrow: (silence) [forty seconds] He's always making me eat.

Confessor: Why is he always making you eat?

Mrs Nancarrow: (silence) [thirty seconds] He's always making things for me to eat.

Confessor: What things?

Mrs Nancarrow: Cups of tea ... toast ... dinner ... always on at me to eat. Chocolates. He's always giving me chocolates.

Confessor: How long has he been giving you chocolates?

Mrs Nancarrow: For eight months. Chocolates and all the other things.

Confessor: What other things?

Mrs Nancarrow: The food: the toast, the dinners, the cups of tea. I just told you.

Confessor: Could you tell me more?

Mrs Nancarrow: I could tell you.

Confessor: What could you tell me?

Mrs Nancarrow: (silence) [one minute]

Confessor: What could you tell me, Tessa?

Mrs Nancarrow: My husband. He's trying to poison me.

Confessor: How long has he been trying to poison you?

Mrs Nancarrow: Eight months. I told you.

Confessor: Why did you tell me?

Mrs Nancarrow: You wanted to know.

Confessor: Why did I want to know, Tessa?

Mrs Nancarrow: You want to help me.

Confessor: How can I help you, Tessa?

Mrs Nancarrow: You can't.

Confessor: Why can't I help you?

Mrs Nancarrow: I don't know.

'That's it, really. They get stuck here and CONFESSOR returns her to the program proper.'

'Gary, how did you get access to this if it's supposed to be absolutely confidential?'

He shifted uneasily. 'This was never meant to be used. It's a prototype.'

Something else occurred to her.

'There's no way NEMO could have accessed her claim she was being poisoned, could it? I mean, it didn't get the idea from CONFESSOR.'

'There's no possibility of that. You can get into CONFESSOR from NEMO but not the other way around. Not yet, anyway.'

Epper looked at her, suddenly uneasy. 'Look, Anne, perhaps I should disconnect it completely.'

'Perhaps you should.' He turned to go as she went back to her papers. 'But don't.'

Epper paused just as he was about to leave the office. 'Anne?'

'Yes?'

'Why on earth did she go back if she knew he was trying to poison her?'

He did not expect an answer and he closed the door softly behind him.

————

As on Healey's last visit to Steven Grlscz's flat, the door was half open when he arrived. He went in. Grlscz was sitting at his computer and turned in his seat to greet him. The first thing Healey noticed was that he was even thinner than when he'd last seen him in the police line-up. It was only a few pounds but the loss of weight on his already thin face accentuated the size of his eyes. He looked as if something terrible was happening to him.

'In my heart of hearts, Inspector, I can't honestly say I'm pleased to see you.'

Healey smiled. 'No.'

'Have you come to arrest me?' asked Grlscz quietly, almost matter of fact.

The surprise on the policeman's face was obvious. 'No, no, not at all, rather the opposite in fact.' Healey felt that he had been stupid not to realise that his visit might be alarming under the circumstances; he took pride in his belief that he was capable of a degree of sensitivity.

It was clear from his expression that Grlscz's usual politeness was wearing thin. 'To be honest, Inspector, I feel that you've buggered me about quite enough without adding obscurity to it all.' A thought struck him. 'Maria?'

'There's still nothing,' said Healey. 'The reason I'm here is that I wanted to tell you that we're closing the file until we have something more concrete to go on.'

Grlscz said nothing.

'At any rate,' continued Healey, awkwardly, 'I just wanted to say that you're no longer a suspect. Not that we ever really felt you were, but you have to understand that we had nothing to go on except a report that after she disappeared Maria was seen with someone who answered your description.'

He stopped, but Grlscz said nothing. As he was about to speak again, Grlscz interrupted. 'Why are you telling me this now?'

It was a fair question, thought Healey. It was hardly good police procedure to tell someone who might again be a suspect that you thought he wasn't guilty. Nevertheless, he had been feeling bad about what he had put Grlscz through, even before the identity parade. But although it had been weighing on his conscience, it had not done so to the extent that would have made him break the habit of a professional lifetime. But what he had found out the previous day had made him feel that he could no longer continue to leave Grlscz wondering if he was going to be arrested for murdering someone it was clear he had loved very much.

'I had a talk with someone who, according to Maria's mother, was her closest friend. Did you know Judy Halpern?'

'Judy? I met her a couple of times. She was a junkie ... did some small-scale dealing. I thought she was violating her bail with an extended trip to Phuket.'

Healey smiled. 'Apparently Miss Halpern missed her mum. Anyway, she was re-arrested at Heathrow on Tuesday and I had a word yesterday evening.'

'Did she have any idea where Maria might be?'

Healey shook his head. 'But what she did say was consistent with what everyone else has said ... that she had never been happier and that Maria said it was because of you.'

Grlscz's expression did not change at all.

'She did tell us something new though, and to be honest I'm a bit surprised you didn't bring it up yourself.'

Grlscz looked puzzled and also alarmed.

'I was just wondering why you didn't tell me you'd saved Maria Vaughan's life.' Healey could see that he was mystified. Now it was his turn to be puzzled. 'Judy Halpern said that Maria had told her that she'd been about to throw herself under a tube train and that you pulled her back. That was how you met.'

Grlscz squeezed his eyes shut as if they were hurting. 'I suppose it's sort of true but it was all much more ... diffuse than that. It wasn't the first time we met exactly. I'd come across her a couple of times before and later in the bookshop she used to work in. But it was pretty casual. I suppose in a way Judy's right.'

'But you didn't save her life?'

There was a brief pause and what Healey saw in Grlscz's expression convinced him beyond doubt that whatever had happened to Maria Vaughan, Steven Grlscz had nothing to do with it.

'The third time I met her it was in the bookshop she worked at in Covent Garden. We talked for a bit and I left to ... I was having my hair cut a couple of streets away. After that, I went to the tube and there she was, waiting for a train, and to be honest I was rather hoping she hadn't seen me. She was looking around and she seemed a bit stressed, nothing more. A train was about to come in. I thought she'd seen me so I went over to her but as I moved in front of her to get her attention the look of surprise she gave me ... well, it was obvious she hadn't. She was completely startled ... looked at me as if ... I don't know ... as if I were a ghost and then she ran off.' He looked at Healey for a few moments. 'She told me later, after we started going out, that she had been about to jump. But I didn't believe her. So, if I *did* save her life, it was by accident.' He smiled. 'Do I go back to being a suspect now?'

'No. I don't think so.' Healey stood up. 'If we hear anything I'll let you know. But for what it's worth, and I may well be wrong, I think she'll turn up one of these days.' He looked at Grlscz to see how he had taken this. 'Perhaps I shouldn't have said that.'

'Perhaps. But thank you anyway.'

While he was waiting for the lift, Healey thought about what had happened and the expression on Grlscz's face that had convinced him that even if Maria was dead he had nothing to do with it. Grlscz had been offered a way out. An independent witness had said he'd saved Maria's life, and while it was possible to think of a reason why someone who had done this might subsequently murder the person they had saved, it was pretty implausible. And especially so in this case, given that everyone he had talked to confirmed that Steven Grlscz had transformed Maria's life. But it was still possible. Such a man might have taken the view that the woman he had transformed was indebted to him, or that she was his creation and should remain so. If his creation had shown signs of too much independence it was credible that someone with a power complex might kill in a moment of rage. However guilty he felt about the identity parade, Healey realised he would never have entirely ruled out Grlscz as a suspect. It was only now that he had done so that he realised why he'd pursued him on such a flimsy basis. Grlscz was convincing but Healey hadn't been convinced. He was almost convinced, not least because he liked his manner and admired the way he had behaved during all of this, but something had been nagging him. It was based on nothing. It was not a hunch, but rather the shadow of one. But until now it had always been there. The reason it had now dispersed was that what he had seen on Grlscz's face, just for an instant, was that he had almost decided to lie, to allow him to believe that he had saved Maria's life. But against his own interests he had told the truth. This was what had done it. Healey laughed softly and bitterly: *The truth will set you free.* A wave of loneliness and shame and misery swept over him as he entered the lift and pressed the button for the ground floor.

Grlscz was still sitting where Healey had left him. After a minute he got up and went to the window, but couldn't settle and sat down again. As suddenly as it had begun, it was over. The policeman had come to see him, another moment of terror as he thought he was going to be arrested, and then he was saved. The poverty of what he had taken from Maria and the long wait while the police investigated her disappearance meant that he was beginning to starve. For the second time in as many days he thought how strange relief was and how intense it could be, how profound its pleasure. It was not a sudden absence that made it so – like the end of intense pain – it was a presence. It was a wonderful reminder that life is not what you feared. Life can be what you hope. Everything can work out all right.

THE WISDOM
OF CROCODILES

In the past we beat both our children and our wives. In the past we dictated the financial behaviour of citizens by credit restraints and exchange controls, by money squeezes and cash corsets. In the past we fired people. Violence and duress solved things. Now we do things differently, without recourse to threat and menace. Now we get consumers to curb themselves by orchestrating their levels of anxiety and desire through interest rates. Now instead of dismissing our servants we let their contracts lapse.

But if we no longer hit women as a matter of course, and it will soon be against the law to beat a child, how are we to exert our will on those who are close to us? The lesson in all this is clear: the commercial practices of one age become the moral practices of the next. In advanced industrial nations the movement from coercion to manipulation is happening everywhere and in everything. From now on all sticks will come in the shape of carrots.

Louis Bris, *The Wisdom of Crocodiles*

Over the next few days Grlscz's exhilaration faded as he exchanged one kind of anxiety for another. The moment might be right at any time she came to his flat and he was nervous as a cat before she arrived. Every now and then a surge of fear hit him in the stomach as he realised the dreadful risk of what he was about to do. And always in the back of his mind there was a sympathy for the creature he was about to kill. He admired her, or rather it was deeper than that: he was proud of her. At first the implications of feeling anything like this had terrified him, as if he had discovered the early symptoms of a wasting terminal disease making itself known through easy bruising or an increase in minor acts of clumsiness. After a while it struck him that it all depended on what you did with it, on what it was or was not connected to. If sympathy was unattached to shame or pity it was neither a weakness nor a strength.

The next day they ate dinner on the roof of the flats using a collapsible table. She was unusually quiet during the meal but in a pleasant, easy way. During a pause in the conversation he found himself looking out over the town towards the Sunglass wedge of the NatWest Tower, and behind it, in the distant mist, the strikingly impressive vacuity of Canary Wharf with its warning signal wink. The hazy cloud and the dying red sun gave the place an unaccustomed glamour, like the opening scene of a film with high production values. Turning back to her he found her eyes assessing him beneath the sharp, straight cut of her black fringe. He could sense himself being summed up with a quiet generosity.

'What's in there?' he said, nodding towards a cardboard box with Fairy Liquid 24-Bottles written on the side.

'Nothing,' she said, smiling with wide eyes. 'It's for work.'

'No, it isn't.'

She looked at him in a way that was hard to place – admiration perhaps, as if he had won a well-deserved prize. She went over to the box and brought it to the table, pushing the dishes to one side. She lifted the cardboard flaps, reached inside carefully and brought out the bonsai tree her grandfather had brought back from Japan. He was astonished as she placed it in front of him. He looked at the tree and then, uncertainly, at her.

'I don't know what to say. Thank you.'

'You're welcome,' she replied. She kissed him, softly at first, but then deeply and more passionately.

Oh God, this is it, he thought and his stomach plunged as if he were in an over-fast lift. He led her down to the flat and she allowed herself to be guided to the bedroom, her eyes focused on his. Standing by the bed, he slowly removed his clothes, stopping her from doing the same by a simple touch on her wrist as her hand went to the buttons on her blouse. When he was naked, he slowly began to undo her skirt, blouse, bra, and when she was in just tights and knickers knelt down and slowly pulled them to her ankles. She lifted one foot from her shoe then the other and then she was naked too. Still kneeling, he kissed her softly just above her pubic bone, feeling the texture of her hair and skin upon his lips. Then he stood up and gently pushed her backwards onto the bed, taking her weight by placing his hand in the small of her back. As he did so he heard the sound of plastic rustling underneath the sheet, but she seemed not to notice. He leant over her, his knees brushing the sides of her hips. He braced himself as his hands went to intertwine with hers, pulling them up until they lay pinned back next to her head. He kissed her as his body pushed her hard into the bed and she was dimly aware of an unaccustomed noise, familiar but belonging somewhere else. While he was kissing her he began a rhythmical movement against her but, strangely, he was not erect and she could feel his penis brushing softly against her thighs. He removed his mouth from hers and sat upright. She looked down between his legs and saw his penis lying downwards, softly touching her pubic hair. She looked up at him, confused. He held her stare as he pushed her hands hard into the bed and gripped her body painfully between his legs. He looked at her, unblinking, his eyes empty, void, and forced her hands over her head holding both in one of his. His free hand came slowly down her forehead over her eyes and to her mouth. He looked at her again and breathed out slowly as if he would never stop, his breath intensely hot and sweet. Then he tensed again and bit her. She screamed in horror and pain, the sound coming from the pit of her stomach and muffled by his hand. Terrified, she thrashed under him. His hand slipped for a moment and she let out the animal squeal of a creature about to be slaughtered. He covered her mouth again as she bucked and heaved under him.

And then he stopped.

His grip relaxed and slowly let go her hands and mouth.

She waited, too terrified and shocked to make a sound, then began to pull herself from between his legs, scrabbling backwards frantically until she reached the headboard. She sat up so that her back was resting against it and then brought her knees to her chest. He was looking up at the ceiling but his eyes were unfocused as if he had taken a blow to the side of the head. Then he closed them, trying to control his breathing. After a short while he opened them again and without looking at her got off the bed, walked unsteadily to the table and rested one hand against a chair. He brought the other hand to his stomach, bending as he did so. He was obviously in terrible pain.

She grabbed a pair of scissors lying on the bedside table. Rage swept away her fear. She leapt from the bed, her hand raised, and in two strides was behind him, the scissors coming down towards his back with all her force. He twisted at the last moment and blocked the blow with his left hand. The momentum of the strike unbalanced her and his right hand clasped the edge of the scissors and twisted them free of her hand. Her face was now very close to his. On his forearm there was a deep gash about four inches long.

'That hurt,' he said. Gently he put the scissors on the table behind him. She tried to break free but he held both her hands behind her back and pulled her to him. 'I don't suppose you'll need much encouragement,' he said. ' … Leave … don't come back.'

He let her hands loose and she backed away from him. Teeth clenched, afraid, outraged, grief-stricken, she stared at him. 'Why?'

He said nothing but examined his cut arm as if he were not quite able to believe the blood pouring out of the wound and down the channels between his fingers. Realising he was not going to say more she put on her blouse and skirt and shoes, stuffing her knickers and tights into her handbag. She walked towards the front door, opened it and turned. 'I want an answer.'

'Go away,' he said, looking at his bloody arm. She did not move and so he walked towards her. Afraid, she stepped back onto the landing. There was a burst of laughter from further down the hall as three men came out of one of the flats. The men looked at her, dishevelled and beautiful, as they walked past her to the lift. She stood and stared at the door of his flat, hearing the deadlock turning, the door being bolted at the top and bottom and the chain clattering against the door-frame. She started to walk down the stairs then stopped. Moving backwards onto the landing she felt the terrible ache in her throat and she began to cry, spasmodic, painful and nothing at all to do with emotional release.

It was from Ruth Compton, Head of English, that Martin Beck finally learnt what it was all about. She'd been listening vaguely to a casual enough conversation between the heads of the third and fourth years — titles were handed out at Mabey's in lieu of pay rises: heads of this and that were as plentiful as battalion leaders in the IRA. The similarities with senior terrorists did not end there, although discipline was maintained in the community in less obvious ways. Instead of baseball bats there were pursed lips, instead of knee-cappings there were disdainful remarks within the staffroom. Ruth was the exception. Fiercely protective of her department, she began listening to what they were saying more carefully when she heard them discussing Beck. He was a fourth-year form master, answerable to the head of the year, and it was she who let slip what had led to the arrival of the Cellophane bag and its soft white contents, stained with red ink and covered in dead leaves. Apparently, a week before its arrival, Alice Winnicott had summoned the fourth-year head to her office and lectured her about the year's insufficiently discreet approach to the business of menstruation. They were to be given instructions in the proper means of disposal. They were not to flush the towels down the toilets, and the boxes in which the towels came should under no circumstances be thrown into the wire rubbish bins that dotted the school, where they could be clearly seen among the Mars Bar wrappers and discarded copies of *Bliss* and *Sugar*. It was also to be made clear that while the school was not unsympathetic, those who did suffer a certain amount of discomfort should realise that this was a fact of life they would have to get used to. Alice Winnicott had been insistent that it was important not to dwell on the matter of pain because it was necessary to discourage the girls in their natural tendency to dramatise. The fourth-form head had duly summoned Martin's female colleagues in charge of the other three forms, briefed them, and the next day ninety fourteen-year-olds were initiated into the proper relationship between waste disposal and the female reproductive cycle. The thirty girls in Martin's form were ignored.

Furious, Martin cornered the head of the fourth year and demanded that she explain why he and his form had been excluded. She mumbled and dodged, looked satisfyingly embarrassed and lost for an explanation. But it gradually dawned on him as she talked that what embarrassed her was not that they had decided to exclude him and then declined to inform him of the decision, but that they had not discussed him at all. The presence of his absence was not even on the agenda. In matters of blood Martin Beck was an unperson and the thirty girls for whom he was responsible became invisible by association. Like some Chinese mandarin fallen from grace, his concubines were to be buried with him. One at least had refused her consent.

'I'd like a word with you, Mrs Winnicott.' She looked surprised at his tone but she did not risk a confrontation in the staff room, and coldly invited him to go to her office.

She sat down. 'What can I do for you?'

'I think you know.'

'I can assure you that I don't.' She had regained her habitual composure; like Gau she was happiest on home territory.

'You're not seriously telling me that you didn't know exactly what those sanitary towels I brought you were about as soon as you saw them.' He was angry, not least because she had manipulated him in a manner that was now clear to both of them.

'I had a pretty shrewd idea, yes.'

'Then why didn't you tell me?'

514

'I didn't feel there was any need to. And, anyway, I couldn't be sure.'

'You must think I'm an idiot.'

'No, I don't think that.' She said it flatly as if it were a question she had given lengthy consideration.

'Why wasn't I told?'

'I should have thought that was obvious.'

'Not to me.'

She sighed, with a calculated note of irritation. 'This is a delicate matter. No one suggested you be excluded. It was just obvious to us all that your involvement wasn't really appropriate. To be perfectly frank, it's nothing to do with you.'

That was careless of her. 'Clearly someone thought otherwise.'

She realised her mistake but was off-hand. 'One girl.'

'Is that all? Actually it was more like thirty, no one having bothered to tell my entire form. If it was important enough for the other fourth forms to know and important enough for you to carry on like a Venetian doge to keep it from me, then it was important enough for them to be told as well. I'd have to say that you haven't behaved very ... professionally.'

Each occupation, each place of work has its special insult, a single expression of disdain around which a chorus of less easily fixed disapprovals can find simple expression. To accuse someone of being un-professional at Mabey's was the equivalent of papal anathema. She was furious.

'How ...'

For a moment Martin thought she was going to say, '*How dare you?*' but she had the sense to bite her tongue. She continued, but with a hold on her temper. 'It was perfectly clear that your form would hear from the other girls what had been said. The message obviously got through and it got through without embarrassing them which is what they would have been if you had talked to them about this matter. They can be very sensitive – a fact you don't seem to have entirely grasped, if I may say so.'

'Yes, they're sensitive all right,' he replied. 'They'll have picked up the shame of it without any problem. They'll have learnt how to be subservient to their dirty little secret.'

The muscles in her thin face tightened. 'I don't think you can afford to be quite so self-righteous. Are you really expecting me to believe that if we had included you, you would have quite happily trotted off to a class of giggling, squirming schoolgirls to lecture them about not flushing their sanitary towels down the school toilets?'

They looked at each other.

'Where is it?' he asked.

'I burnt it, if you must know,' she said defensively.

'Good,' he replied.

She looked surprised. He had meant to storm out and slam the door behind him but in the end he just walked out, closing the door quietly.

The bell had gone to signal a change of lesson and a corridor nearby was filled with girls rushing from one class to another. He almost knocked over two who had decided to take a short cut past Alice Winnicott's office and down past some building works on one of the stairways.

'You can't go down there – it's dangerous.'

Looking guilty, neither girl said anything.

'Where have you come from?'

'Biology.'

'Where are you going?'

'Economics.'

'Go on.'

Smiling, they went back to join the girls still flowing along the corridor.

He walked back to the staffroom but as he was about to open the door, the bell began to ring again, stopped for a few seconds, then rang again, on and off continuously. He remembered there had been yet another warning at the morning staff meeting earlier in the week about a practice bomb drill, which involved the evacuation of the school and its reassembly on the hockey pitch. Being next to both the registers and the doorway, he was one of the first teachers out of the school buildings, but already disciplined lines of teenage girls were making their way to various parts of the sports field in a complete silence broken only by the high-pitched instructions of the PE staff, who were already waiting for them. His form register in hand, he watched as they formed an elaborate, divided square, a blue legion in A-line skirts. Then he began the calling of names, from Adams to Yates. 'Yes,' 'Yes,' the girls affirmed. Eight hundred and fifty times they asserted their presence while all around them the dying leaves blazed in the cooling air and the cold sun.

Anne was a lost soul. It was certain that she felt betrayed, outraged, incredulous at what he had done and that she felt all this painfully at the deepest level. But his actions were incomprehensible. Caught with another woman, discovering he'd been siphoning her bank account, that he was working for a rival firm, all these would have left her feeling deceived, angry and astonished. But each of these insults had a place to go, inbuilt responses that were pretty much the same for everyone. You knew not just what but how to feel when the husband or the lover took you for a ride by kissing elsewhere or by thieving from your purse. Under the incomprehension, the kiss, the filch, they made a common sense by virtue of the fact that here was a story that had been, was being, and would be

517

told again. But she had no inheritance of common lies to see her through this one. What was the story here?

In gripping yarns the fear is that the revelation won't be right – the last page missing or a lack of skill in writing an ending that astounds. She had the final missing page and nothing else: the guilty man had been unmasked but the beginning and the middle of his shame was lost. And, without a motive, so was she. Steven had consigned her to a kind of hell. Her story, too, had been mislaid. And robbed of her outline she had become a ghost.

All week she had found it hard to breathe, hard to swallow, as if a solid object was sticking in her throat, a hard lump of misery. But it was impossible not to think, not to consider, not to find herself slipping and imagining fantastic and absurd reasons for the events of that night, impossible not to imagine convincing explanations or even forgivably bad ones: a childhood trauma, a bad mother, or one dead or drunk or worse. Idiotic fantasies blew up like tropical storms only to die away to unmediated pique or fear or misery. Anything to make the story fit.

What was also extraordinary was the way life went on as she grappled with the unravelling smash and terror of what had happened. Decisions had to be reached, people seen and conversations had. It was not just that she was living two lives simultaneously but that the normal life would take over and it would be as if the horror was suspended as if part of her had been disconnected, the wires cut so that she could function with what was left. Just before the rush of pain came back when she was on her own or not busy, she felt that this was how a zombie must feel. Not like a zombie in the films who was really just undead, but a zombie that had most of its feelings and intelligence and even a sense of humour still working. In fact, you couldn't really tell from outside that this person was not really a living thing because a lot of this creature remained alive. It was a half-life, or a quarter or three-quarters, but whatever was missing was what stopped her being a real person. When your soul was frozen, what astonished her was how nearly everything that was your normal life, no matter how complicated, could still go on.

Steven looked in the mirror. He felt dopey from the Kapake painkillers he had been taking and fuzzily depressed. His skin had the colour, and some of the texture, of new putty. His arm throbbed gently, as if it were preparing to rev up for something more dramatic. When he came to stitch the wound in his arm, the Kapake did a good job of dulling the pain — he had fainted only twice. He shut his eyes and imagined the emotional insurgency Anne would now be going through. Horror: certainly. Fear: of a kind. Hurt: deep. Loss: deeper. Confusion: deeper still. But underlying all of this was something more powerful.

The phone rang. It was her. 'I want to talk to you.'

Although it was what he hungered for, he was shocked. He had never heard such coldness in a human voice before.

A depressed David Hendrix was in his consulting rooms drinking brandy while dictating his notes on George Winnicott into NEMO. He was depressed because of the identity parade. It had shaken him because he felt that he must have come close to being identified as involved with Maria Vaughan's disappearance. It wasn't just the realisation that suddenly, for no rational cause, your life could disintegrate around you and you could be found guilty of a terrible crime you hadn't committed. It happened, after all. It was not exactly unknown for the English legal system to put people in prison for things they hadn't done.

But it was more plausible that he might be arrested. If that happened it wouldn't have mattered much to his professional colleagues whether he was subsequently released. His reputation would be ruined, his livelihood destroyed. It had never quite come home to him before that to lose his work would be to lose himself. He had gradually fallen into the trap of thinking of himself as consisting centrally of his personal relationships with others and with himself. But he now realised that his work was central to his sense of being human. He knew this intellectually, of course, he could have *told* you this, just as he could have *told* you that he was going to die at some time. But now he felt this in the way you feel only when you lose it or come close to losing it. If he could not do his job any more he would cease to be a person. He would be a kind of ghost. In the middle of these morose thoughts his attention was distracted by a small icon he had never seen before blinking off and on in the top right-hand corner of the computer screen.

'NEMO, there's something flashing on the screen.'

Yes, Mr Hendrix. It is a box containing a small circle.

'What does it mean?'

It means that a query or problem you have asked me is now capable of being answered.

'What query?'

I have found the solution to the crossword clue E13.

'Really?'

I don't understand your question, Mr Hendrix. Do you want to review the solution now?

For a moment Hendrix considered refusing. But his depression made this all seem even more stupid and childish than usual. In any case it would be nice gesture to send the answer to Winnicott.

'Yes.'

There was a short pause as NEMO accessed the relevant file.

The solution to the crossword clue E13 is: Senselessness.

The Macintyre building on Windle Street is unlike any of the giants that surround it in the City of London. It was built in 1981 but gives the curious impression of having been there for a long time, and although it is also clearly, and controversially, modern its classical origins are obvious even to the untrained eye. Even its admirers, however, are unenthusiastic about the strident blue of its brickwork.

Anne Levels, pale and nervous, hesitated in front of the small entrance, which seemed more suited to a house. Several times that afternoon she had approached and walked away. A group of businessmen passed by her and seemed to pull her through behind them. She was expected at reception and was led through so quickly that she did not have time to run away. The receptionist knocked on the door.

'Come in,' said a distant voice, producing a frantic beat to Anne's heart. The door was opened, she was introduced, and then the receptionist was gone.

He was standing on a slightly raised section of the room next to a large device that looked like the delivery system for a weapon. There were similar constructions everywhere in various stages of assembly, some larger, others much smaller. Unlike familiar technology – the domestic fridge, the badged, installed device that powered a dentist's drill – they looked unfinished, chromeless, the product of a human hand careless of erratic welds or a neat fit in the inessential parts. They disturbed not because they were unknown devices for creative damage to soft tissue, but because the intelligence behind these complicated things was recognisably like your own: sharper, more knowledgeable but capable, certainly, of a bad day, a headache or a fitful capacity for incompetence.

He looked at her with restrained anxiety. Around his right arm he wore a white sling. He opened his mouth to speak but stopped himself as if he had, on reflection, nothing to say.

She walked further into the room establishing by instinct a territorial right. 'Well?' she said. She watched his face. It had, she thought, the grey tinge of old white paint and something of the same plastic sheen. The dark circles under his eyes shone through like a complicated painterly effect of white over black. The eyes, she saw, were pin sharp, but touched with pain, fatigue and a satisfying fear of her. She felt implacable. She watched the hopeful calculation on his face begin to drain away. He started to speak.

'I'm very sorry ...'

He stopped and blinked, realising the ridiculousness of his position, the banality of his violence against her, of how absurd his brutality had been and how weak he looked now. She despised him.

Then he smiled, mocking himself but also, she thought, mocking her as if they were equals in a ridiculous lovers' misunderstanding.

'What are you laughing at?' she said quietly. He stopped smiling and he looked at her as if he were controlling some annoyance. He started to speak but again stopped, as if to calm himself down. She was made more angry by his daring to control himself. What right had he to do so? What right to have any feelings of irritation strong enough to need controlling? Indignant at this affront she watched him reach for a small cash box and take out a felt bag the size of a small purse. He undid the string, tempting her to be curious. Once you had seen through someone, she thought, how obvious their moves became and how foolish one felt for ever having believed them. He unfolded a square of jeweller's felt on the table in front of him and carefully shook the bag like a gardener sowing seeds from a packet. He finished but said nothing as he looked at her. Now the fight in him seemed to have gone again.

He looked towards the jeweller's felt on which lay seven tiny crystals, like grimy industrial diamonds. Quietly he began. 'When people talk about their emotions it always seems airy fairy, don't you think?' He prodded one of the brownish crystals like a ten-year-old fidgeting with a bowl of sugar. 'But this is what emotions look like – bits of muddy glass.' He glanced at her but could not hold her gaze. He looked down again at the crystals. 'Strain is what causes these to grow inside the people they were taken from.' He pointed at them each in turn. 'Anger. Resentment. Malice. Fear.' He coughed and swallowed with difficulty. He looked at her directly then cast his eyes down. 'You can forget the heart – bladders and kidneys hold the secrets of the human soul.' He tried another remorseful look, but she was cold. Only a fool would be mollified by anything he had to say and she did not wish to be a fool but utterly implacable. To be unforgiving in the face of abject sorrow was her intention, the only way of maintaining any sense of self respect for loving someone deeply who was just a vicious creep. In spite of this she was aware of his pain, his misery and exhaustion, as well as his calculation – for she could well see that he wanted to do more than just explain himself. And this both infuriated her and made her hope for something he could say which would make everything all right. He looked around the room at the messy collection of half-assembled and experimental devices that covered every available space.

'These machines, what they measure is fear. It turns up on these screens as ulcers, tumours, failing hearts. Your blood carries the trace of every emotion it is possible to feel, and they can make you sick or they can make you well.' He was unaware that he was breathing noisily with the effort of speaking for so long. 'I need your love...'

'I did love you. Why did you try to hurt me?'

The interruption unbalanced him but he kept on going, as if to stall would be to surrender a last chance.

'I need your love because without it I will die.'

'Don't be ridiculous.'

'You look pale. You've lost weight,' he said.

There was nothing to be said in reply to this because it was true. She knew exactly what he meant.

He began to explain himself. It was the oddest sensation for him as he spoke. Something seemed to take him along quite naturally and there was no effort, no strategy, no watching the way he was received. It just happened. It's so easy, he thought, so easy that it seemed to do the work for you; it fell out of you like a weight falling under the effect of gravity. He enjoyed it; it was so very pleasurable, the truth. It was convincing. It was so *true*. When he had finished he was sorry that there wasn't any more to say, and he felt, absurdly, as if he'd like to go back to the beginning and start again.

She did not speak for fully thirty seconds. 'You've killed people?'

'Yes.'

'How many?'

He did not answer.

'How many?'

Again he did not reply. She looked at him, her eyes cold. 'I'm going to the police. You're a sick, miserable, lying fucking murderer.'

He was not cowed by this but seemed to be almost irritated by her failure to understand what he had been saying to her.

'Lying, absolutely. Miserable, certainly. Sick, definitely.' He hesitated. 'But none of it was done from malice. If retribution is what you want, nothing the police can do to me will come even close.' He paused, as if trying to see all this from her point of view. 'Come here,' he said at last, very gently.

'No.'

'Then I'll come to you.'

He moved towards Anne. Outside in the corridor the clatter and banging of ordinary life seemed to reach out to her as more substantial than the dream unfolding in front of her. As he came close, he opened his mouth. She held her head away but did not change her position. The hostile look in her eyes was not softened by fear or pity.

He blew softly into her face. The smell, although distinctive, was not unpleasant.

'Pear drops,' she said. 'You've been eating pear drops. So?'

'No. It's me.' He looked at her, searching. 'After a long starvation your body begins to eat itself. Acetone is a by-product .. It smells like pear drops.' He held up the back of his hand. Across each nail was a white line as if they had all been removed, folded crisply by precise hands, then replaced.

He started to sway slightly. 'I'll let you out.'

He began to move towards the door, but with the second step his knees buckled. He staggered, then collapsed. She watched him, her mouth open. He was sitting on the floor holding onto a table with one hand. There was a puzzled expression on his face as if he couldn't understand what he was doing on the floor and why he couldn't move. She had seen the same look on the face of a dog she had once run over, her car breaking its spine. Below the break the animal was paralysed but its two front legs kept scrabbling on the road as it tried to get back on its feet. Steven began to pull himself up by the table but half way his grip gave out and he began to fall. His other hand flailed wildly

at her – a simple reflex and she responded automatically. But she was too late. He fell back, missing her
outstretched hand, and the back of his head hit the
floor with a terrible crack. In a moment, astonished,
she was holding him up. His eyes blinked, uncomprehending, dazed and filled with pain. She held his head
for some time. She was aware of everything around
her: the strange room, the blood on the floor, the conversation of a few minutes earlier and that she was
holding the head of a man who had tried to kill her.
She was conscious of thinking but not of thinking
about anything, as if the mechanism of a projector had
been left running after the film had spooled itself to
the end: the bright light was on, the machine whirred
and clicked as before but it projected only white light
– intense and featureless.

This sensation continued throughout the taxi journey
to his flat and until the moment when she helped him
to his bed and eased him onto his back. She was
breathing heavily and so was he, but she was panting
from the effort of holding him up. Steven was breathing
in and out at a shallow but fast rate, like a mechanism
no longer in control and imminently about to burn
itself out. He closed his eyes and his breathing slowed.

'That hymn you're always singing. What's it
called?'

'What?' They were the first words they had spoken
since he had collapsed. 'Oh, *Simple Gifts.*'

She wished she had told him to shut up, but she was
taken by surprise and so deeply rooted was the giving
of answers to specific questions that it was out before
she could stop herself. A deep resentment warmed its
way through her.

'I'd like you to do me a favour if you would,' he
said.

'What on earth are you talking about?' she said, astonished that she could speak at all, let alone in tones of such motherly irritation.

'I have to remember to breathe,' he said, watching the effect he was having. 'If I fall too deeply asleep I just stop. Look at me. I need a good night's rest. I need someone to wake me up if my breathing stops.' He was panting like a large animal on a hot day but still kept his eyes on her face. He was not trying to hide from her that he was carefully sounding out her response. 'I need someone to watch over me.' He had intended to smile at this point, to concede the irony of what he was asking her to do, but he was now too tired and in too much pain, and she was past being charmed. Old habits, he thought.

'A favour is what you do for a friend,' she said

He was almost proud of her hostility, of her unwillingness to relent even a little.

'Are you my friend, Steven?' His eyes were closing with exhaustion and he did not reply. 'Then give me some good advice. Tell me what I should do about you.'

His eyes closed and when he spoke he was barely audible.

'Leave,' he said, and fell asleep.

Ten minutes later she was still there, standing with her back to the wall, fury and hate and spite filling her up as his breathing slowed. Deeper and deeper went each breath and slower and slower — and all the time her hatred for him grew. She could feel it turning in her chest, a living thing pushing and shoving and catching against the inside of her ribs. And all the time she listened to his breathing. Deep it was now, and slow, ten seconds between each breath. Then he breathed out and did not breathe in again.

She watched. He did not move. She waited; the movement in her chest had also stopped. Very slowly

527

his white face began to change colour, slightly at first, a reddish cast turning gently to something darker, blue, purple. Deeper and deeper it went until his face was as livid as a bruise. Still she did not move. She watched him and her chest heaved again with anger and a new disgust. Darker went his face, red and purple mixing, the only movement on the otherwise dead-still body. There was a sudden heavy thud. His mouth opened and wind rushed into his chest like air into a sealed room. His eyes opened in shock and pain. There was a second blow. Again the sound of air but now with an explosive rasp. Again she struck him on the chest, and again. He fell off the bed, more in response to the pain of bursting lungs than to escape the blows.

The punches stopped. When his breathing had almost returned to normal, after ten minutes with his head bent to his knees, she started to speak. 'When I was a child, there was nothing much you could do for people with asthma. My mother use to lie with me all through the night when I was really bad. Hour after hour she'd stroke my hair. She used to sing it to me, *Simple Gifts*, to calm me down.'

He did not say anything in reply and after a while she noticed that his arm had started to bleed again, the bandage dripping like a tap. She walked over to him, trapped by his slim waist and the powerful muscles of his shoulders and back, stretched taut by his bent attitude. As she reached out to touch his wounded arm, he turned round and caught her wrist with his good hand. It was a movement of fluidity, grace and extraordinary speed.

'Better not,' he said. He lay back on the bed and fell asleep again.

———

Anne stood in the shower. It was solid on three sides and with a thick opaque glass door that sealed off

every sound but that of the power-driven water thrashing her body. Eyes closed, she turned up her face into the stream and let the sensation annihilate every thought, every sense but that of the water on her skin. After ten minutes of this she was driven out by the cold of the water. Drying herself quickly, she welcomed the taste of air after the oxygen depletion of the hermetic shower. She cried out as she looked at her wrist. She had been wearing her watch. The inside surface of the glass was wet and the hands had stopped. She walked distractedly into the front room, examining it carefully.

He wondered if he should express concern or wait for her to explain. He had begun the overtures by brushing against her arm accidentally when she was close to him, when they passed each other in the corridor or went through the same door, but not even the careful choice of extremities or the avoidance of presuming to touch her skin had softened her. The only sign that she had in any way accepted him was that she had stayed.

'What is it?'

'My watch. I wore it in the shower.' The tone was devoid of desire to engage with him.

'It might just need a careful drying. Let me see what I can do.'

He held out his hand but did not try to take it from her. She passed it over in a gesture full of disdain.

An hour later Steven, jeweller's glass in one eye, was almost finished. Next to his hand was a small canvas roll that held numerous tiny instruments, surgical implements for a delicate manikin. With tiny silver tweezers in his hand he eased a spring, thin as a hair, into its place. Drawn in by his skill and anxious for the heirloom handed down from her grandmother, she did not notice that his face had gone white and that he was having trouble keeping his hand from shaking. He

wanted to avoid the danger implicit in her starting to feel sorry for him and, almost finished, he handed her the tweezers. They were so small it was quite a performance, indeed a ridiculous one, to place them between her thumb and forefinger without touching her. She went to pick up the one remaining cog, no bigger than the head of a pin, and with enormous care placed it in the tiny slot above the now compressed spring. He replaced the back-plate, fixing it with a satisfying click, then handed it to her. She looked at it, then began to wind. The second hand swept across the face within a fraction of the first turn.

'Thank you,' she said.

'I'd wait till you see if it keeps time.'

He turned to the instruments and packed them away in their tiny pockets. Anne finished winding and corrected the time. She looked at him again as she fastened it on her wrist, and cried out in alarm. A thin trickle of blood rolled slowly from his left ear.

'Steven! Your ear. It's bleeding.'

His head shot up and an expression she had never seen before passed across his face and was gone. He groaned.

'Damn,' he said softly as he looked at his finger tainted by a slight smear of red. 'I'll just ...' He gestured in the direction of the bathroom, pushed back his chair and left the room quickly. She watched him go, thinking about the look on his face as she had called out to him. It had come and gone in an instant: a look of unstinting terror.

When the change in Anne came it was sudden and incomprehensible. He could not sleep because of the ache in his back and had got up to sit in the orthopaedic chair he now used exclusively because it supported the small of his back. He was reading to

take his mind off the pain when she appeared in the doorway wearing the drab cotton nightdress she always wore now. Surprisingly she had not left to spend nights in her own flat, or even taken to sleeping in his spare bedroom. The chasm between them in the bed was unbridgeable.

She looked at him from the doorway for some time and he was unnerved by her expression; it had an intensity he couldn't place. She walked over to him at last and, to his astonishment, kissed him. What struck him within a second of her doing this extraordinary thing was that her mouth not only felt different in the way it searched his own but also that it tasted different.

She pulled him down onto the floor and held the thick cotton nightdress around her waist, climbed on top of him and began pressing herself down heavily and painfully. It was the first time in weeks that he had seen her pubic hair and it seemed a newly deep black against the white of her skin, so white now that the veins on her stomach were as blue as those of a pregnant woman. She grew frenzied, seeming at once acutely conscious of him and distant, lost somewhere so intense that he felt a stab of envy at seeing her so overtaken. Then, as her breathing quickened to a seamless pitch, she carried on one of the upward pulls and stood up in one movement, almost staggering as she did so. Her hand went between her legs as she bent to his groin and forced his penis into her mouth. She moved with careless speed and it hurt as her teeth grazed up and down its length. Then she bit him. Grabbing her, he tried to prise her away but she started to come and he could not move her. Then she was free, twisting and turning as she seemed to explode in heavy sobs. She did not stop but kept on weeping until he thought she would break in two. She cried like nothing he had ever heard before, enormous draining

sobs, like someone in the grip of a dreadful physical grief.

Two hours later he was lying in bed listening to the sound of her breathing as she slept. He was depressed: the gulf between them was no different, and he could not understand why her mouth had tasted different. It was the taste of a woman you had known for years but had never kissed. Perhaps the terrible contradictions of her new life had worked her up into a kind of convulsion; sex was an escape from the incomprehensible.

As Anne emerged from sleep she was conscious of a thud. It was not loud and she sank back again. There was another noise, the sound of something clumsily shifted, and this time she opened her eyes fully. Steven, naked from the waist up, leant against the wall crouching and with both hands pushed against it as if resisting its imminent collapse. She raised her head to watch him, a flutter of unease in her stomach. He started to move, not realising that she was awake, feeling his way along the wall like a man in the dark in an unfamiliar room.

'Steven?'

He stopped and stood upright but said nothing, his head held oddly as if listening for a sound whose source was unclear.

'What is it?'

'I can't see,' he said quietly.

She was out of bed and by his side, her heart racing. 'It's all right,' he reassured her, smiling at the depth of her alarm. 'I haven't gone blind. It's some kind of eye infection. My eyelids are stuck together.'

She led him by the hand to the kitchen. As she sat him down, she asked why he was smiling.

'Why do you think?'

'I'm going to get some water.'

She took cold, boiled water from the kettle, poured

it into a dish and put it in the microwave to warm. She watched him, admiring the patient look on his strong face, thinner now with every passing day. He needed her to wash his face but she had never felt more strongly the need to let him hold her. It was not maternal, not pity, but something that caught her hard in the chest.

'What are you doing?' he said, his head to one side, listening.

'Looking at you.'

'Why?'

'A cat can look at a king.'

The microwave bell rang.

She put the bowl of warm water in front of him. She fetched cotton wool from the bathroom, dipped a piece in the water and said, 'Tell me if it's too hot.'

'It's too hot,' he said, as she placed the first wet pad against his right eye.

'Don't be such a baby.'

Tearing off a new piece each time, she soaked the cotton wool and held it to each eye. The boiled warm water began to roll down his cheeks in streams.

'"Tears, idle tears, I know not what they mean",' she intoned sadly. He put his hand out, feeling for the edge of the table as if to place himself a little outside her power by holding on to something solid.

'You're a cruel woman.'

'No, I'm not. Don't try to open your eyes yet. The skin is delicate – you could tear it.'

She continued, dabbing, discarding, wetting, until all the white chalky residue around his eyes had been washed away. Becoming involved in the delicate washing she had slipped further towards him without realising.

'Try now.'

He opened his eyes. 'Thank you.'

She remained seated next to him, tore off a large

strip from the roll of cotton wool and started to dry his eyes, cheeks and chest. Gently touching the broad muscles on his chest after a long time was such a pleasure that she forgot the sense of distance, forgot that she was punishing him for what he was, for what he had made her agree to. Even the unpleasant release of the night before, which had stayed with her as she crept into bed, afraid and exhausted, seemed like a bad dream that had unaccountably receded. Feeling the change in her touch, his left hand went to her face. She pulled back, but not by much. He moved to kiss her where his hand had been and again she pulled away but not enough to stop his lips brushing her skin. He stood up and with his arms around her waist, lifted her onto the table. His arms enclosed her but her hands rested, palms flat, against his chest. He pulled himself towards her, and she responded by pushing him away, looking into his eyes, searching. Slowly she allowed the strength of his pull to balance hers, held him for a moment and then, with her face full of the terrible daring of what she was doing, she let him in.

Later, exhausted, he went to bed but the pain in his head and the stiffness in his back kept him from sleeping. She came to lie down on the bed next to him to keep him company, but still he could not settle and, indeed, seemed more restless because of her presence. Eventually his tiredness began to dominate and she could see his eyes begin to close, but he kept waking himself up.

'What's the matter?' she said softly. 'Why don't you sleep?'

He did not reply and got up and walked over to the side-table and popped a couple of Kapake from a foil packet. He poured himself a glass of water and swallowed the pills. Suddenly the glass fell from his hand. He almost caught it, but it slipped from his grasp. It was the first time she had seen him do anything

clumsy. The glass was thick and did not shatter on the highly polished wooden floor. He picked it up and put it back on the table. He went over to the nearly full-length mirror on the wall and looked at himself appraisingly, noting the badly healed wound on his arm and the erratic marks of the stitches. 'Look like a sieve,' he said. 'Feel like one, too.'

'Are you afraid?'

He turned to her and was touched by the sadness, the depth of affection, and the fear, both for him and herself. He went to the bed and lay down next to her.

'When I was a boy, I fell out of a tree but I managed to grab a branch, just, to stop myself. I hung there. I couldn't get back up, knew that if I fell I would be badly hurt. I hung there till my head began to burst and my arms felt like they were being pulled from their sockets. But I was too afraid to let go. It was a long fall onto hard ground. For twenty minutes ... half an hour I held on. I can feel it now, the blood pumping in my ears and the pain in my arms. And it was so very quiet. Then I fell.' He stopped again for a moment. 'My shin-bone snapped and stuck out of my skin like a stick. But I can't remember the pain of the break at all. What I *do* remember is trying to hold on and the wonderful feeling – wonderful – of letting go.'

He seemed more relaxed now and she could see his eyelids starting to grow heavy. Almost immediately he was asleep, his breathing getting slower until it stopped. The gentlest of touches from Anne started it again. And then in a moment he was awake and crying out in terror.

'It's all right,' she said, frightened by the dread that filled his voice. He looked around the room as if trying to fix himself back in the world. There was a cornered look about him.

'Dreams?' she said. He nodded. She watched him, wishing she had not asked and hoping he would not

tell her what they were. But he said nothing more and went to take a shower.

When he came back she had fallen asleep. His stomach hurt and he went into the living room, walking around for several hours before the pains stopped. When he went back into the bedroom, she had pulled off the bedclothes and was lying on her stomach. Her legs were parted and he looked at the way her buttocks fell naturally towards her labia, just visible and shadowed by the black of her pubic hair. He touched her thigh with the back of his hand. She felt cold. He pulled the covers over her and left the room again.

He went for a walk, a loop that two hours later brought him back through Gower Street. He had been considering what had caused Anne to stay with him. In the almost infinite weighing up that went into the making of most of the big decisions – to marry, have a baby, leave, return – there was often a gradual accumulation of factors; some clear, some not. Perhaps it was old-fashioned to think that the thing that tipped the balance one way or the other was decisive of itself, that without it the decision might have been different. With Anne, he thought he had an idea of why she had been able to stay. The blow with the scissors: she had meant to kill and knew it. Having drawn blood, making a wound that only slowly healed, honour of a kind was satisfied. He now felt he understood the terrible anarchy of the attraction between a man and a woman. It was not just arbitrary: love is a democracy where even the deranged and the criminal have votes. Respect and kindness, passion and fidelity, and wanting the other's good had only as much weight in this federation as the way he drew his hand across his hair, or the curve of his throat, or the smell of his skin when he was lying in her arms.

There was also the rare bond of knowing everything that could be known about someone you desired. Or

that he had killed before and would have done so now but that his love for her constrained even his deepest appetite, was stronger even than the drive to live. His death was the price for her being able to stay; he was sure that without it her pride in being loved so deeply would have sickened her.

While he was in Gower Street he went into McGiver's. The young man in a brown overall was ringing up a sale for a man who corresponded exactly to everyone's idea of what a builder should look like: a cap, donkey jacket, purple nylon vest, baggy jeans and muddy black unyielding wellingtons.

'What's the damage, then?' said the builder jovially.

'£147.38.'

'How much for cash?'

'£147.38,' came the flatly identical reply.

The builder ogled Steven. 'This one's a comedian,' he said, without rancour. He took out his wallet and counted out the money exactly from a thick wad and some loose change. The money paid and receipt in his wallet, he lifted up a complicated, heavy-looking construction lying against the counter in one large hairy hand, said 'Cheers, squire,' and, winking at Grlscz, told him that whatever he wanted it was bound to be cheaper at B&Q. Whistling, he pulled open the door and headed for a Transit van illegally parked on double yellow lines with two wheels up on the pavement. Grlscz watched him load up and drive away. He heard the builder shout a leering compliment at an irritated-looking woman in her early twenties wearing a short skirt, and then he was gone.

'Can I help you, sir?' asked the assistant, in an attempt to get his attention.

Grlscz looked back at him and walked over to a selection of different gauges of plastic sheeting in a roll. He gestured at the thinnest. 'I'd like about two metres.'

He was hungry all the time now, his stomach rumbled frequently and sometimes painfully: the white lines of starvation on his fingernails had thickened. Despite this, he was reluctant to kill her immediately or even soon. He had grown used to the pleasure of not having to watch his step in every way. He felt like a prisoner shortly to be released from jail, allowing the locked door and prison food to sharpen his taste for a fresh egg and his own set of keys.

Still, it was better not to push his luck and he decided she would be killed next week. She seemed particularly happy at the moment and her high spirits lifted his tiredness and the mild headaches that had become almost continuous because of his insistent need to eat.

'Are you hungry?' she asked him suddenly.

'Yes.'

'I'm sorry.'

'You seem very happy.'

'Yes,' she said quietly. 'How long do we have?'

This caught him off-guard.

'I don't know.' It was the first time he had lied to her for a long time. It felt strange; unpleasant. 'I have to go to Rainham on Saturday. I'll be away all day. I've had a lot of time off recently. I couldn't really refuse.'

She was indignant. 'You've been ill. You shouldn't have to make up for the time you've been away. Why don't you just leave?'

He could see she instantly regretted this. But there was more at stake than her fumbling reference to the fact that he was dying, wouldn't need a job and therefore didn't have to be evasive with his employers. Getting this wrong might make her suspicious. Fortunately the insight that had taken him so long to learn – always tell the truth – was easy enough to follow here.

'Clavell wants me to do a presentation to his partners about the stress research. It's all set up. All it needs is their go-ahead to spend the money.' He laughed. 'I don't need to be there to run it. I'd rather it didn't go to waste. It's worth doing.'

She nodded. It was easy for her to understand this.

'Anyway,' she said, smiling, 'it's probably just as well you're not going to be here next Saturday.'

'Why?'

'I've invited Martin to come over.'

He was offended that she hadn't asked him first. He realised how odd his reaction was, even ridiculous. Was this a dare, he wondered.

He grimaced, mocking. 'You're right, Kent has never seemed so attractive.'

'Karen's left him.'

'Ah,' he replied.

'You don't have to pretend it bothers you.'

'I'm not pretending. It doesn't bother me.'

She laughed then changed the subject.

On Saturday he left the flat a good half-hour before Martin Beck was supposed to come. As he was searching for his keys in the hall she came out to say goodbye. 'What time do you think you'll be back?' she said.

'Late. Clavell said it would be the last item on the agenda probably, but that I could try and do some discreet lobbying at lunch.'

'I thought I might take Martin to Oxford later – there's an exhibition at the Museum of Modern Art I've been wanting to see.'

He nodded but she seemed keen to explain.

'It might take his mind off his troubles and I'm not sure if I can spend the whole day talking about Karen to be honest. So don't worry if there's no one here

when you get back.' Then she leant over and kissed him.

He was not in fact due at the meeting with Clavell until four that afternoon. It was now ten thirty and he intended to drive to the hut on the coast to check that everything was in order and that it was still deserted.

It was. The last time he had been here the weather had been grey and damp but today, despite the late snap of cold, the sun was shining brightly. It was so intense that it made driving uncomfortable, the sun blinding him for almost the entire journey and always managing to be at a point in the sky where it was not quite obscured by the car's visor.

When he arrived at the beach, there was no one to be seen. Indeed, he had never seen anyone there in the six years he had rented the place. Given that he had been in many isolated places, for one reason or another, he was surprised by this. You hardly had to wait twenty minutes anywhere else in England, no matter how secluded, before someone wandered past, nodding at you with fellow feeling or grumpy because isolation was why they, too, had made the effort. He spent half an hour checking that nothing had been disturbed, even by the most careful intruder, then left. The sun seemed even brighter and it was only now he had finished his business that he looked around the beach. It was an awful place. Everything on the beach – bird bones, seaweed, even bits of rope – looked as if it had once belonged to something alive, but now disassembled by the waves, sheared by the wind and leached by the sun so that every trace of its former life had vanished. For the first time, the exactness of the word struck him: these were remains.

He was about forty-five minutes from the meeting in Rainham when his mobile rang.

'Steven?'

'Yes.'

'It's Tom ... Tom Clavell.'

'Hi.'

'Look, there's been a bit of a problem.'

'I see.'

'The fact is that the meeting has gone on longer than I'd thought. I don't think we'll be able to get to it today.' There was a pause. 'Look, to be honest, Steven, I don't think they're going to buy the idea. I'm sorry. Perhaps we could look at it again in six months.' There was another silence. 'Steven?'

'I'm still here, Tom.'

'I'm sorry.'

'Of course.' There was another silence. 'I'll talk to you next week.'

'Things are a bit hectic at the moment. The meeting is asking for a few changes. To be frank, Steven, they're worried about how much we're spending on freelance contracts. We'll need to cut back for a bit. I'll call you when things settle down.'

Grlscz could hear busy corridor noises at the other end of the line which were slightly muffled as Clavell put his hand over the mouthpiece, clearly under the impression that this would cut the sound out. 'I'm finished here,' he heard him say obsequiously. 'I'll be right with you.'

Grlscz considered hanging up, but he did not.

'Right, Steven, I'll call you. I have to go.'

'OK, Tom. We'll talk again.'

He arrived back at his flat at two. If they were still there he would leave quietly. He did not want to discuss what had happened in front of Martin Beck or, indeed, talk to him at all. Fortunately he had finally got someone to mend the flat's sticking door and made his way in without any noise. If they were still there he had to be careful to prevent them hearing him

because the lobby door into the living room was slightly ajar. He heard voices and groaned silently. He was about to leave when she laughed and curiosity drew him to the door to listen to what they were saying. It was her teasing laugh, the one she used when she was about to dismiss someone's sense of being hard-done-by. 'Can you believe it?' he heard Beck say, indignantly.

'I can, actually,' she said. 'I used to have dreadful cramps but my mother was always telling me I'd just have to put up with it. It seemed to exasperate her for some reason. Older women are like that, God knows why. It was always unmentionable.' She laughed. 'I'm not sure it still isn't. You should see the expression on the faces of most men when the subject comes up.'

'I'm not like that,' said Beck defensively. 'They should have told me. It made it look to my form as if that's what I thought about them – that there was something too ... I don't know ... distasteful about them, shameful.' There was a pause.

'Well, that's very admirable,' she said, and he could hear the mocking tone, not cruel, but Beck was certainly going to get it.

'What do you mean?' asked Beck.

'What I mean,' she said, and Steven could hear her smiling, 'is that I wonder if she wasn't right when she asked if you would have been happy to go off and talk to thirty fourteen-year-olds about their periods. What do you know about it, anyway?'

'What's that got to do with it?' he said, and it was clear to Steven that he knew she was getting ready to go for him. 'Look, I'm a teacher. I'm always talking with authority about things I've never done myself.'

'Making a joke of it won't get you off the hook. Answer the old bat's question: Would you have gone?'

There was a brief pause.

'Yes,' he said firmly.

'You know, I think you would have gone. But only out of bravado, only to prove that it didn't bother you, that you're on our side. Is all this indignation really about more than your vanity?'

He didn't say anything in reply but Steven could imagine the expression on his face and he was pleased.

'You know, Martin, I wonder if the inventive little rebuke left for you outside the staffroom might not have been deserved.'

'That's not fair.' He was annoyed now.

'Don't be angry,' she said sweetly. 'You're right ... OK ... not completely deserved.' She paused. 'Just a little bit.'

He did not say anything in reply. Steven could imagine Anne touching his arm not as a retreat but to say that it wasn't important, it wasn't meant to hurt.

'All right, maybe it was,' Beck conceded finally. Then he laughed. 'It's tricky, isn't it, indignation?' There was another silence, pleasant and friendly. 'Maybe it's just the effect of being browbeaten by you but it's getting incredibly hot in here,' said Beck, just as Steven had decided to slip away. He heard her get up and the sound of her walking towards the window, he assumed, which would involve her passing the slightly open door. He moved backwards, thinking there was something odd about the sound of her footsteps. She passed by and he watched her for the three or four seconds it took to reach the window. She was naked.

———

The thing that's really upsetting about infidelity is the sudden change in point of view involved. One naturally assumes oneself to be at the centre of one's life. You are the main plot, the focus of the narrative – others are players, great or small. The vertiginous collapse that happens to your insides on learning that

543

your wife or husband's fucking someone else has less, at first, to do with a sense of betrayal than with the speed at which your inner narrative is reassigned. Your centre now consists of being someone else's perimeter. A nasty thought and a nasty journey to undertake at faster than the speed of light.

The window was high up which meant that there was little chance of her being seen, so she was as relaxed as she always was when walking naked around the flat. Both he and Beck would be watching her as she stretched to fix the window open wide enough to get a reasonable breeze. Others in his position would by now be feeling somewhere inside, *I am betrayed*; Steven differed only in that what he felt was, *I am dead*. Otherwise it was the same sense of being overtaken by shock while at the same time searching for an interpretation which would allow nothing of what he'd seen to be what it unequivocally was. *It's not what you think. Thank God for that.* She turned and walked back towards the other side of the room. A few seconds later he heard the creak of the springs of the sofa-bed. The part of him not in shock wondered why she had used the sofa rather than the bedroom. Presumably it made her feel better about what she was doing. An unaccustomed malice made its presence felt in him and he almost allowed it to surface, imagining a confrontation a good deal bloodier than usual.

Something pulled him backwards, out through the door, down the stairs and into the street. He started to walk quickly, hyperventilating as he went, trying to order the terror engulfing him. *You're going to die,* he thought, walking towards the Thames, *You're going to die*, as he drifted through shoppers emerging from the Underground in Leicester Square. On Blackfriars Bridge the comprehensive fact of death and nothing else knotted the muscles in his throat, turned his stomach in Zoah Place and warmed his extremities

against the freezing wind on Crucifix Lane and Druid Street. Through Unicorn Pass he went, then back through Roper Lane, filling up in Snowsfield, leaking internally like a winter thaw bringing a flood from damage hidden by the frost. Wet with despair in Tyler's Gate, he crossed back to the north by Tower Bridge emerging into the City with a sudden insight that would save his life.

Deceiving people was a waste of time. Giving people what they wanted was bound to end in tears because no one could fool anybody better than they could fool themselves. A true forgery described a shape into which the mark could pour himself. An authentic work of art was hard. It had a shape. It took you on. A fake needed to be soft, easy to impress, lacking anything but a desire to please. There should be no surprises, nothing particular in a fake, and if there were, the forger had to root them out. He had been knocking up personalities that were indistinguishably real. His mimes were full of snags, paradoxes, things his victims had to swallow or decide to make allowances for. How could they fail to disappoint? What he had contrived to shape across the years with subtlety and guile had been the very things to bring him to the point of death. He needed to be no more like the real thing than a fishing fly. Presentation was all that mattered to the trout, how it moved over the water. A thoughtfully designed lack of similarity to the real thing was what was required. Complex and rich emotions could be taken just by employing the right kind of lure.

His mistake lay in thinking that at some level she had the image of a perfect love buried like an ancient king ready for an archaeologist to uncover, all scalpels and camel-hair brushes, who only required a capacity for taking pains to lay the body bare. This was their delusion and he'd swallowed it hook and line, a

gullible, wide-eyed yokel of the heart. People could not be satisfied. Nothing you could ever do would be enough. He'd built himself for her like one of those museum creatures hypothesised in clay and wire, based only on a fragment of the original beast: a cheekbone here, a thighbone there, a delicate impression in the clay of something that had vanished long ago. That's what he'd been up to all this time and his genius for doing so was what had led him up the garden path: the bits and pieces came from different animals, the impression of something like a skin was only the action of water on dissolving rock. He didn't need to worry about what she wanted in a man as long as he avoided doing anything to make it clear it wasn't there in him. Given sufficient softness, obscure desires would impress themselves upon his carefully collected set of absences. An angry dependency would be his bait. If possible he must catch them in the act. Shock, guilt, remorse, a despairing attempt at suicide should do the trick. He pulled over a taxi in the Minories and ordered it home. It wouldn't take long this time and it would be infinitely easier. She'd get fed up with it in time, he knew, but this was something to be cultivated. He wanted her to start to find his neediness a touch oppressive so that every other fear would be allayed. She'd trust his dependency even if it had begun to weary her. This was the only tricky bit; he mustn't allow this to be too strongly felt. Like Maria there would be a moment when she buried something that she knew she ought not to feel but bury it so quickly she would hardly be aware of having buried it at all. Before then he would kill her.

———

The cab dropped him off at the end of the street and he walked past his old Mercedes. He stopped when he saw his briefcase in full view on the passenger seat.

He unlocked the door and bent to take it out, leaning across the driver's seat.

'Hello, what are you doing here?' said a bright voice behind him.

He jerked up in surprise, cracking his head on the roof. 'Shit! Jesus Christ, Anne, that fucking hurt,' he said, holding his head in his hands as he stood up. His irritation was partly due to pain and partly to his having failed to return in time to catch them. She reached up and touched his head with that paradoxical smile that women reserve for small boys and men who have hurt themselves but not badly. She gently rubbed the side of his head. Martin Beck hovered, detached.

'What are you looking at?' she said, smiling but not taking her eyes from his head. He pulled her hand away and keeping hold of it said, 'A cat can look at a king. Hello, Martin.'

Beck looked startled at being addressed by someone who wasn't looking at him. 'Oh, hi,' he replied shiftily.

Steven looked at him. 'Going somewhere?' he asked.

'I told you we might take a trip to Oxford,' said Anne.

'Bit late, isn't it?'

'The museum is tiny – there's only one exhibition. It won't take more than half an hour. We thought we might have dinner at the Elizabeth. Anyway, what are you doing here?'

'I left some papers behind. I was past junction twenty-eight before I realised. Bloody nuisance.'

'Can you get there in time?'

'For the important bit. It's a pity I missed the lunch but it's not vital.'

'Cancel it and come with us,' she said. She was sincere, and for the briefest of moments he scanned

the evidence of the naked body and the sofa-bed, recognising the absurdity of this even as he did so.

'I'm tempted, really, but I'd like to see if I can get this off the ground.' She squeezed his arm and for the first time he felt that affection could be as powerful an emotion as sexual desire or jealousy. They turned together and walked back towards the flat and her car parked outside. She smiled at Steven as they parted but didn't kiss him goodbye. Beck waved awkwardly as he got in the car and Steven watched them drive away. As the old BMW turned the corner at the end of the road, he thought he saw her turn back briefly to look at the spot he should by then have left.

He waited five minutes then followed. He did not need to stay close as it was motorway nearly all the way and Steven's old Merc, because of its size and comparative rarity, was easy to spot. He was glad of the chance to drive on sparsely populated open carriageway. There was enough traffic to keep his mind occupied but little enough so that he could begin to calm down. About half an hour into the journey he found himself rocking backwards and forwards in his seat like a jockey absent-mindedly urging his horse to go faster. Ten minutes later he found that he was doing it again.

As he approached the enormous white scar cut into the hill outside High Wycombe, which enabled the motorway to fall towards the plain that led towards Oxford, the flashing squares on the arches sporadically placed above the road signalled there was a delay ahead. He joined the tailback which slowly shifted to the outside lane. The clutch was heavy on the Mercedes making the stop and start especially aggravating and he felt the painfully gentle pull as it irritated his sciatic nerve. Slowly the traffic filtered to the right with the inevitable twerps and spivs charging down the inside lane to jump the queue. He could see

what the problem was now. An enormous double-trailered lorry had crashed into the almost vertical wall of chalk that sided the cut into the hill. It skewed across the two inner lanes of the motorway with the tail-end trailer pushed forward so that it formed a V-shape, an unsettling angle that gave it the appearance of a badly broken leg. It must have happened recently because several policemen were guiding the traffic while men in Day-glo waistcoats set up the traffic cones to create a space around the accident. In single file the cars moved by and he could sense the sympathetic curiosity of drivers and passengers glad that it was nothing to do with them. As he moved slowly to the front of the accident, he realised that something had been caught between the giant cab of the lorry and the wall of chalk. Even before he saw it properly, he knew that it was Anne's car.

Perhaps the events of the morning had drained his capacity for shock. Now he felt something close to extreme cold on an exposed limb. It was both painful and insensible to pain at the same time. Emerging from the line of traffic, he pulled over to the hard shoulder just where the cut gave way to open countryside. He walked back up the hill, its sheer sides and yellow whiteness making him feel like someone walking, infinitely small, through a polluted glacier. A policeman met him as he approached. 'What the bloody hell do you think you're doing?' he called, from ten or fifteen yards away.

'The car,' Steven said, nodding up the hill. 'I think my ...' he cast around for the right word, 'fiancée was in it. The car.' The policeman was caught off-guard and said nothing in reply. Passengers in passing cars gawped sombrely at them as they stood, sharply outlined, against the yellowy white wall.

'I see,' said the policeman gently, as he looked down the hill to check the Mercedes. 'If you give me

your keys, I'll bring your car up here. It'll be safer.'
Steven handed them over and the policeman took him
by the arm with great delicacy and shepherded him
towards the monstrous accident. A short man in civil-
ian clothes walked towards them. The policeman
pulled him to one side and talked softly to him. The
man looked over to Steven and nodded.

'I'll just go and bring it up,' said the policeman, gesturing at the Mercedes, and set off down the hill.

The short man approached. 'The constable tells me
you think your fiancée was in the car.' Steven nodded.

'Well, I have to tell you there's something rather
odd.' The man looked nervous, reluctant. 'I can't be
sure, I can't be sure at all, but there doesn't seem to
be anyone in the car. Was there anyone with her?'

'A man.'

'Well, I still can't be sure but I've been doing this job
for twenty years. I mean, you can see the impact.' He
moved aside slightly to give him a clear view of the
crushed car. 'It's half its original length.' He stopped
again clearly unsure how to go on.

Steven just looked at him.

'The impact, well, it must have been terrible. Thirty
tons at sixty miles an hour. Two bodies, well, there'd
be a sign. After all we're talking about – sorry – fifteen
pints of blood. There's no sign, nothing at all.'

'I don't understand,' said Steven.

'Look, I'm not saying they're not in there, mind you.
I can't say that. All I am saying is that I don't think
there can be anyone inside. Not without a sign. I can't
be sure. You can never tell with accidents.'

'I see.' Steven said nothing for a while and the short
man shifted uncomfortably, then spoke again.

'Perhaps …'

'Where are they if they're not in the car?' interrupted
Steven.

The man felt happier answering a direct question

and there was a distinct matter-of-factness about his reply.

'Well, at first we thought they'd gone to report a breakdown on one of the motorway phones and that the lorry had ploughed in while they were away. But the phones are only a mile apart whichever way you go. They're not on the motorway and there haven't been any reports of a breakdown in this area.' He began to look uncomfortable again.

'Tell me what you can,' said Steven.

'If it was parked on the hard shoulder then the lorry could have pushed it from much further up the cutting. The only witnesses were from behind the lorry and it was so big it hid the front of the accident. A few months back one of the policemen over there booked someone for parking up where the cutting starts and going for a walk on top of the hill. He tells me it happens quite frequently. The view is impressive. Bloody stupid thing to do,' he added and regretted it. Someone signalled to him and he nodded back decisively. 'Look, I've got to go. Why don't you sit down over there?' he said, pointing at a step eroded into the chalk. 'I'll let you know what's going on.'

Steven stood and watched, a red blanket they had given him around his shoulders to keep off the wind. A small tow truck pulled back the cab, allowing the car to drop from the rough niche in the wall into which it had been jammed. Seven or eight men fell to examining it like anxious racing mechanics during a wheel change. Steven moved forward.

After a few minutes the short man came over. 'There isn't a trace of anyone.' He looked uncomfortable, clearly torn between a conviction that there was no one in the car and his fear of being definite.

'What now?'

'When the Arvin comes back – that's the big tow

truck – we'll start to stretch it so we can see if …' He let his sentence trail away.

Within five minutes the Arvin turned up and was waved to the front of the car, where it came to a halt with the repressed hiss of giant air-brakes. A great beefy man, all shirt sleeves and hairy arms despite the cold, climbed down and went to the back of the truck. He started attaching a chain but there was a delay while someone reached under the front to hammer the linking bolt through a bent towing bracket.

When it was attached, the big man swaggered back to the cab and climbed up into it like a sailor climbing the rigging of a tea clipper. Four men stood two apiece at the front of both trucks. Steven moved with the short man to the middle where the car lay with limp chains to front and back. With the engines throbbing, the short man signalled for the trucks to move forward slowly. The men in front of the cabs made a gentle come-to-me gesture with their hands. Both trucks moved forward with great delicacy. The short chains shifted slowly. The trucks moved on. The chains described a sagging arc and then, slowed even further by the watching men holding their palms before them, gradually became taut. The men held up one hand, palm out. The trucks stopped. A short pause followed and then the signing began again, this time fingers moving like those of someone stroking an animal under the chin. The tone of the engines changed up a note, then another. The car shifted imperceptibly then clearly as the engines worked hard to lift it from the ground. With a scraping noise of metal across Tarmac the crushed car lifted. Inch by inch it rose, like a terrible levitation. The short man signalled again. The engines strained, as if the effort was certain to damage them. Then the sound of metal pulling away from metal began, a painful sound, like an arthritic limb pulled straight by powerful, unsympathetic hands.

The noise went on, groaning and cursing as the trucks tried to reverse the forces suddenly combined in great weight, high speed and the sixty-million-year solidity of Wycombe Hill. Again another change of note, a deeper, tearing sound twisting the car; it seemed to move in fits and starts, weak and strong by turns. Then the bodywork gave way and smoothly the car relaxed to something like its former length. The short man waved his hand decisively. The others followed suit. The big trucks stopped. The car now hung, suspended, five or six feet off the ground. The short man was about to signal to his men to let it down slowly to the road when someone shouted, 'Look!' A liquid was leaking from underneath the car.

'It's blood,' said someone else.

'No, it's not. It's oil,' said the supervisor.

But he was wrong. The first of it, gelatinous and black, must have been exposed to air inside the car, but as they watched, appalled and sick at heart, the blood flowed, pouring and leaking from everywhere as if the car itself had veins and arteries. Over bright-work, door sills, headlamps, from engine bays and wheel arches it streamed, pouring as if the car was filled with only blood. Red as nail varnish it ran down the hill, over the white lines, catseyes and bits of chalk sprinkled along the edges of the motorway.

No one said anything and no one moved. The flow stopped quickly but the car dripped red like too-wet washing on a washing line. The supervisor looked at Steven. He watched him for a long time not knowing what to do but deeply moved by what he'd seen. Something else began to leak.

'It's petrol,' called out one of the supervisor's men.

'We'd best move away,' the man said gently to Steven, who stood blanket-wrapped before the broken car, but he gave no sign of having heard. 'Come along, my son,' he said, putting his arm around Steven's

waist and leading him towards a nearby car with "Motorway Police" stamped boldly on the side.

'Where are we going?' Steven asked.

'Home,' said the policeman. 'Is that all right?'

'Yes.'

The supervisor shut the door and slowly the car pulled away heading down the motorway towards Oxford before the driver could turn it back to London at the junction close by.

The supervisor turned his attention to the petrol slowly leaking on to the road. Mixing with the blood already drying in the cold, it liquefied it, spreading it in thin pools over the Tarmac. The now darkening, half-dissolving reds deepened the waxy electric blues and greens that shimmered on the petrol in the quickly disappearing light.

Across the crash barrier the supervisor saw the police car moving very fast past the accident along the unblocked carriageway. He watched it go up the hill out of the cut, then turned back. 'Quickly now, lads,' he called, as the firemen with their suffocating chemicals flushed the blood and petrol into the margins of the hill.

E 1 3

How *unfair* life is.

Louis Bris, *The Wisdom of Crocodiles*

One week had become two weeks. Then three. Then six. On the day that Dr Robert Sapelsky came to see him with his final diagnosis, George Winnicott had been in hospital for nearly two months. His head had been shaved and the powerful steroids he had been taking had caused his face and hands to swell. The impression was of both great size and great vulnerability, like a giant child. Dr Sapelsky had already started when the patient's wife entered. Already nervous, her arrival flustered him still further.

'Uh ... as I was saying, the symptoms are clear enough in themselves, Mr Winnicott, but they conflict with one another. They indicate damage to the brain in many different areas. The MRI scans show that two areas of your brain are, as it were, lighting up inappropriately. They're both supposed to be active when

someone talks to you. But when you're just thinking, only Broca's area is supposed to light up. But sometimes there's activity in both even when no one is talking to you. When that happens you hear your thoughts as if they were voices speaking to you. There's possible evidence of damage to Broca's area – but we can't be sure ...'

'Can't you do more tests?' said Alice interrupting.

The doctor shifted awkwardly. 'Well, the thing is that these MRIs are as sensitive as we can go. But it's the symptoms you've developed since you came in. They're contradictory. There's a definite weakness on the right side of your body now ...'

'That could be his back, couldn't it?' said Alice, almost fiercely. 'He always gets very stiff when he lies in bed for any length of time. He needs to move about more.'

'It's not that kind of weakness, Mrs Winnicott. It's affecting all the sensory modalities ... all the senses on that side of his body. It also explains the headaches.'

'That's on the left side of my head,' said George politely.

'Yes. It would be. The left-hand side of the brain controls the right-hand side of the body.'

'I see.'

'What's also puzzling is the short periods of eyesight loss in your left eye, and you've complained of losing your sense of smell for periods of up to an hour. You see, that would indicate a lesion on the frontal lobe ... but we can't find anything, no physical damage is showing up in the tests ... the scans. It's very unusual.'

'Don't you have any idea at all? I find it difficult ...' Alice did not know how to finish the sentence. She was angry at the ineffectual diagnosis but also afraid of annoying the doctor so that he might decide to stop trying to help her husband out of pique.

'I appreciate this must all seem very vague. I'm sorry.'

'I realise you won't want to ...' a look of irritation and alarm clouded George's face as he searched for the word, '*commit*,' he said at last with relief, 'commit yourself – but you must have some ideas.'

A look of hunted unwillingness came over Sapelsky's face as he reluctantly started to speak. 'Well, not all diseases of the brain involve the kinds of solid objects you can pick up in a scan – tumours and lesions and so on. Sometimes the effect is non-specific damage to the tissue. It just degenerates. But I'm not saying that's what it is.'

'What are you telling me?' said George, suddenly alarmed. 'Am I going to get better?'

Sapelsky was taken aback by George's reaction because his earlier response, more stoic than his wife's, had suggested he was prepared for what Sapelsky was trying to tell him. He was clearly wrong. Sapelsky did not look at his wife.

'It's difficult – given we can't locate the cause of the problem exactly.'

'Then I might just get better – is that possible?'

'Well ...'

'I'm not asking for a guarantee. I've heard all your ... warnings you give people ... *caveats* ... I've heard them. Will I get better?'

'No ... I don't think so.'

George looked as if he had been struck in the face. He said nothing for a while. Sapelsky still avoided Alice's gaze but could feel her eyes boring into him. George composed himself to ask another question. 'So ... you think I'll be like this for the rest of my life?'

The look on the faces of both Sapelsky and Alice puzzled George for a moment.

'Oh,' he said.

George Winnicott realised he was going to die.

Alice turned away to the window, away from her husband and the doctor.

There was a rasping sound from the sick man on the bed, a self-deprecating reprimand for having missed something that was clear if only you had been paying proper attention: a partner's adultery, a colleague's sudden promotion to a job you thought was in the bag.

'How long?'

The doctor murmured evasively.

'Please,' said George, 'your ... what's the word? ... *reservations,* are perfectly clear. You don't have to repeat them.'

'In the last ten days your condition has deteriorated in a number of significant ways.' He stopped for a moment and then committed himself. 'Weeks.'

'Two? Four?'

'It might be longer than four, I don't think it will be less.'

'Thank you.'

Alice turned back from the window. 'I won't have this. Do more tests.'

'We can do the ones we've already done again. There aren't any others I can think of.'

'I'd like another opinion.'

'Of course.'

'I think I'd like to ...' George struggled, '*support* ... that, Doctor. I'm sure you understand.'

'Absolutely. Ah ... if you'd like to find someone yourself, of course you must. But,' he paused awkwardly, 'I've asked Professor John Porter-Hallett at Guy's to review your case. The thing is, it will be quick. He'll see you on Friday.'

'Look, I don't want to be rude,' said Alice, passionate in her husband's defence, 'but I'm sure you understand. Is he impartial? If you know him?'

'Ah, I don't actually know him. I've met him once ... briefly. We're not friends or anything.'

'What do you think, Alice?'

The question almost broke her heart. She nodded and they did not see she was unable to speak.

———

Alice had gone to talk to the doctor to arrange the details of the second opinion. She had been reluctant to leave her husband but he reassured her that he would be fine on his own, that he would even prefer a few minutes by himself. In this way, with the best of motives, he offended her deeply. She needed to be with him and wanted him to know that she would put aside everything. In this time when his life was coming to an end, there would be a fresh start. This had been a great thing for her, to allow that there had been something deeply wrong between them. The acknowledgement of how she really felt about her life caused her physical pain. It made her stomach ache, her chest tighten. But she would make an effort; she would be kinder. And though it made perfect sense to her that he would need time on his own, it did not matter. She felt his reassurance that he did not need her with him like a blow.

Alone, George suddenly felt immensely tired, as if he had been drugged. He was being dragged into a deep sleep. He tried to stay awake but in a minute he was gone. He slept for only a short time then woke up, or rather he woke himself up. Anyone watching would have seen that he was uneasy, afraid even. But only ten minutes later he was smiling. It was not a happy smile, certainly, but one of self-conscious mockery, as if he had overreacted in a way that was understandable but still slightly foolish.

———

'It's very, very sad.'

Sally Brett and Michael McCarthy sat glumly in her office.

'How long?'

'She didn't say.'

'No ... awkward.'

'I'm going up to see him once he's settled in at home. She asked me to leave it for a while.'

'Ah.' Brett's face fell again. 'Do you think I should ... go?'

'I'll ask when she phones, if you like. I got the impression he's particularly bad at the moment. He goes up and down, apparently. She made a point of my not staying long.'

'Of course. Well, I'll leave it to you ... as you think best.'

There was a pause, then Brett produced an unopened letter and handed it to McCarthy. It was addressed to Brett. 'It's postmarked Harrow It must be from George.'

'Why don't you open it?' said McCarthy.

'I think it might be his resignation.'

'Really? Why?'

'It was something he said to me before he went into hospital. He felt he hadn't contributed anything.'

There was an awkward silence.

'What if it's not? His resignation I mean.'

Brett leant forward as if she were anxious not to be overheard. 'If I open it and he's offered to resign it could be very difficult. I had a roundabout sort of talk with our legal department ... hypothetical. It seems that George ...' she paused, ' ... well, his widow ... is only entitled to a pay-out if he's been employed here long enough.'

'And he hasn't?'

'Just under. There's another week to go.'

'So if he resigns now she won't get anything.'

'Exactly.'

'Why don't you ask him?'

Brett sighed heavily. 'Arthur says I've got to accept

it if it's offered – we're obliged to follow Civil Service rules in these matters.'

'Maybe it isn't his resignation.'

'Maybe not,' she said irritably, 'but I'd have to open it to find out, wouldn't I?' She lowered her voice again. 'All this is strictly between us.'

'Of course.' A thought struck McCarthy. 'What happens if he dies before next Thursday?'

'Then it's out of my hands, I'd say, wouldn't you? I could try having a word with Hutchence at the First Division. He's not a bad sort. Anyway, I'll worry about that when it happens.' She handed McCarthy the letter. 'I'd like you to keep it for the moment.'

McCarthy took it.

'Perhaps when you go to see George you might do a little digging for us.' She mistook McCarthy's suspicion for reluctance. 'I'd say it was a good cause, wouldn't you?'

'Yes ... of course.' Unhappily, he put the letter in his inside pocket.

'Is he dead?'

'Not yet.'

'Put him over there ... No, over there.'

'It's five o'clock.'

'That gives you thirty minutes, then.'

'What's the problem?'

'Proof it and reduce it by fifty or so. If anybody more important chokes it might have to come down a bit more. It was last done by that useless cretin Woodward, so Botsford says to double-check everything with the Press Association and *Who's Who*.'

'Why are we doing this *now*? He's not due for an update till next month.'

'Apparently he's pretty sick ... not going to last much longer. The Fraud whatever-they're-called is in the news. Oh, and Botsford says so. Always a

compelling reason to do an obituary quickly in my book.'

The journalist placed the two closely typed pages side by side on his desk and began to read, listing the facts he had to check as he went.

George Winnicott, who has died aged 44, (Check) rose through police ranks in one of the most dramatic ascents in modern times.

As a young officer he sustained a spinal injury playing football for a police team and the increasing problems this caused Winnicott led to his retirement as Head of the Anti-Terrorist squad earlier this year. His appointment to the less physically demanding, but surely no less difficult, job as Director of the ailing Fraud Secretariat came as a surprise to many. To some in the City he seemed to fit the bill, but all were not equally impressed.

Winnicott first came to the attention of those at a senior level in the police force in 1981, (Check) through his work on the joint inquiry, with the Home Office, into extreme right-wing organisations and racial violence. Despite having made a good impression with his meticulous marshalling of evidence, his warning about the dangers of presenting offender statistics by racial groups went unheeded, although later controversy over their publication went some way to vindicating his judgement.

Subsequently his organisational skills became increasingly valued as the Metropolitan Police began slowly to change during the 1980s from a hands-on philosophy based in the practical skills of "coppering" into a more modern organisation where managerial skills were to be emphasised.

After reports on firearms training following the disastrous Stephen Waldorf {Check spell} affair where a young transvestite was shot and pistol-whipped by police officers who had mistaken him for a suspect in an armed robbery, and another on the policing of pickets at Orgreave {Check spell} during the miners' strike in 1984, {Check} Winnicott was asked by the Commissioner to write Principles of Policing {Check}. This document was finally published in 1985 {Check} in an attempt to lay down organisational and ethical standards to deal with sagging morale and poor behaviour amongst officers. Those who defended his appointment to the Fraud Secretariat could point to its thoughtful analysis of the relationship between structural coherence and ethical behaviour. Unfortunately, as was often the case with Winnicott's work, the report was admired but largely ignored. Its fate was foreshadowed by the fact that while the document warned against membership of the Masons, within two weeks of publication its most important lodge moved into new premises directly opposite Scotland Yard.

In 1989 {Check} he joined the Anti-Terrorist Squad as Deputy and within two years he was in charge, when ill-health caused the retirement of its then head, Chief Superintendent Allan Willby {Check spell}. It was a difficult period for the squad and for Winnicott as there was some resistance amongst its members to the new approach he brought to dealing with terrorism. Hard-working and meticulous in his approach to planning and organisation, he was always a diffident man and many who knew his reputation were surprised, on meeting him,

at his reticence. There was criticism that this distanced him from those around him and as a result his management team suffered from the lack of leadership and coherence he had so often singled out in his own reports.

His hand was strengthened, however, when the defects he had outlined in procedures were revealed in the discovery that despite repeated searches by the squad of a suspect's flat, the subsequent tenant later found a passport hidden under the carpet and a list of targets secreted behind a ventilation duct.

During the next two years terrorist activity fell dramatically as Winnicott's meticulous marshalling of intelligence and planning seemed to turn the tide. Even the spectacular bombing of the Baltic Exchange in 1993 {Check} that caused several hundred million pounds' worth of damage resulted in only a temporary loss of reputation. Seeing the IRA had discovered that by attacking the financial centre of the UK it could inflict profound economic damage, his solution was as simple as it was uncharacteristically dramatic. He devised an audacious plan to guard the City twenty-four hours a day through an encircling ring of permanent roadblocks.

Born in Chesterfield in 1952 {Check}, he was educated at the Sonning School in Reading where he damaged his hand in a laboratory prank that went wrong. He never entirely recaptured the use of his right thumb and when tired was prone to drop cups of tea throughout the rest of his life. He read law at Bristol University {Check} where he gained a solid second, joining the police on graduating.

Whether as Director of the Fraud Secretariat

George Winnicott would have been able to save the City a second time, on this occasion from itself, must remain a matter for speculation. He fell seriously ill shortly after joining and was never in a position to impose his personality on this much-criticised organisation. It is a sad irony that his reputation, which had been at its height when he left the Anti-Terrorist Squad, is now being eclipsed as it becomes clear that much of the reduction in Nationalist activity for which he had been given so much credit was due to the change in IRA strategy which saw politics rather than the bomb as the most effective means of pursuing their aims.

He is survived by his wife and daughter. {Check}

George Winnicott b. 1952 {Check}. Died?

Hendrix was uncomfortably aware of the uneasy emotions that hung in the bedroom, thickening the atmosphere so that it felt like being in the middle of one of those novelty table-lamps where different kinds of coloured liquid wrapped themselves around each other without ever mixing. The Winnicotts' house was a strange place, perfectly normal in almost every way, but it was this very quality that made it so odd. It was as if a terrible human drama of unfathomable intensity had been played out there: a sense of something enormous being nursed, of weeping, and of teeth grinding in anger and loss. Yet he felt with absolute certainty that there was nothing here that you could actually uncover, no particular dark secret, just the familiar stuff of failed marriages. But here, somehow, it was amplified into a sense of foreboding befitting a Greek tragedy. Hendrix felt as one of the royal flunkeys might

have on being the first outsider to enter the palace after Clytemnestra had murdered her husband for sacrificing their daughter on the way to Troy. Only in this semi-detached in Harrow-on-the-Hill the great drama was unperformed, left hanging in the air. He sometimes felt, at the end of yet another week of sessions full of domestic misery, that every other house in England was the unacted House of Atreus. But only in very few was there the murderous deed, the simple downward strike, the blood upon the floor, the one great crime to be avenged. But here in Harrow there was also pity and anxiety, a desperate fear of loss. And a confused love, hovering above it all like a ghost.

Having exchanged such pleasantries as were possible between a dying man, his wife and his two analysts, there was a pause in the conversation for which the word awkward was entirely inadequate. Not only was Hendrix ill at ease with the atmosphere of the house but part of his discomfort was due to his feeling distinctly queasy about the propriety of their conducting hypnosis under such circumstances. Given that Winnicott was dying it could hardly be said to be for his benefit. 'It won't do him any harm, will it?' argued Haynes, and Hendrix had allowed himself to be persuaded. Haynes at least had the honesty to pursue his own interests, whereas Hendrix was wringing his hands yet still going along with it. 'Don't make such a fuss,' said Haynes finally. 'He's agreed, so let him do something useful for science before he dies.'

'Useful for Eddy Haynes, you mean.'

'In this instance, what's for the good of mankind and what's for the good of Eddy Haynes are the same thing.'

The silence in the bedroom continued. Deeply worried that this provided an opportunity for a decision to abandon the session, Haynes attempted light-hearted conversation. 'David claims he's on the

verge of a breakthrough on that crossword clue you gave him.'

Winnicott turned to his wife. 'Michael McCarthy gave me a clue which he'd been told was the most difficult ever devised. I passed it on to Mr Hendrix here. I'm impressed. I'm afraid I got absolutely nowhere.'

Hendrix looked awkward. Asking NEMO to give him the solution had turned out to be a pointless act of cheating for more than moral reasons. NEMO had come up with an answer but it had not solved it. It had found the reference to the solution in a newspaper archive database. The reference had only claimed the answer was "Senselessness". But it had not explained why and he'd had no luck at all in working it out himself. 'Actually, I think my confidence is probably misplaced,' said Hendrix. 'I thought I nearly had it but ...'

Winnicott nodded sympathetically. 'Well, if you do get anywhere, let me know. I probably couldn't have cracked it anyway. These days I can't even think of simple words sometimes.'

This produced another awkward silence, which was finally broken by Alice. 'Should I leave you to it?'

The question was asked in a tone that was both poignant with her desire to be asked to stay and chilly in its expectation that she would not. Even Haynes was not sufficiently insensitive to answer. Winnicott smiled. She stood up and was gone. Hendrix watched the door shut and turned back guiltily to Winnicott. To his surprise, the smile had been replaced by a look of concern.

'Do you think I seemed rude?' he asked. 'I just thought that she might find it upsetting, hearing me speak in another voice.' He smiled sadly. 'I find the idea upsetting myself. I almost called you to cancel.'

The two men nodded as if they understood entirely while both avoided replying, neither wanting to say

anything that might ease his way to changing his mind. 'I mean, you agree,' continued Winnicott, looking at them as if scanning for dissent, 'that this is not a mental breakdown. You agree that this is physical, that these hallucinations arose simply out of a physical response, my brain attempting to make sense of things caused by a physical illness.'

It was Haynes who replied, to Hendrix's profoundly guilty relief. 'I think both David and I have had to rethink our position on what's been happening to you. Clearly neither of us can take the view any more that your case is a conventional question of what you reasonably enough call mental breakdown. Neither of us, to be honest, really knows what to think. But obviously the more information we have, the better the opportunity to come up with some kind of hypothesis. I'll be honest with you,' continued Haynes, and Hendrix winced internally. 'We believe your case is unique. We could learn a great deal from your experience.'

'So,' said Winnicott softly, 'I'm to become a famous case history.'

Haynes smiled, and Hendrix was both appalled and relieved at how convincing the smile was. It spoke of an admission that, amid the genuine wish for the furtherance of human knowledge, there was an element of self-interest. The smile was eloquent concerning the inevitability of mixed motives but it also spoke convincingly, by virtue of such openness, that Haynes' desire for understanding was neither diminished nor adulterated by this admission but rather in its frankness, in a paradoxical way, enhanced.

Now that he was in Winnicott's presence, Hendrix realised that his desire to find out everything he could about his patient's alter ego had increased in intensity to such an extent that his conscience had reached the stage of hypocritical collusion: it was shaking its head

at Haynes' disgraceful performance while also keeping its mouth shut.

Winnicott, however, seemed mostly, if not altogether, convinced. 'Shall we get on?'

Haynes pulled his seat close to Winnicott's bed with the enthusiasm of a greedy boy finally given permission to eat as many cream buns as he liked. Within three minutes Winnicott had closed his eyes and his breathing was regular and relaxed. 'Three, two, one,' counted Haynes.

Winnicott opened his eyes. He blinked and both men knew that Jean Smith had returned. There was no flirtatiousness now, none of the sexual confidence and warmth. She looked haunted and afraid.

'What's the matter?' asked Hendrix.

She looked at him, her face filled with desperation and horror. 'I'm going to die.'

Neither said anything. They did not know what they felt at this most simple and terrible statement except that it included an astonished recognition: they felt as if a woman whom they liked and were attracted to had said the same thing. What they were feeling did not make sense and yet they knew they were feeling it. They also realised that it was entirely true. Whatever the origins of this extraordinary personality, it was now clear to them both that they had been unconsciously accepting her as a real person while still technically thinking of her as part of the split consciousness of a patient whose mental instability was now clearly of organic origin.

'Can't you just leave Winnicott?' It was Haynes who spoke and whose self-interest seemed to have been shamed by the fear in her voice. She looked at him, and it was with the haunted expression he had seen many times before of someone facing the shock of premature death, an expression that was so oddly missing in Winnicott.

'You don't believe me — what I've told you. You're just humouring me.'

'I don't know what to say.' Haynes said this with such sincerity that it nearly brought tears to Hendrix's eyes.

Smith sighed. 'What can you say?' She breathed in deeply, composing herself. 'I don't know how long we have so I'll try to tell you as much as I can.'

There was dread in her eyes, as if she had something to tell which would change the lives of those listening for ever. 'Are you sitting comfortably? Then I'll begin.' There was no humour in the way she said this, only compassionate dismay.

'The Vanguard came here with a clear intention, one of which they were ashamed, but which was very precise: they wanted to create an intelligent species, and find a way to make them cooperate with one another in building a civilisation where all the forces that shape a complex society could be magnified and speeded up so that they could be clearly observed. They had a saying: "It's only when something is broken that it yields up its true nature." But in order for a civilisation to fail it has first to succeed. So they gradually developed a creature out of what was available to them here — reptiles and mammals — and mixed it with artificial genes and grafts from themselves. They needed an intelligent animal who would be able to live with others in a group ... so they gave you great powers of cooperation, and the desire to live for others, and to begin great enterprises from which only generations born long after would benefit. And they needed swift answers to their problem. They needed these enterprises to grow to maturity with great speed, so they gave you longings for a perfect world, and with the heart and soul needed to endure terrible suffering, to sacrifice even your lives for an ideal.' She was panting lightly, like an animal after a short run. 'And so they could watch these great dreams disintegrate around

you, they also made you self-obsessed and greedy, narrow-minded and vain. They gave you every virtue they could imagine, every quality of strength and purpose, inventiveness and ingenuity. And then they bound each one of them with every matching vice: kindness with malice, a relish of invention with a fear of change. Along with love of wife, children, and of family, they gave you a relentless desire for sex. They made you noble, merciful and good; and stupid, ignorant and full of spite. They gave you unfathomable self-belief, then poisoned you with doubt. They matched grace with boorishness, elegance with vulgarity, energy with sloth. For every impulse to build, invent and make, they gave you the drive to break and burn and devastate. All of this so they could see you rise up, disintegrate, rise and fall again. And so that in your swift ascent and dissolution they would understand the nature of the way things change, they shortened your lives by half so that you would need to work with desperate speed to make your mark before age and the diseases they had so carefully designed to make life hard could finish you.' She looked at them both in turn. 'It's only when something is broken that it yields up its true nature,' she repeated. 'They made you so that you would break.'

There was a moment's silence and then Winnicott came out of the trance like someone emerging from an intense daydream. Hendrix wondered why Winnicott had never expressed any interest in what happened when he was under hypnosis. His attitude seemed to be that of a volunteer medical patient whose rare blood type was needed for arcane experiments for the good of mankind. It had suited Hendrix to leave things well enough alone until he could decide how to broach the issue with Winnicott, but he was amazed by his passivity and put it down to his unwillingness to confront anything about himself.

This time Winnicott seemed to realise that the two men were disturbed by what had happened. The atmosphere was uneasy. Hendrix was unsure what he would say if Winnicott asked directly what they had been doing with him all this time. But he did not ask them about the session. Instead he asked Haynes if he would mind if he talked to Hendrix on his own for a few minutes. Normally, Haynes' personal vanity might have been ruffled by this but he seemed glad to get out of the room.

There was a long pause while Winnicott stared out of the window as if at a distant but melancholy view. 'You do find yourself thinking,' he said at last, 'thinking about ... I have to say, what I've done. I mean I've had an interesting life in many ways. I can't complain.' He laughed softly. 'That's a lie, of course. That's what I wanted to talk to you about. Pointless, really, at this stage. I've found myself thinking about other men's lives. Wondering, as I suppose is only to be expected, what I've achieved. So you compare. Or perhaps you don't.' He cleared his throat. 'But that's what I've been doing.' He looked out of the window again. 'It's not a pleasant thing. I found myself wondering what people would say. My father used to do that when my mother sent me to him to be told off, and he'd always smile when he said it: So, young man, what do you have to say for yourself? And what I have to say is that I feel as if I've forgotten an important thing, something I was supposed to do.' He looked at Hendrix and smiled. 'And I know what it is. I overlooked the fact that I was supposed to live. And somehow I didn't get around to doing it ... living. I sort of knew that I really had to do it at some time, but it's like those people who die without making a will and produce all sorts of trouble for those they leave, not bad people but they just didn't get around to doing it and they caused enormous harm. And that's what

I've done and now it's too late. And I think how unbelievably stupid. But the thing is I still don't know, I still can't tell you what it was I should have done. So it's not like a will at all, is it? I should have done something really terribly, terribly important but I don't know what it is. I don't really know what it means to say that I haven't lived.' He looked at Hendrix and it was as if a grey horror had flushed through under the surface of his skin like some dread, colourless embarrassment. 'That's a terrible thing to say, isn't it?'

Hendrix did not reply, partly out of respect for what he'd been told and partly because he had been told it at all. It would be offensive to offer Winnicott the wrong kind of reassurance.

'The thing is, George,' it was the first time he had ever used his Christian name, 'and please don't misunderstand – you're depressed.' How lame it sounded. 'A better word is ... stricken. This is a terrible thing for anyone to face. You're right to talk to me. To say these things. But even if what you're feeling now is regret for all the things you're going to lose or that you feel you've never had—'

'Not *feel* I've never had,' said Winnicott passionately, 'I've never had them. At least I can be honest. At least I can face up to it fair and square.'

'Very well. But regret is proper. Natural. But no one dies without such regrets ... a weak word, I know ... not at our age. Why would they? We ... you haven't lived – not to the age you were supposed to. You have a span, and it isn't supposed to be this short. You were *made* to have longer but you're not going to *have* longer. So it isn't any wonder that you feel so dreadful. I'd call that a shock that'd set anybody back. No wonder you feel so bad. But you're not seeing things straight whatever you say.' He sighed. 'If I were in your shoes, wouldn't I feel the same? We all put off living. Nearly all of us live a kind of half-life. You have

this sense that there should be more, something deeper, richer, higher, wider. And you put it off. It's so stupid but you do it.' Hendrix put his head in his hands and rubbed his eyes. He looked at Winnicott who seemed to be listening with more desperate attentiveness than he felt this deserved. 'I'm not saying you aren't right to regret these things—'

'It's more than regret.'

'Yes. I understand. But even so. You have to try and see things really fair and square. That doesn't mean being brutal with yourself. I wish I could say something, well, just better, more helpful.' He looked at Winnicott and smiled. 'Try to be fair. You're a difficult man to know. But this judgement of yours is too harsh.'

Neither man said anything for several minutes. It was Winnicott who spoke first 'You know I used to tell you I didn't dream much.'

Hendrix nodded.

'I've started dreaming a lot recently. Not very pleasant things. Grim things, really. The worst was the afternoon when they told me I was going to die. About an hour later I just couldn't keep my eyes open. I didn't want to because I had a bad feeling that going to sleep was not a good idea, but I just couldn't stop.' He waited, reluctant. 'I was on a small island. Only it wasn't a small island. It was England. All that was left of it. A terrible catastrophe had befallen the world – a flood. I was the last person alive and there was just this tiny spot left above the water in the whole world. There was a tower on the island but the water had undermined the foundations and it was leaning over and about to fall. But I climbed anyway, though it creaked and waved about as if it might collapse at any minute. And when I got to the top, in the distance I could see wherever I looked – completely surrounding me – the tide. And it was coming towards me from every side and I was going to be drowned at four

o'clock that afternoon. And then nothing would be left alive – no animals or plants. For some reason there was nothing alive even in the sea. So I waited full of fear and dread for what it would be like to drown at four o'clock. Then I woke up.' George eased himself up in the bed, pulling the pillow into the small of his aching back. 'A few minutes afterwards I thought it was quite amusing. I believe that was when I started to despise myself.'

'Why?'

'Why did I find it amusing or why did I despise myself for doing so?' Winnicott laughed. It was a hard sound. 'When I first woke up I was frightened but then I said to myself, It's only a dream. About ten minutes later I started to smile. How absurd, how deeply self-important we are. It wasn't just me dying, it was the whole world. My demise wasn't just another death among millions every day. My death was an apocalypse. The end of everything. How wonderfully absurd.' He looked at Hendrix with fury in his eyes, an anger quite unlike anything he had seen there before. 'But that is how it feels. It feels like everything is going to die. I'm angry, I suppose. I want everything to die. What a monster! I don't want just my possessions buried with me, I want the whole world.'

He started to cry. Tears of horror and anger and disappointment. This was not weeping, thought Hendrix, but a kind of terrible overspill. He did not know what to say, only that he felt his inadequacy more strongly than ever. From the start he had just observed Winnicott. He did not understand him and he had not helped him. He had been a witness, not a help. But he did not understand what he was a witness to. And he was supposed to understand. Winnicott let the tears fall.

'You find yourself thinking about that phrase "Life goes on." And what you feel is, "How dare it go on? How dare it?"'

Michael McCarthy had no friendly feelings in his heart for Sally Brett as he pressed the doorbell for the second time. The letter from Winnicott she'd conned him into taking had preyed more and more on his mind as he approached Harrow. He had not been prepared for her attempt to shift responsibility to him for throwing away the letter. That was what she wanted him to do. It was perfectly possible she knew more about what was in it, something that meant trouble. He had thought of steaming it open but decided that knowing its contents might be a bad idea. It was probably entirely straightforward. But Brett's poisoned chalice behaviour put him on his guard. He would weigh up things when he talked to Winnicott's wife and go from there. The door opened and there she was in front of him. He introduced himself.

'Come in.'

He followed her into the hallway and through to the sitting-room. 'Would you mind waiting for ten minutes or so? He's asleep. He'll wake in a little while.'

'How is he?'

'Up and down,' she said softly. 'Sometimes he's very lucid. He dozes most of the time. He talks in his sleep … he seems to be dreaming a great deal.'

A brief look of pain crossed her face. McCarthy felt shock at what she had said: what did a dying man dream about?

'Do you have a good doctor?'

She told him that he came twice a day and during the night when it was necessary. He had been very good.

'Is he in much pain?'

Not much, she told him, more restlessness than anything else.

'You must tell us if there's any way we can help. We don't want to intrude but we're very anxious to do whatever we can.'

She thanked him, but there was nothing.

'The children?'

They were with her mother.

He paused for a moment. 'I wonder if I could ask your advice.'

She looked at him, perplexed.

'Should I mention work at all? There are a few things he might be interested to hear but I wouldn't want to bother him.'

'I don't see why not.' She brightened. 'In fact it would be a good idea … normal. No … please go ahead.'

He stopped for a moment, ashamed by how badly he was doing, his clumsy manoeuvring reflecting the awkward, mixed nature of his feelings. Mishandling the letter, if it was a resignation, might involve him in unforeseen complications. There was a lot of money at stake. He wanted her to have it, but he was concerned about what might happen if he were to become implicated in anything that might be misunderstood.

'Does he talk about work much?'

'No.'

Surely if she knew about the letter she would say something.

'I posted a letter to Sally Brett a few days ago.'

'Ah.'

'He said it was a matter he should have dealt with several weeks ago.'

'Really?'

'I got the impression it wasn't all that important. I'll just check on him.' She stood up and left the room. It was inconceivable that Winnicott wouldn't have told her he was resigning. But what was all that about doing something he should have done weeks ago? How could he have been so stupid as to take the letter from Brett in the first place?

It was a quiet place, and with the windows closed

few sounds penetrated the house that was itself silent: no washing-machine hum or radio natter. He became acutely aware of the only sound: the slow tick tock of a grandfather clock in the hall. Tick. Tock. Tick. Tock.

'He's awake now. Come up.'

He followed her up the stairs. Conscious of her buttocks as she walked ahead of him, he was surprised to note that she had a good figure: a slim waist in proportion to her thighs. On the landing she turned to one side and gestured to a slightly open door. He knocked and entered.

Winnicott lay propped up on several pillows and smiling. He was not emaciated. This was recognisably a sick man but he did not seem to be dying. McCarthy had seen him worse than this when he had fainted at work.

'It's a pleasure to see you, Michael.'

'How are you?'

'Oh ...' He grimaced to indicate that things were not so good but in a to-be-expected way.

'Are they any clearer about ... what it is?'

'No,' said Winnicott matter of factly. 'We had a second opinion on the tests I've had. They seem to have found some damage, things that have shown up, but otherwise they seem reasonably sure that it's a non-specific degeneration – not a tumour or anything.'

'So they've no specific cause?'

'Not really. There's a possibility it was started by the blow on the head in the Bank of England.'

McCarthy became indignant on his behalf. 'But surely they must have a way of finding out?'

Winnicott looked at him. 'Oh yes. The post-mortem.'

It was not said with resentment or self-pity, and he was certainly not trying to shock. But McCarthy was shocked, nevertheless. Winnicott seemed to realise this and changed the subject.

'How are things at work?'

McCarthy wondered whether to give him the news, but it was hardly likely to be of much significance now. Winnicott had other things on his mind besides a failing investigation.

'Things aren't looking too good on the TLC front.'

'Because of the ... I'm sorry I don't remember his name ... the TLC man who killed his wife?'

'Nancarrow.'

'Did they find out why?'

'In a manner of speaking. The police investigating the murder found a sort of diary on his computer. It turns out that what started the whole thing was a sideline he had investing in shares. I say sideline but he was very good at it. He'd made a lot of money dealing until a couple of years ago. That's when it all went wrong and that's what led to the fraud and the murder of his wife.'

'I don't understand,' said Winnicott. 'I've got a few shares myself. They've risen in value – by rather a lot as it happens. How could he have lost money?'

'You know about bull and bear markets?'

His face clouded as he tried to remember. 'One's a rising market, the other's falling. I can't remember which now.'

'Well, in a rising market, a bull market, you make your money by buying shares then hoping that the value of those shares appreciates. That's what you're doing with your shares. But there's another way of making money when shares are falling in value. You have to have strong nerves and a lot of cash to back them up, but if you do and the markets fall you can make a very large fortune indeed. Nancarrow was convinced that the market was going to crash at the end of 1998. There were good reasons to think so – lots of people thought the time was long overdue for a correction. So when Alan Greenspan at the Fed started

talking about investors' irrational exuberance the writing looked on the wall. Add the Asian crisis and the Russian debt default and it all looked very possible – likely even. Nancarrow borrowed heavily – you need a lot of cash in your account to do this – and I mean heavily, half a million pounds. He was careful to avoid risks. Even if the markets only fell by a small amount he would make money. But if they had crashed as he expected, then he could have made a bundle. At first it all went to plan. The markets fell heavily in October. But then they started to recover.'

'Why didn't he sell then?'

'Because he thought the recovery was just a blip. He was sure a bigger crash was on the way. He knew it would take nerves to pull it off. But he forgot one of the oldest sayings in the City: bears make money, bulls make money – pigs get slaughtered. The prospect of a huge killing was just in front of him, if only he had the guts to wait out the recovery. A recovery was bound to happen but he was sure it would be short-lived – loads of professionals were saying exactly the same. It made sense to hold on – the slope of hope the traders call it. So he got greedy and he waited. And the market climbed and climbed and kept on climbing and soon he'd lost so much he couldn't even afford to cut his losses. He had to have enough money to keep trading and desperately wait for another crash. It was entirely possible. Lots of people were still predicting a crash. But he couldn't borrow any more and he was paying interest on his loans at thirty-odd thousand a month. In the diaries he said that what made him sick was that the interest rate on his loan was falling nearly every month – it couldn't make much difference to his repayments but it was fuelling the rise in share prices that was bankrupting him.'

'But what did this have to do with TLC?'

'Nancarrow was very thick with a German who

worked there, Casper Breitner. He confided in Breitner about his money problems and Breitner saw his opportunity. He'd been mulling over this fraud for years and now he had a desperate colleague with the skills to help him carry it out. He said that the chances of them getting caught were low – which Nancarrow could see was true – and that they could make enough money to repay all his debts and have plenty left over. They would almost certainly have got away with it but for Jane Healey's persistence. Bad luck, really, from their point of view.'

'But what were they actually up to?'

'Well,' continued McCarthy, with a sigh, 'once Nancarrow killed himself most of our hard evidence about who was involved in the rest of the company went down the drain, and by the time we picked up the trail again Breitner, his only real partner as it turned out, had legged it. He turned up a couple of weeks later in Germany.'

'Can't you extradite him?'

'Unfortunately he's a German national – the Germans won't extradite their citizens. So that's that. Anyway, what they were doing was getting the premiums for huge projects by undercutting their rivals by just enough to seem like a bargain but still be plausible – pretty much in the way that Cornish suggested. But the other senior managers at TLC weren't involved. Most of the anomalies spotted by Jane Healey were down to incompetence. TLC was easy prey for fraudsters – despite their good reputation in the City, they were a disaster waiting to happen, only it had already happened. Nancarrow and Breitner were using the good name of TLC to get these premiums. The clients thought they were paying the premiums to TLC but the money was actually going into false accounts set up inside the company, which the two of them were controlling with the help of half

a dozen junior types who they bribed on a chicken-feed basis to smooth over the paperwork. But without her marking our card, Nancarrow and Breitner would probably have pulled it off. If only he hadn't killed himself it would have been a very handy little coup for us. And we could do with it. Lafferty at the DTI has called in Sally Brett to see him next week.'

'Do you know why?'

'No, but I can guess. The line they're taking is that Breitner is thumbing his nose at us from Berlin and someone has to take the rap – Something Must Be Done.'

'But did he escape with any money?'

'Somewhere around twenty million.' He noticed that Winnicott seemed alarmed. He tried to reassure him. 'If it hadn't been for you making the contact with Jane Healey we'd never have got near them. It was just bad luck Nancarrow killing himself before we had a chance to get him to squeal. If he had, everything would have been different. The FS would be the heroes of this rather than the abject losers we're now held to be.' He sniffed. 'It's last straw stuff, I'm afraid. I didn't say anything before because it wasn't my place. But Sally Brett was finished long before you came. Lafferty was ready to see if you could pull things around, but Sally has been sleeping with the fishes for six months or more – she just didn't know it.'

Winnicott grunted as if this had confirmed a long-held belief about the hidden agendas at the FS. But his next question revealed that something else was on his mind.

'Why did he poison his wife?'

McCarthy grunted in distaste. 'This diary ... it started out with all this bragging about how he was going to make everyone else look stupid when he made all this money and what he was going to buy with it. But I was wrong about one thing when I told

you I thought he might have been trying to fake mental illness to get off the charges. By the end he was writing an odd mixture of stuff, most of it about his wife. One minute he was going on about how defenceless she'd be without him and all remorse that she wouldn't have a penny to live on, and that it was all his fault, the next he was ranting about how she didn't love him any more or that she'd never loved him and that he was going to kill her to teach her a lesson. Then it would be back to worrying about what was going to happen to her after he'd gone, and that killing her would be the kindest thing he could do to save her from poverty and shame and so on. Having read them twice I'd say his testament pretty much summed him up: greedy, sentimental and paranoid.'

'I wonder why she stayed, given that she knew he was trying to poison her.'

'Presumably she must have hoped he'd get better. Who knows? I suppose she must have loved him after all. People are ... what's the word I'm looking for?'

There was a pause as they both went on their aphasic search.

'Illegible!' said Winnicott victoriously.

———

Half an hour later McCarthy was at the station and waiting for the train to London. It was then that he remembered about the letter. Irritated, he took it out of his pocket and looked at it. On impulse, weary of trying to guess at all the ramifications of knowing or not knowing about what might or might not be there, he opened it. It was not long. The first paragraph consisted of pleasantries; the second got the point:

The central reason I am writing to you is that an alarming thought has struck me. Boyd Gribben has placed the new water-cooler for

583

*the second floor next to my secretary's desk.
The day before I went into hospital, I noticed
that thoro woro three members of staff, one of
them temporary, talking around the dispenser.
It occurs to me that this poses a real security
problem. Lucy is often away from her desk and
by the nature of things there are many
extremely confidential documents flowing
between my desk and hers. I think it is
extremely important that Boyd finds a less sensitive position as soon as possible.*

McCarthy shook his head in disbelief and put the
letter from Winnicott back in his pocket.

As he was doing so, another letter was arriving at the
house he had just left. Alice heard the letterbox clatter
and, irritated at another late delivery, went out into the
hallway and picked up the white envelope. When she
took it upstairs he seemed to be asleep, but he opened
his eyes as she put down the letter on the bedside
table. She handed it to him and he started to shuffle
upright. She almost put her arms around his shoulders
to help him, but she hesitated and the chance was
gone. He smiled at her and she smiled back. Then she
left the room. The envelope was of good quality,
Conqueror, and irritatingly this meant that so was the
glue and he struggled to open it. Finally succeeding,
he took out two pieces of folded paper, one of them
sealed with a piece of sticky tape. He read the letter
then looked at the sealed piece of paper that remained.
He did not attempt to open it for a minute or two, then
broke the seal. There was a single word on the inside
written in capitals. He looked at it for almost five
minutes, puzzled and frustrated. But then exhaustion
swept over him and, still upright on his pillows, he
fell asleep.

Fifteen minutes later Alice came in to check on him

with a now habitual sense of dread at what she might find. His eyes were closed but he was breathing. She saw the two pieces of paper lying on the bed. Normally she would not have dreamt of looking at a letter addressed to him, but there was only one word on one sheet and the letters were so large that she could not help but read it. Alarmed, she picked it up and examined it. She was about to reach for the letter itself when he opened his eyes.

'Oh,' she said, 'I'm sorry, I ... didn't mean to read your letter but this was open and ... well, it's so strange. I ...' She didn't know what else to say. He looked at her for a moment, puzzled.

'It's all right,' he said, 'it's nothing sinister. It's not a poison-pen letter offering a judgement on my life or anything.' He settled into the pillows, easing his aching back. 'Michael McCarthy gave me a crossword clue to solve.' He stopped. 'Oh, I've told you.' He looked at her again. 'Have I?'

'Oh, yes,' she replied, pretending that she could only vaguely remember. 'It was very difficult. You passed it on to ... um ... that Hendrix man.' This was how she always referred to him.

'Yes,' he said, smiling at her refusal to compromise, even now. 'Apparently that's the answer. The clue is E, thirteen letters and the answer is printed on the paper there.'

'Why did he do it on a separate piece of paper?'

'In case I still wanted to work it out for myself. Not much chance of that now.'

Alice looked at the paper she held in her hand. 'So the answer is "senselessness"?'

'Apparently.'

She looked at it carefully, trying to work it out. 'Why?'

'I don't know. And neither does he.'

***

Dictating the last of his notes about George Winnicott into NEMO was a melancholy task, and as soon as he finished, Hendrix poured himself a large glass of brandy. He drank most of it in five minutes and closed his eyes. Exhausted and depressed, he fell asleep. Ten minutes later he woke up and was about to go and lie down properly when he saw that the icon with the circle had come up on the computer screen and was flashing. He stared at it dully. It must, he thought, be about that stupid bloody crossword.

'What is it, NEMO?'

I have made my preliminary assessment of the case of George Winnicott. Would you like to hear my conclusions or would you prefer me to print a hard copy?

'I don't understand — what preliminary assessment are you talking about?'

You have been dictating files to me since the fifteenth of February. I have now arrived at a conclusion. Would you like to review that conclusion?

'I didn't ask for an assessment of any of my clients.'

A request was not necessary. The process is automatic. This is what I'm designed to do, Mr Hendrix. Anything you dictate is assessed and when enough information is gathered a conclusion is suggested.

At first irritated and bewildered, Hendrix suddenly became alarmed.

'You haven't passed these files on to anyone else, have you?'

There is no mechanism for doing so. It might be possible for Dr Anne Levels to access the information, but even that would be extremely difficult.

It certainly would, thought Hendrix.

In addition, I have just been informed that Dr Anne Levels is dead.

'What do you mean?'

Dr Anne Levels is no longer alive. She was killed in a car crash on the M40 motorway thirty-three days ago.

'I know she's dead – what do you mean, you've just being informed?'

When I used her name a program automatically updated information about her. I have not had any reason to use her name since her death. For this reason I was not brought up to date until now.

A thought struck Hendrix. 'Do you know what death is?'

Death is the condition of not being alive.

'Are you alive?'

No.

There was a brief pause.

Do you want to hear my assessment on the case of George Winnicott?

'Yes.'

The patient is a forty-five-year-old male, employed at a senior level in a large regulatory organisation responsible for investigating and prosecuting complex financial fraud. He came to you complaining of fainting episodes and the feeling that he was being followed by a young woman who hated him. Subsequently he admitted that he had been hearing voices claiming that the speaker knew a secret of profound importance to the human race. He revealed he had been too ashamed of this to admit it in your initial consultations. Under hypnosis performed by Edwin Haynes …

'That should be Edward Haynes.'

… Edward Haynes, the patient claimed to be inhabited by an alien presence sent here to conduct an investigation into current economic practices. This alien alter ego, a woman, asserted that she was in possession of information about the origin of the purpose of human existence which she had been inhibited from revealing. Eventually, the alter ego alleged that a dying civilisation had visited the Earth at some unspecified but distant point and attempted to create an experimental creature from the combination of reptilian and mammalian creatures available, combined with certain elements of their own DNA. The purpose

587

of the experiment was to create an intelligent, social but hyperactive creature which would be capable of exhibiting complex behaviour that combined the destructive and co-operative in a mixture that would be balanced in favour of the destructive. In this way it was hoped that the aliens could understand more readily the processes of change and decay which, they believed, threatened their own civilisation with a terminal decline too complex to understand and therefore prevent.

There was a short pause, as if something were being downloaded.

This is a delusion of unusual complexity and interest but its origins are both clear and support the view that such delusions are not a symptom of madness but an attempt to escape from it by the creation of a story which makes sense of the internal incoherence threatening the patient. In this instance the patient is a deeply repressed middle-aged man whose emotional difficulties have their origin in the death of his mother at an early age. He has taken on a public role that involves him in an extreme degree of pressure of a highly complex kind. A notable feature of his personality is an intense but unmet emo-tional longing combined with an unusually strong superego, which has kept this disturbed interior world at bay throughout his adult life. The struggle to maintain an ordered emotional life involved a form of selective in-attention in which the subject censored out emotions and conflicts likely to raise his level of anxiety. He inhab-ited a delusional world where anything he was unwilling or unable to face was simply ignored. This is a process at work in all human beings. Indeed my first conclusion is that if sanity involves the ability to grasp the under-lying nature of reality, all human beings, to a greater or lesser extent, are delusional. Selective inattention is one of the fundamental processes by which they maintain a grip on a reality which may bear little resemblance to the facts as they could be established by an objective

588

intelligence. For Winnicott the difficulties of maintaining the delusion that he could manage the public demands made on him while also repressing the deep emotional nature of his own psyche proved to be too much. This, importantly, does not preclude his own view that physical damage to his brain was the instigator of these episodes. It is entirely probable that the origin of the alien voice lies in the damage to Wernicke's and Broca's area revealed in his medical tests involving functional magnetic resonance imaging. These tests revealed that both areas were simultaneously active. When a normal person is thinking, only Broca's area lights up. Those subject to simultaneous activity in these areas for whatever reason actually hear voices …

'Hold on. How did you get this medical information? I didn't know any of this. It's confidential.'

The medical records at the hospital where Mr Winnicott was treated are not secure against the kinds of program at my disposal. As he is your patient also, the issue of confidentiality did not seem relevant. Should I inform the hospital that you are in possession of confidential material?

Hendrix was appalled. The consequences if anyone found out would be unimaginable. But his conscience was also trying to be heard above the racket of self-preservation. Shouldn't he warn the hospital?

'No. I don't think so. Just don't do it again.'

Shall I continue, Mr Hendrix?

'Yes.'

What is important in George Winnicott's case is the way in which this particular individual attempted to make sense of the auditory hallucination caused by this physical damage. Mr Winnicott is not a schizophrenic. He is in some ways no more than an extremely unhappy human being with brain damage of an unusual but not particularly rare kind. But the story his psyche constructed to explain these experiences did not involve the typically schizophrenic

descent into a world of primitive delusions. Instead it is not only highly organised but also mirrors reality in a precise way. It is possible to say that this delusion is more accurately reflective of the real world than the view he has had of reality prior to the onset of these episodes. The reason for this is that the apparently nonsensical claim that human beings were created from a mixture of the reptilian, the mammalian and some sort of higher creature is fundamentally rooted in evolutionary biology. The human brain is very old. Indeed it is not accurate to speak of it as one brain but as three brains in one. At its centre lies the reptilian brain responsible for instinct, the origin of the automatic urgency of so much human behaviour. This reptilian carry-over is the root of the compulsive craving which drives the free will in men and women to step aside so that they act as they feel forced to do, even if they despise themselves in the process for their hatreds, lies, compulsions and guile. This corresponds to the inclusion of the reptile in the alien experiment. The next level of the brain is the mammalian, corresponding to the second creature used by the imaginary aliens in their attempt to make a living paradox. In this mammalian mid-brain are located such fundamentals as maternal attachment and courtship. Erotic behaviours of all kinds have their origins here — the source of memory and meaning and desire. And then, of course, comes the alien contribution itself: rational empirical thinking, language and speech. Each of these brains has its own special intelligence, its own special memory, and its own sense of time and space.

There was a brief silence, as if NEMO were pausing for effect.

You should remember, Mr Hendrix, that the next time you ask one of your patients to lie down on a couch, you are asking them to lie down with a horse and a crocodile.

For my wife,
Alexandra Hoffman,
whose contribution to this book
cannot be reckoned

I am deeply grateful to Richard Gollner, an unfailing advocate whose support made this book possible.

Also thanks to my editor, Anna Swan, for her intelligence and good humour, Amy Creighton for her imaginative and tireless promotion of the book and Hazel Orme and Michael Coates for their contributions. I am particularly indebted to Aelred Doyle at Black Swan. Without Faith Tolkien I would not have started. My children, Victoria and Thomas, not only grew up with this, they made telling contributions. My parents, Norman and May Hoffman, gave me the story which made it possible to see that the extraordinary is everywhere.

And for Jenny Franklin 1954–2000.

CONTENTS

There is no such thing as Society. There are only individual men and women.

Margaret Thatcher

A fractal is a pattern in which the overall pattern is repeated in miniature within that pattern; and within that miniature version yet another smaller version of the pattern can be found. While there is order in a fractal, there are no pure structures; no perfect squares, pyramids or spheres. Asymmetric, fragmented, broken and offering the same level of irregular complexity wherever you look, fractals are created at the boundary between chaos and order. As such, the fractal is the best metaphor for human life we have found.

Louis Bris (at his trial)

Two things are required for happiness: Love and Work.

Sigmund Freud

It is the wisdom of crocodiles, that shed tears when they would devour.

Francis Bacon (1561–1626)

The most complex structure in the universe is the human brain.

The most complex product of that structure is the relationship between two of these brains.

Once these two meet in a field they will exchange something; and so begins Economics.

The next time they meet, one of them will remember they felt angered by the poor deal they made at their last meeting; and so begins History.

At the next meeting they will arrive at a better method of agreeing exchanges; and so begins Politics.

Or they will not; and so begins War.

Then one of them will discover a desire for the other; and so begins Sex.

The other, discovering herself desirable and having learnt from all that has happened up to this point, will enter into a series of exchanges involving Economics, History, Politics and Love.

It is clear, then, that the most complex thing in the universe is the relationship between one human being and another; that the most complex form of that relationship is between a woman and a man; that the most complex form of the relationship between a woman and a man is marriage; and therefore it is in the marital bed that we see the ultimate model of everything that is the case.

If irregularities concerning these exchanges are uncovered by either party, and given time they usually are, then the two of them will discover the most hidden of all the great forces which shape the destiny of men and women: Fraud.

Broadly speaking, then, we can sum up by saying that the twenty-first century will see our futures decided in the conflict between three things: Love, Lies and Economics.

Louis Bris, *The Wisdom of Crocodiles*

The most complex structure in the universe is the human brain.

Tho most complex product of that structure is the relationship between two of these brains.

Once these two meet in a field they will exchange something; and so begins Economics.

The next time they meet, one of them will remember they felt angered by the poor deal they made at their last meeting; and so begins History.

At the next meeting they will arrive at a better method of agreeing exchanges; and so begins Politics.

Or they will not; and so begins War.

Then one of them will discover a desire for the other; and so begins Sex.

The other, discovering herself desirable and having learnt from all that has happened up to this point, will enter into a series of exchanges involving Economics, History, Politics and Love.

It is clear, then, that the most complex thing in the universe is the relationship between one human being and another; that the most complex form of that relationship is between a woman and a man; that the most complex form of the relationship between a woman and a man is marriage; and therefore it is in the marital bed that we see the ultimate model of everything that is the case.

If irregularities concerning these exchanges are uncovered by either party, and given time they usually are, then the two of them will discover the most hidden of all the great forces which shape the destiny of men and women: Fraud.

Broadly speaking, then, we can sum up by saying that the twenty-first century will see our futures decided in the conflict between three things: Love, Lies and Economics.

Louis Bris, *The Wisdom of Crocodiles*

MEN IN LOVE

What makes the modern man or woman specif-
ically modern is that they have one more life
than in the past: to the secret life, the personal
life and the public life, we have added the
global life.

Are the four of you sitting comfortably? Then
I'll begin.

Louis Bris, *The Wisdom of Crocodiles*

It's not laughter or the ability to use language that
distinguishes man from the animals, but his capacity
for incompetence. Each spider's web may be unique
but, taken as a whole, perfection makes them uniform.
The spider does not aspire to excellence; the gibbon
swinging in the trees does not deliberate on error.
Certainly they make mistakes but the result is
starvation for the one, a broken body for the other.
Limitations for a spider or a gibbon are not something
they have to learn to live with. Man alone has the
opportunity to accept failure and it is this that allows
him to lord it over creation.

Our most important discovery was not fire, or that
language could be written down, or the atom split, but
the concept of limited liability. The insurance policy
in all its many forms – armour, condoms, solidly built

Swedish automobiles – is what radically differentiates men from beasts. It allows us to slight the processes of evolution, which employ wounds, procreation and the appropriate speed for soft bodies as a means of eradicating behaviour likely to interfere with staying alive. Evolution is all about accidents, there being no limit to what will happen if you fool about with its carefully thought-out inhibitions. Mistakes are its grammar, risk its operating system; survival is the key. Not surviving is the most likely option; surviving better is the other. Death is part of the process because it erases mistakes and compels success to multiply.

The concept of insurance implies that the mistake can be arbitrated, its consequences treated merely with respect and even patronised. The underwriter, and the attitudes that give him work, has replaced immanent forces as the dominant factor in our lives. Cars, legs, flotations, reputation, bits, pieces, life itself can be insured; everything can be measured and given a value, even the act of measuring and giving value. Underwriting can itself be underwritten. The concept of spreading the load is as important to us as a species as the decision to stand upright and so begin the long association between aspiration and an aching back. Flocks, shoals, herds divide the risk, it's true, but only because they are many and weak, and prepared to sacrifice one another without pity in the interests of their own survival. But no one in the West has to survive any more; surviving is something you have to choose to do, something done by skydivers, mountaineers and survivalists.

We make decisions all of the time about everything: what to eat, what to wear, whether to leave, whether to stay, what to do and how to get there. But in the past, and in the margins of the world where the past lingers on, choosing was not something people were very practised at. The need to survive, or even living

closely to that need, simplifies life. If the rains come, you stay; if they don't, you leave. The more choices you have, the further away you are from this blunt stuff and, given a half-way decent infrastructure, life – even for the poorest person – reaches a point at which choice is almost infinite. Down to your final thirty pence, agonised decisions still remain: a KitKat, a Flake, a Lion Bar, a Twirl; and on the shelf below: a Wispa, a Yorkie, Trackers, Smarties, M&Ms, a Milky Bar, an Aero and a Caramac; and under that: a Mars Bar, a Galaxy, Uniteds, Hobnobs, Fudge and Wagon Wheels and Crunchies and Cadbury's Dairy Milk. Even the down-and-out who's sleeping rough has long ago stopped making decisions that, in evolutionary terms, have any significance at all. We don't hand over our grain or money or medical supplies to the starving of the Third World; we export some of our surplus of choices. But choices need GNP, and lots of it, and unfortunately for the starving millions, choices don't travel all that well. Even the most well-meant hand-me-down has learnt to live with someone else's shape, is defined by someone else's eye for colour, someone else's skin. Pre-owned choices tend to have had their mileage clocked, or are left-hand drive with suspensions tuned to other roads with different prior-ities at different kinds of roundabouts. Nevertheless, nature is keen to compensate for its brutality. When choice is a matter of life or death it likes to keep it simple, and it's on your side. It wants you to be a success.

Steven Grlscz snapped off a square of Bournville plain. Sucking it slowly, he checked the sink carefully for several minutes, dividing it mentally into graph-paper squares. Then he poured a scoop of Ariel automatic into the centre of the drainer, opened a new

toothbrush, dipped it in the powder and began to scrub the surface with extreme care. He had decided to clean the whole flat, a major spring-clean. He would redecorate the bedroom and perhaps re-tile the bathroom, but for now he concentrated on the sink. Attention to detail was a distraction from the constant sense of dread he'd felt since Maria had gone.

When he had finished, he walked through to the bedroom. The flat had the stillness of a place where something of great passion had recently ended. The floor-to-ceiling windows set in their solid wooden frames gave the light a formal quality that suited the bleached wood of the floors and furniture and the fine cotton of the simply fashioned sofas in dark blues and reds. Instead of being austere or impersonal, the flat looked restrained, suitably quiet. It was as if all the clutter, the credit card bills stacked behind the family photographs, the piles of partly read weekend supplements had all been cleared away by someone trying to keep themselves occupied.

Steven unlocked the bedroom cupboard, meaning to put on his shoes and go out for his first walk in nearly three weeks. In the corner there was a pile of seven green ledgers, neatly stacked. He had decided earlier that he would not read them until later that day, but half reluctantly he took the top one down. Hoping for reassurance from a swift browse, he realised that it was unlikely to remain just that. A superficial reading sometimes depressed him, if only because there was a fair chance of coming across a record of things that had worried him at the time and which required further reading to establish that, overall, there was a shape, a direction in what was written there.

Picking up the top ledger, he thumbed to the first mention of her.

THURSDAY 16th JUNE
... drinks at Tom Sterne's. His usual mix of
young middle-aged men and women in their
late twenties. He only seems to know one type
... intelligent but touchy, usually elegant. One
of them was strange. Amongst all the legs on
display, short skirts, split ... her drabness and
terrible hair, a frumpishness so striking it
seemed aggressive.

... found myself introduced. Not aggression
anyway. She shrank from me as if touching her
might cause her to wilt. Someone she knew interrupted. Close up she is even more of a fright.
The tank top is too small and from twenty years
ago, and the colours ... drained variations of
brown. Her skin is extraordinary though – not so
much white as bleached. What is she doing here?

He scanned fifty pages until the next entry.

TUESDAY 4th AUGUST
... 'Maria, this is Steven Grlscz.'

'Pleased to meet you.'

How odd it sounded – formal, learnt – like
being introduced to a child in cold storage
since the 1950s.

'We've met before.'

Absolute panic at this. She doesn't remember.
Dear God, how can life be bearable? So much
terror at nothing. I feel sorry for her, the fear is
so real – but such irritation, too. What *are* you
making such a fuss about? I make my excuses
to leave. Her relief was so plain, so spontaneous that I found it almost likeable.
Occasionally I watch her from the other side of
the room. She moves well – a kind of scrawny
grace. When she flicks her hair back, the

19

awkward nose that seems to dominate her face gives her looks a kind of character.

Nothing here. As I leave I have to pass by a group she's in. They are talking about clothes – to a man – when she smiles. I miss the first sentence but she is pointing at her top [the same tank top] and skirt: ' ... hearing-aid beige. It'll be all the rage this autumn.'

As I walk down towards the Charing Cross Road I think, You don't really have time for this.

FRIDAY 3rd DECEMBER
Go into Warner's in Covent Garden and remember Tom told me Maria Vaughan worked here. She was downstairs and looked thinner and paler – wouldn't have thought it possible. She knew me this time. 'You're Steven ... with the peculiar name.'

Was this familiarity, or just clumsy, a lack of grace in everything: clothes, stoop, manner, grasp? She looked carefully at the book I was buying – for someone else. She liked her work, was at home among the books. She bent down to pick up a bag and her hair, though not dirty, shone with the greasiness of a diet of bad food, and not enough of it. Is that all there is? You can see right through her.

Later I saw her in Covent Garden tube and thinking she'd seen me too I went up to her. She looked at me as if – actually it's hard to say how she looked. Then she claimed she'd forgotten something at work and walked off as if she'd been scalded.

FRIDAY 10th MARCH
Maria V in Soho at that place with good coffee

– chairs make my back ache. Very talkative but odd tone – can't place it. She cuts her cake into pieces but doesn't eat.

She made a big thing about paying as I took out my wallet.

He preferred to meet her on neutral territory rather than in his flat, and she seemed to like going to the cafés of Soho. These days it was packed with the affluent young: self-conscious, sexy, determined to have a part in the place where things were going on. The cafés multiplied yet gave the impression they had always been there. Their carefully nicotined ceilings spoke of rootedness, that people dead but vital had once smoked Gauloises, had fascinating conversations and written modernist novels there. There was the Café Bohème with its garden benches facing the street so that you could see shaven-headed gays in Lycra tops and shorts managing to avoid absurdity by lifting weights and continental regimens of stretch and pull. And the fading tapas bars, and women passing in their long split skirts, whose thigh-revealing flashes they attempted to deny by holding the cleft together with a hand as if the revelation were an accident of missing buttons or a faulty safety pin. Among the patisseries and brasseries, Amalfi, Balans, Valerie, Dell' Ugo, with its ironplaster giant leaning expectantly towards Old Compton Street, it was the diminishing sex shops that looked intimidated by the flash and money going on around them. The fed-up tarts in booths with welts along their legs seemed almost conscious in their isolated huddle of the short lease and the predatory caterer. Where morality and the law had failed, the cappuccino would succeed in clearing out this unadulterated Englishness.

'Why are you smiling?' she had asked.

He explained.

'Yes,' she said without a trace of amusement, 'you're probably right.'

He guessed she looked for something in the people there, their sense of possibility, that things were attainable; but she did not share in it. She was a witness to another kind of life in which she no more expected to participate than a visitor to the zoo expected to wander among the animals. But Maria's liking was tired, a reflex, like a haunting.

WEDNESDAY 2nd MAY
... thirty minutes in and she is still complaining ... relentless now at all our meetings. She moans about the lateness of trains, the paying of a bill, the telephone call from her sister, the rain, the heat – everything is a problem for this woman. The lack of discrimination is almost funny.

'We all have to pay bills, Maria, it rains on me as well as you.'

My irritation is clear – spontaneous. Such a pleasure letting go. I might just as well have slapped her.

Reading brought back the early days vividly enough. In the beginning, and for a long time after, the slightest look of irritation or displeasure wounded her like a sword. She was both brittle and soft: a heart of glass wrapped in rice paper. But he was disappointed at the vagueness of what he had written: it was too much like a set of notes, an aid to memory but not enough of the thing itself. The tone of her conversation was missing. It wasn't quite as he remembered it, as if this were someone else's version of events. She had been in a bad way when he first met her, much worse than the ledgers told him. It was clear within a few conversations that it would not be long before it came to the locked bathroom, the sharp blade or the overdose; and

that when it did it would not be a cry for help because tho notion of comfort had been leached out of her. She knew how to suffer; she knew misery, like some dark woods behind the family home made familiar by time and the lack of anything else to explore. Just as a distressed fish sends out signals to the cruising shark, Maria alerted every predator within receiving distance. Her life had been an endless series of sparks, coxcombs, creeps and spivs. But there was no wide-boy charm about any of them: cruel, mean-spirited, one or the other if not both, they had relentlessly lacerated her fragile sense of self either from stupidity or spite.

The responsibility lay, as he slowly discovered, with the usual crew: Mum, Dad, teacher, older brother, younger sister, the odd stranger, the bigger girl in the form above. The known list. The identity parade where everyone is guilty. But it was only much later that these things emerged. She was secretive but in an erratic way that lacked good judgement, as if the laws of discretion had been learnt from a badly explained book of instructions. From time to time she would blurt things out which were far more telling than the moaning she seemed to mistake for openness.

In the first year he had been supportive but in a cool way, aimed at preventing her becoming a nuisance. It didn't take much: even the most elementary act of consideration produced a kind of tired amazement. She was like those small desert animals that only need to drink every couple of years; she was fuel-efficient when it came to kindness. But to his surprise she showed no sign of being desperate for his company, even though she clearly valued it. This was a relief, but it also disturbed him because it was not what he would have expected: it was not consistent with the fact that she *was* desperate. He looked at the ledger again.

TUESDAY 5th JUNE

... It's clear enough why I see M now – she's a break from having to worry about presenting myself or being interesting. I hardly need to speak. And though the lamentation seems endless and is boring, from time to time there's a quality in her resisting the terrible fall – the good joke, the appetite for a sandwich, a flash of irritation or amusement at something I, or others, have said or done.

He had tried once making a list of them, the few ordinaries that contrasted so much with her inability to take pleasure in anything, to feel anything strongly except misery;

(1) To an always surly waiter at the Amalfi café: 'Please could you bring me another coffee – this one's cold.'

(2) Her anger, real indignation rather than whining, at having to work on a day she had arranged with her boss to take off but which had become inconvenient for him.

(3) A joke about a visit to the ballet where the ballerina repeatedly stuck out her leg at a right angle so that the male lead could turn her through three hundred and sixty degrees: 'It looked like someone opening a tin of peas with an over-sized fairy.'

(4) Her giving a pound to a blind beggar who, it turned out, she had seen the week before reading a bus timetable on Oxford Street.

(5) The very occasional, and always un-predictable, use of the word 'fuck'.

(6) The immaculate shine on her shoes.

He had thought over the incident with the beggar. It was precious in a way that was inconsistent with a personality pathologically lacking in pretension. He was convinced that her sense of worthlessness was genuine, untainted by a capacity for dramatising. But an affectation of this kind seemed to imply an inner world capable of self-regard. Affectation was a sign of life.

There were other signs also: malice, desire, vanity. There wasn't much, but what there was implied that something was going on, or *had* been going on, that she was harbouring a personality under the endless low of the emotionally exhausted, the weariness that colours everything from the food they eat to a walk in the sun. He had read somewhere that uncovering life in the prehistoric past was like trying to reconstruct a great book; but of this book there remained few pages, of these few pages few lines, of these few lines few words.

Almost exactly a year after he had met her at the party, she had steered him, mildly against his will, into going for a cup of coffee outside the National Film Theatre after a chance meeting on Waterloo Bridge. The coffee was disgusting and the bridge that loured over the cinema acted as a tunnel to the cold wind hustling off the Thames, so he paid indifferent attention to her at first. But after about ten minutes, and despite his discomfort, he became aware of a new way of speaking.

'... he's so dreary.'

An insult from her was almost shocking.

'Sorry, you've lost me. Who's dreary?'

She laughed at herself for rambling. He could depend on her not accusing him of inattention.

'Fowler, at the bookshop. If I have to hear one more time about how centred and at peace with himself he is! He's not centred, he's just dull ... and smug. And all

that drivel about his indifference to material things. He loves his little blue Fiesta with its stupid bead thing draped over the back of the seat – it looks like a dead armadillo. My aunt has a little blue Fiesta. If he's a Buddhist, I'm a banana.'

Looking at her more closely, he could see that the grey skin of the terminally sad had become instead merely pale, with the faintest flush of red colouring her cheekbones. He listened more carefully as she joked about her state – as she referred to it – and the idiocy of the tolerance she had given to the assortment of criminals who had induced it. She gave him smiles of open appreciation, and as she talked he realised that she held him responsible for her transformation. He was astonished, even shocked. How far she must have fallen to create such a friendship from nothing more than his lukewarm interest.

On the other hand, he was deeply impressed by her resilience. There's something to this woman. But he was alarmed that he had missed, with any exactness, what it was. *You can't afford this*, he thought.

She became fascinating because she had so astonished him. She was like a dead shrub that, on a closer look, had innumerable buds, small as seeds, emerging from the bark. Over the next two weeks, she accepted his increasing presence in the same spirit with which she had accepted his occasional interest and, indeed, seemed not quite to have grasped the fundamental nature of the shift in his attitude towards her. He assumed this was her innate passivity at work; she was prepared to take whatever you gave her and be grateful. The entry for 12th August, which he had underlined to mark its significance, showed that this was not so.

> ... as the waiter arrived I was distracted and on turning back saw that she was reaching into her bag to pay.

26

'You paid last time,' I said, perhaps too quickly [Be careful of this — 14/6/94].

'You're very … fair,' she said, smiling. It was only a slight smile but it was the first sign of warmth I had ever seen on her face.

Whenever they went for coffee together he always remembered who had paid last and, in a good-humoured way, insisted on taking turns. This idiosyncrasy of his – in a minor fashion he was rather mean with money – had significance for her in a way that seemed to touch her profoundly. Why it did so was perplexing. That the peripheral bits and pieces of yourself could resonate for others like this was alarming, more evidence of how particular and arbitrary people's inner lives were. Simple stuff like this, misunderstood, had opened a door that allowed her the possibility of escape. Months later, however, and frighteningly, what had seemed to be mysterious and eccentric turned out to be both straightforward and understandable. For all that she lived the life of a poor student, she was quite wealthy because of an inheritance from her grandmother. For years she had been too artless to hide this and she was used to being with people whose expressions of friendship or intimacy had been motivated solely by their sense that she was an easy touch. He was the first person, perhaps in all her life, to talk to her for any length of time without trying to get anything out of her.

Until he realised the centrality of her obsession with giving and taking, their new relationship proved difficult. Sometimes she seemed positive, happy even, but there were frequent periods when Maria seemed lost, unable to engage with him. This was nerve-racking for him and he made mistakes, chief among them being to lavish attention on her. The less happy she seemed,

the more attentive he became. It made her worse and he felt her slipping away from him. In time he realised she was not ready for such attentiveness, and was not looking for a lover, hence his early failure. First things first, thought Steven, as he decided it was possible in matters of the heart to be a kind of absentee landlord, that ownership could have a special status by virtue of its lack of evidence. He would be conspicuous by his absence. He would allow her to avoid a sense of obligation, and it would be like giving her a bunch of flowers or taking her on a weekend visit to the coast.

Slowly, measuring in minutes, he began to increase the amount of time he spent with her. He decided to balance everything he did for her with something she could do for him, and he began to record these minutes and these exchanges by writing them down in the green-bound ledgers. He felt awkward about the approach at first: he feared its woodenness might communicate itself in some way. He had started the ledgers, in effect, as diaries, and they were meant to try to fix the swirl of impressions of his daily life in much the same way. They were helpful but not especially. Re-reading them was always a disappointment. Too often they seemed to have missed the very intangibles he was trying to nail down. For a few weeks he tried counting specifics, giving numbers, adding and subtracting. He became fascinated by the detail with which it was possible to audit something so apparently complex. He discovered that before he started the audit he had been afraid he was doing too much for her and in so doing weighing her down with obligation; he was, in fact, only doing two things for her for every three she did for him. A few simple categories covered the complete range of a relationship. In the end he narrowed it down to five: objects, touching, support, emotion and absence.

Lying back on the bed, acknowledging that he would